Acknowledgments

This time around we'd like to thank Kate Salter for emergency hospitality above and beyond the call of duty, and Eli, Hawg, Joe, Mike, Ray, and the other Joe—especially Hawg and Ray—at Wayland Automotive in Wayland, Massachusetts, for taking good care on short notice of our injured minivan.

A DESPERATE SITUATION

"Damn!" Len's voice crackled again over the intraship speakers. "They're alongside us now."

"Shoot them!" Zeri ordered.

"With happiness, my lady, but we're unarmed. Merchant, remember?"

"Damn," said Zeri in her turn. In a quieter voice, she said, "Herin?"

For a moment there was no answer; then he answered her in a voice that sounded distracted and far away. "Yes, cousin?"

"I don't want to be captured and taken back to Lord Natelth," she said. "It would humiliate me and disgrace whatever was left of the family. Don't let it happen."

"We're working on it, Zeri."

"I wasn't thinking about that. I was thinking that you probably know how to—well, to put a quick end to someone."

"Yes. That too."

A Working of Stars

✦ ✦ ✦ ✦ ✦

**Debra Doyle and
James D. Macdonald**

A TOM DOHERTY ASSOCIATES BOOK
NEW YORK

This is a work of fiction. All the characters and events portrayed in this book are either products of the author's imagination or are used fictitiously.

A WORKING OF STARS

Copyright © 2002 by Debra Doyle and James D. Macdonald

Edited by Patrick and Teresa Nielsen Hayden

A Tor Book
Published by Tom Doherty Associates, LLC
175 Fifth Avenue
New York, NY 10010

www.tor.com

Tor® is a registered trademark of Tom Doherty Associates, LLC.

ISBN: 0-812-57193-2
Library of Congress Catalog Card Number: 2001050753

First edition: April 2002
First mass market edition: July 2003

Printed in the United States of America

0 9 8 7 6 5 4 3 2 1

*This one is for all the squad members of EMS North and
the folks at Upper Connecticut Valley Hospital.*

A Working
of Stars

Prologue

On a world not his own, in a life he had never anticipated, Arekhon sus-Khalgath sus-Peledaen slept—and sleeping, dreamed. In his dream he knelt in the meditation chamber of the starship *Night's-Beautiful-Daughter,* where he had not gone in his waking body for over a dozen years. His staff, a cubit and a half of black wood bound with silver, lay on the deck in front of him, and all around him the *Daughter* vibrated with the urgency of her passage through the Void.

Arekhon wondered what he was meant to do. Had he only now begun his meditation, here inside his dream, or had he just ended it? He couldn't remember; but somewhere outside the chamber, an alarm began to sound.

He picked up his staff in his right hand and got to his feet. Outside the chamber, the alarm bell continued its steady, pulse-note chime. He found the door and opened it, and stepped through—not into the harsh illumination of a starship's passageway, but into the Old Hall at Demaizen, and the warm golden light of an autumn afternoon.

Garrod syn-Aigal sus-Demaizen—great Magelord, Voidwalker, and finder of worlds—had taken the land and fortune that were his inheritance, and had used them to build a Circle strong enough and dedicated enough to carry out the greatest of great workings: to bring together the two parts of the sundered galaxy, crossing the interstellar gap and healing a rift that had existed since the unimaginably long ago. Arekhon had left the sus-Peledaen fleet and his family altars to become a part of Lord Garrod's Circle, and when the working demanded it of him he had left his native world as well.

He had walked through the Old Hall in dreams often enough since then, in the years after the Demaizen Mage-Circle had split apart in fire and blood, but never as now, with the weight of knowledge bearing down hard upon him. In these rooms, he had grown from a sus-Peledaen fleet-apprentice with a knack for seeing the *eiran* and making luck to a working Mage in Lord Garrod's Circle—and now he came back to them with the sound of the *Daughter*'s alarm bell following him wherever he went.

Sometimes in his dreams he saw the Mages of Demaizen as he had known them before. On those nights he sparred with Delath or Serazao in the long gallery, or talked of space and stars with Kiefen Diasul, though in the waking world both Del and 'Zao were dead, and Kief had betrayed all of them years ago. Tonight, though, was different. Instead of Delath or Serazao, the dream gave him Iulan Vai.

Vai—the last-come member of the Circle, who had brought *Night's-Beautiful-Daughter* from her employers, the sus-Radal, to save the Demaizen Mages from utter destruction, and who had stayed behind on Eraasi in order to repay the debt. Arekhon found her in the long gallery, with its tall, westward-facing windows and its racks of exercise mats and limber practice staves. She hadn't altered her appearance since the last time he saw her in the flesh. Under the touch of the afternoon sun, her dark hair still glinted with rusty-brown highlights, and she still clothed her compact frame in tunic and leggings of ordinary black.

"Iule," he said—though she had always refused the forms of affection, even with those who might have had a claim to use them. "What are you doing here?"

"Looking for you. Did you think you could go away forever?"

"I didn't think I had a choice."

"You didn't," she told him. "Not then. But everything changes, and we have to change with it."

As she spoke, the light from the westering sun struck the windowpanes at a new and sudden angle, dazzling his eyes for a moment. When the glare died, he wasn't seeing Iulan Vai any longer. Another woman looked at him in her place: an older woman, whose thick black hair was shot through with wide streaks of iron-grey, and whose skin was the color of burnished copper. Not Vai, though like Vai she wore plain black and carried a Mage's staff, and not anyone else he recognized.

"Do I know you?" he asked her.

"Not yet," she said. "But soon." Outside the long gallery, somewhere in the rooms—and the life—that he had left behind him, the sound of the *Daughter*'s alarm changed from a bell note to a strident metallic wail. "You have to leave now. It's almost time."

Natelth sus-Khalgath sus-Peledaen stood with his back to the observation deck of his orbiting shipyard and stronghold, his face only a few inches from the armored glass that gave the deck its name. The world of Eraasi lay before him, a great globe against the starfield, black in the vacuum of space, stars glittering all around it. The sunset line lay across the world, on the left as he looked at it, the darkened crescent alive with city lights.

He knew that elsewhere, hidden beyond the bulk of the planet, the citadel of the sus-Radal fleet-family circled Eraasi in an orbit exactly opposite to his own. But Natelth, secure in his own place, hardly thought of the sus-Radal. He led, and the other star-lords followed; and if he started hopping on one foot, before long Theledau sus-Radal would be bouncing around on his head.

Natelth heard the swish-click of the doubled inner airlocks that isolated the observation deck from the rest of the station, but he didn't turn. He would have known who was approaching him even if the armored glass had not shown him her reflected image. His sister Isayana, joining him in the safety of exile from the planet's surface, had come bearing news.

He hated living on the orbiting station.

He watched Isayana's reflection approaching, not a twin of his own, but close enough that he and she had often been mistaken for such when both were young: the same square frame and strong features, the same black hair now going grey. Isayana's light-colored garments appeared stark against the black of space, under the dim light of the room. The reflected light of Eraasi provided all the illumination here. The observation deck held no chairs, no furniture, no decoration. When Hanilat and the station slid under Eraasi's nightside, then he could dial up the lights. He could. So far, he never had.

"What's happening?" Natelth asked his sister, after she had walked, ghost-silent, to his side.

"Not much," she said. "The launch of *Fair-Wind-Rising* will be on time."

She fell silent, looking down at the world where they had both been born, and where they could never live at ease again. Star-lords they were, as their family had always been, but never so much as now.

"We'll need to spend some time in Hanilat before the end of the year," he said. "Working out of the family house."

"The security people will hate that," Isayana said.

"I know."

Another long silence.

"Have you heard any word from any of the other fleet-families?" Isayana said at last. "About some kind of cooperative arrangement for dealing with problems down on the planet?"

Natelth's face hardened. "There's no cooperation between star-lords."

"We're living in changing times, Na'e. What was true a generation ago isn't going to be true forever."

Natelth turned to look at his sister. The empty observation platform stretched out to his right, the light from Eraasi bringing up the profile of his face, his right side in shadow. "And how do you propose to bring about this new era of cooperation?"

"We need to make alliances," she said. "Alliances based on trust, not fear."

"With the likes of Theledau sus-Radal?"

"Thel isn't a rival," she said. "He hasn't been building warships for almost five years now; maybe he's waiting for you to notice that he's not a threat."

"He's still there," Natelth said. He turned back to the window and gestured expansively across the face of the globe below them. The orbital shipyard was in geosynchronous orbit, the starport city of Hanilat lying forever directly below them. Whatever the space station lacked in comforts for the soul—and Natelth thought that it lacked most of them—at least here he could see strangers approaching from a long way off. "Down in Hanilat, waiting for me to make a mistake. And if he isn't building warships, it's probably because he's working on something else. I would be."

"We have larger enemies than the other fleet-families, Na'e," Isayana said. She hadn't stopped looking out, her feet square to the flat expanse of armor glass. A late-season storm washed over the southern ocean, but Hanilat, approaching its own sunset, had a cloudless sky. This station would be visible soon to those who lived and worked below. "We both know it. The other families know it, too. You, me, the sus-Radal, everyone."

She turned to face him, then, and laid a hand on his shoulder. "What will the people of Eraasi do, when the people of Garrod's world come back across the Gap to deal with us?"

"Garrod was a meddling fool," Natelth said. "And I was foolish enough to help him."

"All done before we knew, and beyond recall." Her hand continued to rest on his shoulder. "Will you come and inspect *Fair-Wind-Rising* with me?"

"I suppose I should," Natelth said, and turned his back on the glittering world outside the armored glass windows.

Arekhon awoke into darkness. The hour was well past moonset, so that the starlit rectangle of his bedroom window took a long minute to resolve into a patch of grey against the black. The furniture—bed, nightstand, chair, desk—took a little longer to emerge from the undifferentiated night. When he could distinguish the outline of the half-open closet door,

over on the far side of the room, he got out of bed and began
to dress.

His clothes were on the chair where he had laid them out
before retiring: garments of local cut, but made in the plain
black and white he had always preferred. He'd never grown
accustomed to the colors of this world, its alien dyestuffs
and yet more alien aesthetics, and after a while he had given
up trying. He put on shirt and trousers and a loose jacket,
then hesitated a moment before pulling on his boots. Stock-
ing feet would have been quieter, but far less dignified. Arekhon had nothing against suffering embarrassment in a good
cause, but he had no desire to suffer it unnecessarily.

He picked up his staff and fastened it to his belt, then stood
for a moment, thoughtful, before opening the drawer of the
night table and pulling out a hand-sized object shaped like a
flattened cylinder. He slid the pulse-gun into the inner pocket
of his jacket, then shut the drawer and left the room.

The lower floors of the building were silent and empty. In
the town houses of Arekhon's childhood, the night hours had
belonged to the *aiketen,* the constructed intelligences in their
metal shells; it had been impossible for anyone to move
about in secret without first subverting the quasi-organic servitors. They didn't have *aiketen* here on this side of the interstellar gap. The men and women who did what should
have been a construct's labor—and who worked late and rose
early—slept in a warren of small rooms high up under the
mansion's gabled roof.

No one lived on the bottom floor except for Arekhon. He
was, at least nominally, a scholar-savant under Mestra Elela
Rosselin's patronage, and entitled to maintain private chambers elsewhere at her expense. But those closest to the Mestra
knew him—by face if not by name—as the man responsible
for House Rosselin's domestic security, and they would expect to find such a one keeping his quarters under the Mestra's roof. Arekhon, who had known the Mestra when she
was still Elaeli Inadi syn-Peledaen, considered himself fortunate in the arrangement.

The stairs ascending from the mansion's lower level were
dark and narrow. Arekhon went up them with the familiarity
of long practice, and up the next set of stairs as well. These

were wider, and lit by a night-glow in a niche halfway along. The door at the top answered to a palmprint scan; Arekhon was one of the people it recognized. He placed his right hand against the pad and the lock clicked open.

He passed through one darkened room, noting the dim shapes of chairs and cabinets and pieces of unobjectionable art, all unchanged since his last visit, and through another, this one a private office similarly unaltered, before he came to another door with a palmprint scan. Again he touched the pad, and, when the lock answered, opened the door.

Elaeli was awake, though it took him a moment to spot her in the unlighted room. She wore a loose bedrobe of dark fabric, and—standing as she did a little to one side of the window—seemed at first like a part of the curtain that had been drawn aside. She looked around as he entered.

" 'Rekhe," she said. "I was wishing I dared to go looking for you. I couldn't sleep."

He crossed over to where she stood, and put an arm around her, so that she could lean her head against his shoulder. She was as tall as he was, and her light brown curls were soft against his cheek.

She still wore her hair short, after the style of the sus-Peledaen fleet—it was almost the only part of her past she'd been able to hang on to, he supposed. Arekhon had let his own black hair grow out long when he left the fleet for the Demaizen Circle, and he hadn't cut it since, but Elaeli had more reason that he did to cherish the older style.

She'd been a bright young light in the sus-Peledaen fleet—Pilot-Principal on the first exploratory voyage to make contact beyond the Edge—until Lord Garrod and the Demaizen Circle had conscripted her into the service of the great working. Arekhon was never sure whether her political maneuverings here on Entibor sprang from honest ambition in search of an outlet, or from the need to bury a past that hurt too much to remember.

"I'm here now," he said.

"I miss you when you're away downstairs."

"This is the city," he said. "If I stay in your rooms for the whole night, the servants will officially know, and if the servants know, the scandal-rags will have it by nightfall."

"Damn the scandal-rags." She sounded tired, worn down with waiting for sleep that hadn't come. "Fourteen years I've been here, 'Rekhe, and I still don't understand this place."

"Don't try. Just ride the luck, and trust it to carry you in the right direction." Which it would do, Arekhon reflected; he had expended considerable energy over the years in working the *eiran* for this world, and for Elaeli Inadi syn-Peledaen. The threads of his own luck were tangled and untended by comparison. He would probably come to regret that one of these days, but not yet.

She made a disgruntled noise. "The Provost of Elicond doesn't believe in luck. He favors persistence."

"I know." Nothing could make Arekhon like the idea of the Provost's visit—Elaeli needed the Provost's support in the complicated political intrigues of the Federated Quarter, and the Provost had asked for a gene-link with House Rosselin in return. "Make it the three weeks requested, and that's an end," he said, more to himself than to Elaeli.

"I hope that's long enough to suit him," Elaeli replied. "Because three weeks is about all I can handle thinking about."

"Tell him all the security arrangements are for three weeks, and that it's too late to change them. Put the blame on me if you have to."

"That's hardly fair."

He didn't bother telling Elaeli that nothing about their life together was fair; she already knew that as well as he did. Instead, he told her, "I'll be absent from the city by then. Venner—" his second, a clever and ambitious young man from the rough side of An-Jemayne "—has already been briefed on everything, and you can trust him to handle whatever comes up."

"If you trained him, 'Rekhe, I'm sure he's good." She leaned against him for a moment in silence, looking out at the dark, and then said, "As soon as the Provost is taken care of, I'm going to the country and staying there for a while . . . will you stay there with me?"

"Yes," said Arekhon. Elaeli's summer cottage was isolated enough that the scandal-rags didn't bother with it—at least not for something as commonplace as bedroom gossip. Arekhon thought of the pleasure of waking beside Elaeli in the morning sunlight, and sighed.

You have to leave now, the woman in his dream had told him. *It's almost time.*

He did not think that she had been speaking of the house in An-Jemayne.

1:

Herin Arayet sus-Dariv took his rented groundcar around the last curve on the uphill drive to Demaizen Old Hall. The burnt-out shell of the ruined building reared up against the sky ahead of him. A little later, he saw a line of rusting metal hulks drawn up in good order on the overgrown gravel driveway, with clingvine spreading over them and tall stalks of field weeds springing up around their treads.

He slowed the groundcar into a careful approach. He'd taken his usual precautions before setting out on today's errand—a pocket-pistol concealed inside his jacket, a knife hidden up his sleeve, a note to the family's Agent-Principal filed among his personal effects—but he knew that against Magecraft, such measures would do him little good. And whatever had happened to the line of blasted and shattered assault vehicles had been a Mage's work.

Nobody knew, or at least nobody admitted in public to knowing, exactly who had sent the private assault team up against Garrod syn-Aigal and his Circle. The incident had taken place during the period of civil unrest that had disturbed Eraasi's main continent over ten years before; but Demaizen had been an independent Circle during that period, supported by Garrod's private fortune and not tied formally to any particular faction or institution. True, they'd had an informal connection to the sus-Peledaen fleet-family—Lord Natelth's younger brother had been one of the Demaizen Mages, and members of the Circle had taken part in the sus-Peledaen exploratory voyage to the far side of the interstellar gap—but such a connection should have given Demaizen more protection, rather than less.

The one thing Herin could say for certain about the attack was that neither side had survived the encounter, and that no guilty parties had revealed themselves by coming in to clean things up afterward. The house and grounds had passed into the hands of the Wide Hills District Wildlife Protection League, according to Lord Garrod's testamentary wishes; and the League so far had operated strictly within the boundaries of its charter, leaving the ruined Hall untouched.

Herin wasn't surprised. What the Mages wanted had a way of happening. Garrod had wanted the Old Hall left alone, and alone it stayed, unaltered except by the elements. No graffiti marked its smoke-stained walls, and no empty cans or broken bottles littered the shadowed ground beneath. Even the local adolescents, it seemed, chose to go elsewhere for their amateur debaucheries.

He left his groundcar parked in the driveway and made his way up the front steps of the Hall and through the great, broken doors. Inside was more destruction, cracked brick and burnt wood and more than once a disturbing glimpse of something that looked like bone. He found the door that his contact had told him about, a small one that opened onto a service stairway, and started down the narrow steps into the basement.

"Syr Arayet."

The voice came from the darkness ahead of him. It was low and not unpleasant—a woman's voice, he thought. A moment later, a light came on in the corridor. After a few seconds, he realized that the pale, apparently sourceless glow actually came from a Mage's staff in the woman's right hand. He couldn't see her face, and it took him another few seconds to realize that the blank, reflective darkness underneath the hood of her black cloak was in fact a spacer's ship-combat hardmask.

"*Etaze,*" he said, using the term of respect for a Magelord of high rank. Maybe this one was merely somebody's Circle-Mage, disaffected enough to send along a request for a personal meeting. But if she was not—if she was the First or even the Second of a major Circle, whether in Hanilat or in one of the fleets—then she would need polite and careful handling. "Your message reached me only a short while ago. I came as soon as I dared."

The woman chuckled, a surprisingly warm sound to come from behind the dark plastic of a combat hardmask. "You mean you came as soon as you'd made sure that my message was genuine. Nobody's ever called you a fool, Syr Arayet."

"I must need to work more on my presentation," he said. "What is it you wanted to talk with me about?"

"I heard that you were interested in what became of the Demaizen Circle."

Herin nodded. "I've only heard the rumors, and I'm curious."

"That all happened a long time ago. Why start asking questions about it now?"

"Call it a hobby," he said. "The past informs the present, and so forth."

There was a long pause. Herin could feel the woman's gaze assessing him from behind the unrevealing hardmask.

"A present," she said finally, "in which the sus-Dariv are debating whether or not to deploy private ground security forces as an auxiliary to their fleet arm."

He said nothing, though he was uncomfortably aware that the damp, cobwebby basement of Demaizen Old Hall was the sort of place in which a too-curious researcher could conveniently disappear. Lord Garrod's Circle had died there, as far as anyone could tell, and nobody had come to gather up their bones. Another body moldering away in the dark would probably never be noticed.

"Don't worry," she said, as if his hidden trepidation had somehow manifested itself around him like an aura. For all Herin knew, it could have. Mages saw things like that, where other people saw nothing but plain air. "I still have some standards. If I'd wanted to do you harm, I wouldn't have come up with anything half as melodramatic as this."

"I'm relieved to hear it, *etaze*."

"I'm sure you are," she said. "Now for the reason you came here: Ask me your questions, and I'll answer them. At least, as much as I can and may."

"Very well," said Herin. "What happened to Lord Garrod's Circle?"

"Who sent the killers, do you mean?"

"Well, yes."

She shrugged. "The first time? No one knows. They're all dead."

"Yes, I know . . . what do you mean, 'the *first* time'? There was a second attack?"

"When the rest of the Circle came back from across the Gap Between. But the Hall had already burned down by then."

Herin felt a brief flicker of intellectual vindication. Investigating the destruction of the Old Hall had been a personal project. If he'd made it official, he would have had some trouble justifying his interest in a bit of recent history that the family's less irregular agents had chosen to overlook. Already, though, he had retrieved an interesting bit of previously uncollected knowledge—two bits, if he counted the implication that the identity of the second group of attackers, unlike that of the first, was not unknown.

"You must have a theory about why the initial attack failed," he said.

"You think that this—" she used the hand that held the glowing staff to describe a vague circle, presumably meant to include the entirety of the Hall "—was a failure?"

"If the attack had been a complete success, somebody would have taken credit for it. Nobody ever did." Herin paused. He'd never intended to keep up his current pose as a hobby-researcher for very long—it was a means of gaining entry, and little more—but he shied away from revealing his true interests quite so bluntly. "I think that whoever sent in the strike team was afraid. Those assault vehicles up there were blasted by Magecraft. They had to have been; there's no record anywhere of the Demaizen Circle having weapons.

If one of Lord Garrod's Mages survived long enough to do something like that—"

"—then he or she might still be alive," said the woman. "And still angry."

"Yes."

"A good theory."

"I like to think so," said Herin. "What I don't know is who he was."

"Or she," said the woman. She gave a quiet laugh. "If it will make your mind easier, I can tell you that it wasn't me."

"Can you tell me who—?"

"Delath syn-Arvedan died in the first attack," she said. "So did Lord Garrod and Serazao Zuleimem."

He knew the names of the Demaizen Circle, both the ones who had stayed behind on Eraasi and the ones who had gone exploring with the sus-Peledaen across the interstellar gap; he'd made it his business to find out when he began his researches. And he could do subtraction in his head as well as any man.

"Diasul," he said. "Kiefen Diasul."

Iulan Vai stayed behind in the shadows and watched the sus-Dariv agent make his way out of the ruins and back down to the overgrown drive. He'd come to her for this meeting, not the other way around, and she wasn't sure what that meant. She'd heard rumors that someone was asking questions about the Old Hall, and about Lord Garrod's Circle—maybe she wasn't the sus-Radal's Agent-Principal anymore, but she hadn't cut all ties with her old contacts in the shadow world of information gathering—and she had taken steps to make certain that the questioner made contact with her.

Herin Arayet sus-Dariv had not been what she was expecting. To begin with, he wasn't a hireling. He was a family member from one of the inner lines, and probably well-off enough in his own right that he didn't need to work at all if he lacked the inclination to do so. She wondered what had induced him to take up his peculiar hobby. Was he moved by concern for the family good, or by the pleasure of finding out secret things—or had somebody high up in the inner family trained him for the work?

He was suited for it, Vai conceded, at least inasmuch as nobody would take him at first glance for one of the sus-Dariv. That family ran to slightly built blonds and redheads, especially in the inner lines, and Syr Arayet was dark and wiry and at least a head taller than the average. Something about the man continued to nag at her as she withdrew from the ruins of the Old Hall and made her way back to Demaizen Town.

She kept a rented room there, upstairs from an all-night staples-and-sundries shop. The name on the lease wasn't hers, of course, except in the sense that she'd created the identity and used it off and on for over a decade. She'd wanted to have a bolt-hole available somewhere outside of Hanilat, and it had made sense, or so she told herself, to set one up where she could keep an eye on the Old Hall as well. The manager of the sundries shop collected the rent and watched over the place for her when she was absent.

The cloak and hardmask Vai had worn at the Old Hall were out of sight in her daypack by the time she reached town. The staff wasn't as easily concealed, so she didn't bother. As far as the townspeople were concerned, her local persona claimed affiliation with a minor Circle someplace in Hanilat, the kind of Circle whose members all had day jobs and only came together for fellowship and the occasional minor working.

She stopped in the sundries shop to buy a pack of candles and exchange greetings with the night clerk, then went on upstairs to her room. She'd told the store manager that she was a field investigator for the Wildlife Protection League, using the small apartment as a place to rest and write up reports in between assignments, and she'd fixed up the room with that identity in mind: locally purchased secondhand furniture mixed in with a scattering of folk-art pieces from the Antipodes and the northern territories; bedspread and curtains made of hand-spun fibers block-printed in traditional patterns; maps and journals and data readers covering all the available flat surfaces.

She'd thought for a while of painting a proper meditation

circle in white and black on the wooden floor—nothing in the terms of her lease said that she couldn't, and people would be unwilling to gainsay a Mage in any case—but in the end she had decided not to. The landlord would have to refinish the surface if she did that, and there was no point in giving him extra work. A chalk outline scrawled on the floor served well enough for her purposes, and scrubbed away easily afterward.

Vai shucked off her daypack and tucked it out of the way beneath her local persona's cluttered desk. A pottery bowl at one end of the desktop held the stub end of a stick of chalk, along with a flick-top lighter, a spool of black thread, and half a dozen small, weathered stones. She stood for a moment undecided, then picked up the chalk and used it to inscribe a circle on the polished wooden floorboards. Nobody would be surprised if the Mage upstairs chose to meditate upon a private intention. They would assume that she held the shop and its environs in her thoughts as well, and would be, if anything, grateful.

The cabinet in the kitchen nook held a quartet of cheap glass candleholders. She fetched them down and set them out around the perimeter of the chalk circle, then unwrapped the candles she'd bought in the store below and put one in each holder. The rest of the candles went into the cabinet. Then she took the flick-lighter from the pottery bowl and used it to light each of the candles in turn.

A quick tap on the desk's control pad, and the lamp that had come on when she entered the apartment clicked off again, leaving the room lit only by the yellow, unstable candle flames. Vai stepped into the circle she had drawn, and knelt.

As always when she did this, she felt keenly the absence of the rest of Demaizen's Mages, the dead and the estranged and the unimaginably far away. She needed them here with her, needed their greater strength and their longer training as she opened herself to the vision of the *eiran*. The silver cords of life and luck came to her sight hesitantly at first, in wisps and tendrils. She let herself watch them, and tried not to think about them overmuch. If she focused her attention on them too soon, they would fade, and all her careful non-effort would be lost.

Herin Arayet sus-Dariv.

The name emerged unbidden out of her thoughts, not as a distraction but as something to be dealt with, a part of the unsettled state of mind that had led her to this meditation in the first place. She considered the name, and marked how the words insinuated themselves into the weave of the *eiran* as she watched. The silver threads caught hold of the name, and ran in and out of it like vines on a wrought-iron fence.

Vai smiled at their eagerness. The *eiran* knew Syr Arayet, whether Syr Arayet knew them or not.

She considered the matter a little longer, then pulled on the cords enough to twist and lodge them yet more firmly into the man's name and his place in the pattern—working the luck, just a little, for a man who was, in some sense, a colleague in a dangerous profession. And if more should ever come of it than that, well, the universe had a strange sense of humor sometimes, and she herself had first come to the Demaizen Circle as a spy for the sus-Radal.

Satisfied, she let her thoughts move outward from the troubles of the present, following the *eiran* as they traced their patterns through time and space. Arekhon sus-Khalgath had seen the pattern of the great working, the binding-together of the sundered galaxy, both as it stood now and as it would come to completion—but 'Rekhe was on the far side of the galaxy and not likely to be coming home soon no matter how much she wished for him.

She needed him, though; the working needed him. The Circles were changing, moving away from what they had been . . . *we served all of the people once,* she thought; *it was that way even when I was a child. Now the fleet-families and the merchant-combines want to make us tend the luck for them alone and not for the whole world, and I don't know enough about the old ways to set things right.*

I don't even know if it's possible to set things right. Some things, when they change, can't be changed back.

The tangle of *eiran* closest to her hand and mind had brighter and darker threads in it. She tugged at one of the dimmer lines, hoping to tease it out of the mass and straighten up at least a fraction of the disarray. When she pulled on the thread, it grew brighter in response.

Under the surface of her meditation, curiosity stirred and came to life. This was a new thread, stretching away out of the local tangle and leading off into strange and uncharted realms. Something different was coming into the working—something fresh and unanticipated, yet at the same time very old and very strong.

Something dangerous.

The sun was rising over the hills beyond Rosselin Cottage, and a light mist hovered between the branches of the spring-green trees. Arekhon had risen early, after his custom when he was here alone. He sat in a wicker chair on the screened-in verandah, sipping at a mug of the hot bitter liquid the people on this world drank for a morning stimulant.

Elaeli's summer cottage, she'd told Arekhon once, had been Elela Rosselin's first home on Entibor—part of the fictitious identity that Garrod syn-Aigal had made ready for her, knowing that the great working would bring her to it in time. Remote, isolated, and rustic, the cottage had provided a safe haven from which to launch a political career, and Elaeli had used it to play politics with a will.

"I was planning to be Fleet-Admiral for the sus-Peledaen," she'd said to him, "back before Lord Garrod conscripted me into the great working and then marooned me on Entibor with a bankroll and a fake identity. I couldn't leave all that ambition behind just because I wasn't with the fleet anymore; I had to do something, or I'd go crazy. And when I came here, politics was what there was to do."

The cottage itself was a rustic, sprawling building, built of wood and painted white, that floated like a low cloud on the brow of the mountain, against the forest's edge. At the moment, except for Arekhon himself, it was deserted. Elaeli was in the city, entertaining and being entertained by the Provost of Elicond; and it was better for everybody's peace of mind if her chief of domestic security—who was not, officially, her lover—stayed away until the Provost had finished his business and gone home.

As a domestic arrangement it was less than ideal, but far better than nothing at all. They'd had a little over ten years of it, by local reckoning. Arekhon tried to do the arithmetic for converting the passage of time into Eraasian measures, and gave up when he couldn't remember the exact ratio of one planetary year to the other.

At the moment, though, he was content. This world was fair, and this country house was fair, and here, when her business with the Provost was done, Elaeli would be joining him. For a little while, at least, they could pretend that nothing would ever change—though the time he'd had here with Elaeli would never be long enough, and the time he'd spent away from the homeworlds was far too long.

But both times are the same, he thought. *Like the Void, where all times are the same time . . .*

". . . and all places are the same place."

The words were Eraasian, but marked by a strong accent, as though the speaker had learned the language as an adult. Turning, Arekhon recognized the strange woman who had come to him in his dream of Demaizen Old Hall, displacing Iulan Vai and telling him that he would know her soon. One of the wooden floorboards creaked faintly as she stepped forward out of what might have been a shadow left over from the night.

So she was real, then, and a Void-walker as well, one of the powerful Mages who could journey alone and unprotected through the no-time, no-place that lay beneath the physical universe. Garrod syn-Aigal had also been a Void-walker, earning the nickname "Explorer" because of the worlds he had journeyed to in that fashion, marking a way through the Void for the ships that would follow; for that reason, Arekhon was less startled by the manner of his visitor's arrival than by the fact that she had spoken to him earlier in his dream.

Seen in the unexpected flesh, she wasn't tall—perhaps half a head less than Arekhon's own moderate height, even in the sturdy boots that she wore with her white shirt and black trousers—but compact and trim with muscle. The staff she carried in her right hand was a cubit and a half of ebony, bound and ornamented with silver wire.

"Who are you?" he asked.

"My name is Llannat Hyfid," she said. "I'm your last student."

"Llann—" He stumbled a bit over the unfamiliar syllables. The words weren't Eraasian, or any other language that he was aware of. That meant nothing, given that a Void-walker could be from anywhere, or any when. If such a one had deliberately sought him out, first in dreams and then in the flesh . . . he tried the name again, this time with better luck. "Llannat."

"If the name gives you trouble," she said, "you can call me Maraganha instead. Some people find it easier on the tongue."

"Maraganha." The name meant "from the forested place" in Eraasian, which told him something, at least, about his mysterious visitor—and as she had promised, its syllables were easier for him to say. But the woman herself remained an enigma. "I don't know you. And I've never had a student."

"You were—you will be—quite a bit older then."

Arekhon shivered, even though the morning was warm. He remembered how it had felt to look upon Garrod syn-Aigal sus-Demaizen as a great Magelord in the vigorous prime of his life, and know that the same man would in time become the white-haired idiot the Circle had already left behind on Eraasi. The thought of Maraganha or anyone else looking at him in the same manner was profoundly disturbing.

"I said something like that to my own teacher once," he told her. "When Garrod came back through the Void to show the rest of us the way to Entibor. But there aren't any Mages on this world, Maraganha. Only Adepts, and they're a cold and solitary lot."

"It's their way." Maraganha came forward and took a seat in the other chair, the one that was usually Elaeli's, and laid her ebony staff across her knees. "I was one of them, until it didn't suit me any longer. My fault as much as theirs; I've known Mages who would do well in an Adepts' Guild-house—"

"I've seen it happen," Arekhon said. "It's not for me."

"Here you are, though, as lonely as any Adept in the galaxy."

"None of it was my idea. I had a Circle once, but it's broken and scattered across the interstellar gap."

"Scattered, maybe," she said. "But not broken."

He shook his head in protest. "I don't know that. How can you?"

"My first teacher was called the Breaker of Circles. Believe me, I know all about these things."

He sat for a moment in silence, not looking at her, gazing out into the flower-scented dawning. Then he said, "I'm not sure I like my future very much, if it has people in it with names like that."

"It's all part of the great working. Did you think that putting the galaxy back together was going to be a quick and easy job?"

"If I ever thought so," he answered, "it didn't take me long to learn otherwise. And if that's what you're here for, you've come a long way to tell me something I already know."

"Well, I didn't come here for the sake of sitting on your front porch and admiring the view," she said, rather more sharply than before. "I've got forests at home that I can look at."

"Why, then?"

"I dreamed about you last night for the first time in—let's just say, for the first time in a long while—and when I woke up I had a feeling you were going to need my help. So I walked the Void until I found where you were waiting."

"*That's* certainly clear," he said. "Did you happen to see what kind of help I was going to need?"

Maraganha shrugged. "It's as clear as I can make it. And I'm afraid the universe didn't bother to give me specific instructions."

"I don't think anything scares you, *etaze*." He gave her the title without thinking, and wasn't surprised when she accepted it as her right. If Maraganha was a Void-walker, then she'd have to be the First of her Circle as well. For all her superficial friendliness and ease of manner, Arekhon knew that he was looking at one of the great Magelords—Garrod syn-Aigal's equal and perhaps even more.

"You'd be surprised," she said. "When I was young, I was scared to death of everything, and scared of myself most of all. That's the biggest part of what you taught me, in fact—to trust in what I knew and what I was."

"I'm glad that I was able to help. Or will be able to, as the case may be." He shook his head. "If we're going to keep on talking like this, we need better verbs."

"I can't help you with the verbs," she said. Then she looked at him straight on, and her voice had the same firmness and surety it had held in his dream. "But whatever else it is you're planning to do—I can help you with that."

"My Circle," he said. There was no chance, not after all this, that his dreams of late had been mere homesickness, born out of a wish that his life here with Elaeli could be something other than what necessity had given them. This was the great working, that he had pledged himself to finish when he was still the Third of Garrod's Circle, and there was no escape from it. "I need to find the rest of my Circle on Entibor, and take them home."

It was the damned ship-mind again.

Lenyat Irao—known to his cousins and most of his work-aday associates as Len—watched in disgust as the display on the chart table flickered. *Fire-on-the-Hilltops* was an old ship, a one-man light-cargo carrier purchased secondhand from the sus-Radal after that fleet-family had upgraded all of their own vessels to the new style. Len had known she was obsolete on the day he bought her, but that was how the game was played. New construction was for the star-lords, and everybody else took what was left over.

Still, he'd expected the *Fire* to hold together long enough for him to finish paying for her. And it was starting to look like—absent a complete flush-and-renewal of the ship-mind's quasi-organics—that wasn't going to happen. Lately she'd been growing reluctant to interface with anybody's charts but her own, and if that kept up, there went any hope of getting another decent contract.

The display blinked on and off and on again one more time, then settled down. The false-color display took on a three-dimensional aspect, the orbital lanes in blue, the world in yellow, and the marker-buoy in white.

"Finally," Len said. "Took you long enough."

As usual, he addressed his ship not in the Hanilat-Eraasian that he'd learned in school, but in his milk tongue, the language of Eraasi's antipodal subcontinent. The Irao had never intermarried with outsiders, and Len's knife-blade nose and yellowish-hazel eyes would have passed without remark in the homeland that his family had left a hundred years ago.

With the chart finally stabilized, he went to work setting up the *Fire* for emergence from the Void. The marker he'd asked for was a deep one, out at the farther limits of Eraasi's normal-space travel lanes. He'd have a long crawl past the outer planets, doing it that way, but he wasn't hauling perishable cargo and safety was better than speed.

For a good enough contract, sure, he'd pop out of the Void close in over Eraasi, and risk having one of the big fleet-families take him for an unlawful intruder and respond with force. He'd gotten his latest contract through the sus-Dariv, and *Fire-on-the-Hilltops* was listed with their fleet for the duration of the current voyage, but that wouldn't help much if a trigger-happy guardship captain decided not to bother with asking for his papers.

All the *Fire* had aboard this time was mixed-lot bulk cargo: transport, not trade, most of it, and not big enough to warrant a fleet-family's direct attention. Independents like Len handled the small jobs, and the urgent ones that couldn't wait for a convoy or a fleet courier, but the star-lords would come down hard on any pilot they suspected of working without a contract—"in the grey," as the slang term had it.

"Hard times, old girl," Len said to the *Fire,* as the ship-mind chewed its laborious way through the calculations for normal-space emergence. "Hard times. You and I, we were born too late."

There had been a time, not more than a generation or so ago, when a family working in the grey could gather enough ships (by trade or purchase or outright capture) to put a *syn-* or even a *sus-* in front of their name and have it stick. Len had daydreamed of it himself in his boyhood, back when he was the space-happy one among all the cousins. He'd pictured himself taking the family out of the groundside shipping and transportation business and into the stars, making them syn-Irao and star-lords and a fleet-family in Hanilat. Then he grew up, of course, and understood that those days were gone.

He took the figures the ship-mind ground out for him and entered the series of commands that would pass them to the *Fire*'s navigational console. "Emergence in five," he said, and keyed in the final sequence. There was only the ship-mind to hear him, but he'd learned to observe the formalities during his training days, when he'd served as hired crew aboard fleet-family ships.

A little while later he felt the disquieting inner sensation of Void-emergence pass through him like an oily wave. The distinctive hum and vibration of the *Fire*'s passage changed in response. Even if he'd somehow managed to sleep through the emergence, he would have known, by the sound and by the feel of the ship around him, that *Fire-on-the-Hilltops* was moving through normal space.

It was eight hours before he heard the distress signal. He had the *Fire*'s search-and-scan routines set to a tripwire sensitivity these days—a lowly contract-captain couldn't be too careful. They repaid him this time with a clamoring alarm and, when he put the signal onto ship's audio, a voice:

"This is sus-Dariv's *Garden-of-Fair-Blossoms*," it said, and the synthesized clarity of its pitch and elocution raised up all the fine hairs on the back of Len's neck. The only thing in space with a voice like that was a ship-mind, and if the ship-mind alone remained able to put out a signal, something very bad had happened aboard *Garden-of-Fair-Blossoms*. "If you are receiving this transmission, know that we are in distress and call for aid. We beg of you, make all speed to our location at—" There followed a warbling noise that Len recognized as the *Garden*'s ship-mind transmitting its reference coordinates directly to the ship-mind of whatever vessel might be listening. Then there was a pause, and the message started all over again.

Len hit the Transmit button on the *Fire*'s communications

board. *"Garden-of-Fair-Blossoms,"* he said. "This is contract carrier *Fire-on-the-Hilltops.* Try to hold on—I'm coming as fast as I can."

He turned back to the navigation console. For once, the *Fire*'s ship-mind had behaved itself properly. The false-color display now included a flashing amber dot—the *Garden*'s reference coordinates. He contemplated the symbolic representation briefly, then checked the alphanumeric readout and tapped in his course-query. More numbers and letters came up in reply, and the false-color display shifted, then shifted again after a second query and a second response.

After the third query, he said aloud, "I think you've got it this time, old girl."

The *Fire*'s ship-mind didn't have an internal speaker. Instead, the alphanumeric display at the navigational console reset itself to zero, then said, THIS COURSE CONTRADICTS PREVIOUS EXPRESSED PREFERENCE FOR NORMAL SPACE RUNNING DURING ERAASI APPROACH.

"That was then," he said. "And this is now. I'm not going to drag my feet through normal space on my way to answer a distress call, and neither are you."

2:

ERAASI: HANILAT
ENTIBOR: ROSSELIN COTTAGE

Rain had fallen since before sunset on the grounds of the Hanilat Institute of Higher and Extended Schooling. No surprise there—the city was in the deep middle of the winter wet, and heavy, wind-driven rains came on schedule every afternoon.

Today's downpour had only intensified with the fall of night. Someone not familiar with the Institute's paths and walkways might have gotten lost looking—as Kiefen Diasul was looking—for Quantret Hall. Quantret was built in the same old but not ancient style as most of the Institute's other structures, and the buildings all had much the same size and outline in the wind-lashed dark. The sign near Quantret's front entrance, set well back from the street and half-overgrown with night-blooming clingvine, was scarcely visible even in daylight.

But Kief was no stranger to the Institute grounds. He had come to Hanilat as a young man scarcely out of his basic schooling, and had studied the stargazers' disciplines at the Institute for more than a full hand of years; he had first trained as a Mage in the Institute's own Circle. He remembered the fastest way across campus from the Ten Street transport stop to Quantret Hall: down the brick-paved Long Diagonal, around the side of the tall brick Thalassic Studies Building, then across Quantret's back parking lot and down the three concrete steps to the little door that led directly to the sub-basement.

The Circle had met in Quantret Lower Level B when Kief was a student, and according to his researches, it met there still. Esya syn-Faredol was the First now. She had been only an unranked Circle-Mage when he left. Well, so had he been, but he had gone to the Demaizen Circle after that, and she had not.

The Institute's Circle worked the *eiran* to promote safety and tranquility on campus, a low-key and not especially demanding task. Demaizen, on the other hand . . . Demaizen's Mages had crossed the gap between the homeworlds and the rest of the galaxy, walking through the Void and marking a path for starship navigators to follow. That had taken a great working, paid for in blood and pain and lives. If the Circle here on campus had ever done such a working, neither tradition nor official record made any mention of the fact.

There was a puddle of muddy water at the foot of the steps. Kief halted on the last step above the puddle, and set down his daypack on the wet concrete. Then he shed his long weather coat and draped it over the slick metal handrail. The Mage's working robes that he'd been wearing underneath—and that had made his public transport ride a stuffy ordeal—tumbled free and fell loosely around him. He felt suddenly cooler, almost cold, and told himself that it was the result of taking off the sweltering coat.

Kief bent and unfastened his daypack. Inside the pack lay an ordinary ship-combat hardmask, done up in smoky grey plastic and black enamel. He took out the mask and put it on.

The harsh glare of the incandescent lamp over Quantret Hall's rear basement entrance dimmed to a muted glow. Kief drew in a long breath of satisfaction between his teeth. The hardmask had been a matter of practical necessity at first. In the work he and his Circle did for Natelth sus-Peledaen, it was not always convenient for his face to be seen and recognized. Only later had he become aware of the other advantage that the mask conferred: In the diminished light, the silver threads of the *eiran* stood out clearly, a dense network of them, looping and interweaving in a pattern as familiar to him as the lines on his own palm.

Garrod's working. The last, great working of the Demaizen Circle, still ongoing even though the Old Hall at Demaizen was nothing but rubble and the Mages themselves were dead or scattered across the galaxy.

All but me, Kief thought. *Anyone else would say that I've done well since then. I have another Circle; I am a power that not even the sus-Peledaen can ignore; but Demaizen will not let me go.*

Tonight, though, would see his old Circle's hold on him broken, and the pattern of the great working ripped asunder for good and all. So far as Kief knew, nobody on Eraasi had ever tried to do what he was planning to do, once he got to the room in Quantret Hall's sub-basement where the Institute Circle met—nobody else had even considered the possibility of doing it, and there had been Circles working on Eraasi for as far back as history and legend ran.

That he could think of it at all, Kief supposed, meant that he was not entirely sane. This possibility failed to surprise him; he sometimes thought that he hadn't really been sane, at least as his younger self would have understood the concept of sanity, since the day the Old Hall burned.

It didn't matter. If he failed tonight, he would be dead, and his mental health or lack of it would soon be forgotten. And if he succeeded—

If he succeeded, then everything would change.

Kief unfastened the staff from his belt and held it loosely at the ready in his right hand. With his left hand, he pushed open the sub-basement door.

The door opened onto a stairwell. Light came from an amber-colored Emergency Exit sign bolted to the wall. Through the dull grey faceplate of his hardmask, Kief saw how the glowing silver threads of the *eiran* had followed him in here, too. He grimaced behind the hardmask.

Soon, he told the pattern of Demaizen's working. *I'll be rid of you soon.*

He started down the stairs. Five steps . . . ten steps . . .

twelve. The door at the bottom was locked. He struck it once with his staff, lightly, and it swung open.

The corridor on the other side, like the stairwell, was a dark space lit only by the amber glow of the Emergency Exit sign. The darkness didn't matter; Kief had been here many times while he worked at the Institute, and he knew the way. He let memory take him past the first doorway, and the second, before stopping at the third.

This time it was no light tap he gave it, but a full-strength blow, backed up with all the power at his command. The door ripped open and slammed against the wall on the other side.

The room within was as he remembered it from his Institute days: black floor tiles, with a large circle of white tiles set in the middle; walls and ceiling also dead black; thick white candles burning at the compass points outside the circle; and inside the Circle, Mages kneeling in meditation.

None of them were masked, of course. They had no need, here in their safe meeting place, of the anonymity a hardmask could provide, and their bare faces were pale white blurs inside the hoods of their robes. He spotted Esya at once, in the First's position, and stepped across the boundary of the white circle to stand in front of her.

"Esya," he said.

She hadn't yet gone deep into the working; the sound of her own name was enough to rouse her. She lifted her head and looked at him across the ring of kneeling, black-clad figures. He could tell from her face that the hardmask wasn't enough to conceal his identity. She'd always had a good memory for voices and postures.

"No more names," he said before she could speak. "We have business together first."

She wet her lips. Kief remembered that habit of hers, too, and knew that it masked a surge of apprehension. The Circle's routine had been unexpectedly broken, and Esya had never dealt well with unscheduled change.

"What kind of business?" she asked.

"I've come to offer you a choice."

"A choice?"

"Yes," he said. "Either you give me your Circle, or we

can make a working together, you and I, and let the *eiran* decide."

"Why should I do either one?"

"Because you're not strong enough to hold the Circle once they begin to doubt," he said. "And they're doubting you right now."

She didn't answer, and he knew that she was testing the *eiran* and the temper of her Circle, trying to judge for herself whether he spoke the truth. Kief knew what she would see. The Institute's Mages were barely more than dilettantes these days—maybe they'd give their lives to a working if the cause was dear enough to them, but not for the sake of Esya syn-Faredol.

But he had liked Esya more than a little, once upon a time, and for a few moments longer he allowed himself to hope that she would take the easier way. Then she rose from her kneeling position and stepped into the middle of the Circle with her staff in her hand.

"All right," she said. "We'll work it out together, as the universe wills."

He strode forward and passed between two of the kneeling Mages to meet her in the center of the ring. "As the universe wills."

The Void-walker Maraganha had spoken to Arekhon in fluent—if strongly accented—Eraasian, so he had assumed, perhaps irrationally, that she could speak Entiboran as well. He discovered his mistake later that same day when he took her into the town nearest Elaeli's summer cottage in order to purchase some locally made items of clothing. Maraganha's voice shaped words that Arekhon didn't understand or even recognize, and the *eiran* twisted like snakes in the air around her, making meaning.

"Denli tappak, amjepin bi veppis?"

Do you have one like this, but without the bead trim?

The shopkeeper didn't seem to notice anything amiss. "Are these more like what you're looking for?"

Maraganha looked at the indicated garments and smiled. *"Ea."*

Yes.

Outside the shop, Arekhon said, "How did you do that?"

"It's a knack," she said in Eraasian. "You could probably do it yourself if you tried. Most people don't even notice it's happening."

"Most people aren't Mages and Adepts. What language was that?"

"Standard Galcenian," she said. "It's not my birth tongue, but it's the one I was speaking when I picked up the language trick. One bit of knowledge sticks to the other."

Arekhon said, "I've heard of Galcen."

"Don't tell me that place already thinks it's the beating heart of the civilized galaxy."

"I'm afraid so," he said. He thought of asking her how she had come to learn the languages of Galcen and of the homeworlds, but not of Entibor, but something in her manner suggested that he wouldn't get an answer if he tried. He tried another line of inquiry instead. "How long from now is Galcen still thinking that?"

"That's not a good question to ask," she said.

"Because too much knowledge of the future is dangerous?"

"Because all the Entiboran dates I've ever heard of are in regnal years," she said. "I don't know enough of your local history to match them up with anything standard. So any answer that I give you runs a big risk of being nonsense."

"I see."

"Also, too much knowledge of the future is dangerous."

"Then I'll suppress my curiosity," Arekhon promised her—he might as well be virtuous, he reflected, since Maraganha plainly had no intention of revealing anything. He changed the subject. "Are you ready to go looking for Mages, *etaze?*"

"Call me Maraganha. Too much deference, and I start wanting to jump out of my own skin."

"Maraganha," he said. "Are you ready?"

"As ready as I'll ever be," she answered. "Let's go."

Iulan Vai waited in the rain and shadows outside the town house of Theledau sus-Radal, watching the night wind drive the raindrops slantwise in the glow of the streetlamps. The wet-season nights in Hanilat, which those local to the district found chilly, felt comfortably warm to Vai, who had come of age in Eraasi's high subarctic forests. Nevertheless, she wore a hooded cape of unlined watertight material—not so much out of deference to the weather as to the custom of the city—as well as a half-mask in stiff black cloth. That, also, was a custom of the city these days. The wearing of masks had come into vogue during the civic unrest of a decade earlier, and while the fashion had subsided among the greater middling class of people, those who lived at the extremes of Hanilat society—street urchins as well as star-lords—still kept the practice alive.

For Vai, the mask was also a necessity of her name and calling. It would not do for a passerby to catch a glimpse of her features and recognize one of the supposedly dead De-maizen Mages. Someone might spot her lurking masked and hooded near sus-Radal's doorstep, but if they did, they would say nothing and hurry on. She might be a sneak thief looking for a purse to snatch in faceless anonymity, or she might be a sus-Somebody on her way to a lovers' tryst. These days in Hanilat, prudent people asked no questions.

When the road was clear of loiterers and passersby, and had been so for long enough that casual watchers at the darkened windows of other houses could be presumed to have grown bored and moved away, Vai drifted—still in shadows—up to the sus-Radal's door.

As always, she used the private side entrance with the lock keyed only to close members of the inner family and its most trusted employees, and passed through without disturbance. The hour was late enough that most of the stairs and hallways inside were darkened. The night before, Theledau sus-Radal had entertained guests at dinner until the small hours, but not now.

Once inside, Vai removed her mask and tucked it under one arm, then made her way unchallenged to the room at the top of the house where the attic had once been. The room answered to another purpose these days. Thel came from the same far northern district as Iulan Vai, and he followed the ritual of his native country even in subtropical Hanilat.

To those of the north, the moon was holy, and proper worship lay in keeping watch over her movements. The upper room, its ceiling replaced by a circular dome of clear glass, was Theledau syn-Grevi sus-Radal's temple and observatory. At this hour of the night, on this day of the lunar month, Vai could usually depend on encountering him in the moon-room—alone, most often, since those of the sus-Radal who were native-born to Hanilat had their own ways of tending the family altars.

Vai had also been raised in the northern worship, but she had left it behind her when she came south to be Theledau's eyes and ears in Hanilat. When Thel became head of the sus-Radal, he had rewarded Vai's service by making her the fleet-family's Agent-Principal. So high a promotion often brought with it an adoption into the outer family, the syn-Radal, but Thel knew better than to offer her such a thing. It would be an insult, when only the lack of their common father's acknowledgment had kept Vai's name from being inscribed along with Thel's on the inner-family tablets of the sus-Radal.

Thel was standing in the center of the darkened moon-room when Vai entered. There was no moon visible tonight to flood the room with silver; heavy clouds obscured all but the faintest of reflected city light, and the driving wind threw the rain in heavy spatters against the glass dome.

Turning at the sound of her footsteps—she had made no effort to mute them—Thel brought up the room lights with a gesture toward the control panel on the nearby wall. The increased illumination showed her a square-built man with hair the same rusty black color as her own, though in his case the black was liberally streaked with iron-grey.

"Vai," he said. "What kind of trouble have you brought me tonight?"

" 'Trouble'?" Vai feigned indignation; she might not be Thel's Agent-Principal any longer, but their relationship was still close enough to allow for a good deal of familiarity if she chose to exercise it. "Why do you always ask me about trouble?"

"You're a storm-bird," he said. He gestured at her sable garments. "These days you even dress the part."

She lifted one corner of her cloak and let it drop again into folds at her side. "All black and fluttering? I suppose I do. But if all I bring you is bad news, blame it on the times and not on me."

"From which I take it the news isn't good this evening, either?"

"I don't know," Vai said slowly. "It's been a long time since I've done any of your official security work; and I don't know what your Agent-Principal may have advised—but speaking as a Mage, my lord, and one whose Circle owes you a debt: You're right; there's trouble coming. Tell your fleet-Circles to practice and be ready."

"Be ready for what?"

She gave him a brief, rueful smile. "That's the heart of the problem. I'm not sure. But I'm not the only one who's noticed it. The sus-Dariv are taking an interest as well."

Thel frowned. "The sus-Dariv aren't a threat—they stay out of politics and stick to trade, and believe me when I say that I wish the sus-Radal could do the same. What about the sus-Peledaen?"

"You and I both know," Vai said, "that the sus-Peledaen don't take an interest in the problem because the sus-Peledaen *are* the problem."

"You never used to be that blunt when you worked for me."

"I never used to be a Mage, either, when I worked for you. I've seen the *eiran*, Thel, and they're changing. The patterns are different now, and the Circles and the fleet-families and all of Eraasi are being drawn into them like fish into a net."

"What am I supposed to do about it?"

"Do what you're doing now," she said. "Whatever it is that's keeping the *eiran* around you moving. Keep the sus-Radal free as long as you can."

He nodded slowly. "You don't really think we'll be able to stay out of it, do you?"

"Not this time," Vai said. "Something new is beginning, and it isn't good."

◆

Ayil syn-Arvedan snapped shut her mail-reader and sat for a while frowning at the closed cover. She had studied the stargazers' disciplines at the Hanilat Institute for almost two decades, and had taught them as well: a quiet life, and one much to her liking. She'd seen what too much passionate involvement did to people. Going to the Mages had killed one of her brothers years ago, and—if this latest angry communication from her older brother Inadal was any clue—the current round of city-versus-country, star-lords-versus-everybody politics was fast eating away at the other one.

The old land-families didn't have the influence they used to—well, they hadn't had *that* for a couple of centuries, but now the urban bankers and merchants who'd made common cause with them were losing power as well. Her brother thought that outside trade alliances would strengthen the mercantile party against the fleet-families. Ayil considered that idea to be foolish optimism: a few off-planet traders might make big talk about their independence, but none of them had crossed an Eraasian fleet-family in years—not since sus-Peledaen warships had left a space-bombed scar across the heart of a rival world's largest continent.

She would write to her brother, she decided, and tell him what she thought. In the morning, after she'd had a chance to sleep on it first. This was a wild and rainy night, with a strong wind for the season and the barometric pressure heading steadily downward. Not a good night for composing a tactful letter to the head of the family, asking him to back away from a losing fight.

A gust of wind drove the rain hard against the windows of her Institute Towers apartment. She was three floors up, on a level with the swaying treetops. Light from the streetlamps and from the watch-out glows embedded in the sidewalks didn't make it up this far, except for the occasional glimpse through tossing branches.

She was looking out of the window when the door-tone sounded: the low, gong-like note of the outside building directory, rather than the light chime of her own apartment's sounding-pad. Somebody had come to the Institute Towers in this weather, and at this hour, to call at her address. *An-*

other lost drunk, she thought, reluctant to answer the summons. *Or some kind of student prank.*

On the other hand, she did give out her home number and address to those students whom she was advising directly. If one of them needed help badly enough to come asking for it in person—

"House-mind," she said. "Answer."

"Answering," said the apartment's house-mind, and she heard the click of the voice connection opening as the gongtone sounded for a second time.

"Who is it?" she asked.

At first she heard nothing in reply except what sounded like ragged breathing. Then—"Ayil?"

Not a student. A student would never call her by her personal name, not if he—the speaker *was* male, she thought—not if he had come here needing a favor. A prankster, maybe, using the unwanted familiarity to frighten her.

"Who is it?" she demanded again, more sharply.

"Ayil . . . it's me. Diasul."

"Kief?"

"Yes. Let me come up?"

She knew the voice by now, the name and the accent together bringing back memories of earlier days. She'd shared office space for a while with Kiefen Diasul, back before he'd left the Institute to join a Void-walker's Circle—her late brother Del's Circle, in fact, which she supposed gave Kief at least as much claim on her late-night attention as one of her wayward students.

"Are you all right, Kief?" she asked. "Do you need me to call someone for help?"

"No." Too fast, too firm—something was wrong, she thought, no matter what he said. "I don't need help. I just need . . . I don't know. Someplace to rest for a while. It's been a . . . it's raining sheets and buckets outside tonight, Ayil. I'm soaked with it."

"Come on up, then. House-mind: Open exterior."

She heard the noise of the downstairs door opening. Then the voice connection clicked shut, and she had to wait uneasily for the sound of the elevator, and footsteps in the hallway outside her own apartment. At least, she reflected, if she was going to have an unexpected visitor from the past, the luck had brought him to her on a night when everything was fairly tidy. She had books and papers strewn all over the place, of course, but Kief had been a scholar once himself; he'd be used to that.

The sounding-pad chimed. "Open," she said to the house-mind, then raised her voice as the door swung open. "Come in."

Kiefen Diasul stepped over the threshold into the entry-way. He hadn't changed much since the last time she'd seen him—he was older, of course, but his early-greying brown hair still hung in loose curls down to his shoulders, and he still wore the same pendant earring of rock crystal and twisted wire that he had affected during their officemate days. He was wearing the black garments of a working Mage, and he hadn't lied when he said the rain was coming down in sheets; the heavy fabric of his robe looked sodden with it. He moved carefully, as though his joints and muscles protested the effort, and his face was grey and exhausted.

Ayil hurried forward. "Come on in . . . you're leaving pud-dles all over the foyer."

"Sorry."

"It's all right. Did something happen to your weather coat?"

"Left it behind. Outside Quantret."

"Don't worry about it; I can send somebody to fetch it tomorrow." She touched his wet sleeve. "Let me hang this over the watercourse in the necessarium until it stops drip-ping."

She thought at first that he would refuse, but she kept hold of the sleeve. After a few seconds, he let out his breath in a faint sigh and allowed her to help him out of the wringing-wet garment. He had his staff with him—she should have known that he would, she thought. Even the members of the Institute Circle, who wore their Magecraft lightly, as an av-ocation rather than a life's obsession, kept their staves close by them at all hours. Kiefen Diasul clipped his staff onto the belt of his street clothes as soon as she lifted away the rain-heavy folds of his robe.

She left him standing in the foyer and carried off the robe

to the necessarium, where she left it hanging from the drip bar. When she returned to the entryway, she found that Kief had wandered into the dining nook and was sitting in one of the cheap plastic chairs that had come with the apartment.

Considerate of him not to spoil the good upholstery, she thought. And then, as she got a look at him for the first time in a good light, *He needs warming up in a bad way.* She went over to the preserving-cupboard and pulled out a canister of pale leaf.

"*Uffa?*" she asked.

He nodded, not looking up from his contemplation of the tabletop. "Please."

She fiddled about with the *uffa* makings, putting water on the stove and filling a strainer with the dried curly leaves. As she worked, she said, "What was it brought you back to the Institute? Some kind of Circle business?"

She thought he wasn't going to answer, he was quiet for so long. But just as she was about to give up the inquiry as a bad job and talk about something else, he spoke.

"Yes."

"Oh." She got a cup down from the shelf over the sink and balanced the strainer over it. She could hear the kettle beginning to sing a little as the water inside grew hot. Finally she said, "I never asked . . . for a long time I didn't even want to think about what happened at Demaizen . . . did you keep Lord Garrod's Circle together? Afterward, I mean."

"No."

Curiosity warred in her briefly with the pain of memory—but she was a scholar, with her own driving passions, and curiosity won. "Whose Circle *do* you work with, then?"

Now he did look up—straight at her, with what might have been a warning in his glance. "There was a time," he said, "and not so long ago, either, when that question wasn't in bad taste."

"Del certainly never made any secret out of belonging to Demaizen," she agreed. As she'd half-expected, her brother's name drew a reaction from him, as if she'd touched on a painful memory. She decided to give the matter another push. "Have things changed that much since then?"

"Are all you people here at the Institute really that sheltered?" He asked the question lightly, but the expression in his eyes was bitter.

She shrugged. "You studied here yourself. You should know."

"Yes," he said. He didn't say anything more for a while. The kettle boiled, and she poured the hot steaming water over the strainer of *uffa*. Tendrils of steam curled upward, and the kitchen nook was suddenly full of the sharp, invigorating scent of fresh-steeped leaf.

When the water had taken on the proper golden color, she dumped the leaves from the strainer into the garbage and gave him the cup. He sipped at it, lowering the level bit by bit for several minutes. She watched him and said nothing. At last he sighed, put down the cup, and said, "It's probably on record somewhere . . . I'm with one of the sus-Peledaen Circles these days. Lord Natelth's younger brother was Second at Demaizen for a while, so there was a connection when I needed one."

"That's good. Say whatever else you want to about the sus-Peledaen—they take care of their own."

"Yes." She thought he might be going to say something more, but instead he fell silent and went back to his cup of *uffa*. She waited for him to finish it, watching him fade visibly with exhaustion as they talked of Institute gossip and other inconsequential matters. After he'd finished the last of the *uffa*, she cleared away the cup and the strainer, then left him to check on the robe hanging in the necessarium. When she returned, he was nearly asleep sitting up at the table. She touched his shoulder lightly to rouse him.

"It's coming down like a waterfall outside," she said, "and the wind's picking up. I'll make you up a bed on the couch and you can catch the bus in the morning."

He shook his head as if to clear it. "You shouldn't—"

"—shouldn't help out my old officemate and the friend of my brother? Don't be silly, Kief. It's practically my duty to put you up for the night."

His protests faded; there plainly hadn't been much heart in them to start with. She fetched sheets and a pillow and turned the couch into a makeshift cot, shifting aside two folders full of student examinations in order to clear off space. That done, she retired to her own bedroom.

But sleep, for Ayil, was a long time in coming. Instead, she lay awake thinking about what she was going to have to do next. The unfinished argument with her brother about the long-term viability of his political goals would have to wait. More important, right now, was that Inadal should know what she had learned tonight: There had been blood on Kief's robe, quite a lot of it, rinsed out by the flowing water in the necessarium and staining the rough tiles of the watercourse beneath.

His "Circle business" had included a major working—one that had ended in serious injury, had perhaps even required a death. And it had brought one of Lord Natelth's Mages onto the Institute grounds.

The sus-Peledaen were up to something, without a doubt. Which meant that their enemies, her brother and the others of his faction among them, would need to keep close watch.

3:

ERAASI: HANILAT; ERAASIAN FARSPACE
ENTIBOR: CAZDEL

So far, the morning promised to be an ordinary workday in Hanilat. Grif Egelt, the sus-Peledaen Agent-Principal for Internal Security, arrived at his office in the fleet-family's ground headquarters carrying—as was his invariable practice—a tall serving of yellow-leaf *uffa* in a paper cup, purchased from one of the sidewalk vendors outside. The habit dated from Egelt's early years in the sus-Peledaen employ. In those days, the *uffa* pots in the headquarters building only had red, because the head guy liked red leaf and no one knew when he might drop by. Egelt had grown accustomed to decanting the morning's tall cup into his desktop warmer, then nursing it along for hours until he had the chance to get himself another round of yellow at lunchtime.

These days, the *uffa* brewed at ground headquarters came in both red and yellow like it did everywhere else, because Natelth sus-Khalgath sus-Peledaen had moved up to the orbital station and all his visits to the ground office were scheduled days in advance. Natelth's sister Isayana came and went regularly—she did liaison work with a lot of the family's ground-based tech contractors—but from what Egelt had seen of that one, the *uffa* in her cup could be bright green and she wouldn't care, or perhaps even notice.

The change in the leaf, Egelt reflected, was just one more indicator of the general decline of ground headquarters. The building had once housed the main offices for everything the sus-Peledaen fleet-family did that wasn't managed by the big man personally—the Finance Division, the Division of Research and Development, both the Internal and the External Security Divisions, and a host of others—but most of them had suffered a downgrade to "Eraasi Branch" during the big reorganization following Lord Natelth's move to the orbital station.

The Internal Security Division had escaped that much humiliation, at least. But the External side of the family's security operations had moved up to the station with Lord Natelth—and the head of External had moved up into the syn-Peledaen—while Internal Security had not.

Egelt took the executive elevator up to the Internal Security floor. The division's second-in-command, Jyriom Hussav, was already checking the main board in the outer office for updates. The wall-sized flat-display currently showed a detailed street map of Hanilat. Colored glyphs—violet for favorable indicators, green for items of possible interest, and bright yellow for dangerous or urgent situations—dotted the city grid. Based on the display alone, Egelt reflected, today was shaping up well. Plenty of violet dots and no yellows, and just enough green dots to make life interesting.

He joined Hussav at the board. "What have we got?"

"Not much, for a change." Hussav was a Veredden Islander, short and dark by Hanilat standards, with curly black hair and a thick mustache. Standing next to him tended to make the fair-skinned and much taller Egelt feel like an illustration from his grandmother's old *Peoples of Eraasi* textbook; nevertheless, the two men had worked well together for several years. Hussav pointed to a cluster of green dots in the port district. "The sus-Radal are still pushing at us and trying to penetrate our operations, but the level of activity hasn't changed markedly, so it's probably just routine snooping."

"Get some people on all those incidents," Egelt said. "Maybe they're just going through the motions over there—

but if they happen to find something that gives when they push it, they're going to push even harder and move right on in. We can't afford for that to happen."

Hussav entered a series of notes on his textpad. "Got it."

"Anything else?"

The second-in-command jabbed his stylus at another green dot. "More disaffected mutterings among the landed gentry. Country nobility come to town, for the most part."

Egelt frowned. "Analysis doesn't make it yellow?"

"No. Consensus is more hurt ego at work than actual grievance—and no real power to act. And the threat's too diffuse; they don't like the other fleet-families any more than they like us."

"For now, at any rate." Egelt understood the power of a hurt ego. It had made him head of Internal Security, when his predecessor—denied the outer-family adoption given to his External counterpart—took early retirement in the wake of the great reorganization. "Keep watching them." He turned his attention to the largest cluster of green dots, in the area around the Court of Two Colors in the downtown entertainment district. "How's the sus-Dariv situation?"

"Stable, for the moment," Hussav said. "But it'll be interesting to see what kind of policy changes come out of the big meeting."

"I assume we've got people on the inside taking notes."

Hussav nodded. "Right. We've been working them up through the ranks for a while now."

"Good," said Egelt. "Keep me posted—the sus-Dariv may not be pushing us at the moment, but they've got enough money and resources to become a real problem if they ever change their minds."

Arekhon and Maraganha found Ty at the Cazdel Guildhouse. Locating him hadn't been difficult; Ty had never made any secret of his whereabouts, and he and Arekhon had kept up a sporadic correspondence over the years.

Diplomatic relations between Cazdel and the Federated Quarter hadn't been particularly good lately, but so far the peace accords were holding. Arekhon was able to secure passage for himself and Maraganha on a commercial jumpshuttle for a suborbital hop. They picked up a glidecab at the Cazdel shuttle port, and Arekhon instructed the driver to take them to the Guildhouse.

"You do business with those people?" the driver asked.

"Sometimes."

"Better watch it. They mess around with things to make stuff come out right. Right for them, anyhow. They don't care so much about the rest of us."

"I'll bear that in mind," said Arekhon. It was yet another strangeness of this world that he'd never grown accustomed to: the idea that people who could see the *eiran* would not work with them on behalf of others. Next to him in the rear of the glidecab, he saw that Maraganha looked disapproving, though whether it was the driver's prejudice or the local Adepts' indifference that had moved her, he couldn't tell.

The Cazdel Guildhouse, despite its formal name, turned out to be an ordinary-looking commercial building with offices below and apartments above, located near the middle of town. Arekhon knew from Ty's letters that the house sheltered almost two score men and women—enough to fill more than one Circle, had they known how to work in that fashion.

In the Guildhouse lobby, a gated wooden railing blocked the way to the offices and meeting rooms beyond. The young woman at the desk behind the rail wore simply cut garments in dusty beige. From her age and general demeanor, Arekhon placed her as a student of sorts, assigned to gate duty as part of her training.

"You two have business here?" she asked.

He nodded. "We need to talk with one of your people . . . Ty, his name is. He knows that we're coming."

"Wait in Room Five, down at the end of the hall. I'll let him know that you've arrived."

She touched a control on the desk, and the railing buzzed as the gate lock opened. Arekhon and Maraganha passed through and went on to Room 5, a bare conference room furnished only with a table and a number of uncomfortable-looking folding chairs. A lecture board and a rack of light-markers covered most of one wall; the board was powered down, revealing nothing. There were no windows.

Arekhon unfolded one of the metal chairs and sat down at the table to wait. Maraganha hesitated, then did likewise.

"You're shading the truth a bit, you know," she said.

"By not mentioning you when I sent the message?" He shook his head. "With all respect, *etaze*—Maraganha—that's a bit more strangeness than I felt like explaining in an open text."

"You know, I used to wonder whether you were naturally secretive or if it was an acquired habit."

"And now?"

She laughed quietly. "I'm beginning to suspect you were born that way."

"My sister would probably agree with you. She had the sorrowful task of raising me after our parents died—my brother Natelth had to take over the family at the same time—and she said later that she found it easier to instruct and maintain a house full of quasi-organics than to bring up one infant sibling."

"She sounds interesting," Maraganha said.

"Perhaps you'll meet her when we . . . ah, here comes Ty."

The youngest surviving member of the Demaizen Circle hadn't changed much over the years, at least externally. He still wore his hair cut short in back and long over his forehead like a Hanilat street tough, and dressed like a laborer-for-hire—albeit one who wore plain grey and black and carried a long wooden staff.

Arekhon looked at it and raised an eyebrow. "What became of the staff you used to carry?"

"I put it away," said Ty. He propped the long staff in the corner and unfolded another of the metal chairs. In Eraasian, he added, "How about you, 'Rekhe? I don't see you carrying a staff at all."

"No, you don't," Arekhon replied in the same language. "Not in public, anyway."

"Why not?" Ty looked over at Maraganha. "She does."

"Maraganha *etaze* is a Void-walker and a great Magelord," Arekhon said. "On the other hand, as far as most people know, I'm Mestra Elela Rosselin's chief of domestic security—which means that I'm part of the furniture. If people begin to think of me as one of your Adept friends, or as something else that works like one, then they'll start to notice me, and I don't want that."

"It would be a bad idea," agreed Ty. "Especially if someone also notices that you've been working the *eiran* for the Mestra's benefit. They don't like that around here."

"So I've heard," Arekhon said. "This world would be better off if they did, I think."

"Like we did for Eraasi? I remember how well *that* turned out." Ty's cheeks reddened as he spoke. "And now you've brought a Void-walker into the Guildhouse, and they'll notice the disturbances in the *eiran* for sure."

"Give me credit for some discretion, child," Maraganha said. "I've spent more time in Guildhouses than you ever will, and I think I know how to avoid scandalizing the inhabitants."

Ty looked hard at her. "I don't know you," he said at last. "I don't know why you're with 'Rekhe and I don't know where you come from. Is there a reason why I should believe you?"

"Because you're one of those who can see truth or falsehood in the *eiran* if you bother to look." She met Ty's gaze squarely. "I came here across time, space, and the Void because the great working wasn't done with me yet . . . and it isn't done with you, either."

"She's right," Arekhon said. "The working isn't finished. We have to go back."

"There's no 'have to' in it for me. You expect me to drop everything and follow you back to Eraasi?" Ty shook his head. "I have a place here, 'Rekhe, and I don't want to lose it. Not without at least a fighting chance that it won't all have been for nothing."

"What would it take to convince you?"

"Narin," Ty said. "She was always the strongest of us, except for Garrod; stronger than him, maybe. The only reason she didn't hold rank in the Circle was because she never wanted it. If you can find Narin and persuade her to come along, then I'm in."

◆

Zeri sus-Dariv had been attending her family's annual business conclave every year since she'd reached her sixteenth birthday—old enough to enroll as a fleet-apprentice if she so desired, or to leave her family's altars and train with the Mages, though not of age to hold a family commission or Circle membership. Zeri didn't want to be either a fleet officer or a Mage; since she had to study *something* until she reached her majority, she claimed to be an aspiring merchant-administrator—an entirely reasonable choice for a member of the family's senior line. As part of her apprenticeship, she went to the meetings and observed her family's internal politics in action, and found them dead boring.

Almost seven years later, she hadn't changed her opinion. Not even holding the current meeting in the private conference area of the Court of Two Colors, Hanilat's most exclusive hostelry and dining place, could make Zeri feel more than a passing interest in the matters at hand. Some years she'd lasted as long as the full week; this year she gave up trying on the fifth day.

She remembered the moment clearly afterward. She'd been at the late-afternoon snacks-and-*uffa* break in the Court's Grand Reception Hall, where the working members of the sus-Dariv, the men and women upon whom the inner family relied for support, stood about in gossiping clusters on the black-and-white tessellated floor that gave the Court its name. Tables on the long side of the room held trays of food—small sausages wrapped in flaky pastry, grilled miniature vegetables on wooden skewers, cubes of hard white cheese, and slices of *neiath* fruit drizzled with bittersweet syrup—flanked by giant copper urns full of both red and pale *uffa*.

The pair of outer-family administrators with whom she'd been working all afternoon—first generation syn-Dariv by adoption, which meant they were ambitious up-and-comers—had been talking about differential rank and compensation scales for the last half-hour. The conversation seemed to press down upon her like a pillow, vast and formless and smothering. What was she doing here, anyway? She'd missed this month's theatre-arts group meeting already—

She caught sight of her cousin Herin filling a crystal mug

with *uffa* at the nearest urn. With a skill honed over years of family conclaves, she detached herself from the two syn-Dariv and bore down upon her cousin.

"Herin!" she exclaimed, as soon as she came within earshot. "This is the first time I've seen you, this whole session—have you been avoiding me?"

"Not on purpose," he said. He added, "I didn't get here until today, as it happens."

"Lucky for you. Where were you all that time?"

He filled a mug with pale *uffa* and handed it to her. He knew her tastes well enough to omit asking for her preference, which was handy if a bit unsettling when she considered that they'd never been particularly close. "Here and there," he said. "Studying."

"Studying what?"

"Private security forces, mostly," he said. "And how they're being integrated into different family structures."

"Ah." That was the main issue facing this evening's open session; it had depressed her a little that more people hadn't been talking about the problem earlier. "How *are* they being integrated?"

"As a general rule?" He drained the last of his mug of *uffa* and filled it again. "Badly. Either they're not exploited well enough or they're a danger to the family that supposedly controls them."

"I suppose that means you're going to vote against establishing a sus-Dariv strike team," she said.

He nodded. "The odds of it working as intended aren't very high."

"I suppose not . . . look, Herin, will you take my proxy for that vote when it comes up? If I don't get out of here soon I'm going to suffocate."

"Of course," he said.

She set down her mug and searched through her folder of conference materials until she found a stylus and a slip of paper with which to write up the formal authorization. He tucked the finished note inside his shirt. That done, Zeri gave Herin her thanks and a smile of farewell, then began working her way through the crowd to the door.

The Court of Two Colors had its main entrance on High Port Road—a wide, elegant doorway, all thick black glass with burnished silver fittings, for the honor of the guests. The Court had other ways in and out, however, plainer and more utilitarian ones, for the use of suppliers and workers and maintenance personnel. The pleasure of Hanilat's best and highest was not to be sullied by interruptions from those who made that pleasure possible.

The service entrances to the Court had their own feeder network of alleys and unloading bays, kept brightly lit no matter how dark the night outside. Beyond the entrances lay the Court's working spaces—kitchen and laundry and storage and maintenance. In one of the offices on the kitchen level, the Court's chief-provisioner Mielen Tabbes sat going over a copy of tomorrow's planned menu, with a printout of the contents of the larder ready to hand.

"Snowdrifts in tangleberry sauce?" he asked, his finger tracing the menu item. He brought up the Court's master recipe index on his desk reader, and moved to the entry for snowdrifts. "Glacial ice. The standard is glacial ice."

The larder list showed only four pounds of glacial ice. Hardly enough for a table full of star-lords, should they get the hunger on them for berried snow. Refrigerator ice could be substituted, but not at the Court of Two Colors.

Tabbes drew a line through the menu entry to show that he had not approved it, then moved on to the next item, a gallimaufry of tenderwort in cream. Tenderwort was on the delivery list for tonight, very good, because it didn't keep. The list showed a truckload from the Ridge Farms Produce Cooperative going to Loading Dock 3, and from there to the low-humidity storeroom. Perhaps it had already arrived. Tabbes would check later.

What would have been a slow crawl of a month or more in normal space was barely an eyelash-flicker spent transiting the Void. Len Irao didn't even have a chance to get properly apprehensive about guardships and other hazards of an off-lanes emergence. The *Fire* took him into the Void and out of it again as smoothly as he'd ever known her to go. Even the usual brief disorientation was less marked than usual, although he supposed that could be the result of having other things on his mind—such as the question of what kind of disaster could have done such damage to a fleet-family vessel that only its ship-mind was left to signal for help.

Normal space after emergence didn't give him any clues, or at least not at first. Then the *Fire*'s proximity alarm sounded, and he felt the ship change course abruptly. As soon as the acceleration let up, he checked the navigational console. The false-color display now showed a patch of what looked like amber fog where the marker for the sus-Dariv ship had been, and the alphanumeric readout said, SENSORS REPORT DRIFTING DEBRIS. STAND BY FOR UNSCHEDULED EVASIVE MANEUVERS.

"Damn," he said. "I hope we haven't lost them."

The communications console obliged him by coming once more to life. "This is sus-Dariv's *Garden-of-Fair-Blossoms*. If you are receiving this transmission, know that we are in distress and call for aid. We beg of you, make all speed to our location. . . ."

Maybe the *Garden*'s luck wasn't gone after all. If its ship-mind could still function, the sus-Dariv ship was probably not one of those bits of drifting debris *Fire-on-the-Hilltops* was busy avoiding. He set himself to instructing the ship-mind in a search pattern that would increase their chances of finding *Garden-of-Fair-Blossoms* in an expeditious manner.

Several hours and a number of unscheduled evasive maneuvers later, the navigational console began to blink and hoot at him. SEARCH TARGET FOUND, reported the alphanumeric display. SENSORS REPORT VESSEL'S DOCKING RING INTACT.

Len drew a deep breath. The next few hours, he suspected, were not going to be pretty.

"Initiate docking procedures with *Garden-of-Fair-Blossoms,*" he said, and went to don his pressure-suit and otherwise make ready for an extended period of extravehicular activity.

Before long, he was waiting outside the airlock of the

Fire's docking hatch. He felt the ship twisting and rotating as her maneuvering rockets brought her into proper alignment with the opposing vessel. Then came an audible *clunk* as the two ships mated, followed by the sound of the *Fire*'s airlock cycling through. Then the amber light over the airlock door turned to violet, and the door swung open.

Len stepped in and waited patiently for the door to close again and the lock to cycle him through. Then he repeated the process in reverse for the airlock and door on the opposite side.

That done, he stepped out into a fearsome scene: *Garden-of-Fair-Blossoms* was a ship of the dead.

Some of them, in combat dress and hardmasks, lay tumbled together where they had stood in ranks for boarding. He didn't know what kind of weapon had struck them down, except that it had burned them like a sudden fire. Others, farther along the ship's main corridor, had died under the blows of boarding pikes. Even the ship's bridge was a small slaughterhouse. Len was glad that he had worn his pressure-suit; the *Garden*'s air supply was intact, but he had no desire to smell the aftereffects of such carnage. The sight of it alone was bad enough.

He stood at last before the ship's main console and turned the speaker volume on his pressure-suit up as high as it could go.

"Ship-mind," he said. "Is anybody on board here still alive?"

The synthesized voice of the ship-mind spoke again. "Analysis of internal sensor data suggests at least one possible survivor."

Not here on the bridge; that was certain. "Where?"

"Localizing the data now. Please follow the flashing guides."

A yellow light on the bulkhead by the airtight door started to blink on and off. He went back through the door into the passageway outside; another light was blinking on the bulkhead there, telling him to go left. More flashing lights appeared as he needed them, directing him steadily inward toward the heart of the ship, the most protected spaces. The raiders had been in these passages, too; more than once his feet, clumsy in the magnetized soles of his pressure-suit, stumbled over bodies.

He found the survivor in the ship's infirmary. The medical *aiketen* there had continued their work even with slaughter going on around them. Len supposed that the sus-Dariv fleet-apprentice who lay beneath the armor-glass lid of the stasis box, cocooned in a delicate web of balanced energy, had been left for dead by the mysterious invaders, and had made her way to the infirmary with the last of her strength.

Len spoke again to the ship-mind. "How long can the stasis box maintain her like this?"

"Indefinitely," the ship-mind replied. "Subject only to the need for a reliable power supply."

"If I open the lid, can the *aiketen* revive her long enough to answer questions without killing her for good?"

"Consultation with the infirmary's quasi-organics is required in order to answer your question."

"Consult away."

Silence once again filled the infirmary. Somewhere in all that lack of noise, presumably, the ship-mind and the medical *aiketen* traded data back and forth.

At last, the ship-mind said, "The *aiketen* are allowing the box's energy fields to lapse for a brief period. Please ask your questions as concisely as possible; the patient's condition cannot be supported for long outside stasis."

Len undid the clamps and lifted up the lid of the box. As he did so, the shimmering web of energy faded, and he got his first good look at the survivor of the attack. The girl was a fleet-apprentice, as Len had guessed from the bits of uniform he had glimpsed earlier, and as the ship-mind had intimated, she was in a bad way. Most of her torso was covered by one of those mysterious burn wounds—this one looking as though it must have been delivered at point-blank range—and her right arm and shoulder had been stabbed and hacked at by a boarding pike.

As the *aiketen*'s supporting web faded away, the fleet-apprentice drew a shuddering breath. Her eyes snapped open.

"Who—?" The word came out in a painful whisper.

"Lenyat Irao. Captain of the light-cargo carrier *Fire-on-the-Hilltops*." The thought came to him that his pressure-suit, with its blank-faced helmet, must look disturbingly like ship-to-ship combat gear, and he groped for something to say that might give her confidence. "I'm under contract to the sus-Dariv for this run, so that makes us temporary kin."

"Good." The fleet-apprentice's eyes drifted closed. She lay there without speaking, while Len watched her ravaged chest rise and fall in shuddering, irregular breaths. After a while she seemed to gather strength again and went on: "You can take back word."

"I will," said Len. "But—what happened? If I'm going to take back word, I have to know."

"We were attacked. Thought it was another family's ship, challenging us for cargo . . . met them at the airlock, all in proper form. . . ."

"I know how it goes." Len had stood to meet a boarding party more than once himself, in the time he'd spent as hired crew on the family ships. "And it doesn't look like they followed the rules."

"No. They burned us where we stood." Even now, the echo of that first outrage colored the girl's thready voice. "I've never seen weapons like that. Anybody left standing . . . they cut them down. Ran through the ship like fire and a flood together."

"Do you know why?"

The fleet-apprentice shook her head painfully. "They never said anything. And they didn't take anything, either . . . some stuff from here they tossed out into space. And their ships have guns. I heard them talk about blasting the convoy into pebbles."

"They did. Your ship is about the only thing left."

"Why?"

"Why did they leave the guardship intact?" Len had been wondering that himself, ever since he saw the first bodies lying sprawled on the deck outside the airlock. He'd seen enough on the bridge to give him a theory. "Before they left, they had your ship-mind set the *Garden* on course for a transit home in normal space. That means they want somebody to find this ship eventually—but not right now. Right now they want to use the fact that she's disappeared."

"Good idea," said the fleet-apprentice. Her voice was fading badly now. "For a pirate . . ."

"You've managed to spoil it for them," Len said. "The *Fire*'s old, but not that old. I can get your word back home a long time before this ship reaches Eraasi."

". . . family . . . be grateful . . ."

Len doubted that; bringing bad news never made anyone loved. But he said only, "I don't have a proper infirmary on board the *Fire,* so I'll let the stasis box put you back under for now. You've got a long trip ahead of you, but at least you won't have to be awake to get bored by it."

The fleet-apprentice's eyes had drifted closed, but now she opened them again. "Something else . . . to tell the family. The pirates . . ."

"What about them?"

"They didn't wear . . . ship's colors. Black and grey, like nobody. Nobody's. But after I fell . . . they were careless. I heard them talking. Heard names."

She stopped talking then, and he thought that she'd run out of breath to speak. The voice of the ship-mind clicked on again and said, "The *aiketen* report vital signs are slipping. They advise resuming stasis maintenance."

"Not yet!" It was the girl, speaking in barely a whisper. "Wait. The names. I remember . . . they said 'sus-Peledaen.' Natelth·sus-Peledaen."

4:

Serpent Station—blazing hot and dry for one half of the year, chilly and dry for the other—was the main sus-Dariv installation on Eraasi's antipodal subcontinent. The family did most of its construction work there, having seen long ago the wisdom of not competing for labor and material in the same market with the sus-Radal and the sus-Peledaen. The current fashion among the fleet-families for throwing away money on permanent orbital stations had not impressed the sus-Dariv, who still preferred to lease commercial space-docks on an as-needed basis; meanwhile, Serpent handled repairs and shipbuilding for the fleet.

Port-Captain Aelben Winceyt, commanding officer of Serpent Station, usually ate breakfast alone. Fleet-family custom prevented anyone of lesser rank from joining him unasked, and Winceyt couldn't afford to play favorites—or even appear to be playing favorites—with his invitations.

For a while he'd shared the Station's high table with the commanding officer of *Sweetwater-Running*, before the *Sweetwater*'s repair work was finished and the ship left geosynchronous orbit over Serpent for one above Hanilat Starport. Winceyt had enjoyed the company. These days, for lunch and dinner, he had a list of the other officers at the Station, and was patiently working through it one name at a time. When he finished the whole list, he planned to randomize it and start over.

Setting aside its social drawbacks, however, Winceyt was happy with his posting to Serpent. Combined with his adoption into the outer family, the promotion marked him as a rising officer in the sus-Dariv fleet, one who only needed the seasoning of a ground-based command before being given a ship of his own. Granted, the Antipodean summer temperatures made him suspect that when the senior fleet officers referred to seasoning, they meant "dried, smoked, and heat-cured," but that was a minor problem as long as the Station's environmental controls kept on working.

And the food here was good—far better than shipboard rations, and interestingly different from any of the main-continent cuisines. Today's breakfast was paper-thin griddle-cakes wrapped around a filling of salt-apple relish, made by a kitchen staff that could have held its own against any in Hanilat.

Well, maybe not at the Court of Two Colors level, Winceyt conceded. *But almost anything less than that.*

The thought, and the day's date, sufficed to remind him of the only other cloud on his contentment, the fact that he was too new in his post as commanding officer of Serpent Station to get away with taking personal leave. Had matters been otherwise, he could at this moment have been attending his first general conference as a member of the sus-Dariv outer family.

That would have been a good way to celebrate his promotion. Now that he was outer-family he could respectably begin thinking about other long-term commitments, such as courtship and marriage—and while the women of the Antipodes were good-looking and superficially friendly, as a group they had little desire to abandon their homes and family altars for a life in distant Hanilat. Fellow-members of the syn-Dariv, though, were unlikely to have such objections.

Oh, well. No hurry. We have time.

Breakfast done, he left the dining hall for his office—a matter of going from one low concrete building to another, almost identical one. Already the air outside was hot and dry, under a sky of deep, cloudless blue. Today looked like being another scorcher.

Command-Tertiary Yerris was waiting for him in his office with a textpad. "Sir. Summary of the message traffic."

Winceyt glanced at the pad. Nothing unusual there—most of the entries were copies of messages going in and out of Hanilat. There was only one heads-up for Serpent: A message-drone had come in overnight from *Garden-of-Fair-Blossoms,* letting the family know that the main trade convoy was entering the Void for the last leg of its journey home, with a list appended of ships needing repair and refitting.

"We'll need to set up a schedule for rotating stuff in and out," Winceyt said, tapping the message with the blunt end of his stylus. "But the big job is still going to be upgrading the engines on *Golden-Flower-Crown,* and we're ready for that."

In fact, he had been requisitioning and stockpiling the necessary parts and equipment for the anticipated overhaul ever since coming to Serpent. The main engine assembly had arrived by ground hauler just two days ago, and now occupied most of Construction Hangar 2. A major refit was always time-consuming, and a cargo ship lost the family money every day that it was in the yards.

"Rigging-Chief Olyesi says that she can start as soon as you give the word," Yerris said. "All three of the heavy work platforms are cleared and rigged for lift."

"Excellent," Winceyt replied.

Turning around *Golden-Flower-Crown* rapidly and efficiently would be a good start for his outer-family career. And maybe next year he'd feel settled-in enough at Serpent Station to take leave for the meeting in Hanilat.

"Finding Narin," Arekhon said, "isn't going to be easy."

He and Maraganha were in a small café near the Cazdel Guildhouse, sharing a midafternoon meal of hot bitter-root tea and sweet pastries. The Void-walker paused in the act of pulling apart a flaky piece of spice-bread, and asked him, "What exactly makes it hard?"

"Well, for one thing, I haven't heard from her in almost ten years."

Maraganha winced. "That could make things difficult. Any idea why she decided to vanish?"

"Not in any great detail," Arekhon said. "She never cared much for writing letters in the first place, and the last message I got from her was a voice-note saying that she was sick of trying to explain the *eiran* to Adepts and was going off to look for honest work."

"That's when you lost track of her?"

"More or less," he said. "She wound up somewhere in the Immering Archipelago, but I don't know anything more than that. There's a limit to what the search services and the public datanets can tell you, especially if the person you're looking for is a powerful Mage—and Ty was right about Narin being powerful. She was the First of her own Circle once, before she came to Demaizen; if she's vanished deliberately, we may never find her at all."

"Don't spook her, then," Maraganha advised. "Stay away from working the *eiran* unless you have to."

Arekhon poured more of the bitter-root tea into his cup. There were some days, and this was one of them, when he missed the sharp tang of good red homeworlds *uffa* more than words could tell. "We'll have to go to Immering, then, and check the local records—and I can tell you right now that they're going to be a mess. The Immering islands seem to have been everybody's favorite invasion spot for the last five or six decades."

"And open warfare has a nasty habit of blowing holes in people's filing systems," said Maraganha. "Oh, well. Let's go to Immering and see what we can reconstruct."

Inadal syn-Arvedan let himself into his room at the Wintermount Guesthouse and locked the door behind him. The house-mind brought up the lights as soon as he entered, and he saw that the hostelry's *aiketen* had left him the midnight supper he'd requested, a tray of smoked meats and small breads and relishes set out on the side table along with a flask of wine. He hung up his damp weather coat, then sank gratefully into the deep-cushioned leather chair next to the table and broke the seal on the wine.

It was summer wine, pale and sparkling; he poured some into the glass the *aiketen* had left with the supper tray and drank it off. The drink's tingling sharpness cut through the fuzz of talk and exhaustion that the day's business had left in his head, and he set the empty glass aside. He'd finish the wine later, after he'd eaten, when he was ready to sleep. Now, however, he wanted to have the meal he'd been too busy to stop for all day, and he wanted to think.

The Hanilat Ploughmen's Club, where he had spent most of this afternoon and evening, had been for almost a century the main meeting place for Eraasi's agrarian and mercantile families. In past decades, when the powers of the star-lords and the ground-based interests were more in balance, very little had actually gone on inside the club—socializing mostly, and the occasional private business arrangement. These days, however, the conversation at the Ploughmen's Club had a tinge of desperation in it. The fleet-families were growing ever more powerful; soon now, if nothing happened to stop them, they would overshadow the city and country interests completely.

Talking isn't enough, Inadal thought. *If we don't work to counter the power of the star-lords, we may not survive them . . . and we* are *Eraasi, in the end.*

Politics had never been Inadal's first love, or even his second. He could happily have spent his entire life in Arvedan, overseeing the family estate and only coming to Hanilat for shopping and holidays. But the times weren't good for that. At least a few of the men and women he'd spoken with at the Ploughmen's Club had seen things his way; but they didn't have a plan.

The room's communications console sounded its two-note chime, interrupting his thoughts.

"House-mind. Answer the call and play it aloud." The console speaker clicked on. He said, "Hello?"

"Inadal?" It was his sister Ayil's voice. "I tried calling you at home first but they said that you were here in town."

"Business meetings," he said. "Very dull ones."

"Don't patronize me. I know exactly how dull those meetings really are." Her tone changed. "I learned something last night, and I think you need to know it."

"What?"

There was a pause, as if Ayil were collecting her thoughts. "You do know that one of my old officemates left the Institute to be a Mage in Delath's Circle."

The name of their late brother, killed years ago in the destruction of Demaizen Old Hall, still had the power to cause Inadal a brief, sharp pang. "I remember you telling me something like that once."

"Well, I saw him again last night."

"Alive?"

"Of course alive. Del was the one who could see spirits, not me." Her voice caught a little, and Inadal reflected that he was perhaps not the only member of their family who could be stricken with unexpected grief. "Kief is with one of the sus-Peledaen Circles now."

"He's no friend of ours, then. The sus-Peledaen are star-lords to the bone."

"I don't think this is one of their fleet-Circles," Ayil said. "It's something else, I'm almost certain."

"What do you mean?"

"He was with the Institute Circle last night . . . they always meet then . . . and he slept on my couch afterward because he was too tired to go home. I think there was a great working, Inadal; I saw the blood on his robes."

"They're Mages, remember. It's what they do."

He heard her give a faint snort. "Not the Institute Circle. It's common knowledge they haven't done a great working in over a century."

"Are you saying that your old officemate is up to something that his sponsors don't know about?"

"I'm not sure," Ayil said. "But Kief never thought that highly of the star-lords back when I first knew him—his family were all merchants—and I can't see him changing his opinion of them now."

Isayana and Natelth sat in their private withdrawing-room aboard the sus-Peledaen orbital station. Far below them, in

Hanilat, it was night; just as it was ship's-evening here on the station. They were listening to music after dinner—not recorded or synthesized music, but local talent, an amateur consort drawn from instrumentalists among the resident fleet-family and hired crew. The actual musicians were several decks away, playing for a small audience in one of the recreation lounges; the music in the private withdrawing-room was piped in over ship's audio.

Isayana was only half-listening, if that; she liked music as a background to thought, but didn't care much for nuances of performance. Tonight she was fiddling with a draftsman's pad, idly sketching and erasing designs for *aiketen* and other specialized devices that might never get built.

She looked up from her pad and glanced over at her brother. Natelth was going over the sus-Peledaen convoy and construction schedules, trying to fit everything together so that the orbital yards produced enough guardships to run all the trading voyages the family needed. The process didn't seem to be working tonight. He swept his stylus through the latest entry, frowned, and shook his head.

"Problems?" she asked.

"Complaints. The orbital yards claim to be stressed by the pace of new construction."

"Well, are they?"

Natelth's frown deepened. "Their performance is not deteriorating."

"Not yet," she said. "If our supervisors are any good, they're spotting the warning signs before the decay sets in, not after."

"We don't promote and adopt incompetents. But we can't afford to halt our shipbuilding efforts, either—not when the sus-Radal and half a dozen other families are fattening their fleets."

"There's always farming out the nonsecret work to commercial shipyards," she said. They'd had this argument many times before, in one form or another, but she still felt obliged to try.

"No."

"It works for the sus-Dariv."

"We are not the sus-Dariv," he said. "We are the sus-

Peledaen. I don't want outside interests getting involved in our fleet construction."

"We've used commercial yards for repairs and refitting."

"Only when there was no time and no alternative. If I'd had a choice, we would have brought all the work in-house four decades ago."

"We don't always get the choices we want," she said. "And we surely didn't get them back then."

She hadn't thought about those days for a long time. It had been a dark, violent period, when she and Natelth had been fighting hard just to keep the control of the fleet-family in the hands of the sus-Khalgath line. Their parents were suddenly, unexpectedly dead; their late-born sibling Arekhon was an orphaned infant thrust into Isayana's care; and all of Hanilat seemed firmly of the opinion that Natelth sus-Khalgath was by virtue of his youth unfit to rule the sus-Peledaen.

Showing people otherwise had taken the greater part of a decade, but they had done it, she and Natelth against the world. He ran most of that world, these days, but sometimes Isayana thought that he had absorbed those early lessons in control and suspicion a bit too well.

In the service lot behind the Court of Two Colors, a Ridge Farms produce truck was backing up to Loading Dock 3. Inside the truck's canvas-shielded rear compartment, five men sat beside a metal drum, some four feet high and two across. These were men who took no chances: they had their own handcart with them.

The truck did not contain tenderwort. That cargo had been dumped unceremoniously by the roadside some twenty miles outside the city limits of greater Hanilat—as had the driver and his assistant. They would not be found before dawn, by which time bigger news would already be filling the morning feeds.

"Hey, Gesri," said one of the men in the back. His current name, adopted for the occasion, was Daryd—his mother had certainly never called him that, but then, he hadn't used his birth-name in years. Daryd was an older man, dressed in the impeccable clothing of a legalist or an administrator. In addition to being the leader of the men in the truck, he also functioned as the team's outside interface: If his people ran into someone officious, Daryd could official back until the others got clear. "What's eating you? You're sweating, man."

"I'll be all right," Gesri said. "It's the way this truck is moving. I get sick."

"I hope that's all it is."

The truck eased to a stop with a light bump. The driver hit the back of the cab twice. Daryd stood up.

"It's showtime," he said.

"Then let's move," said the bombmaker. He also had a true name, but no one had called him by it for a long time now. In the shadowy world where the team functioned, he was known only by his expertise. "There's three hundred pounds of nasty in that thing. Until it's armed, we're in deep if we're caught, and with nothing to show for it."

"Where do we want it?" asked another of the men.

"Down low as we can get," the bombmaker said. "And as close to the center as we can get, over in the wing with the main ballroom."

Two of the men opened the canvas back of the truck while the other two rolled the drum onto the handcart. Working together, they backed the handcart gently onto the dock. The metal door rolled up and they were in.

"Fish sauce," the no-longer-ill Gesri said. He passed over a clipboard to the lading-clerk. "Where do you want it?"

"Larder A-Twelve," the clerk said, not looking up from the work on his desk.

"This way," Daryd said to his crew. The four of them, with Daryd leading, walked down the corridor to the right. "Ahead should be a door, then a ramp down to the left."

Once they were out of sight of the people at the loading dock, Daryd brought out an inertial tracker. He'd gone over the Court's floor plan before the start of the operation, but he hadn't dared do a recon, for fear of getting caught. Getting caught would have boosted security, and maybe moved the sus-Dariv conclave to some other venue. So this live run was also the first and only.

The door they were looking for—which was not the door

of Larder A-12—was where it should be, and the lock was simple. Now they were where no honest delivery man would ever be, so speed was even more essential.

They closed the door behind them, relocked it, and jollied the handcart and its burden down the ramp into another corridor. This one was all white, full of bright incandescent glows, with pipes for steam and chill-water running overhead, along with the gas lines and the communications feeds.

Down the ramp—to the right—another set of corridors. Daryd was counting the paces and watching his inertial. The main supports for the building would be near here. An explosion would take them out, would take out the building, collapsing it. An outside bang with much bigger fireworks wouldn't have half the effect.

"Here," Daryd said finally.

He stepped back, and the bombmaker stepped forward. "Take off the cover."

Gesri whisked away the drum's canvas traveling robe. Thus revealed, the metal of the container gleamed in the light. The drum had no top. Inside it was a simple circuit with a timer, and beside the circuit a chemical vial, and beside *that* a drop bolt. The electric timer was the main component. It had batteries and an electric blasting cap, sunk into the explosive bricks ranged around the inside circumference of the drum.

"Time," the bombmaker said.

Daryd checked his chrono. "Fifty-eight minutes."

"Fifty-eight minutes, check," the bombmaker said, and dialed in the number. He pressed the button.

Nothing visible happened; but slowly, internally, the timer began its count.

In fifty-eight minutes, if nothing went wrong, the hollow shape of the drum's explosive load would turn into incandescent gas moving at many times the velocity of sound, with a volume far too large for the corridor to hold without cracking. And even if the timer didn't work—things go wrong, after all, and luck holds for some people and not for others—there remained a second, chemical circuit.

"Fifty-eight minutes on the primary." The bombmaker selected a sixty-minute chemical timer from a group in the leather roll he pulled from a pocket. The timer was a slender metal cylinder made of copper at one end and white steel at the other, divided at the midpoint circumference by a brass ring. He checked the printing on the chemical timer. "Sixty minutes, as advertised."

Daryd checked his chrono again. "Let's move it. We don't have all night."

"Patience," the bombmaker said.

He pulled a pliers from another pocket and crimped the copper end of the chemical blasting cap. That would break the vial of acid inside. After a while the acid would eat through to where the initiator was, and much else would follow.

The bombmaker punched the steel end of the timer into a soft blasting brick, placed opposite where his electrical timer was counting down. Two initiators, more luck.

One more thing to do: the mechanical, the failsafe, the booby trap. In this case, a gravity bolt that would fall if disturbed. The bombmaker pulled back the spring-loaded hammer of a mechanical initiator, and held the hammer in place with a long piece of flat metal.

"Now," he said. "And be careful. If I lose my grip on the shim, none of us will stay alive long enough to notice what happened."

The other men—except for Daryd, who couldn't get his hands dirty, in case somebody should notice that the grime under his fingernails didn't match his respectable business garb—rocked the drum off of its cart and turned it over. Carefully, they lowered the open end of the drum, with the metal shim across it, down onto the floor.

Once the drum was in place, the bombmaker pulled the shim out. Slowly. Carefully. A click, and he held his breath. Then it was done.

"Right, then," he said. "Anyone tries to moves that drum before time, up it goes."

5:

ERAASI: HANILAT

His cousin Zeri, Herin decided, might look like nothing more than a nicely rounded bit of yellow-haired fluff—but she was quite a bit smarter than she appeared. She'd made a neat escape from a largely pointless evening, not to mention the remainder of the afternoon working sessions, while at the same time ensuring that her vote was counted on the only issue of any actual importance. The folded paper with her authorization on it crackled stiffly inside his jacket as he made his way to the banquet hall from a roundtable seminar on kinship parity. He didn't have any interest in the subject—he was high enough in the inner family that the work he did was not done for rank or recognition—but he'd attended the seminar out of a sense of duty.

The banquet, of course, would be excellent; the Court of Two Colors could hardly provide anything less. The debate to follow, on the vexed issue of private security forces, would be acrimonious, but would settle nothing, even with the weight of Zeri's vote added to Herin's own.

A flicker of motion caught at the corner of his eye outside the leather-covered double doors that led from the conference area to the banquet hall.

He looked in the direction of the anomaly, only to have it vanish; a second later, it was teasing at him again. This time he was more careful, using his peripheral vision to watch the thing, whatever it was. He was rewarded with a glimpse of what looked like pale, glowing thread, that sometimes trailed on the black-and-white patterned carpet and sometimes appeared to float in the air above it.

Very odd, Herin thought. People who worked in the Mage-Circles spoke of the *eiran* as looking like silvery thread; but he had never been a Mage, or even trained for one. He wasn't supposed to be seeing the *eiran* for the first time at a business conference in Hanilat.

But now that he'd spotted it, the glowing line wouldn't go away. It curled and snaked about, twisting in and out among sus-Dariv and syn-Dariv alike. Herin was seized by the thought that it must be trying to find him, personally, by some kind of touch. Before he could think better of his action, he stepped around a knot of gossiping life-sciences savants and let the questing silver thread wrap itself whiplike around his ankle.

An electric sensation passed through him with the contact. This was luck, all right—strong and real, the pulsing current of life itself. Next to it, the furnishings of the Court of Two Colors, and the chattering crowd outside the banquet hall, seemed diminished and pale, like objects from a lesser order of existence. He marked how the thread of the *eiran* wound away from him, through the room and out the farther door, and felt it pulling at him to follow.

This is definitely something new, he thought. And because Herin Arayet sus-Dariv was an inquisitive man by nature as well as by profession, he gave in to the urge and let the silver cord draw him away from the banquet hall.

Chief Provisioner Tabbes looked at his chrono, then touched the intercom for Loading Dock 3. "Has the tenderwort arrived?"

The voice of the lading-clerk came back over the link. "No, sir."

"No? Ridge Farms was supposed to get it here an hour ago at the absolute latest!"

There was a moment of silence, in which Tabbes fancied he could hear the lading-clerk shrug before answering, "Nothing's come in at the loading dock in the last hour except a drum of fish sauce."

"We didn't order any fish sauce," Tabbes said indignantly. He would need to have words with the people at Ridge Farms, if their order department had become capable of such confusion. "Where did they put it?"

"A-Twelve."

"Leave it be, then. I'll go over the order myself later and see if I can figure out where they went wrong. Fish sauce, of all things. . . ." Tabbes was still seething with irritation. "We don't need fish sauce. We need tenderwort, and the menu's gone to the printer already. Let me know if anything looking remotely like tenderwort happens to show up in the next ten minutes."

A restlessness seized him. Rain tonight, hardly low humidity. A whole shipment lost, possibly ruined.

Tabbes decided to walk down to the loading dock and check things out on-scene. It was always possible that the fatal error had occurred not in the order-processing department at Ridge Farms, but somewhere at the Court's end of things. Perhaps the tenderwort had already arrived unnoticed, and was now being allowed to sit there wilting in the heat. If so, the parties responsible would need to be singled out and disciplined, perhaps even discharged with prejudice. The Court had a reputation to keep up.

He stood and left his office, heading for the loading docks by way of the managerial corridors. The restricted-access halls and stairways provided the Court's upper staff with expeditious routes to all the key service areas, without the delays that might come of encountering other workers along the way. He was on the second level, and heading at a quick pace for the passageway that opened onto the general loading area, when he rounded a corner and saw a polished metal drum standing untended in the middle of the corridor.

Tabbes came to an abrupt stop. "What in the world?"

He looked at the drum. No markings on the outside. Nothing to show where it had come from or what it contained.

"This isn't right at all," he said to himself, and hurried to the belowstairs security office in one of the small rooms opening off of Loading Dock 1. "There's a big drum of something-or-other in the managers' corridor," he said to the officer on duty. "And it doesn't belong there."

"Probably one of the janitors left it," the officer said. "They'll get it in the morning."

Tabbes had a thin set to his lips. "No. It doesn't belong, and there wasn't anyone around. I want a qualified person to come take a look at it."

"All right," the security officer said at last. "I'll come look. But it's probably nothing but some trash that didn't get picked up."

Tabbes led the way back to the corridor with the drum. He unlocked the management-only doorway, and then went down the ramp, with the security officer following close behind. They could see the drum waiting for them up ahead, under the glaring lights.

The two men were perhaps twenty feet away from the drum when the timer's fifty-eighth minute passed. The bomb-maker was good at what he did: Both of his backups proved unnecessary.

By strict count—if victims are divided one from another by fractions of a second—Tabbes and the security officer were the first two victims of the blast. Could they have watched with slow-motion eyes, they would have seen the drum first bulge around its center, then split with great vertical tears, black against the yellow light inside. But they never had the chance. Instead, the overpressure from the expanding gas took them and hurled them down the passageway, stripping flesh from bone and pulverizing the bone afterward.

The *eiran* led Herin away from the private areas of the Court of Two Colors, and down to the pavement level. He let the silver thread draw him, unresisting, through the heavy glass doors and past the gatekeeper-*aiketh*, and from there to the street.

Night had fallen outside, and the glowing thread stood out against the darkness like a line of silver fire. Herin wondered if any of the passersby hurrying along to their transit connections or their evening appointments also saw the *eiran* as he did—or was that beckoning silver thread intended for him alone?

He followed it across High Port Road, weaving in and out of the vehicular traffic and through the press of pedestrians on the other side. There, in the shelter of a recessed doorway, the *eiran* left him, dissipating like fog and taking its strange compulsion away with it into the night.

That was certainly peculiar, he thought, in the instant remaining before the world as he had known it came to an end.

There was a noise—an enormous, unexpected noise—and the whole Court of Two Colors swayed as if struck by a giant fist. The right-hand side of the building, the side holding the grand ballroom, collapsed downward. Dust rose in a vast cloud; water spurted from broken mains; electricity sparked from severed cables. The high-velocity shock wave touched and killed everyone in its path, as far out as the middle of High Port Road.

The left side, where the public restaurant and the guest rooms were, swayed and canted but did not collapse and—judging strictly from its effects—the shock wave was more attenuated there. After the explosion, silence fell; though it could have been merely a temporary deafness. Tongues of fire began to lick at the wreckage. Emergency vehicles with lights and sirens—all the power of a city come to deal with a hurt—arrived soon after that.

Herin watched, unscathed. And all that he could think of, beyond the fact that the *eiran* for some reason wanted him alive, was that somebody else had definitely wanted all of the sus-Dariv dead.

Theledau sus-Radal had plans. Iulan Vai knew that as soon as his summons reached her Hanilat message-drop:

Come to the office tonight. The usual hour.

She wasn't as high in Thel's private councils as she'd been back in the old days, when she'd been his Agent-Principal and the sus-Radal's eyes and ears in Hanilat. She was a private person now, and worked for the family only when asked, and only if she saw fit to do so. Nevertheless, her unannounced visit of the previous evening had apparently moved the head of the sus-Radal to a decision of some kind.

She came to Thel's headquarters a little after dusk, slipping into the tall building through the service entrance with her dark hair wrapped in a day laborer's kerchief. Here in the downtown business district, she didn't need the concealment of a hardmask and Mage's robes. If anybody noticed her, they would take her for one of the maintenance workers who followed after the building's *aiketen* and took care of those jobs that fell outside of the servitors' limited instruction sets.

Thel was waiting for her in his top-floor office. He nodded a greeting to her as she entered. "Vai."

"Thel," she replied.

He had the windows uncovered and the room lights dimmed, the better to see the last glow of the sunset and the first emerging stars. Vai knew that he hated working late—it meant taking a chance on missing the hour of lunar observance. Thel had always been devout, but his years in equatorial Hanilat had made him, if possible, even firmer in his adherence to northern ritual and custom.

"What have you got for me?" she asked.

"After our talk last night, I decided I needed to show you something." He pressed a control on his desktop and an image appeared, hovering in the air above the polished wooden surface. "This is what the family's engineers have been working on for the past five years."

Vai frowned at it. "A *rock*?"

"An asteroid," he said. "On the surface, at least. Inside—"

He pressed another control. Half of the image peeled away, leaving a cross section riddled with caves and tunnels like an insect mound. He plucked a stylus from the desktop holder and used it for a pointer. "Living quarters, docking and construction space, observation and recording equipment . . . even accommodations for a working Circle."

"Is this a natural object?" she asked. "Or did your engineers make it from scratch?"

"Natural to start with. But they've worked on it extensively."

"It'll make somebody a nice observation post once it's operational."

"That's the general idea."

"Ah," said Vai. "Who's going to be observed? Our friends the sus-Peledaen?"

Thel smiled. "We already have agents in place for that. No, this is for watching the planets on the far side of the interstellar gap."

She contemplated the floating model for a while in silence. *'Rekhe would have loved to play with this thing,* she thought, with a rare pang of nostalgia. "Something this big, you're never going to keep word of it from getting out."

"It doesn't really matter if people think that we're building something like one of the sus-Peledaen orbital stations," he told her. "We've already got one of those in progress anyway, as a decoy. What's important is that nobody suspects where we've been building this one."

"You built it all the way over there?" The plan, she had to admit, was alluringly audacious. Audacity, however, brought along problems of its own. "How did you shuttle the workers back and forth without being spotted?"

"One rock in space looks much like another," he said. "The people on the transport ships know the truth, of course, but we've been sticking with family for this project—no hired crews and no contract carriers."

"Word will get out eventually. It always does."

"By that time, we should already have a string of bases in place. And they'll be mobile, not fixed. If a particular location is compromised, the base in question can—"

An eye-searing flash lit up the darkness outside the office windows, followed an instant later by a thunderous blast that rattled the glass panes and sent Thel's heavy ceramic stylus-holder skittering across the desktop. The floating image of the asteroid base wavered and winked out.

In the after-silence, Vai heard Theledau drew a sharp breath before demanding, "What was that?"

"Explosion in the entertainment district. Big one." She found herself at the window, not quite aware of having gotten there, looking out at the city. The night sky was full of orange flames shot through with clouds of white steam and heavy black smoke, and the flashing lights of emergency vehicles made streaks of bright purple and hot amber on the streets below. "I can't pinpoint exactly where from up here."

"Give me a moment." Thel was at his desk already, working the buttons and touch-points. She knew that he had to be forcing his way into the fire and security information grid with the brute force of a star-lord's personal level of access. "Hanilat Emergency Response puts the explosion at the Court of Two Colors."

"The sus-Dariv," Vai said at once. "They've been meeting at the Court all this past week. The attack has to have been aimed at them."

"This time." Thel was working the controls on his desk again. The sigils for all the various branches of sus-Radal family security flared to life on its glossy black surface, shifting under his hands from low-threat violet to flashing max-pri yellow until the entire desktop seemed aflame.

When he was done, he sat down heavily in the chair behind his desk. A few minutes ago, showing off the family's latest project, he had looked confident and satisfied with the world; now he just looked tired.

"If you're right," he said, "then nobody is safe anymore. The rules of the game are changing—and we'll have to change with them, or die."

Herin stood in the doorway of a building not far from what had been the Court of Two Colors, watching the wreckage burn. Training and instinct said that he should go—that he should put as much distance as possible as fast as possible between himself and the death some enemy had meant for him and his family—but for a long time he found himself unable to turn away from the destruction.

The night air was full of smoke and chemicals and the noise of sirens. Searchlight beams crisscrossed the darkening sky, and the flashing amber and violet lights of a dozen or more fire and safety vehicles lit up the street at ground level. He knew already that the rescuers weren't going to find anybody alive—not in the conference rooms, at least, and none of the attending sus-Dariv anywhere. The *eiran* would not have manifested themselves to somebody like him, at his age and without warning, for anything less than a total disaster.

Zeri, now, had rescued herself without knowing it. The easy luck that had always let her slide out from under unwanted obligations without causing trouble had played a trick on her at last. But Herin couldn't give himself a like credit for his own survival. He had been found—singled out—caught by the *eiran* like a fish on a lure, and what little he knew of the Mage-Circles suggested that if the *eiran* had him, they were unlikely to let him go.

I do not need this, he thought. He tried to laugh at the sudden absurdity of his situation, but the breath caught in his throat halfway and he was sobbing instead. He closed his mouth tightly and forced himself to stop. *Especially not now.*

He took one deep breath, then another, and tried to think about what he ought to do next. Find Zeri, maybe. She would need to know what had happened. He shook his head. *She'll hear about it soon enough.*

Something teased at the corner of his vision, wisps and threads of silver that faded as soon as he looked at them directly. He kept on watching the public-safety workers toiling in the debris of the Court of Two Colors, and waited. It didn't take long for the *eiran* to come back. This time the shift and flicker of light resolved into a line of blue-white fire trailing off into the shadows—another message, he supposed, from the capricious forces that had pulled him away from death a little while before.

Herin moved out of the doorway and let the silvery threads draw him away through the periphery of the crowd. This time they didn't vanish until he was well away from the street where the Court of Two Colors lay burning.

He took a closer look at his new surroundings: deserted alley, no streetlights, big industrial buildings all around. A far cry from the ultra-fashionable Court.

"I get the idea," he said aloud. His voice sounded hoarse and shaky, as though it belonged to somebody else he'd never met: Herin Arayet sus-Dariv, talking to the *eiran* like a drunken Magelord. Shock and grief could do that sometimes, leave a man bare to the universe in ways he hadn't been before. Sometimes the changes went away as the trauma faded; sometimes they were forever; but it was never a wise idea to ignore them. "It's time for me to lie low for a while."

The idea sounded like a good one. All he needed to do was find a place to hide out in. Then he could wait until enough time had passed that the destruction of the Court of Two Colors was yesterday's news—and until the *eiran* either went away or told him to go do something else.

Vai waited for half an hour after Theledau had left the office building, then started home herself. She had more than one bolt-hole in Hanilat—places that, because she was by nature cautious, not even the sus-Radal knew of—but she ignored all of them and headed instead for the Five Street transit hub. The city was not a safe place tonight, even for someone who carried a Mage's staff, and she would rest better on the railcar to Demaizen than in a downtown bed.

A light rain had started falling while she was indoors, diffusing the light from the streetlamps into a yellow glow. Over on the other side of the city, the Court of Two Colors still burned, painting a smear of sullen orange across the overcast sky, and the night air was full of the stink of smoke and chemicals.

That was another reason she wanted to get out of Hanilat. The events of the night had set the *eiran* to stretching and interweaving in new and restless patterns, and she could feel the will and intention behind them.

Partway to the hub, she became aware that the *eiran* of the city were changing around her as she walked—directing her attention not to the elusive pattern of the current working, but to something else. She let her eyes unfocus a little, and was rewarded by a glimpse of silvery cord, a tantalizing wisp of light that curled and twisted its way into the shadows of a nearby side street. The light flickered and blinked out as she watched; a few seconds later, it flickered back on again.

Vai smiled in spite of herself. Somebody, it appeared, was trying very hard to remain inconspicuous and escape public notice, and the *eiran* were not cooperating. In fact, one could almost say that the *eiran* were actively seeking out her attention in the matter.

But if they're expecting me to follow a come-hither look into a dark alley, she thought, *they're going to have to think again. The sus-Radal trained me better than that.*

Still, Vai had to admit that the incident had piqued her curiosity—and she didn't think that it was part of whatever working had struck against the sus-Dariv. She applied her mind to another part of the extensive training she had received from the sus-Radal in earlier days, and came up with a mental map of this portion of Hanilat. The side street up ahead was one that she'd used as a shortcut more than once in the past, since it connected at its other end with the major Three Street transit corridor, but it was sufficiently dark and out of the way that a person with a need to stay unseen might find it a useful hideout.

If she could trust the *eiran*, whoever lurked in the shadows had most of their attention turned in this direction. She had plenty of time before the last railcar left the Five Street hub; she could afford the time to work her way around to the alley's Three Street entrance. Maybe the lurker would be gone by then, in which case she could simply cut back through the alley shortcut and continue her journey home.

Or maybe the lurker would still be in there hiding—and she could find out what kind of person the *eiran* had seen fit to bring to her attention.

Be honest, she told herself. *You're all keyed up, and you want to do something for a change instead of watching it all happen.*

Maybe. But that's not going to stop me.

Going around the long way to the Three Street entrance took about fifteen minutes, long enough for the lurker to be well away if flight had been his intention. Vai unclipped her staff from her belt and entered the darkened alley.

Finding him was easy after that. He wasn't running; in fact, he'd settled himself in for the night in the sheltered corner between a trash bin and a flight of concrete steps. If the *eiran* hadn't been swirling and twisting about him like threads of spun sugar, she would never have spotted him. As it was, she ghost-footed up to within a few feet, cleared her throat politely, and spoke.

"Who are you hiding from?"

Somebody had definitely trained him: He was on his feet and reaching inside his jacket for a weapon almost before she'd put the final inflection on the sentence.

She said, "Please don't do that," and let her mind release a little of its collected energy, so that the staff in her hand began to glow.

He lowered his hand again, slowly and carefully. In the glow from her staff, she recognized Herin Arayet sus-Dariv—his hair in disarray, his eyes still wide and dilated in the aftermath of shock, and his skin and clothing covered with a fine layer of pale grey dust.

"Ah," she said. "I can see why you might not want to be found tonight."

He looked at her intently. She thought that he might be planning to make a break for the mouth of the alley—he was still on edge, and probably not as rational as he thought he was—but he didn't. Instead he said, "I know you. You're the Demaizen Mage I talked with at the Old Hall."

"You have sharp eyes, considering that I was wearing a mask at the time."

"Sharp ears, actually. Your voice is the same."

She made a mental note to remember that for the next time she went incognito, then said, "I know what happened tonight at the Court of Two Colors. How close were you to the blast?"

"Too close." He stopped, drew breath, and began again. "Across the street. I'd left the building a minute or two earlier. . . ."

She nodded. "Right. And you're sure that you happened by coincidence to leave the building before the bomb went off."

"No," he said. "Something else happened." His eyes flicked sidelong to her glowing staff. "It was the *eiran*. I'd never seen them before, and they came looking for me and pulled me out of there just in time."

"That explains a few things," she said. "Like what the

eiran were doing when they showed up wanting me to come in here and look for you."

"Oh?" He was finally relaxing a little, which was good—less of a chance that he'd try to overpower her and bolt for the main thoroughfare, or reach again for the weapon inside his jacket. "What were they doing?"

"They were bringing me a Mage," she said, "and you a Circle."

6:

Arekhon and Maraganha took a shuttle-hop to the city of Tifset, on the main island of the Immering Archipelago—"This can't be cheap," Maraganha said; and Arekhon replied, "It isn't. But the money I've saved here on Entibor isn't going to do me any good back on Eraasi."

"Don't spend all of it," she told him. "You never know what may happen."

In Tifset, they spent several hours going through the paper archives—raw data, unscanned and unprocessed. It was slow, dreary work. Arekhon possessed only a basic reading knowledge of Immeringic, and Maraganha's trick with the *eiran* didn't work on the written language. They ended up dividing the job accordingly, so that he read, painstakingly, all the reports and files and ledgers, while she talked to the clerks and secretaries.

Their efforts paid off, eventually, in the tax records for Gifla Harbor, a small fishing port at the isolate southern end of the archipelago. One Narin Iyal, a resident alien with birthplace self-listed as "Amisket in Veredde," had dutifully reported and paid last year's taxes on money earned as a crew member aboard the deep-sea fishing boat *Ninefold Star*.

"I should have guessed it when she talked about honest work," Arekhon said to Maraganha. "She ran the Mage-Circle for Amisket's fishing fleet before she came to Demaizen."

The tax form gave a residence address, 14 Upper Shore #2b, but no voice number. Arekhon thought of calling the general information office for Gifla Harbor, then thought better of it. His command of the island language was sketchy at best. He could read the Immering tax records, provided that he knew what he was looking for to start with, but conversation—especially over a voice comm with no help from expressions or gestures—was another matter. And Maraganha's knack for languages, they had already determined, did not work well over communications lines.

Instead, they booked seats on one of the hydrofoil island-skimmers, and arrived in Gifla Harbor early the next morning. After some confusion with street maps and half-understood directions, they found 14 Upper Shore—a weather-beaten tile-and-stucco house broken up into apartments—and Arekhon knocked on the door of #2b.

After a minute or two, he heard grumbles and the sound of movement from within. The door swung open, revealing not Narin but a stranger, a stout man who wore a loose bed-robe over work trousers, and smelled faintly of fish and stale beer. He scowled and said something in Immeringic.

"I'm sorry," Arekhon said, in his own halting version of that language. "Narin Iyal—is she here?"

"No. Not here." The man had switched to An-Jemaynan, although his grasp of the Federated Quarter's main language was even shakier than Arekhon's knowledge of Immeringic. "Gone. Last winter."

Arekhon sighed in exasperation. If Narin had moved on from Gifla Harbor, there was no telling where she might be. "Gone where? Do you know?"

The man muttered something in Immeringic that sounded like either a curse or an invocation—the gesture that went with it was one that Arekhon didn't recognize, and that could have belonged to either. In An-Jemaynan, he said, "Nobody knows."

Maraganha stepped forward, just enough so that the movement drew the man's attention. "Is there anyone we could ask?"

After a moment, as if reluctant, the man said, "Fishing Office. Maybe. Now go away."

Zeri sus-Dariv yawned and stretched her way out of a sound and dreamless sleep, then sat up in bed and raised her voice for the benefit of the house-mind.

"Kitchen! Fix me some toast and red *uffa*."

The kitchen's synthesized voice came back to her. "I hear."

She rose and made her way down the hall to the necessarium. Compared with the house in which she had been raised, Zeri's apartment was cramped—scarcely more than two rooms, not counting the necessarium and the kitchen nook—but it didn't lack for comfort. After a session of hot mist followed by a cooling waterfall had coaxed her the rest of the way to wakefulness, she put on a light morning-gown and thin-soled slippers and went to have her breakfast.

The late-morning sun shone in through the half-curtained windows of the apartment's outer room. Zeri sat down in the high-backed wovenwood chair where she usually took her meals, and the household *aiketh* floated in from the kitchen carrying a tray. The servitor construct—a quasi-organic node of the house-mind, encased in a roughly cylindrical shell of metal and plastic—hovered on its counterforce unit a handspan or so above the green and yellow carpet.

"As you required," the *aiketh* said.

"Excellent," said Zeri, after the *aiketh* had unfolded the legs of the tray to make a table. "You may go."

The *aiketh* floated off. Zeri applied herself to the toast and *uffa*. She was not quite halfway through the meal when the entrance monitor chimed an alert and spoke.

"Fas Treosi is here with urgent news, and requests admittance."

She felt a stirring of curiosity, not unmixed with guilt—had the conclave actually decided something noteworthy, after all? "Let Syr Treosi come in."

She heard the door opening, and a moment later Treosi

appeared: an elderly gentleman, the very image of a respectable legalist, his coat and trousers of sober grey a silent reproach to her own informal dress.

"My apologies for being so late in breakfasting," she said to him, and gestured toward the wovenwood guest chair. "Please join me for *uffa,* at least."

"I don't want to trouble you—" Treosi began.

But the *aiketh* was already bringing up another tray, this one bearing a cup and saucer, and placing it beside his chair. Then the servitor took the pot of *uffa* from Zeri's tray and filled Treosi's cup with the steaming red liquid.

"You see," Zeri said lightly, "it's no trouble for me at all. Now, Syr Treosi—what brings you to my door, of all places, so early in the midmorning? Has some unforeseen disaster cut down all the senior family and left no one standing besides me?"

To her astonishment—followed, a heartbeat later, by the slow crawl of increasing fear—Fas Treosi's face went pale. "Yes," he said. "You are Zeri sus-Dariv sus-Dariv, the oldest living survivor in the senior line."

"Explain," she said. She knew better, seeing Treosi's face, than to ask if this was a joke. "Please."

"An incendiary device," Treosi said. "During the late meetings . . . somebody must have known who would be there. If you hadn't chosen to leave early . . ."

"Yes," said Zeri. She'd meant to look in on her theatre-arts group, but the conclave had left her feeling dull and out of sorts. She'd gone home instead, to read a journal article called "Civic Turmoil and Public Art: A Window of Opportunity?" and play solitaire against the house-mind. Pure slackness on her part—Cousin Herin would have said so, and only half in jest—but she was alive because of it, and he was dead.

"I can't possibly be the only one left," she said in desperation. Her mind didn't want to shape itself to comprehend the idea of complete destruction, because comprehending it would mean that the news was real. "Somebody else *had* to have missed the late meetings. Great-uncle Beven—he wasn't there at all that I remember. Somebody said he hadn't been feeling very well."

"Apparently not," said Treosi. "His household *aiketen* found him dead this morning."

"Killed?"

Treosi gave a minute shrug. "Without further examination, who can say? You are the head of the family now; if you want to order—"

"What would be the point?" She set down the cup she'd been holding ever since Treosi made his first, bald announcement. There was a puddle of red *uffa* in the saucer—she didn't remember making any sudden movements, but she must have done so all the same, if she'd spilled it like that. She laced her hands together in her lap, hidden under the breakfast tray so that Treosi would not see them shaking. "He's gone. So are the rest of them. Anybody left is away with the fleet. We have to call the convoy home and sort things out."

"I'm sorry," said Treosi. He was shaking his head, and his expression had not lightened. "I didn't get the chance to finish telling you—"

She had been cold; she was growing colder. Cold inside and out. "Finish it, Syr Treosi. What else happened last night?"

"The trading fleet is lost."

"What! How—?"

"Pirates, out beyond Ruisi. The guard and attack ships were destroyed, the cargo haulers boarded and left empty. The final message drone from *Path-Lined-with-Flowers* came in-system before midnight."

"I see." Piracy had always been a key element of the game of trade as the fleet-families played it, but seldom piracy so complete and so disastrous. "Did the *Path* recognize any insignia or fleet-livery?"

"Black only," said Treosi. "And the boarders never unmasked. The attackers may have been hired crew for some group who either didn't know enough or didn't care enough to follow proper custom; the message drone was sent by the ship-mind, and didn't include speculation."

"Clearly we have an enemy who cares nothing for custom," Zeri said. She clasped her hands even more tightly under the shelter of the lacquered tray. "It would have been more convenient for everybody if I *had* stayed at the meeting. I was never intended to be head of the family."

"If I may offer a suggestion—"

"Please."

"The outer family and the junior lines are relatively intact despite the losses of the past few hours. Your wisest course would be to approach one of the syn-Dariv, or perhaps the Arayet—I can make a few recommendations, if you don't actually have a preference—with an offer of contractual alliance."

"I don't think so," she said.

"You have to do something," Treosi protested. "Soon, before the other families notice the absence of control and move to devour you."

"Someone is devouring us already," she pointed out. "Our fleet is weaponless; our senior line is destroyed . . . if I were to find a capable man and make him head of the sus-Dariv in every important respect, with his line to be senior after I'm gone—that's the kind of agreement you were thinking of, wasn't it?—how long do you think the rest of the fleet-family would last?"

"But what else is there to do?"

She had shocked him, Zeri could tell; he hadn't thought that she would reject the idea. She wondered briefly which of the ambitious junior families had seized the moment, in the midst of flame and consternation, and solicited Treosi's ear.

It didn't matter. The star-lords were not universally loved in Hanilat, for all that their ships and trade had made the city prosperous, and kept Eraasi the dominant force in the homeworlds. They had enemies among the newer mercantile families, and among the members of the old land-based aristocracy—and now one of those enemies had discovered the way to take a fleet-family down.

Without ships, and without the cadre of trained managers and administrators that had been lost in the disaster, the collapse of the sus-Dariv was inevitable. The candles on the altars would burn out, the family tablets would go untended, and all the people who depended on the sus-Dariv for their place in society would be left without protection.

We have the money to rebuild our fleet, she thought, while Syr Treosi was remonstrating with her across the breakfast tray. *But we don't have the time.*

"Go to Natelth sus-Peledaen," she said at last. *If this comes down, in the end, to the star-lords against the rest of Eraasi, we need the most powerful ally we can get.* "Tell him that the head of the sus-Dariv wishes to speak with him on a matter concerning our two families."

The Gifla Harbor Fishing Cooperative had its headquarters in a whitewashed stone building with a weather station on the roof. The building directory listed an Overseer of Ships and Crews, whose office, when Arekhon and Maraganha finally located it, turned out to be a single large room occupying most of the building's top floor. One wall of the office was mostly windows looking out over the waterfront; the other three walls were covered with charts and notice boards.

Maraganha nodded in the direction of the woman working at the biggest and least cluttered desk. "That one's probably the Overseer," she said. "You try charming information out of her while I complain to the clerical help about the way you've been dragging me from island to island on a missing-person search. I'm going to abuse you shamefully and claim that you're my nephew."

"I always wanted a favorite aunt," Arekhon told her, and went to talk with the woman at the big desk.

"You are the Overseer of Ships and Crews?" he asked.

The woman looked as if she recognized his An-Jemayne accent and scorned it. "Yes."

"I need information, if you have the time, on a certain crew member of the fishing boat *Ninefold Star*."

"The name?"

"Narin Iyal."

The woman's expression changed from scorn to something he couldn't identify. "She is gone."

"Yes. I need to know where she went."

"She is not here. She is gone."

"Where?" asked Arekhon. "Do you have an address?"

"Gone," the woman repeated, then made an exasperated

noise and switched to An-Jemaynan. "*Dead,* you understand? *Gone.*"

For a moment Arekhon could only nod in reluctant comprehension. Then he found his voice and asked, as steadily as he could, "What happened?"

The woman shook her head. "This office does not say."

"Do you—does this office—know?"

"We do not say." The woman turned away from him and pulled a file folder out of the tray on her desk, deliberately cutting off his inquiry. "My sorrow if she was your friend. Now I have work to finish."

Arekhon tried to say something in protest, but the words caught in his throat. He stood for a while in silence, waiting for the woman to say something more, but she kept on working as though he were not there.

Finally he gave up and went away. He was almost out the front door of the building before he heard Maraganha's footsteps coming up behind him.

"I think I got a lead on something," she said.

"So did I. She's gone and we're fucked." Arekhon knew that he sounded ungracious, but he didn't care; he was still trying to absorb the shock of hearing so abruptly about Narin's death.

"I don't know. The clerk I talked to—he knew there was more to the story than the Overseer was letting on. I could feel it."

"Oh."

"So I leaned on him a little. Not enough to disturb the *eiran* much; if anybody looked, it would just be the language trick working again."

In spite of himself, Arekhon felt a stirring of curiosity. "And then?"

"He said that if we wanted to know what really happened, we should ask a fisherman by the name of Juchi Haris."

"Did he say why?"

Maraganha shrugged. "Only that Haris doesn't go out on the boats anymore—and he was one of the crew members on *Ninefold Star.*"

◆

The wall speaker in the workroom chimed, and the house-mind said, "Your brother has arrived from the orbital station, and asks for your attendance in his office."

Isayana sus-Khalgath reluctantly laid aside the needle-tipped drill she'd been using on today's part of her current spare-time project—retooling a basic medical dispensary *aiketh* into a high-level biotech assistant. Strictly speaking, the household emergency closet didn't need such a specialized piece of gear. Anything beyond the scope of the *aiketh*'s original instruction set would properly be a matter for the family's physicians. But Isa wasn't really happy if she didn't have a device of some kind to tinker with, a small piece of the universe to fine-tune until it shaped itself conformably with her desires; nobody would be surprised that she had set herself to such an apparently needless task.

Her other brother—'Rekhe, who was dead—had been the same way when he was young, building models and constructing small ingenious devices. Then he had grown into a Mage, and had worked with the *eiran* instead, making patterns with the lives and luck of the people around him, until his own luck had failed him at last.

Resolutely, she put the thought of Arekhon away—no point in courting bad luck through brooding on it—and considered the house-mind's summons. It was odd for Natelth to come down from the station; as much as he disliked living there, he liked the isolation and improved security more. *Whereas I could live on the station year-round and be happy,* she thought, *but what I do needs the quiet and obscurity of a dirtside life. Life these days is just full of little ironies.*

Even odder than Natelth's presence, however, was that he should ask for his sister's attendance in the middle of what was, for him, a working day. She had no direct voice in fleet decisions—they had divided up the work of the family that way between them in the beginning, when it had been just the two of them against all the star-lords on Eraasi, even against the rest of the sus-Peledaen—and if her own security had been the issue, the house-mind would have already informed her. The quasi-organic intelligence inhabiting the town house knew quite well who had built and instructed its defenses.

"What's the problem?" she asked the house-mind. "Has something gone wrong in the fleet?"

"It's a matter of family, Lord Natelth says, and of some urgency."

"Ah." Deftly and rapidly Isa cleared away the debris of her mechanical experiments. "Tell him I'm coming."

Natelth was waiting for her in his office. Her older brother's black hair had gone grey over the last few years, but he was still a vigorous and attractive man—solid and square-shouldered, the same height as Isa but heavier in bone.

He rose from behind his desk and gestured her toward the office's bow window, where two chairs and a low table over-looked the streets of downtown Hanilat. A pot of *uffa* perched over its heater on tripod legs, steaming gently; a pair of crystal glasses waited alongside. Natelth seated himself in one of the chairs and filled the glasses with red *uffa*.

Isa took the other chair and drank three sips of the *uffa* for politeness' sake before saying, "So what is this family problem you're so eager to talk with me about?"

"Strictly speaking," Natelth said, "it's not a problem at all; it's an unexpected opportunity."

"What kind of opportunity?" Isa asked warily.

"A chance to increase the size of the sus-Peledaen fleet by at least a third, without incurring significant extra expense."

She sipped at the *uffa* again. It was the family's own leaf, spicy and rich and brewed up to a vivid crimson. "Um. It sounds good, but if it were that easy you wouldn't be bothering to consult with me about it. So what exactly do we have to do, in order to carry off this masterstroke?"

"Not we," said Natelth. "I. The head of the sus-Dariv has offered me a personal marriage alliance, their inner family to be junior line to ours."

"Who *is* the head of the sus-Dariv now, exactly? To hear it on the gossip channels, everybody who was anybody in the whole family was wiped out at the Court of Two Colors."

"There's always somebody left standing," Natelth said. "In this case, head-of-family defaults to Zeri sus-Dariv sus-Dariv—she's inner-family, senior line, and it's pure luck that she went home early that night."

Isa tried to recall what, if anything, she knew about Zeri sus-Dariv. The answer was, very little: a vague memory of a youngish woman, pretty without being beautiful, met once at an arts-and-letters party somewhere in Hanilat. Isa had been bored by the company—too many talkers and not enough doers—and had left as soon as she politely could.

"And you want to know if I think you should take the offer?" she said. "That's up to you, Na'e; I can't help you there."

"I won't lie to you—the proposal is a tempting one. The sus-Dariv assets are impressive even if their current luck is not."

"Somebody tried to kill her," Isa said. "You may be marrying into enemies you don't even know."

"Let me worry about that," Natelth said. "I've dealt with our enemies before. The harmony and order of this household, on the other hand, are not something I'm willing to throw away. You have a right to be consulted before I decide."

"I don't know—let me think." Isa ran her hands through her hair, dislodging the stylus she had put there for safekeeping some hours earlier. Automatically, she caught the writing implement and jammed it back into place, still thinking. The sus-Dariv girl had been living alone in a small apartment, or so she'd said at least twice during the few minutes Isa had spent conversing with her. She would not have any idea how to manage a multiple-node house-mind and a full staff of *aiketen*. Which was just as well; someone with even a modicum of knowledge could get in the way and cause all sorts of trouble.

"You should marry," Isa said finally. "But this house stays mine to run. The sus-Dariv woman can come here or live elsewhere, however you please, so long as she doesn't interfere with anything."

Arekhon and Maraganha tracked down Juchi Haris in the Blue Nipper, a waterfront tavern with a pair of ragged claws outlined on the front window in azure light. At night, Arekhon suspected, the place was probably something of a dive.

Now, in the middle of the afternoon, it was all but deserted. A vidscreen on one wall flickered with the shifting images of a dramatic program he vaguely remembered had been popular three years ago in An-Jemayne; the voices had been done over for translation into Immeringic.

According to the bartender, Juchi Haris was one of the late-afternoon regulars. "He misses a day now and then, but that's about all."

"We'll have a drink, then," Arekhon said, "and see if he shows up."

He bought a pitcher of beer and settled in with Maraganha at a table near the back. He'd been willing to work the *eiran* if he needed to, in order to bring *Ninefold Star*'s former crew member into his net, but such drastic measures turned out to be unnecessary. The drama playing on the vidscreen hadn't yet reached its temporary conclusion before a man came up to the table and sat down in one of the empty chairs. The newcomer was gnarled and white-haired, and wore a fisherman's pullover and heavy trousers; when Arekhon said, "Juchi Haris?" he wasn't surprised to receive a nod in return.

"That's right. I hear you people have been asking questions about me."

"Yes," said Arekhon. "I ask pardon if we have offended. But Narin Iyal was a friend of ours."

"So I'd gathered," Haris said. His An-Jemaynan had an accent different from the local one; Arekhon supposed that, like Narin, he'd drifted down to Gifla Harbor from someplace else. "Buy me a drink, then, and we'll talk."

For answer, Arekhon held up the empty pitcher where the bartender could see it, then pointed to Haris. That done, he settled back in his chair and said, "One thing I have to know—they said at the shipping office that Narin was dead. Is that right?"

Haris nodded. "That part was the truth, I'm afraid."

The barkeep brought over a fresh pitcher of the bitter local brew, along with a clean glass for Haris. The fisherman took a long pull from his glass and went on, "Thing is, there's all kinds of dead."

"You'll get no argument from us on that," Maraganha said softly. "We've been around. Tell us the rest of it."

"All right." Haris drew a deep breath. "We were crew together on the *Star,* me and Narin, trawling for dabbers and flakes in the Immering Drift. The *Star* wasn't the best ship ever to come out of Gifla—she was old, and her engines were cranky—but she wasn't the worst one, either. Cap'n Sellig knew how to get the most out of her, when to push and when to let it go, and there never was anyone like him for smelling out the fish. Narin said that he was a lucky man, and maybe she was right—he did well enough off the *Star* to cash in his shares and buy a house on the mainland, and that's more than you can say for any of the rest of us."

He looked out at the middle distance for a while without speaking. Arekhon said quietly, "Go on."

"So *Ninefold Star* got a new captain. I won't name him, because it wasn't his fault that he couldn't handle the *Star* like Cap'n Sellig did—he wasn't all that bad at the work, and who knows, he might have matched Sellig, given time. Narin worried about him, though; said he wasn't well matched to the ship's luck, whatever that means—"

"She said things like that often?"

"Yeah. Claimed she'd left the mainland because nobody there believed in luck. Is that true?"

Arekhon thought of the Adepts of Cazdel, who refused to work with the *eiran,* or even to admit of their existence. "I'm afraid so."

Haris shook his head. "Takes all kinds, I suppose. Anyway, there we were . . . old ship, new captain, and a season's worth of fishing to get done . . . when a big storm blew up in the waters south of the Drift. We'd kept our ears open for the weather reports, so we knew it was out there, but all of the projections had it passing well to the east of us, and the captain wanted to stay out one more day and top off the catch before running back to Gifla."

"That's cutting it close," Maraganha said.

"His job to decide," Haris said. "And the dabbers were running in shoals thick enough to beach a dinghy on . . . I'd have done the same thing, maybe. We'd have been all right, too, if the storm hadn't turned, and instead of passing to the east of Gifla it came bearing straight down on the island instead, with *Ninefold Star* right in the way. We tried to make a run for it, but by then we were taking green water over the bow and couldn't make headway. Maybe Cap'n Sellig could have gotten the engines to come through for him, but I don't know. A big sea came aboard and took the main hatch cover, then another one right after filled the hold, and we started going down."

The old fisherman took another long pull of brew before continuing. "Everything went fast after that. We barely had time to launch the life raft and get all the crew aboard. The captain was the last to leave, or at least that's what I thought. Narin had been with us up on deck—but when we counted heads on the raft, she wasn't there."

Haris's glass was empty; Arekhon refilled it with more beer from the pitcher and said again, "Go on."

"I'll tell you the truth. At the time, all I thought was that it didn't really matter if she was gone, because the rest of us would be coming right along after her—the storm wasn't letting up and we hadn't managed to get off a distress call before the *Star* went down. What happened next . . . I heard about it later from the rescue team, before the Fishing Office had a chance to decide that it hadn't really happened that way at all."

"What do you mean?"

"When the *Star* quit making her regular reports, the Fishing Office knew that she was in trouble—but this was the worst storm to hit Gifla since the end of the last war, and all hell was breaking loose on shore. The *Star* wasn't the only vessel overdue or not reporting, and Dama Jerusa wasn't going to throw away one of her teams on a random search for an old boat that had probably lost its comm rig in the blow.

"And then—" Haris paused "—this is the part you aren't going to believe, but everyone saw it and they swear that it's true—then the office door slammed open and Narin Iyal came in, soaked to the skin and dripping rain and seawater onto the floor like a sponge.

"So Dama Jerusa says, 'Is *Ninefold Star* back in port already?'—thinking maybe Narin had hiked up to the office to make the report—and Narin says, 'No. She's gone down eight miles nor-nor'east of Skeppery Reef.'

"Then she turned around and left again without saying

another word. Dama Jerusa might have ignored her—but too many other people had seen and heard, and Skeppery Reef was right in the middle of where they'd have gone looking for us if they'd decided to do it on their own. So Dama Jerusa sent the rescue team out into the storm like it was all her own idea from the beginning, and sure enough they found us . . . all but Narin, and no one ever saw her again."

"Was her body ever found?" Maraganha asked.

"No."

"I see," said Arekhon. "And that's why the people in the Fishing Office won't talk about her?"

Haris nodded, and took another long swallow of beer. "That's right. It's one thing to pull off a rescue because your office crew made some good calculations. Pulling it off because a ghost came in and gave you directions—that's something else."

"It wasn't a ghost," said Arekhon. "She was really there. She was a great Magelord, and she walked through the Void from Skeppery Reef to Gifla Harbor, all for the sake of her shipmates on *Ninefold Star*."

And she tried to go back, he finished, in the privacy of his thoughts. *But without her Circle for an anchor, she was lost in the Void.*

"Eh?" Haris said. "What's this 'Magelord' mean?"

"Nothing," Arekhon replied sadly. "Here, it means nothing at all."

7:

ERAASI: HANILAT
ENTIBOR: ROSSELIN COTTAGE

Wearing masks was the fashion in the city these days, at least for people doing business in places and in company they might not want to acknowledge later. The Hanilat Ploughmen's Club didn't see much of their type; its members had all known one another for years, sometimes even for generations. The doorkeeper-*aiketh* admitting the afternoon's first outside visitor was not equipped to feel surprise that she chose to wear a hard-shell half-mask covering her features from forehead to below the cheekbones. The human functionary who escorted her to a table in the private cardroom was another matter, but he was too polite, and too well trained in his work, to let his opinions show on his face.

Isayana sus-Khalgath took the offered chair and settled in to wait for the man she had come here to see. He was entering the dining room now, a big square-shouldered man with tanned skin like a farmer's—though she supposed that common farmers never dressed so well, or had membership in an exclusive club like the Ploughmen's. His eyes widened for a second when he saw that she'd come to the meeting masked, but the rest of his face didn't change.

He took the seat opposite her at the table. "I don't suppose you want me to welcome you here by name."

"It wouldn't be wise."

"I can understand that." He took a pack of cards out of the table drawer, broke the seal, and began to shuffle them. "We can play a round of break-and-braid while we talk. Five hundred points, or two-fifty?"

"Two-fifty will do." She waited until he had dealt them each a hand of cards, then continued. "I've heard rumors that you don't care for the sus-Peledaen."

He picked up his hand of cards and sorted them. "There might be some truth in that. It's not personal, though."

"I'm relieved," she said. "On what grounds, then?"

"The world isn't what it was when I was young," he said. "It used to be that the merchants and the landed families were what held everything together, and not the star-lords."

"Times change. When *I* was young, we didn't know for certain that there were Mages on Ninglin. Now half our ships' crews are from there."

"And your big ships never touch the ground at all," he said. "That's the part I don't like. If the sus-Peledaen rule everything, and rule it from space, who's left to take care of things on the ground?"

"A good point," Isayana said. She'd made it to Natelth himself, in fact, and more than once, during his push to extend fleet-family control out beyond Eraasi's orbital space. He hadn't listened—ironic, given her brother's own dislike of working at or visiting the family's strongholds outside of planetary gravity, but Na'e had never been one to let personal comfort or affection get in the way of what he saw as the family's best interest.

And he'll never be persuaded that what he sees is wrong. Especially now that he's managed to annex the sus-Dariv family assets as well.

Isayana laid down her first three cards. Their values made a good start on a braided line. syn-Arvedan could opt to continue the braid, or to tear it apart, depending on the cards in his own hand and upon whether he felt like playing this hand in the slow, cooperative mode or the fast and vicious one.

Break-and-braid was a lot like life that way, she reflected.

You never knew in advance which version the other person was playing, and a game could change modes two or three times before the end.

Syn-Arvedan laid down two cards—building on the braid, Isayana noted with interest. Maybe it was the only thing he could do with the cards he held; maybe it was a preferred style of play. Either way, she could take it as a good omen.

She said, "What do you think? If the fleet-families can't take care of planetary matters, then who should?"

"You know my opinions on that issue already," he said. "At the moment—considering that you were the one asking for this meeting—I'm curious about yours."

She pulled a card out of her hand and laid it down, stretching the braid even further. "I believe that you and I have some feelings in common."

He paused, his hand already touching the next card, ready to pull it out and lay it down. "Somehow, I don't think you went to all the trouble of arranging this meeting so the two of us could play cards. What is it that you want?"

"An alliance," she said. "I have certain projects—various investigations and ongoing researches—that are withering away under my brother's disregard. I need somebody outside the family to sponsor them."

His hand moved away from the card he had initially chosen, and pulled out another. He laid the new card down—still building the braid—and said, "If I'm going to sponsor any researches, I want first refusal on the fruits of them."

"Of course," she said. Three cards from her hand this time, extending the braid yet again, and she was out for this hand. "If the syn-Arvedan want to make themselves into the first family on Eraasi—and take on my brother while they're doing it—they're going to need the help. We have a bargain, then?"

"An arrangement." syn-Arvedan looked at the cards on the table. Isa knew from his earlier hesitation that he had at least one breaking card left in his hand. This would be his last play; with it, he could either destroy their braid or tie it off. He put one of his cards into the discard pile, and laid down the ones remaining to tie off the braid. "Yes. We have an arrangement."

The journey by island-skimmer back to Tifset took place in subdued quiet. Arekhon had lost his taste for idle conversation after the interview with Juchi Haris, and sat hunched and brooding on one of the open-air deck-benches. Maraganha left him alone and spent most of the trip looking out over the rail at the open ocean and watching the seabirds wheel about overhead. They were about fifteen minutes out from Tifset when she came back and sat down next to him.

"We have to go back to the Guildhouse," she said. "The one in—where was it?—Cazdel. Where your friend lives."

Arekhon found the thought a painful one, but he nodded. "You're right. I have to let Ty know what happened to Narin. He doesn't deserve to hear it secondhand."

"No—but that's not the reason we have to go back."

"Then what is?"

"You do know that she isn't dead, don't you?"

The sea breeze gusted and blew his hair forward across his face. One of the seabirds let out a long, harsh cry as it arrowed past him and down to pick up something from the froth at the top of a wave. He drew a careful breath, reminding himself that he was talking with a Void-walker and a great Magelord—who might not necessarily see the universe in the same terms as other people—and said, "What do you mean exactly, that she isn't dead?"

"You said yourself that Narin Iyal must have gotten lost in the Void, while she was trying to get back to her shipmates in distress."

He nodded bitter agreement. "And died there. Yes."

"You're forgetting—time means nothing in the Void. If she *was* lost, then she still *is* lost."

"And you're proposing that the two of us go looking for her?"

"You and I," said Maraganha. "And your friend from the Cazdel Guildhouse."

"Just the three of us?" He was hard put to keep the disbelief from his voice. "The last time I saw a Magelord walk any distance through the Void, it took a great working to accomplish the fact, and the Second of our Circle gave his life to it."

"Some techniques get easier with practice," she said. "As it turns out, Void-walking is one of them. But actually bringing a person back takes help."

Len took *Fire-on-the-Hilltops* into Eraasi nearspace nice and slow. He'd already made one risky close-in Void-translation, and had no desire to push his luck with a second—not so long as he was on record as a sus-Dariv contract carrier in a system where the sus-Peledaen warships made regular patrols. He couldn't afford to come to the notice of that particular fleet-family, not until he'd made it safely back to Hanilat and unburdened himself of his dangerous knowledge. Let any of the sus-Peledaen suspect what he knew, and he'd be handed over to their security forces—or worse, to one of their Circles—before he had time to run.

He spent his free time during the approach in expunging all traces of his meeting with the sus-Dariv vessel from the *Fire*'s ship-mind. It was a finicky job, first removing the unwanted memories and then knitting together a fabric of lies and alterations to stretch across the gaps. For once, though, the *Fire*'s age and her general crankiness worked in his favor. Any blips and stutters that remained could be blamed on the vagaries of an obsolete and decaying system.

"I don't want to insult you in front of strangers, old girl," he said as he finished making the last of the changes, "but I will if I have to. If those sus-Peledaen pirates find out our little secret, they'll kill me and break you up for scrap."

To his considerable relief, however, he didn't have to go so far as to speak ill of his own ship. The nearspace patrols let him pass into Eraasian orbit with only routine questions. Nobody paid much attention to contract carriers, after all. They certainly weren't a threat to anyone's security.

He set the *Fire* down on the landing field at Hanilat, and went through the formalities of turning over his cargo to the various parties who had contracted with the sus-Dariv for its delivery. What he learned during the process was disturbing, to put it mildly.

The loss of the fleet was already a matter of common knowledge—one of the guardships had launched a final despairing message drone before falling to the pirates—but the identity of the attackers remained unknown. What was worse, though, from Len's point of view, was that all the people he might have approached with his secret information were also gone. Somebody had wiped the names of an entire generation off of the sus-Dariv family tablets in a single night.

Len found the news of an incendiary device beneath the Court of Two Colors to be shocking but, in light of his private knowledge, not as surprising as it should have been. With all of his contacts in the senior lines lost in one attack or the other, though, he was hard put to figure out what to do next. He had to tell his news to somebody, if only to spread out the burden, but it looked as if all the people who ought to hear it were dead. And under the circumstances, this didn't feel like a good time to ask questions.

Meanwhile, he began the process of looking for another contract. He still had to eat, and he still had to make the payments on the *Fire*. He put his name up on the looking-for-contracts roster at the pilots' hiring-hall, and checked it at least twice a day. On the third day, he found a message posted for him in reply, the offer of a possible cargo, and the time and place for a meeting: two hours before noon, at the breakfast shop outside the gated landing field.

Len was there early, dressed in his good clothes. He ordered a cup of *uffa* and a plate of mixed pastries, and alternately nibbled and sipped while he waited. Precisely on the hour appointed, a man and a woman entered the shop and sat down at the table across from him.

"We understand from the message boards that you're looking for a new contract," the man said. He was lean and dark-haired, and dressed in clothes that looked like they'd been bought secondhand. The woman was smaller and not quite as shabby; and when he looked at her a second time, he saw that she carried a Mage's staff clipped to her belt.

"That's right," Len said, even though the hair on the back of his neck wanted to stand up. Getting involved with the

Circles was never a good idea for an independent, especially these days.

"I did some looking," the man continued. "You worked for the sus-Dariv, your last couple of runs."

"I'm not making a secret of it. If it makes you worried about my luck ... well, I'm here now and so's my cargo. Even it did come with sus-Dariv paperwork."

"Point taken," the woman said. "Unlike our late friends, you appear to have excellent luck."

She had a pleasant voice, but Len could feel the strength in it. He wondered if she and the man were sus-Peledaen operatives, then decided that they probably weren't. The way things were going on Eraasi these days, if these were Lord Natelth's agents they would already have picked him up and hauled him away for questioning.

The man said, more quietly than before, "What we're wondering is whether your luck happened to get entangled—however briefly—with that of the sus-Dariv during this most recent run."

Len set down his *uffa* and stood up. "I'm very sorry, but right now I don't think it's healthy to talk about things like that. I really must be going."

"Stay," said the woman. "Please."

He sat back down, telling himself that it was the woman's politeness and not the strength of her will that kept him from leaving, and not believing himself very much.

The man said, "Don't worry. We're not fleet-family operatives—at least, not anymore."

"Then who are you?" Len asked. "And what do you want to talk to me about?"

The woman smiled. "I suppose you could call us the last of the Demaizen Circle. But my friend here—" she nodded at the dark man "—is sus-Dariv born and bred, my word as a Mage on it. So you might as well tell us the truth."

Elaeli was still in An-Jemayne with the Provost of Elicond—sometimes these things took longer than anticipated, Arekhon supposed—and the summer cottage was empty when he arrived there with Ty and Maraganha. The Void-walker had said already that any place would do for the working in a pinch; here, at least, they wouldn't be interrupted, or need to make awkward explanations afterward.

"There's a cook and a housekeeper," he said. They were sitting together on the screened verandah where Maraganha had first stepped through from the Void. Night had fallen, and the stars were coming out in the sky above the trees. He'd lit a candle, some minutes earlier, and set it on the low table. "But only when the Mestra is in residence. For myself—I don't bother."

"Self-sufficiency is good," Ty said. He looked amused. "Even for the sus-Peledaen."

"I doubt that Natelth kept my name on the family tablets for very long after we left Eraasi."

Maraganha turned her head and regarded Arekhon curiously. The yellow candle flame threw changeable patterns of light and shadow across the dark planes of her face. "Who's Natelth?"

"My brother," Arekhon said. "He and I . . . Natelth doesn't take well to being thwarted."

"He means his brother tried to have us all killed," Ty explained. "And will probably try again if we go back."

"Is that the real reason you don't want to do it?" Maraganha asked. "Because of what might happen?"

"Yes. But not the way you think." Ty looked away from the candle flame, out into the dark. "I had a place to be, when I was at the Guildhouse in Cazdel. If I go back to Eraasi, I think I'm going to lose it. One way or another."

"Only help us find Narin," Arekhon said. "Then we'll talk some more about Eraasi."

"And if Maraganha *etaze* can't help us find her—"

"Then we already have a bargain, and you stay in Cazdel." Arekhon stood up. "Maraganha—is now a good enough time, or would it be better to wait until tomorrow?"

The Void-walker stood also. "Now is as good as tomorrow, and better for being sooner." She looked at Ty steadily until the younger Mage also rose to his feet. Then she said, "Listen to me, both of you. This is something that you need to learn, and learn well enough to teach if you have to. And the first question that you need to ask is how your friend was able to walk to Gifia Harbor from a sinking ship without a Circle to back her."

"It's not the going," Ty said. "At least, that's what all the stories say. It's the coming back."

"I came here without a Circle. And regardless of what you may think, I plan to return home when I'm finished." She turned then to address Arekhon. "This is the part where you're supposed to say, 'Please, Auntie Maraganha, tell us how you did it?' "

"Well, then," he said, "how did you?"

"There's a trick to it—a simple one, once you know the way. You look for an angle, and you turn the corner, and there you are. Like turning the corner in a hall in your own home in the dark."

She vanished, and a moment later reappeared.

"The trick," she said, "is to come out where you left."

"And how do you learn to do that?" Arekhon asked.

"In the Void, all times are the same time, and all places are the same place. So to begin a journey is to arrive."

Ty said, *"That's* certainly full of possibilities for error."

"You're a very perceptive young man," Maraganha told him. "And the chance of going astray is why the Mages in my time are accustomed to setting Void-marks to light their way home. I set my own Void-marks when I first walked here, and they'll help us get back once we've collected your friend Narin."

"If you say so," Ty said. "But this corner that we're supposed to look for—how do we find it?"

"Take my hand, and I'll show you."

She held out her hands. Ty took one, and Arekhon the other—he would have known even blindfolded that it was a Mage's grip, from the strength in it, and the telltale rough spots left by daily practice with a wooden staff.

Maraganha spoke quietly, in the shadows of the darkened verandah. "Now look for the path around the corner, the half-step sideways from here, the journey that has your friend at the end of it."

Narin, Arekhon thought, and watched the cords of the *ei-ran* glow brighter in response to her name. Then he saw the particular Narin-lines that stretched out around the angle in reality. He followed them, and he was through.

The folded slip of paper in Inadal's pocket had arrived at Arvedan Hall with the morning mail. It contained only an address—a residential building not far from the sus-Peledaen town house—a date and time, and the words *Come alone.* Curious, he had returned to Hanilat and done exactly that, leaving his groundcar several blocks away in a parking tower and finishing his journey on foot. The doorkeeper-*aiketh* that let him into the well-kept-up older building was a starkly functional model, its voice the product of a synthesizer module, its casing plain brushed metal.

"Please come this way. The workrooms are on the basement level."

He followed the *aiketh* down a flight of steps, and from there into a hallway that led to a surprisingly well lit and modern laboratory. As he'd expected, Isayana sus-Khalgath was waiting there for him, unmasked this time and carrying a stiff cardboard tube under one arm. In her plain work clothes, with her hair pinned up with a metal clip, she could have passed for a midlevel fleet-family technician and not the sister of Natelth sus-Peledaen.

This laboratory, though, with its long tables, its drafting and mechanical *aiketen,* its well-stocked shelves and cabinets, was clearly her personal domain. The doorkeeper-*aiketh* said, "Inadal syn-Arvedan is here, my lady," and retired upstairs about its business.

He said, "I received your letter. At least, I assume it was your letter—if it isn't, then we're already in more trouble than I want to think about."

"Breathe easily, syn-Arvedan. It was mine."

"Good," he said. "I'm guessing that this isn't merely a friendly meeting for cards and *uffa.*"

"You're right." She uncapped the cardboard tube and pulled out several large sheets of drafting parchment. Spreading the first one out on the laboratory table, she said, "I wanted you to see what I've been working on."

He stepped up to the table and looked. He didn't have

enough technical training to understand most of what he was seeing—his sister Ayil might have, or some of Ayil's friends—but he could follow the summary paragraphs and the conceptual drawings.

Bodies. Not aiketen, *but bodies that live.* He wondered, briefly, if he was standing across the table from a madwoman. Finally, he said, "This is it?"

She shrugged. "Preliminary notes only."

A corner of the parchment tried to curl up again. Almost absentmindedly, she weighted it down with a stone jar full of rulers and marking tools.

Inadal, watching, said, "That's a cumbersome method of storage you're using there."

"The working files are encrypted in the house-mind. I had one of the drafting *aiketen* make these up to show you."

"Ah." He looked at the notes and drawings for a while longer in silence, then asked, "Is your brother aware of the direction your researches have been taking?"

"No."

"I see."

A spot of color rose in her cheeks, and she spoke more rapidly. "Natelth is enamored of inorganic mind components—the materials come cheaply from Ayarat, and the new instruction techniques give us the kind of speed we've been accustomed to getting from gel-based constructs. Not so elegant as before, but . . ." Again, she shrugged. "So I began to think of other uses for the mind-gel, since we weren't going to be using it in our ships anymore."

Not a madwoman, then, he reflected, but a tinkerer, a dedicated user-up of spare parts and unwanted extras. He turned back to the parchment and touched one of the less-confusing sketches with his forefinger. "This would be a medical *aiketh,* here?"

"It could be adapted from one," she said. "For the prototype. Custom-built units would come later."

"These . . . bodies," he said. "Is there any point in making them? What would they be good for, that we don't already have either *aiketen* or true people enough to do?"

"I thought you might have some ideas," she said. "One thing I haven't even put in my notes, although anybody with the right training could probably guess at it—given the right blood to seed the process, the finished body can be a match for anyone you like."

He felt a chill run down his back, a not-entirely-unpleasant sensation. If the syn-Arvedan were going to make themselves into a force of opposition to the likes of Natelth sus-Peledaen, they would need reliable security and intelligence operatives. Doorways of possibility were opening up inside Inadal's mind, and some of the things behind those doors were both dark and tempting.

"Yes," he said. "That does have possibilities. You would be instructing these bodies for their work, I suppose, like you instruct the *aiketen?*"

"The process should be essentially the same," she said. "Of course, I haven't done it yet, so there are no guarantees."

"I understand." He pondered the sketch drawing of the converted medical *aiketh.* "It looks like you'll need a physician—"

"I know that. I have several in mind already."

"—and more than a physician, I suspect that you'll need a Mage. Probably a whole Circle of Mages."

"And that's another problem I thought you might be able to help me with. All of the fleet-Circles answer to my brother these days, whether they admit it or not."

"That will make things difficult, then." He thought about what he'd learned of the Mages from his brother Delath. "The Demaizen Circle could have done it—"

"—but Demaizen was broken when the Old Hall burned." Her expression was sympathetic, and he remembered belatedly that she too had once had a brother in the Demaizen Circle. "I know. And Garrod syn-Aigal died a madman."

"Not all of Demaizen's Mages are dead."

"Diasul?" she asked, somewhat to his surprise. "That one already has secrets he doesn't mention to my brother; I'm sure of it. But I don't think I like him."

"All the same," Inadal said, "he's the only Mage I know of these days who's doing experimental work on Lord Garrod's level."

Isayana sus-Khalgath nodded briskly and rolled up her sheets of parchment. "Then Diasul it will have to be."

The Void was all smoky greyness, a thick fog illuminated by a sourceless glow that came at once from everywhere and from nowhere at all. Arekhon felt the cold of it pulling the warmth from his flesh, and realized a bitter truth—that the *eiran* had shown him the way into this place, but nothing more. The cords of life and luck did not extend into the Void.

"No wonder Narin couldn't find her way home," he said. His voice sounded flat and echoless to his own ears, like a megaviol with dampened strings. "With all her skills and techniques useless, working by instinct and intuition alone . . . a lesser Mage would never have reached Gifla Harbor at all."

"Will and intention are everything in the Void," Maraganha said. "What you will—what you intend—becomes real."

"It can't be that easy," Ty said. "Nothing ever is."

"And the prize for the day goes to the man from Cazdel," she said. "Willing a single thing, purely and clearly—holding a single focused intention—it's not easy at all. Fortunately, gentlesirs, you have the training. We're here to look for your friend, and in the Void—"

"—to seek for a thing is to find it," Arekhon finished. He pointed out into the mist of the Void, in a direction that he defined by an act of will as not-random, and said, "There."

The mists of the Void swirled and parted, revealing a many-branched tree, stark black against a grey background, with the heads of young women impaled on its branches. Thick grey blood fell away in slow drops from their necks and spread out like ink in water on the fog below.

Whose mind, Arekhon wondered, had worked on the Void to give it such a grisly substance? Was the image something from his own dark nightmares, or from Ty's—or was it Maraganha's, a reminder that the Void-walker was, for all her helpful good humor, essentially alien? He pushed the thought away from him; such speculation would only distract him now.

"Look for your friend here," Maraganha said. "If you let fear stop you, she's lost for good."

Arekhon opened his mouth to speak, but Ty was ahead of him, looking straight on at the dreadful tree and asking, "Where is Narin Iyal?"

The head nearest to them opened its grey eyes. Its mouth moved. "Better to ask, where are you?"

A second head spoke as soon as the first was silent. "Better yet to ask what it is that you truly need."

"Do not ask for that which you do not desire," said a third. "For surely then your wish will be granted."

"We don't have the time to play games with oracles," Maraganha said to the head that had first spoken. "Talk straight. Do you know where Narin is?"

"Yes."

"Is she still in the Void, or is she in some other place?"

The head's pale lips turned upward in a smile. It was mocking them, Arekhon thought.

"She is here, and she is not, and she was, and she shall be, and she is not."

"Fine," said Maraganha. She wrapped her fist in the head's long dark hair and pulled it free of the branch on which it was impaled. "Since you know so much, you can come along and show us the way."

The tree dissolved back into the mist from which it had emerged, but the head still dangled from Maraganha's hand. The Void-walker looked back at Ty and Arekhon.

"Follow me," she said, and they began to walk.

It seemed to Arekhon that they traveled through the cold grey mist for hours without discernible progress. His legs grew tired, and his feet ached, but the mist around them never changed—nothing changed, except that every now and again the woman's head, its neck still dripping misty grey blood, would turn to right or left as it hung from Maraganha's upraised hand. When that happened, the Void-walker would change her direction so that the head once more gazed straight forward, and continue on. Ty and Arekhon followed her without speaking.

After an interminable while, there was a noise, coming from what—if this place had distance—would have been somewhere far away. Arekhon thought that it sounded like the noise of the sea, or of breakers crashing against distant cliffs. Then, suddenly, the mist was roiling about them like storm clouds filled with wind, and rushing and curling about their feet like water foaming over stones.

"Here," Ty said, and reached down, his hand going through the layer of nonsubstance on which they stood. Arekhon flung himself down full-length on the illusory ground and thrust his arm through it, and felt a body there, cold, wet, and he grabbed at soggy cloth and pulled, and up into the Void came Narin, dripping wet, blue about the face, and gasping.

She looked from one of them to the other. "Not without my crew," she gasped, "no one dies, not this time," and rolled sideways and down into the breaking mist.

"Catch her! Quickly!" Maraganha shouted, and Ty and Arekhon plunged their arms down again into the foam.

Arekhon touched hair this time, like the woman's hair that Maraganha held twisted in her fist. He pulled, and Ty pulled with him, until Narin rose out of the deep and let herself be gathered into their embrace.

"As the universe wills," said Maraganha, and the phantom head she had carried turned to scraps of grey cloud and blew away on the wind. She laid her hand on Arekhon's shoulder, and he felt them turning the corner again—for an instant he could see the Void-marks shining ahead of them like beacons in the dark—and then they were through, all of them, standing on the dark verandah in the yellow light of a single candle.

Narin said, "My shipmates—where are they?"

"Saved," Arekhon said. "All of them pulled from the water off of Skeppery Reef except for you."

"Why did you bring me back?" she asked. "I wanted to join my crew, be one of them—I was almost there."

"You're part of the great working," Arekhon said. "And it isn't finished yet."

8:

ENTIBOR: ROSSELIN COTTAGE
ERAASI: HANILAT

The next morning, Arekhon begged hospitality for Ty and the others from the Master of the Cazdel Guildhouse, and took them all there together. Ty was glad to be back, however briefly, in the place that had become his home on Entibor, and Narin—having decided that not drowning was, on balance, a good thing—was resigned to staying there with him. Maraganha, for her part, appeared to find the prospect amusing for reasons Arekhon didn't feel qualified to guess.

Having seen to the comfort and accommodation of his Circle, Arekhon returned alone to the Rosselin town house in An-Jemayne. When he got there, the servants told him that Elaeli was gone. The Provost of Elicond, they said, had taken his leave only the day before, and the Mestra had departed also. Arekhon thanked them politely and took one of the household's private aircars to Rosselin Cottage, a familiar journey and one that he feared he was making for the last time.

Elaeli was waiting there for him, sitting in her favorite spot on the screened verandah, overlooking the wooded downslope. She appeared somewhat paler than usual, and tired. Arekhon wasn't surprised; he knew from prior engagements that a visit like the Provost's involved very little in the way of personal pleasure. That knowledge had provided him with a certain amount of consolation from time to time, which he worked hard to keep Elaeli from noticing. She hadn't asked for the life that Demaizen's great working had given her, and she was entitled to make the best of it however she could.

She rose from her chair and came forward to embrace him. He buried his face in the soft brown curls of her hair. " 'Rekhe," she said. "I'm glad you're back."

"I can't stay," he said. It wasn't the greeting that he'd intended, but he couldn't unsay it once he'd spoken. He tried to explain it instead. "The working is too strong. I've found Narin and Ty, and they both agree—" *after some persuasion,* said the voice of honesty in his head "—that we need to go back across the Gap to Eraasi."

She released him from her embrace and stepped away to look at him. "What for?"

He turned his empty hands palm-up, sketching a shrug. "I don't know. But I had a dream that said it was time."

"You never used to dream like that before."

"I had a proper Circle before." For a moment he closed his eyes, feeling again the pang of loss. "Things were . . . more orderly, back then."

She bit her lip. "I shouldn't let you go. If you cross the Gap, you won't come back. You told me yourself that Natelth wanted you dead."

"If I live, I'll come back," he said. "I promised it once before, remember, and I keep my promises."

"That's the problem, 'Rekhe. I don't think anybody can be that lucky twice."

"Nevertheless," he said. "I think it has to be done."

"Nevertheless," she agreed, on a sigh. She went back to her chair and gestured him into its partner a few feet away. After he had settled himself on the gaudy fabric cushions, she gave him a rueful smile and said, "It's true what all the people say, you know."

"What is?"

"That if you take a Mage for a lover, you'll only have to give them back in the end."

He knew better than to deny the charge. "I'm sorry. It's the real reason we leave our family altars, I suppose. The pull of the Circle is too much for us."

She looked at him sharply. "And what if the Circle is gone? What do you do then?"

"Go mad, some of us. Find another, if we're lucky."

"Ah." On the slope below the porch, a long-tailed bird—impelled by some unknown stimulus—burst out from among the leaves and darted across the green background in a vivid, crimson streak. Elaeli followed its motion and subsequent disappearance with her eyes before asking, "So what does that mean for you? Is Garrod's Circle broken, or not?"

"I don't know," he said. "Kiefen Diasul was still alive on Eraasi when I left, and still bound into the working, and so was Iulan Vai. But it's been more than ten years. Anything could have happened."

"I don't suppose there's any way you can talk yourself out of going back there to find out," she said.

"If I could—"

"Never mind," she told him. "I shouldn't be giving you a hard time, after everything you've had to put up with to spend a few years here with me."

"It's had its moments," he said. In spite of himself, he smiled. "I certainly never expected to find myself working as a politician's personal bodyguard."

"It was the only way I could think of to keep you close to the politician's personal body," she said. "And let's face it, you've got a streak of natural deviousness in you that makes you damned good at the job."

"You're kinder to me than I deserve."

She snorted. "Hardly. I've used you abominably, 'Rekhe."

"No more than I used you in the service of the great working."

"You did. We each deserve more than we've granted. Nevertheless, I'm going to ask for one thing more. Come back to me, 'Rekhe. Choose me over the working. Be with me and don't leave."

He sat quietly.

At last she said, "So, you see. We each of us have things

that compel us. So I'll make another request. Return when it's over."

"I swear it," Rehke said. "Living or dead, I will return to you when my part in the working is done, and I will ply the luck for you in the meantime."

"I don't want an *ekkannikh*; no revenant can warm my bed the way you do."

"Nor will I be," 'Rekhe said. "But I have given my word, and I will protect you and all that you have built and will build here, with all my power, in any place or time whatsoever."

"Be careful with words of power," Elaeli whispered.

"I am," 'Rekhe said.

Zeri sus-Dariv had never given serious thought to marriage. She had reached the age of legal independence several years past, and had come at that time into the possession of an income sufficient to let her live as she pleased provided she did not live extravagantly. She had her friends and her occasional lovers; she had her small but elegant apartment; and she did not see how the acquisition of a husband would improve her comfortable state.

Some people thought it a flaw in all of her generation, that they did not make haste to marry and raise up children to tend the family altars. Zeri had looked at the number of her cousins and given it as her opinion that there were, if anything, too many descendants crowding those altars already.

That was before the hecatomb at the Court of Two Colors. If there had been one, just one, minor child of sus-Dariv's inner line closer to its head than she was, she might have secured the same degree of alliance by giving that one over for adoption into the sus-Peledaen. Then she could have gone on by herself to manage whatever remained of the family's affairs, and all without the need to marry.

Instead, she found herself sequestered with Fas Treosi and Natelth sus-Peledaen in the office chambers of the sus-Khalgath town house, under the watchful eye of one of Lord Natelth's own Mages. The three of them—and the Mage—had spent most of the afternoon going over the articles by which, upon the consummation of Zeri's union with Natelth, the sus-Dariv would be subsumed into the sus-Peledaen.

For subsumption it was. Even Fas Treosi's best efforts, as embodied in pages upon pages of legal documents, could not stand against the fact that not enough ships remained in the fleet, and not enough names remained on the family tablets, for the sus-Dariv to continue alone. All that remained was to provide as best she could for those survivors who had depended on the family for their livelihood, and to save what she could of their pride.

"The ships that remain," she said. "Syr Treosi has sent you the list."

The Mage, who up to this point had stood to one side and remained silent, finally roused himself to speak. "A brief list."

"Granted," she said.

"Specifically, two space-only heavy-cargo vessels, one light-cargo landing-ship, three loading shuttles, and a fast courier currently in the yards for repair. Not enough to sustain trade."

She decided that she didn't like the Mage. "No. But let's be honest—if it were sufficient, I wouldn't be here."

Natelth was a square and solidly muscled man, but not particularly frightening except for the fact that he was, quite possibly, the most powerful individual in the homeworlds. Now he only looked amused. "True enough," he said. "Is there something remaining about the ships, then, that we should discuss?"

"It is a matter not so much of the ships themselves as of the ships' crews," Fas Treosi said, in response to Zeri's nod in his direction. "They have had a severe shock—the loss of family and friends, with other changes following close behind—and their morale is correspondingly low. Lady Zeri feels that it would be counterproductive for us to ask them to change their ship-names and fleet colors at this time."

Natelth nodded—not without sympathy, Zeri thought—and glanced over his shoulder at the Mage. "What do you say, *etaze*? Does the luck favor changing the names, or keeping them?"

The Mage gave Zeri a long, measuring look. His eyes were cold, she thought, and there was something in them that she couldn't name. "Change them," he said. "The name should reflect the thing; and the sus-Dariv fleet is gone."

"You hear the man," Natelth said. "Their names and colors to become sus-Peledaen. But this family has always acknowledged good service—nobody will lose rank or seniority by the change, and those who are syn-Dariv will be accepted without question as syn-Peledaen."

Zeri suppressed a sigh. It was, she supposed, the best that could be expected. "So be it," she said, and reached for the stylus.

Isayana had no desire to meet with the sus-Dariv woman before her brother's wedding day. In her opinion, the mere fact that they would be living together under the same roof in no way obliged them to become friends. She waited downstairs in the smaller reception room, out of Natelth's sight and mind, with the household *aiketen* instructed to ignore her presence. Eventually she heard the sus-Dariv's light footsteps coming down the stairs, accompanied by the heavier tread of the legalist Treosi. She continued to wait in silence, and was rewarded a few minutes later with the sound of a third set of footsteps.

She stepped out into the hallway and came, as she had expected, face-to-face with perhaps the most powerful of her brother's Mages. "Syr Diasul," she said. "Well met. I've been wanting to talk with you."

He stopped at the foot of the stairs and looked at her with his strange, half-mad eyes. "I'm flattered. Why?"

"You were a member of the Demaizen Circle. My brother Arekhon's Circle."

Something disturbing surfaced for a moment from the depths of his gaze. "That's not a good name to mention around here. Every *aiketh* and mind-node in this house reports back to Lord Natelth."

"What I speak of in private conversation is my own business," Isa said. "Na'e understands that. But if you feel safer in a null room, I can arrange it—house-mind!"

"Yes, my lady?" said the house-mind over the hallway annunciator.

"Shut off all nodes and receptors in the downstairs front reception room for the next half-hour."

"Working, my lady. Done."

"You see," Isa said to Kief. "Now you can speak your mind in safety."

She turned her back to him and reentered the reception room. A few seconds later, she heard him follow.

"Yes," he said, as the door snicked shut and she turned once again to face him. "I was a Mage in Lord Garrod's Circle. It's not a secret."

"But you left Demaizen to be the First of a sus-Peledaen Circle."

"I left Demaizen because everybody else was dead," he said.

"Arekhon wasn't dead then. Or any of the other Mages who went with him across the interstellar gap."

"I didn't know that at the time," Kief said. "I thought that one of your Circles might take me in for 'Rekhe's sake."

"A good guess, as it turned out," she said. "By the time 'Rekhe came back and got his name wiped off the family tablets, you weren't just one of the common Mages in your new Circle. You were the First."

For a long moment, there was silence. Then he said, "I don't think you appreciate the level on which Demaizen was working. Any one of Lord Garrod's Mages could have done the same thing."

"In fact, I do appreciate it. That's why I'm talking with you now."

For the first time, he looked puzzled rather than suspicious. "What do you mean?"

"You know that I do much of the design and instruction work for the sus-Peledaen quasi-organics."

" 'Rekhe mentioned it once or twice." Kief smiled a little. "Usually when he was tinkering with something himself and explaining how he wasn't actually very good at the work and how his sister could do it better."

"He *could* have been good at it, if he'd wanted to be. But all he really wanted, from the time he could talk about it, was the Circles." She stopped before her voice could get shaky, and forced herself back to the original subject. "In any case, I have a line of research ongoing which needs the assistance of a high-level Mage-Circle during its final stages. And as you've just said, all of Demaizen's Mages were on that level."

Kief looked at her closely. "This is a distinctly irregular conversation we're having, my lady. Which makes me wonder: How does Lord Natelth feel about your new line of research?"

"This is a private inquiry," she said. "Na'e is all for moving the sus-Peledaen outward, making us independent of Eraasi—he thinks it's the only way to keep the family safe, and he may be right about that. But this is still our homeworld, and if all the star-lords follow our lead there won't be anybody left who's strong enough to look after it. Not unless some new faction rises up that can take the star-lords' place."

"Politics," he said. He made the word sound as if it tasted bad in his mouth, and she wondered what had happened to make him dislike it so. "You're working against your own family."

"I'm working for the benefit of Eraasi," she said. "The sus-Peledaen are part of Eraasi, no matter what my brother thinks."

"Ah." Kief turned away from her and began pacing the length of the small room. "And you want me to work with you behind Lord Natelth's back?"

"You aren't even syn-Peledaen," she said. "Nobody at Demaizen was tied to the family that way—even 'Rekhe had himself removed from the formal line—so if you weren't working for the benefit of all Eraasi then, who were you working for?"

"For the benefit of the whole galaxy, if you believed Lord Garrod—which we did. He pulled all of us into his great working, the one that was supposed to end the sundering and heal the galaxy, and those of us it didn't kill are still caught up in it."

"I see. I'm sorry you feel that you can't—"

"I didn't say that." Once again he fixed her with his clear, half-mad eyes. "As you say, I'm not family; and just because I'm First of a sus-Peledaen Circle doesn't mean I agree with everything Lord Natelth says or does. I have to meditate on this. I'll give you my answer by tomorrow evening."

Elaeli's bedroom at Rosselin Cottage was high-ceilinged and cool even in high summer, with tall windows along one side to catch the night breeze, and the other side open to the screened-in porch. When Arekhon came to the door that evening, Elaeli let him in and tapped the catchpad shut behind him. She wasn't in the mood, he suspected, for interruptions. Her long fingers twisted the front of her lounging-dress, and the lightweight fabric slid off her shoulders and down past her hips. She stepped out of the puddle of cloth, fingers already working at the fastenings of her undergarments. By the time she reached the bed, she was naked.

" 'Rekhe," she said, and the sound of his name stroked across his skin like a caress.

He was shedding clothing himself by now, casting aside the sober white shirt and black tunic—not untidily, it wasn't in his nature; but loose and unfolded. The boots took longer; he had to sit on the side of the bed to pull them off. Elaeli knelt in front of him to help, and the moonlight and shadows coming in from the screened porch made dappled patterns against her bare skin.

"Remember when we used to do this for each other?" she asked. They had been fleet-apprentices together aboard the sus-Peledaen guardship *Ribbon-of-Starlight*—and more than just shipmates to each other, even then. She had been 'Rekhe's first, and he hers, and that was a bond that went deeper than any politics.

"I don't remember having this much room in those days," he said.

"No." She pulled off first one of his boots and then the other, her small breasts bobbing with each movement. Her nipples were erect; when he reached out and rubbed his thumb across the sensitive flesh, she shivered all over. "You're overdressed, I think." Her hands came up to unfasten the waistband of his trousers, and it was his turn to draw a sudden gasping breath. Her fingers were long and nimble, and completely without mercy. She worked his trousers down over his hips and onto the floor. "And we certainly didn't have enough privacy on shipboard to do *this*."

She bent her head and took him in her mouth.

He clenched his fists in the bedsheets and tried to draw in enough air for speech. "Not without locking ourselves in a storeroom first. Ela—wait."

She flicked her tongue against him, hard, then drew back enough to say, "What for? I like this."

"You need me to—" he gasped again as her mouth covered him "—work the *eiran*. I need time. Not so soon."

She pulled away and sat back on her heels. In this room of shadows and moonlight, she seemed to be glowing, as though her bare body had been molded out of some luminescent material. "The *eiran*. Are they here? Can you see them?"

"They're everywhere," he said. "Always."

He could see them even now, if he tried, thin lines and wisps of silver tracing across the skin of Elaeli's breasts and flanks and belly like erotic verses in an unknown script. He traced out their shapes and patterns—lightly, lightly, more with thoughts than with hands—and the silver lines shone brighter under his touch, coiling into new designs while Elaeli shivered with pleasure.

He took her hands and lifted her up from her knees, rising to stand with her, embracing her, bare skin against bare skin. He felt the curves and coils of the *eiran* encircling them both, making him burn, making her press against him. The scent of her arousal was like perfume; his own readiness was sharp and salty by contrast.

We are doing this. We are doing this now. Because she needs it; because I will it.

He turned with her, still holding her, still wrapped together in the silvery web of the *eiran*, and laid her down on the bed. He kissed her gently on the arches of her feet, and she moaned; *good*, he thought, and began working his way upward, past her knees—she moaned again—to her thighs and from there to the warm sweet confluence of her sex.

Whatever was denied, he thought, *whatever was circumvented, whatever was put off with lies, it will be manifest.*

He parted her legs and slid inside her. She wrapped her

legs around him, keening in her throat and bucking her hips up to meet his repeated thrusts. All around them the air was glowing, full of changing silver patterns that shone with a light brighter even than the moon.

This, too, is part of the great working, he thought; *this is the shape of our desire.*

Then mind and flesh exploded together in an ecstasy of light, and as he spilled himself into her he heard her call out his name.

Kiefen Diasul lived alone in the caretaker's apartment of the meeting hall where his primary Circle convened for its workings. The drab, worn-out rooms had neither the utilitarian comfort of his student lodgings at the Hanilat Institute, nor the faded elegance of Demaizen Old Hall, but they gave him a place to eat and sleep and take shelter from the weather. The apartment's only luxury was one he had added himself: a small room, closed off from the rest of the space by heavy black curtains. The floor and walls were also black, with the exception of a white circle painted in the center of the floor.

He returned from his meeting with Natelth sus-Peledaen and his disturbing encounter with Natelth's sister knowing that he would have to settle the questions in his mind before he slept. He cooked himself a quick supper of canned flatpeas and sausage heated up in a saucepan, and ate it standing at the counter in the apartment's tiny kitchen. When he was done, he washed the few dishes in the sink and set them out to dry, then went to the meditation chamber.

There was a smoked-plastic hardmask hanging on a peg outside the curtained door. He took the mask and put it on. He'd discovered, over the years since leaving Demaizen, that wearing the mask helped him to see the *eiran* more clearly, cutting out some of the distractions in his visual field.

Mask in place, he stepped into the chamber and let the curtain fall closed behind him. Dim light from the single overhead fixture illuminated the white circle on the floor below. He knelt in the center of the white circle and inhaled deeply, then let the air out again in a long, controlled breath. Either Isayana sus-Khalgath had an information-gathering apparatus that exceeded her brother's, or she was capable of insight on a level that would have done pride to a Magelord. She had offered Kief, unerringly, the one thing on Eraasi besides the power of the Circles that he wanted for its own sake: a chance to thwart Natelth sus-Peledaen.

He told himself that he shouldn't be surprised. She was Arekhon's sister as well as Natelth's, after all, and the gifts that had made 'Rekhe into one of the great Magelords would not have passed her by completely.

That doesn't mean I should accept her offer.

He was already doing something new with the Circles in Hanilat—maybe the first new thing in living memory. When it was all accomplished, he would be in a position to deal with Natelth however he wished, without needing Isayana's help at all.

That doesn't mean I should refuse *her offer, either.*

He saw himself, then, balanced on the knife's edge. Acceptance or refusal . . . he let himself visualize his goal, picturing Natelth discomfited, cast down from his unassailable position and justly requited for sending one member of a Circle to betray another. The intent rose up before him like a mountain against the dark grey of the Void, and he saw the lines of the *eiran* trailing and twisting around it. There was great disorder in them, as though they had not been tended properly for years and years; he would have taken the time to untangle them and arrange them properly if he hadn't promised to give Isayana her answer.

One of the silver threads would be his own, stretching out from the here and now into the indeterminate future. He searched among the threads until he found it, a thicker and brighter line of silver that glinted with flashes of colored light, and laid his hands on it. It was warm under his touch, like something alive. Still touching the thread with one hand, he began following it forward into the Void, toward the dark and formidable mountain of his intent.

It wasn't a mountain after all, but something man-made, a looming ziggurat of black stone with a gaping entrance like a mouth at its base. The silver thread beneath his hand stretched out into the opening.

The answer is in there.

Steeling himself, he followed the thread downward into darkness. For a long time, there was nothing in the dark but the feel of the silver cord and its faint, luminous glow. At last, however, the light around him increased, and he saw that he was standing near the center of a vast, echoing room. He was waiting for someone, apparently; he had his mask on, and his staff hung loosely from his hand.

A figure appeared out of the darkness facing him.

" 'Rekhe," he said, although the newcomer both was and wasn't Arekhon sus-Khalgath sus-Peledaen as Kief had known him before. His onetime Circle-mate had never been that old, and couldn't possibly be that old even now. The man's eyes were the same, though, and the unconscious arrogance of his posture—'Rekhe had always thought of himself as the least prideful of men, and Kief had always found his friend's lack of self-knowledge amusing. "Arekhon."

The other man inclined his head in greeting. "Kief."

"It's been a long time. I always suspected that you'd come back if I waited long enough."

"Well, now I'm there." The man who was and wasn't Arekhon smiled a little. "Or you are here. All times and places are the same in the Void, so I don't think it matters in the end."

Kief said, "I followed the *eiran*. Garrod left his working unfinished, and the path of damage leads straight to this place, wherever it is."

"Or wherever it will be. We're both caught in the working, and there's no way out but to finish it."

Kief looked around himself then, and saw that the single thread of silver that he'd followed into this place had become a dazzling, tangled network of glowing lines . . . a broken, half-completed pattern that he had seen in full only once before, when he and 'Rekhe fought in the Demaizen garden while Lord Natelth's killers watched them from the shadows.

He knew it, though. This was the pattern of the great working. It didn't matter that from day to day he saw it only in part; he didn't need to see the pattern to feel it binding and constraining him.

He raised his staff. "Then guard yourself," he said, and

they took up the struggle again where they had left it.

The combat was brief but grueling. Arekhon, or his vision-shadow, had lost none of his strength and had only gained in cunning. Kief's blows landed on air, or on the interposed wood of the other's staff, while the shadow-Arekhon's attacks came in with punishing force. Then 'Rekhe's last blow came, and struck Kief down so hard it first drove him to his knees, then sent him sprawling.

He pushed himself to his feet, but the body that had fallen stayed behind, unmoving. He turned to look at 'Rekhe. "Am I dead?"

"You followed your own luck to get here, and left all the rest behind. That's no way to complete a working."

He was suddenly filled with a flood of intense regret. "We could have mended the galaxy."

"We still can." 'Rekhe lifted his staff in a gesture that was half-threat, half-invitation. "Come."

"I can't," he said, and felt the substance of his meditation dissolving around him as he spoke. "There are other things that I have to do."

He dropped back into the physical world with a shudder. The meditation chamber was unchanged, as always, and he himself was unharmed—the aches and bruises from his metaphysical encounter would fade quickly, as such things tended to do. The shadow-Arekhon's words remained with him, however: *You followed your own luck to get here, and left all the rest behind.*

And his own luck had not been enough. The struggle in his meditation could have many meanings—it was in the nature of such things to address more questions than just the one that had been asked—but one answer at least was clear to him. Alone, he would never free himself from the great working. To do that, he needed allies. In his mind, the offer of help had come from Arekhon, whom he had known and trusted long ago—but Arekhon was long gone from Eraasi.

Arekhon's sister, however, was not. Kief left the meditation chamber and hung up his mask on its peg outside the door. The clock on the wall said that he had been engrossed in his meditation all night and part of the next day. He had work to do—and a reply to send to Isayana sus-Khalgath sus-Peledaen, putting himself and his Circles at her disposal in the matter of her current project.

9:

ERAASI: HANILAT
ENTIBOR: AN-JEMAYNE

Zeri sus-Dariv's wedding day dawned fair and sunny, one of the rare days of fine weather that sometimes came to Hanilat in the midst of the winter wet. Zeri considered the clear sky to be a dead waste of a good omen—her prospective bridegroom had no more interest in marriage for its own sake than she herself did. She said as much to Rieny, one of the two friends from her theatre group who had come over to assist her in dressing after the customary fashion, helping her into the traditional gown of flame-red tissue and arranging her short blond hair so that it would support the many-ribboned bridal headdress.

"Why does Natelth need to marry, after all?" she said. "He has his sister to keep the house in order—I've met her, and it's no surprise *she* hasn't married; she'd sooner talk to *aik-eten* than people—and he has his younger brother to step into his place if anything should happen—"

"Had," said Rieny. Her long fingers moved skillfully, buttoning up the row of tiny, self-covered buttons that ran up the back of Zeri's gown. She'd already heard Zeri's complaint more than once during the preparations for the wedding, and by now she scarcely bothered to look up from her work. "If you'd troubled yourself even once to think about politics, you'd know that his brother's dead."

"I know that he came back from across the interstellar gap," Zeri said. That had been while she was still pretending she wanted to work for the family someday, and her desktop had been full of the story for weeks.

"He came back," said her other friend, Lyida. Lyida had her cosmetic box in hand, and was busy painting Zeri's brows and lashes to conform to the current mode. "And then he disappeared ... don't squint, there's a dear ... and a while later we heard that all of the Demaizen Mages were dead. Except for his sister, Lord Natelth is every bit as kindred-bare as you are."

"That's what I mean," Zeri said. "The man must have kept himself unmarried on purpose, waiting for something like this to happen."

"It could just be his luck," said Rieny. "The shoes, now ... give me your foot. The sus-Peledaen fleet-Circles are supposed to be some of the strongest ones around, and he gets his luck from them."

Zeri steadied herself with a hand on Rieny's shoulder as she slipped first one foot and then the other into her flamered wedding slippers. "I wish I knew for certain that it was just his luck."

"Oh, dear. You don't think ..." Lyida's eyes were big with concern.

Zeri shook her head. She hadn't meant to voice that particular nagging worry—Rieny and 'Yida didn't deserve the trouble they might get into if they happened to speak of it in the wrong quarter. "I don't *know.*"

"Take my advice," said Rieny. "Don't try to find out." She stepped back and looked at Zeri with her head on one side like an artist contemplating a work-in-progress. "Very nice. 'Yida, are you finished with her face?"

Lyida snapped shut the cosmetic box. "As long as she doesn't go teary-eyed on me at the last minute."

"And ruin all your hard work?" Zeri said. "I wouldn't dare."

"Hold still, then, while we do the crown and ribbons."

Zeri stood unmoving while Lyida and Rieny first secured

the twisted wire coronet in place with hairpins, then began affixing the bunches of long, fluttering ribbons: green and yellow for the sus-Dariv, blue and crimson for the sus-Peledaen, flame-red for the bridal altar, and shimmering metallic silver for the *eiran* that the Mages worked in their Circles. Zeri hoped that the sus-Peledaen Circles were working the luck for her today; all of her family's Mages had died with the guardships of the sus-Dariv fleet.

"There," said Rieny, when the last ribbon was in place. "It's time to go. Syr Treosi is waiting."

Zeri didn't move. She couldn't—she felt as though someone had glued the soles of her bridal slippers to the apartment floor. "I don't want to go."

"Oh, my dear . . . !" Lyida's face crumpled up with sympathetic distress.

Rieny cast a scornful look in Lyida's direction. "Of course you don't," she said to Zeri. "Who would? Call Syr Treosi in here, if you feel that way, and tell him that you won't go through with it."

"No." Zeri drew a long breath, and let it out upon a sigh. Her feet could move again, and she took a step forward, away from her friends' supporting presence. "The sus-Dariv need me to do this. Without it, we'll fall apart and lose everything."

"That's my Zeri," Rieny said, and kissed her quickly on the cheek. "Look them in the eye and smile."

Ayil syn-Arvedan hadn't been accustomed to follow the internal politics of the Institute's Mage-Circle. She knew—in the same general way that she knew Trelu Perres of the Theoretical Quasi-Organics Department was also Comptroller of Lower-Study Admissions and Fees—that Esya syn-Faredol was the Circle's current First; and after the rainy night when Kiefen Diasul had turned up on her doorstep with blood on his robes, she hadn't been surprised to hear that the Ancient Literatures Department was searching for a new scholar to fill Esya's old position. It was the right of every Circle to order its own workings, even if the Institute's Mages seldom needed to deal with any disruption of the *eiran* greater than bad food in the scholars' refectory or rowdy students making noise in the wrong part of town.

But, as she herself had pointed out to Delath more than once, these days everyone on Eraasi lived in unsettled times. She didn't know who had stepped into the position of First of the Institute Circle, but she wasn't surprised, either, to find Kief once again at her front door, this time by daylight. He didn't seem as wrung-out and barely held together as he had the last time, which was a relief, but he still looked too thin and too tired.

"Are you all right?" she asked after she had let him in.

He collapsed onto her sofa and leaned his head, eyes closed, against its cushioned back. "Don't you mean, 'What are you really doing here?'"

"I *am* curious," she admitted. "But right now you look like somebody has been chasing you hard and not letting you sleep."

"An apt description," he said. "But not anyone's fault but mine."

"Good." She took a step toward the apartment's tiny kitchen, speaking over her shoulder as she did so. "You also look like somebody hasn't been feeding you properly. I don't suppose you have an *aiketh* to do that kind of work."

"No. I'm capable of handling it myself."

"Hah. I know you—I shared an office with you, remember? Ready-prepared stuff in cans and boxes. And I'll bet you don't even sit to eat at a proper table."

"Guilty. I admit it."

"Let me make you some bread and cheese while you're here, then, purely to ease my conscience."

"If you insist," he said. "I won't say no."

She got out the brick of sharp cheese from the preserving-cupboard, and the loaf of dark brown homemade bread, and started slicing. As she worked, she said, "So what *are* you really doing here, anyway?"

He sighed without opening his eyes. "You do know why today is important, don't you?"

"Well," she said, "it's the end of the session, for one thing."

"I haven't been a student or a teacher here for almost two

decades," he pointed out. "I've forgotten most of the academic calendar by now."

She set the plate of bread and cheese down on the low table in front of the couch. "And you don't want to find out if the Institute has graduated any nice young Mages for your Circle to snap up?"

"I know the answer to that one already," he said absently. His mouth was already full of sliced cheese. He swallowed and said, "No—today Lord Natelth is marrying the little sus-Dariv. Or marrying the remnants of her family's fleet and all their ground-based holdings. It comes to the same thing."

Ayil shook her head. "Poor girl."

"More than she knows. Her new husband is a hard man."

"So I've heard. He stays away from the Institute, though."

"Be grateful," Kief said.

"I am." Ayil sank into the nearby armchair and set her feet up on its matching hassock. "You're one of Lord Natelth's Mages—shouldn't you be working the luck for his wedding right now?"

"In theory."

She looked at him curiously. "Not in practice?"

"He has the fleet-Circles for that."

"Your Circle isn't part of the fleet? I thought all of the sus-Peledaen Circles were."

"Not mine." He shook his head. "None of mine."

She looked at him thoughtfully. "You work for the sus-Peledaen, but you don't like the star-lords any more than you ever did."

"I don't like it that the Circles have to depend on a star-lord's patronage, or on the goodwill of the community," he said. "Demaizen was independent, so long as we didn't need anything beyond the scope of Garrod syn-Aigal's personal fortune—but then we needed a starship, and for that it was either go to the sus-Peledaen or auction off ourselves and our knowledge like livestock to the highest bidder." He fell briefly silent, thinking who-knew-what unpleasant thoughts. "Maybe we should have done that anyway. It couldn't possibly have made things worse."

"So now you can't bring yourself to work the luck for a

marriage-alliance that stands to give the sus-Peledaen any more power than they've already got."

He nodded. "Something like that, yes."

"Then work the luck for the little sus-Dariv, as you call her. She's another one who's taking herself to the sus-Peledaen because all the other choices looked even worse. If there's anyone who needs luck in Hanilat today, it's her."

This time Kief's pause was longer, and more thoughtful. "You have a point there." He put the last of the sliced cheese in between two thick pieces of bread, the better for carrying away and eating out of hand. Then he stood. "I think I'll go talk with the Institute Circle after all."

Fas Treosi was waiting for Zeri in her apartment's outer room, in the company of two large and impassive guardsmen whose presence he acknowledged no more than he did that of the furniture. He bowed to Zeri and took her arm, escorting her formally down the hall to the elevator and out to the street. Rieny and Lyida followed; Zeri heard them murmuring back and forth to each other behind her, and behind them the muted crackle and murmur of one of the guardsmen conferring with somebody else, out on the street.

The groundcar that waited for them outside was a full-sized wedding-coach, built tall and boxy enough to accommodate an entire bridal party without crushing anyone's gown. Zeri allowed Syr Treosi to assist her in mounting the steps to the passenger compartment. Rieny and Lyida insisted on arranging her ribbons and the folds of her dress after she was seated, and she let them do what they wanted, without protest.

It had taken all of her resolve to break the contact between her feet and the familiar, comfortable floor of her own apartment. She had been content there, desiring—and getting—nothing more from life than a moderate amount of comfort; she should have known that even such ordinary good luck could not last forever unsustained. Now she rode, passively, in the wedding-coach bearing her from home to the place where she would live from now henceforward.

The streets the coach passed through appeared dim and

blue-tinged, a visual artifact of the thick tinted glass in the windows. The wedding-coaches of Zeri's childhood hadn't had dark windows—the brides in their flame-red dresses had smiled out at the world through clear glass. A bride who felt rich in luck might even choose to ride through the streets of Hanilat with the top and sides of the wedding-coach taken completely down, so that the breeze of her passage whipped the ribbons of her bridal crown into a trailing, rainbow-colored cloud. Children would run after such a coach for blocks, hoping to catch a ribbon worked loose by the wind.

When did it all change? Zeri wondered. *Nobody does things like that anymore—instead, we sit in a dim light and hoard our luck like misers.*

The coach rumbled to a stop outside the imposing town house of the sus-Khalgath sus-Peledaen. The driver opened the coach's passenger door, and Syr Treosi once again assisted her on the steps. Rieny and Lyida came down after her, gathering up in their hands the long ribbons of her bridal crown. It wouldn't do for the door of the wedding-coach to snatch away all the bride's good luck as it slammed closed.

The door of the town house swung silently open. A housekeeping *aiketh* hovered on its counterforce unit inside the building. A red light flickered inside the smoky plastic housing of its sensorium, but the construct didn't speak, only extended one of its manipulative members to point the way farther within. On the far side of the vestibule a second *aiketh* waited to show the bridal party down the long inner hall, and a third stood outside the double doors at the end.

So far, Zeri had seen no living guests or servants at all. Somewhere out of sight, without doubt, more guardsmen watched over her safety as she passed from the sus-Dariv into the sus-Peledaen, but they were neither friends nor family and it was not their place to be visible at their work.

The doors swung apart at a touch from the *aiketh*. Syr Treosi slipped his arm from hers and stepped away; Rie and 'Yida let the ribbons fall loose from their hands; and Zeri stepped over the threshold into the sus-Peledaen hall of remembrance.

Her first thought was that she was alone. The closing doors had left her friends and Syr Treosi behind on the other side.

A moment longer, and she knew that she was not alone at all. The room was full of the sus-Peledaen, outer-family and inner-family both. The blue and crimson of fleet-livery was everywhere, in bright splashes against the more sober colors of the other witnesses. But no green and yellow anywhere— among all the sus-Dariv witnesses, from the outer family and the junior lines, there was nobody at all from the fleet. Even from the handful of ships that had survived, nobody had come.

To either side and in front of her, family tablets of wood and slate and bronze lined the paneled walls, reminders of the presence here of all the generations of the sus-Peledaen. Scented candles burned on the offering ledges beneath the tablets, enough of them that they left the pale air streaked with a blue-grey haze. Natelth sus-Khalgath stood before the oldest tablet of all, a heavy slab of stone painted over with glyphs in soot and red ochre. There was one unlit candle on the offering ledge beneath.

Nobody spoke. The sus-Peledaen were one of those families who believed in conducting their observances in silence. Zeri took the splint of burning wood that Natelth handed her, and brought its flame next to the wick of the unlit candle.

With a faint hiss and sparkle, the wick caught fire, and the candle burned.

The room filled with shouts and cheers. The doors opened to admit Treosi and the rest of the bridal party. Natelth stepped forward and gave her the formal embrace of welcome.

"Now you are sus-Peledaen," he said. He was taller and broader in the chest and shoulders than she remembered from the wedding negotiations, and his voice was deeper. "Our luck is your luck, and our strength, your strength, as long as the blood shall run."

Early the next morning, before his resolve could falter, Arekhon left Elaeli asleep at Rosselin Cottage and went back to An-Jemayne. If he was going to take the remnants of the Demaizen Circle home to Eraasi, he had one more person left to find.

This time he didn't need to pay a call at the Adepts' Guildhouse, or fine-comb the Immering tax records. Instead, he rented a hovercar under a false name—his work as Elaeli's head of domestic security had left him almost as careful of his tracks as Iulan Vai—and drove it from the mainland shuttle hub to the An-Jemayne Spaceport Authority, where he looked up a name in the roster of certified starpilots.

His luck in this, at least, held good. Karil Estisk was still alive, and still active in her profession. Better yet, she was between voyages at the moment. He wouldn't have to spend time waiting for her ship to make port.

Her address was a matter of record, and the pilots' roster listed it as current. Arekhon found the apartment block without difficulty, in a moderately well-to-do neighborhood with transit connections to the spaceport. If Karil did in fact live here, she had prospered since their last meeting, or at least she had not suffered material harm from it.

The building directory inside the main entrance gave him her apartment number. He entered it into the directory's keypad, and waited for the tone to sound.

Once . . . twice . . . on the third tone, Karil's voice came over the speaker. "Yes? Who is it?"

She sounded irritable and distracted. Arekhon hoped he hadn't interrupted anything he would have to feel embarrassed about later.

"Arek Peldan," he said, more or less truthfully—he'd used that version of his given name in most of his public dealings since coming to Entibor. "On business."

"Who? . . . never mind; you might as well come on up."

Arekhon didn't think she'd recognized his voice. He took the elevator up to the fifth floor, where Karil's apartment was one of a half-dozen opening off of a central lobby. The door had a spy-eye set into the frame, with a soundpad underneath. He tapped the pad and waited again.

The pause this time lasted long enough for Arekhon to conclude that his face on the apartment's security screen was more memorable than his voice alone had been, and to decide that this part of his quest had been a mistake. He was almost ready to turn away and leave when the door swung open partway and Karilen Estisk glared out at him.

The pilot was a tall woman, with a fair complexion and eyes the color of pale slate. She was wearing a faded velvet lounging robe, and had a damp towel wrapped turban-fashion around her head. That explained some of her irritability, at least, if he'd disturbed her in her bath; but he wasn't foolish enough to think that it was the only reason.

"You're damned lucky I didn't call building security as soon as I saw your face," she said before he could speak. " 'Arek Peldan'—hah!"

"It's one of the names I go by these days," he said. "May I come in?"

She stepped back and opened the door the rest of the way. "Why not?" she said. "If you people are determined to show up unannounced in my life and tear it into pieces for a second time, there's probably nothing I can do to stop you anyway."

"The Circle never intended to cause you harm," he said as he followed her into the apartment. "For the fact that our good intentions came to naught, I can only apologize all over again."

"Right. And are you planning to apologize for damn-near getting me invalided out of the Pilots' Association for mental imbalance?" She turned and glared at him again, and the anger in her voice held echoes of long-past frustration and hysteria. "I tried telling people what happened—I told them about how a bunch of pirates from the far side of the galaxy took my old ship and killed everybody on it but me, and then some of the pirates kidnapped me away to their homeworld and some of the rest of them escaped with me back—and how they were still here, hiding and spying out the land— but nobody believed me."

"I know," he said. "And I do apologize. Making certain that no one believed you was the first working the Demaizen Circle did after coming to Entibor."

"I *knew* it," she said, and slapped him hard across the face.

He took the blow without flinching, though she had enough strength of arm that it was no light love-tap. "I'm sorry," he said. "But we were afraid."

"Afraid? You? Don't make me laugh."

"Yes," he said. "Afraid. Your ships are faster, your weapons are more deadly, your artificial minds—"

"Comp systems."

"—'comp systems,' then—are made out of sand and glass, and cheaply enough that you can throw together a dozen or a hundred of them for the cost in time and labor of a single true *aiketh* back at home in Hanilat."

She looked at him and nodded slowly. "So you—how did you put it back then?—you 'worked the luck.' And I got screwed over."

"All I can tell you is that we tried to do you as little harm as possible. And I know that isn't good enough."

"You're damned right it isn't good enough," she said. "But I'm smart enough to know that it's probably the best I'm going to get."

"There's a lot of that going around."

"You too, eh?" Most of the anger had gone out of her face, replaced by a kind of weary amusement. She gestured toward one of the chairs in the apartment's conversational nook, and seated herself in another. "Come on, 'Rekhe. Sit down and tell me why you decided to show up again after all these years."

She'd used his short-name, which he hoped was a good sign. He drew a careful breath and let it out again. "I have to go back across the Gap," he said. "And *Night's-Beautiful-Daughter* needs at least two at the controls for a long transit."

"You're asking me to go *back*—my word, 'Rekhe, but you've got gall!"

"Will you do it, then?"

"Why should I?"

It was a fair question; but she hadn't directly refused him, either. He took heart from that, and gave her as much of the truth as he knew himself. "For the sake of Garrod's working."

"That's the big one, right?" Her expression was thoughtful, if not particularly warm. "The one your people kept fretting about all the way from here to wherever and back again."

"Right. It isn't finished yet."

"I don't suppose you have any idea when it's going to *be* finished, either."

He shook his head. "Or how much it will cost. All workings need energy to power them, but the great ones can take blood and lives as well. This one . . . we wanted to remake the galaxy."

The corners of her mouth turned up a little—only faint amusement, and at his expense, but better than anger. "You never wondered if maybe you hadn't taken on a bit more than you could handle?"

"We were young, most of us," he said, "and prouder of our strength than we should have been. And Garrod was a man who could ask for wonders."

"I can see that." Curiosity flickered in her pale eyes. "Why again now, and not last year, or a decade ago?"

"I don't know. I thought I was done with Eraasi, working or no working. Lately, though—" he shrugged "—lately, I've had dreams."

"My brother used to have dreams," she said. "But Lenset was always half-mad."

"And so am I, you think?"

"No. You're reckless and high-handed and any number of other things—most of which I could cheerfully have killed you for at one point or another—but you aren't mad."

As a statement of trust, Arekhon reflected, it was something less than enthusiastic. On the other hand, she hadn't refused him. Maybe his luck was greater than he deserved, and Karilen Estisk also remained bound into the great working.

"Then will you come with me?" he asked.

She looked down at her hands. "I'm a senior pilot for InterWorlds Shipping—they took me on when the Swift Passage people let me go, and I can't leave them now."

"That," he said, "won't be a problem. All that's needed is for some plausible organization to contract with InterWorlds for your extended services for an open-ended period of time."

" 'All'?" Her voice sounded a bit strangled. " 'Rekhe, do you have any *idea* how much money that would take?"

"Money's not going to be a problem. If I can arrange for it, will you come?"

"Going crazy must run in my family," she said. "Yes. I'll come."

One by one Zeri exchanged formal embraces with the assembled representatives of the sus-Peledaen, starting with Natelth's sister Isayana—whose touch was distant and stiff—and finishing with a bashful fleet-apprentice in blue and crimson livery. Then the doors of the hall of remembrance swung open, and Natelth took Zeri by the hand, so that they could be the first to leave the room.

Fas Treosi was waiting for her outside with Rieny and Lyida. Tradition said that at this point a bride's friends should rush forward to hug her and claim lucky kisses from the new-made husband, with much laughter and joyful tears all around; but Zeri's husband was Natelth sus-Peledaen, after all, and Rie and 'Yida were stiff and formal in his presence. They gave her careful, tentative hugs, as though they were afraid to wrinkle her gown, and scarcely brushed their lips against Natelth's before drawing away.

The household *aiketh* that had earlier opened the door of the town house floated forward out of the shadows. "If the Lady Zeri wishes to change clothes for the banquet, the bride's withdrawing-room is ready for her now."

Suddenly Zeri wanted nothing else in the world as badly as she wanted to strip the crown and ribbons from her head, and kick away the flame-colored slippers. "Yes, please," she said.

The *aiketh* floated up the stairs on its counterforce unit, with Zeri barely a step or two behind. Rie and 'Yida gathered up the ends of her trailing ribbons and followed close. Outside the closed door of the withdrawing-room, Zeri stopped.

"Lord Natelth isn't here," she told her friends. "You can hug me for real now."

This time they did, and wept as well. Then she slipped out of their embrace, saying, "Go on down to the banquet, please. I can change my own clothes, and I need a few minutes by myself to think."

They made a couple of token protests—tradition again dictated that the bride's friends should assist her with disrobing as well as robing herself for the day—but soon let themselves be persuaded. Zeri waited until they were out of sight around the turn of the stairway, then entered the private withdrawing-room and closed the door behind her.

For a moment she stood there with her eyes closed, doing nothing. If she were at home in her apartment, she would be getting back from her afternoon meeting with the theatre-arts group's finance committee, with plenty of time to take her shoes off and relax for an hour or two before dinner. But she'd sent her regrets to the finance committee days ago, and the workers and *aiketen* from the moving firm were at work in her apartment right now, putting all of her old furniture and other belongings into crates and boxes for storage. By this time next week, somebody else would be living in those rooms, and she would be sharing bed and board with Natelth sus-Peledaen.

Stop whining, she told herself. *You made the choice, and you might as well learn to live with it.*

With a sigh, she began unbuttoning the back of her gown. Then, suddenly, she felt a hand clamp over her mouth, and felt herself pulled backward against a man's chest. She felt his warm breath next to her ear, and the faint roughness of a cheek that had gone a little too long unshaven, and lips that whispered, "Promise not to scream until after you read the letter I'm about to hand you."

His hand was tight over her mouth. She got one of his fingers between her teeth and bit down hard, feeling the skin break and tasting the blood like hot copper in her mouth.

He swore under his breath in a language she didn't recognize, but he didn't let go. Then he said, somewhat breathlessly, "I'm a friend. Your cousin sent me. Herin Arayet sus-Dariv."

"Herin is dead," Zeri said.

He released her then, and she turned around to look at her erstwhile captor. She saw a man, not so well dressed as those she'd spent the morning with, but presentable all the same, with the yellowish-hazel eyes and sharp, fine-boned features that marked his Antipodean descent. He had his bleeding right hand pressed under his left armpit—she was pleased to note that she'd done him some real damage there, enough that the red drops had made a damp stain on the expensive blueweave carpet—while with his free hand he held out a flat envelope.

"Read this, and afterward you can scream if you like," the man said. "My name's Len. Help me help you."

Zeri snatched the envelope from him and backed away, not taking her eyes from the man until she'd torn the envelope open and pulled out a flatsheet. She lifted it, looked down at it, then swiftly up again, then looked down, harder. The message said only, "Trust the man who brings this note. Do not marry sus-Peledaen. Come to me if you can. Herin."

The note was written in Herin's own hand, and it used the sus-Dariv private cipher. Zeri didn't scream.

"Whoever set the bomb and attacked our fleet," she said, "they might as easily have broken our codes if they felt like it. How do I know this isn't from one of them?"

"Your cousin also said that I should tell you that on your twelfth birthday you and he didn't go out to the frog pond to look at the frogs, even though that was what you told your parents afterward."

In spite of herself and the situation, she blushed, and hoped that Herin's sense of the ridiculous hadn't prompted him to tell this stranger the whole embarrassing story. "He could have sent word earlier," she said. " 'Don't marry sus-Peledaen' isn't going to do me much good right now."

"Syr Arayet says that if your legalist was doing right by you, none of the merger contracts come into force until the morning after the wedding night. There's still time."

"Time for what?"

"Your cousin asked me to bring you to him," the man said. "Will you come?"

"Why did Herin send a stranger to fetch me, instead of coming himself?"

"He says that if he's recognized he'll be dead for real next time. Now I'm leaving, with you or without you. I delivered my message—now I'm gone." He bowed his head. "My lady."

Some time later, Rie and 'Yida grew concerned about their friend's welfare, and left the banquet hall to rap on the withdrawing-room door. The door swung open under their touch—and then there was screaming enough at the wedding banquet, for the bride was gone, the window was open, and there was blood on the floor.

10:

Isayana sus-Khalgath was overseeing the replenishment of the banquet tables when she heard the shrieking from upstairs. A moment later, almost before all heads had turned in the direction of the outcry, one of the bride's ladies—the thin, clever-looking one—burst in through the doors of the banquet hall.

Isayana suspected that it was the plump and sentimental lady who had screamed. That one had all the marks of someone who would turn absolutely useless in a crisis. This one, however, pushed her way through the throng of sus-Peledaen family and hangers-on and went straight to Natelth. Isayana couldn't hear what she was saying, but she was speaking rapidly, her words punctuated by sharp, quick hand movements, and Na'e's expression was growing darker and grimmer as he listened.

Another moment, and Na'e snapped an order to the fleet officer nearest him, then left the banquet hall with the bride's lady, heading toward the sounds of hysteria coming from upstairs. The fleet officer took a little longer to pull the sus-Peledaen head of internal security out of the crowd and send him upstairs likewise. Nobody had bothered to tell Isayana what was going on, but that didn't matter; she had her own ways of learning things.

"Stop," she said quietly to the first serving-*aiketh* that floated past her on its counterforce unit. "Attend."

The *aiketh* paused, the crimson light in its sensorium pulsing slightly as it awaited further instruction. Isayana turned so that her voice wouldn't carry into the crowd of agitated guests—some of whom might not, after all, be completely trustworthy—and spoke the override syllables she had given it during its first instruction. The crimson light pulsed faster for a few seconds, then returned to its normal resting beat.

"Now," said Isayana. "Query the house-mind, and all units in contact with it. What has caused the disturbance in the upstairs equilibrium?"

"The house-mind reports a circumvention of security measures in the bride's withdrawing-room," the *aiketh* said. "The window remains open at this time."

"Thank you," Isayana said politely. Even nonsentient quasi-organics deserved courtesy, in her opinion, and it cost nothing to give. Then she spoke the syllables that revoked the override, and the *aiketh* floated on about its business as though she had never stopped and questioned it.

Barely in time, too. She saw Na'e's security chief coming toward her through the crowd of agitated wedding guests.

"Syr Egelt," she said as he approached her. "What's happening?"

"Your brother desires your presence upstairs in the bride's withdrawing-room," Egelt said.

"By all means take me to him."

She followed the head of internal security up the stairs to the private portion of the town house. The door at the top of the stairway opened onto the hall outside the withdrawing-room, and the hall, normally empty of all but household *aiketen* and the occasional family member, was full of people. The bride's two ladies, their message delivered, had been shunted off to the periphery of the action; the short plump one was crying against the thin one's neck.

Natelth stood amid a group of liveried guards, frowning and looking thunderous. Isayana felt a moment's surprise at the sheer number of people in blue and crimson. She hadn't thought that Na'e would bring quite so many guards with him from the orbital station—and these, she realized, had to be only a few of the ones who had come down to the surface, the ones assigned directly to the town house itself.

An army, she thought, suppressing her reflex expression of disapproval. *We have—the sus-Peledaen have—an army.*

"We've got searchers out on the streets already, my lord," one of the guards was saying. "But so far, no sightings and no reports."

Isayana moved forward. The guards recognized her and made way for her to pass. She thought that perhaps they seemed a little grateful for her appearance—she was, after all, almost Natelth's equal in rank, and capable of standing, if need be, between them and his growing anger.

"What is going on here, Na'e?" she asked her brother. "I've heard shouting and rumors, but very little so far by way of an explanation."

"Zeri sus-Dariv sus-Peledaen," Natelth told her, "appears to be missing."

Looking past him through the open door of the bride's withdrawing-room, Isayana could see that it was so. The room was empty, and the window overlooking the flower garden was open. Drops of blood—red in the center but drying into brown at the edges—flecked the blueweave carpet between the door and the window. A single silver ribbon from the bridal crown lay on the floor near the window in a disconsolate curl.

"When was that window opened?" Natelth demanded of the head of internal security.

"I ordered it opened last night," Isayana said before the man could draw down Na'e's wrath by answering. "To freshen the room. The *aiketen* had instructions to close the window before morning."

"Then we want the person or thing who opened it again." Natelth turned to his security chief. "Find my wife and whoever took her, and bring them back. Close the spaceport if you have to."

"I'll question the house-mind as soon as the outcry dies down," Isayana promised him. "But the authorities will have to be notified sooner or later. The wedding guests, I'm afraid, are gossiping already."

"We'll do our own search first. The city watch doesn't have our resources."

"People will say we're taking on the bad luck of the sus-Dariv," Isayana said. "Her family's enemies could be responsible for this."

"Whoever did this wasn't an enemy of the sus-Dariv; they were enemies of the sus-Peledaen. This is a crime against our family—and against me."

"If you say so," Isayana said. She looked again at the bloodstains on the carpet, and felt the stretch and tingle of a new idea taking shape inside her mind. "Na'e . . . will you let me take a sample of that blood?"

"Do you think you can learn something useful from it?"

"Many things," she told him.

And some of them I may even share with you. Some others . . . maybe not.

Arekhon brought his Circle to An-Jemayne spaceport in the early morning, when the low fog wisped along the ground. The two Mages and Maraganha had the rumpled clothing and disgruntled expressions of people who had spent too much time on public transit—a hoverbus from the Cazdel Guildhouse to the transit hub, a suborbital short-hop from Cazdel to An-Jemayne, and yet another hoverbus to meet Arekhon at the port. At least, he consoled himself, none of them looked reluctant or afraid.

The air at the port was thick with moisture, the sunrise a rose shade that bespoke a hot and humid day in the offing. Arekhon, who'd lost his taste for subtropical weather during the years he'd spent with Elaeli in Entibor's Central Quarter, was glad that they wouldn't have to endure it for very long. He'd worried that Karil might lose her nerve at the last minute, but she hadn't let him down; the pilot was standing by the operations hut on the private side of the field, wearing an orange pressure-suit with K. ESTISK embroidered on the tape over her right breast. She carried a helmet swinging loose in one hand.

"I don't know what kind of strings you pulled to do it," she said to Arekhon as soon as he came within speaking distance, "but you've got me hired from InterWorlds Shipping on an open-ended contract. I have to warn you, those deals don't come cheap."

"I'm not worried about the money," he said. "It comes from having relatively few expensive vices."

She smiled. "And I have the current flight plan already filed like you said: test flight; auto-return clicked in, signed for, and ready. You say this trip is supposed to be in-system only?"

"That's the story," he said.

"As in 'the story is a damned lie'?"

"Something like that."

"Right," Karil said. "We have the extra EVA suits on board. They're military surplus, but they've been checked and graded and they're all service-ready." The deep rumble of nullgravs overrode her speech, the sound of a nearby sludge barge tilting itself nose-upward and launching for orbit. After the noise had abated, she continued, "I'm assuming you guys are ready, because we're on minus minutes now. I have a skipsled. You have any supplies you're taking?"

Arekhon shook his head. "Only what you see. I don't want to make it obvious that we're heading out on a long voyage."

"Obvious to whom?" asked Ty. It was the first time he had spoken since getting off the hoverbus and greeting Arekhon by the landing-field gate.

"Spies," said Karil. "Pirates. Other bad guys." She looked over at Arekhon. "Am I right?"

"Yes," he said. "No disrespect to your world, Karilen, but there are people in it I would just as soon not have follow me home."

"I thought so. Let's load up the skipsled and get going."

The pilot walked over to the other side of the hut, where the nullgrav-mounted cargo carrier—an open sled twice as long as she was tall—waited. She stepped aboard and stood at the control pylon, playing her hands across the keypad. A moment later the vehicle floated upward, so that it was bobbing gently on a cushion of air. "Come on up if you're coming."

Arekhon and the others of the group stepped on, and the sled trembled slightly as they added their weight.

"Hold on," Karil said, and they pushed away, skimming over the ground. A couple of minutes later, they arrived at their destination, an in-system surface-to-space transfer shuttle resting on stubby landing legs.

She waved a hand at the bulbous-nosed craft. "This is it for getting us into orbit. Not as good as what I'd like to be flying, but hey, it's what was available."

Maraganha stepped off the sled and walked around the base of the shuttle, taking it in. She laid one hand on the metal, closed her eyes briefly, then nodded and rejoined the group. None of them needed to ask what she'd been doing: there was more than one way to look for the *eiran*, after all, and if Arekhon's Void-walker wanted to do it by touch rather than by sight, that was her business.

"Climb inside and strap in," Karil said. Once they'd all dismounted from the skipsled, she twisted the safety catch on the control pylon and set the sled's autodrive to "return." The sled departed at little over walking speed, going back in the direction of the ops shed.

One by one, Arekhon and the others climbed the ladder into the main part of the cargo shuttle, a large open room filled with passenger acceleration couches. Another ladder led up and forward out of the main passenger cabin.

Karil paused at the foot and gestured at the row of couches. "Your home from here to high orbit. Pick out a place you like and secure yourselves for liftoff."

"I'll come up front with you, if you don't mind," Arekhon said. "If there's room."

"There's room, but I don't see the point."

He shrugged. "I want to watch the departure. Call it sentiment."

"You—sentimental?" Karil shook her head. "You're the most cold-blooded son of a bitch I've ever known, and that's saying something."

Arekhon wanted to protest, but decided, upon quick reflection, that he didn't have the right. Demaizen's great working had not been kind to Karilen Estisk, and he was the working's personification in her eyes, the chief agent of her worst misfortunes. If she'd agreed to join the Circle on this venture, it could only have been out of a conviction that trying to refuse him wouldn't have done her any good.

Which was a thought with more truth in it than Arekhon cared to dwell on at the moment. He followed Karil up the ladder to the control bridge, and didn't say anything.

The pilot swung into the acceleration seat on the right, leaving the left seat for Arekhon. She strapped herself into the safety webbing and began examining the gauges that dotted the panel in front of her.

"Ready for this?" she asked, as soon as her inspection was done. "I have the clearance I need, and it's coming up."

"I'm ready." He glanced at the telltales on the panel. "And it looks like the others are all properly strapped in."

"Then here we go," Karil said, and slid down the launch sequencer switch.

A tone sounded, mind-numbingly loud—the launch alarm. Then the alarm fell silent, and instead an even louder roaring noise filled Arekhon's ears, to be replaced in turn by a trembling sensation. The squares of light that were the windows of the shuttle's control bridge danced a crazy jig in his field of view, and he felt himself pressed down into his seat. Karil had been right, he thought muzzily; this shuttle definitely wasn't the best ride at An-Jemayne spaceport.

Over in the right-hand seat, the pilot was working with the control switches and the twist-knobs, her eyes fixed on the distance and horizon readouts. Arekhon thought suddenly of Elaeli, who had also been trained to do this and who had done it well, and looked away again to watch the sky turn from sunlit blue to violet to black with stars.

"In orbit," Karil said at last, unstrapping her webbing. "Ready to try out those suits?"

Zeri sus-Dariv still didn't know whether she was being kidnapped or being rescued. So far, she felt inclined toward the latter—which, she was prepared to admit, might have more to do with her reluctance to complete the process of becoming sus-Peledaen than it did with any rational assessment of the situation.

Her—abductor? rescuer?—her current companion had treated her with courteous efficiency, turning his back in the withdrawing-room while she stripped out of her wedding finery and put on the loose workaday trousers and baggy overshirt that he'd brought along with him. They'd stuffed the flame-red dress and the bridal crown into the paper shopping bag he'd brought the work clothes in, and taken the bag with them when they left the room by the garden window.

They dumped the bag and its contents into a back-alley trash bin a few blocks away, after she used a fold of her gown's soft-textured fabric to wipe her face clean of 'Yida's carefully applied maquillage.

"I won't make a convincing nobody if I'm walking around Hanilat with a wedding-day face on," she said. "The orange slippers are bad enough."

Her companion—Len, was it, he'd called himself?—pointed at a puddle of something Zeri hoped was only mud. "Walk through that."

"It looks disgusting," she said; but he had the right idea, and she was already stepping into the puddle as she spoke. "And it smells worse. Stage two of this daring endeavor had better include picking up suitable footgear."

"Blame your cousin, my lady. He's the one who put the kit together."

"I'll be kind," Zeri said, "and assume that he was trying not to copy anything he thought I would actually wear."

That had been five city blocks and two transit stops ago, and now she and Len were strolling through Bricklayers' Park hand-in-hand, like a pair of slightly shabby young lovers out taking some fresh air during their noonday break. As a desperate getaway, it was a very low-key, almost slow-motion procedure.

"One would think that we'd be running for our lives at this point," she said eventually. "The sus-Peledaen probably have every watch-patrolman in Hanilat looking for us by now."

"Probably. And if we start running, we'll draw their attention for sure."

"Then by all means, let's not run." They continued along in silence under the rustling shade trees. Here in the depths of the park, the steel-and-glass commercial towers of central Hanilat were barely visible, and the noise of the city was muffled. Eventually she said, "Where exactly are we not-running to?"

"A safe house, or so your cousin says."

"And then what? If I'm running away from my own wedding on Herin's say-so, he'd better have some kind of plan."

"I'm not your cousin," Len said, "but if I were him I'd be planning to wait out the worst of the hue and cry before making another move. The first thing Lord Natelth's going to do is close the spaceport, and there's no point in trying to smuggle you off-planet while that's going on. Not even if we put you up in a metal drum labeled 'preserved greyfish in wrinklefruit sauce' and export you as a local delicacy."

"I don't like wrinklefruit sauce," she said. "Red-wine pickle, yes. Wrinklefruit, no. How long do you think we'll have to wait?"

He shrugged. "Lord Natelth doesn't confide these things in me, my lady. But I'd say not too long. The port can't stay closed forever—sooner or later, cargoes have to start moving or the sus-Peledaen go hungry. And your husband's fellow star-lords won't be much pleased with him, either."

"I can't imagine why," Zeri said. "And all this talk of pickled greyfish is making me hungry. Did my cousin give you enough money to buy something to eat?"

"That part of the bold escape plan seems to have slipped his mind," Len said. "But don't fret about it—I just got paid off for delivering a cargo. I can afford to buy some lizard-on-a-stick for a pretty girl."

Zeri felt herself blush, which was ridiculous considering the difference in their respective stations and the fact that she was wearing Cousin Herin's idea of inconspicuous clothing. She concentrated instead on the pushcart vendor who'd set up his temporary shop next to the path up ahead. The writing on his menu card was in the antipodean script, and she didn't recognize any of the food items being offered.

"Is that stuff really lizard-on-a-stick?" she inquired under her breath. "I'm sure it's absolutely delicious, but I've never—"

He laughed. "Don't worry. It's ordinary spiced sausage.

On Rayamet, now, it probably *would* be lizard."

They ambled over to the pushcart, where Len purchased two of the grilled sausages and a couple of bottles of chilled red *uffa*, and from there they went to a cool stone bench set in the shade of the trees. Zeri took a tentative bite of the hot, highly seasoned sausage, and found it delicious. She hadn't realized how little appetite she'd had for the past few weeks—nothing had tasted worth eating, and half the time she hadn't bothered—but she thought she could have eaten a dozen of the sausages. It wouldn't be right to impose upon Len, though, when he'd used his own money once already to make up for Herin's deficiencies.

Instead, she licked the last of the sausage grease off of her fingers and said, "So when do we go looking for this safe house my cousin told you about? I don't want—"

"—to sleep out in the rain all night?" said an unfamiliar voice. "I don't blame you one bit."

The new speaker was an older woman, trimly built, dressed in an all-black and better-fitting version of the plain work clothes that Herin had provided for the getaway bag. She carried a hardmask in one hand—which implied that she was well known enough in some quarters to go incognito—and she wore a Mage's staff at her belt. Her hair was a brown so dark it looked like a rusty black, and her expression was cheerful and amused.

"Good afternoon, my lady," she said. "Shall we be going, then?"

When Kief returned home from his day with Ayil syn-Arvedan and, later, with the Institute Circle, he found a summons on his desktop waiting for him: a time, now scarcely two hours distant, an address, and a block of encrypted text that served as a signature.

Isayana sus-Khalgath, he thought. *On her brother's wedding day, no less.*

Curiosity as much as anything else spurred him into quick movement. He made the journey across town in street clothes, taking only his staff with him—if Natelth's sister wanted a full-scale working, she wasn't going to get it before tomorrow at the earliest. It took time to gather a Circle, if its members weren't already living under the same roof. There would be messages to send out, and last-minute arrangements to make—somebody would have to cancel a business meeting, and somebody else would have to find a neighbor to take the children; it was no wonder that Garrod had kept everybody together at Demaizen.

Garrod had also possessed a private fortune and nothing else to spend it on, and he hadn't been trying to reinvent the structure of the Circles from the ground up, either. He would never have thought of subordinating another Circle to Demaizen, feeding its energies into Demaizen's working and focusing them through Demaizen's intent. But Kief *had* thought of it—intrigued by tales of the antipodean Circles ending a drought by directing all their separate workings toward the same end—and Kief was doing it. On his own, with no money to speak of, and with an official patron who would undoubtedly be horrified if he realized the implications of what the First of his personal Mage-Circle was doing.

Isayana, on the other hand, wouldn't care. She had her own plans, Kief was sure of that much, and someday Lord Natelth was going to be sorry he'd taken his sister and her skills for granted. Considering the timing, this might even be the day.

The address Isayana had given him wasn't far from the sus-Peledaen town house. She had a set of workrooms on the building's basement level, full of examining tables and biomedical *aiketen* and deep rectangular vats full of quasi-organic gel. She met him there, still dressed in wedding-banquet finery beneath her work apron.

"Kiefen *etaze*," she said, "my brother has a problem. Someone has spirited away his new-wedded bride, and he desires very greatly to find out who."

"Look for somebody with the young woman's best interests at heart," Kief suggested.

She smiled without humor. "We need something more specific than that, I'm afraid. I have a blood sample, and I intend to give my brother a demonstration of forensic replicant technology."

So that's what she was up to: vat-grown bodies to match the quasi-organic minds she built and instructed for the sus-Peledaen. With blood for a seed, she could replicate the form of Zeri sus-Dariv's kidnapper. Except—"You don't need a Mage for that."

"I don't want to stop there." She stepped over to the nearest of the gel-vats and turned on the overhead worklights. "Have a look—I've taken the process as far as I can without a breakthrough, and I want an outsider's eye on it this time."

Kief gazed down at the shape in the gel-vat: blank, undifferentiated, only vaguely human. "I can see why. Whatever you're doing, it doesn't seem to be working."

"This step isn't the one that's causing trouble. You have to expect an unseeded replicant to look like that."

"If you say so." Privately, Kief found the faceless, generic body to be disgusting, but he didn't think that saying so would be a good idea. "The blood seeds it, then?"

"Yes. The process at that point requires a template—I've tried working without one, but when I do that the gel won't stabilize."

"But that isn't a problem?"

"Not particularly. Blood samples are easy to come by— I've been using my own, so far."

Kief tried to picture the thing in the gel-vat with Isayana's face and form. The image was unpleasantly disturbing, and he put it aside with an internal shudder. "So what's the difficulty with the next stage?"

"They're just meat." Isayana frowned at the thing in the vat. "I can make them and give them shape, I can grow them to full maturity—but when I take them out of the gel, they're still nothing but meat."

Good, Kief thought, but he knew better than to say such things aloud. "You believe that this is a problem for the Circles?"

"Yes. I caught myself thinking that 'Rekhe would know what the problem was, and then I remembered that 'Rekhe was dead."

Kief said, "I can tell you right now what the problem is."

"What?"

"The *eiran*. They don't connect to it—they don't touch it anywhere at all."

Isayana looked puzzled, an expression Kief had seen before on mechanics and artificers when something didn't work that by all reason should have. "But the replicant lives, and 'Rekhe always said that the *eiran* touch all the living things in the whole universe."

" 'Rekhe hadn't seen one of these when he said that," Kief pointed out. "Maybe if you'd started it young, let it grow up in the world as a living thing, not forcing it in a vat—"

"This is what I *can* do," she said. "Anything else is ordinary sperm-and-egg work. And why would anybody bother to hire that job done in a laboratory, when the old way is cheaper and easier and almost as dependable?"

Kief could think of any number of people who might want or need the kind of replicant that Isayana had dismissed so lightly, but it wasn't his place to point that out to her now. "If you want to connect this thing to the *eiran*—to make it truly alive—I can only think of one way to do it."

Her expression sharpened. "So you can help."

"In theory."

"What do you mean, 'in theory'?"

"I believe that the only way to make one of your constructs into a living person is to draw a living person out of their old body and use the *eiran* to bind them into a new one." Considered as an abstract problem it was interesting, Kief had to admit. "It would take a Mage to do such a thing—you're right about that—with at least a full Circle to back him up. And I'm fairly certain it wouldn't work unless you had a willing subject."

"I want you to think about how to do this," Isayana said. "Work it out now, so that when I'm ready for you to do it, we won't be delayed by having to make whatever sort of plans and calculations your people need."

Sudden and clandestine—Kief didn't need to see the *eiran* to know that nothing going on here was a straightforward matter. "This is one of those projects that Natelth doesn't know about," he said. "Right?"

"He knows that I'm working for the best interests of the sus-Peledaen."

So Natelth has absolutely no idea what his sister is doing, Kief thought. *Any more than he knows what I'm really doing with the Mages in Hanilat.*

I suppose this is what happens when you set yourself on the way to running an entire world—you spend too much time taking the long view instead of looking at what's going on closer in. A mistake like that could be the death of a man. . . .

"I understand," he said. "Make your replicant, my lady. I'll gather my Circle and begin working out what should be done."

11:

Len sat at the table in Iulan Vai's Hanilat safe house, drinking lukewarm *uffa* out of a kitchen tumbler. Zeri was in the bedroom, changing out of the drab garments her cousin had provided for the getaway, and into other clothing, this time provided by Vai.

"I suppose you got into their customer files somehow," Zeri had said, after a quick glance at the boxes from her favorite downtown boutique. "So much for privacy."

"Privacy's all an illusion anyway," Vai informed her. "And somebody may have already spotted you in the grey work pajamas, so you might as well go ahead and change. There's makeup and hair color in the necessarium if you want to play around with some of that."

Zeri muttered what might have been thanks and disappeared into the bedroom.

As soon as she was gone, Vai grabbed Len's injured hand and pulled it out into the light. "This looks nasty," she said. "Human bites are dirty. If you get an infection in there you could lose the finger."

She was probably right, Len decided. He was surprised to see how deep the wound was, and how sticky with drying blood. He hadn't noticed it much at the time. Excitement, he supposed; it wasn't every day that a mere contract-pilot got the opportunity to carry off a fleet-family heiress from her bridal bower.

He'd probably also left a blood trail all over Hanilat, which could make things difficult before much longer. But Syr Vai was obviously a professional at this kind of work, and so was Zeri sus-Dariv's cousin Herin—even if they were both Mages these days as well. They would know when it was time to cover their tracks and leave the neighborhood. He hoped.

Vai brought him a basin full of warm water and a scrub brush. "You know what has to happen next," she said. "Do you want to do it, or shall I?"

"I'll do it." He picked up the scrub brush and began the painful process of making certain that his bitten finger got thoroughly clean. "Do you have body-glue and bandages?"

"I've got better than that. If you can tolerate *eibriyu*, that is."

"No problems there." A few unlucky people had body chemistry that couldn't handle the quasi-organic healing gel; most people—Len among them—simply couldn't afford it. "If you've got that stuff in your kit, somebody must really love you."

"Never mind where I got it from. Keep scrubbing."

She kept the *eibriyu* in a sealed jar on the lower shelf of the safe house's preserving-cupboard. From where he sat, Len could see that the rest of the shelf was empty; Syr Vai hadn't used this particular hiding place for quite some time. As soon as he'd finished scrubbing the bite to her satisfaction, she scooped up some of the gel on a sterile pad and dabbed it into the open wound.

The gel was pinkish in color, and felt cool and tingling against his skin. Vai put on a light bandage over it, and stood back. "By this time tomorrow, nobody will be able to tell that you got bitten," she said. "Which under the circumstances is just as well."

"I'm all in favor of anonymity, as far as that goes," Len said. "This place here wouldn't be a part of the sus-Dariv property, would it? Because if it is, it's going to be one of the first places people look."

"No, it's not sus-Dariv. Whose it is . . . well, frankly, that doesn't concern you."

"Keeping all the blood inside my skin concerns me," said Len, looking at his bandaged finger, "and so far I haven't even managed that."

"You're doing all right," Vai said. "I should have told you to wear gloves—it wasn't your fault that the little sus-Dariv turned out to have teeth."

"Sharp teeth," said Len, remembering. "And no hesitation about using them, either—I bled all over the sus-Peledaen's upstairs carpet. If I get caught now, the city watch can match me to it in a heartbeat."

"The idea is not to get caught."

"Easy for you to say. Whatever happened to all that luck you were supposed to be working for me?"

"How do you think you made it in through the upstairs window with a wedding in full cry down below?" Vai asked. "Fiddling with the sus-Peledaen security hardware was the easy part of that particular job."

Len felt his temper—already worn thin in places—beginning to fray. "So the help stops now. Is that it?"

"No," said Vai. "I pulled you into this, and I'm not going to abandon you. But working the luck does get harder once other Mage-Circles become aware of what's going on. And the sus-Peledaen have a lot of Circles."

"Do what you can, all right?" Len said. "The last thing we need right now is for some foot-patrolman from the city watch to notice those bandages. If that happens, the next thing you know it's going to be, 'Step right over here, Syr Irao; we have a few questions we'd like you to clear up.' "

"I've got a few of those questions myself," said a voice from the kitchen doorway.

It was Zeri sus-Dariv, back from changing clothes in the necessarium. She was wearing one of the new outfits Vai had provided, tapered trousers and a snug jacket in deep midnight blue—not the sus-Peledaen blue but darker, nobody's family colors this time. Len noticed that she'd also put on more cosmetics, applying the paints and colors with a bold hand; whether she'd meant to disguise herself, or to bolster her self-confidence, he wasn't sure.

She came into the kitchen, but didn't bother to sit down at the table. Instead, she looked across it at Vai with an expression on her face that didn't belong to either the resigned bride or the young woman on the run. She was sus-Dariv, the ultimate holder of his current contract, and right now she looked it.

"First question," she said. "Where is my cousin Herin? If you were going to use his name to make me come with you, then you really ought to have had him available later. Otherwise I might start to think that you've been lying to me all along."

Vai didn't look as impressed as Len felt—maybe she dealt with fleet-family higher-ups all the time. "Your cousin went on ahead to prepare the next stage of your escape. There are places I shouldn't be seen, and people I shouldn't be seen with, and I've empowered Syr Arayet to act in my name."

"Those people wouldn't be the same nicely anonymous people who own this apartment, would they?" Zeri asked. "Exactly who *are* they—and do they even know we're here?"

"This is a safe house," Vai said. "It's mine, to do with as I like and as I need to, and it's been mine for longer than you've been out of school. As for who ultimately owns it, that's a name better left unmentioned—what you don't know you can't tell. All that's relevant right now is that you can stay here as long as you need to."

Zeri's expression grew, if anything, chillier. "You know, I'm starting to get tired of mysterious strangers appearing from nowhere and offering to do me good turns for free. At least Len here has contract-carrier status with what's left of the sus-Dariv, which makes him the closest thing I have at the moment to family. I think I'm going to leave this safe house of yours with him, and I think I'm going to do it right now."

She strode off in the direction of the front door. Len stared after her, then shook his head and, reluctantly, got to his feet.

"I'm sorry," he said to Iulan Vai. "But until I get a new contract, my obligation's to her."

"She feels the need to be elsewhere, and she may be right." Len had expected Vai to be angry at Zeri's outburst, but she appeared more distracted than anything else—as if she were looking at something around him that he couldn't quite see. She made a shooing motion at him with her hands. "Go, go. The last time that young lady ran out on a meeting, the whole building blew up not long afterward."

When Len and Zeri had gone, Vai sat back in her chair, drinking a cup of *uffa*. The girl Zeri was a luck-maker, or a luck-bringer. Time would tell which. The only problem was that luck couldn't be relied on, not for those around her.

The way luck works, Vai thought, leaning back and putting her feet up on the table, cradling the cup in her lap, *is that what seems bad at the time turns out later to be the best that could possibly be. And the bad luck could be very bad indeed for those around the luck-maker.*

So, Vai concluded, she should be off to make some luck of her own. She put down the cup, wiping it down out of habit in order to remove finger and lip prints, stood, and slipped out into the night.

Not much later she had reached the sus-Radal office building. This was the hour of the lunar observance; if her own luck remained equal to the occasion, Theledau would be in his moon-room at home. As far as other watchers might be concerned, she was dressed in the inconspicuous drudge-garb she usually wore to visit Thel's offices—black shirt and trousers and many-pocketed cargo jacket, with nothing except her staff to show that she was a Mage. And it wouldn't take much in the way of working the *eiran* to keep the staff unnoticed in a pinch.

The cipher locks in the sus-Radal building had ceased to hold mysteries for her years ago. She locked all of them properly behind her as she passed through and made her way upward to the top floor. Thel's office was dark and empty, the big executive desk powered down and inactive. The room's security access panel was on the wall by the office door, behind a framed watercolor sketch of syn-Grevi House in midwinter.

Vai opened the panel and made certain that nothing would be triggered by any changes in the room's power flow. Then she crossed over to the desk and turned it on.

A long time ago, or so it felt like to her now, Theledau syn-Grevi sus-Radal had wondered why Vai insisted on re-signing as his Agent-Principal when she went to the Mages for good. At the time, she hadn't been able to explain—most Mages had day jobs, after all, since they had the same financial needs as other people.

That was then, she found herself saying to the absent Theledau as she deftly circumvented the office-mind's security systems and proceeded to make free with the desk's contents. *This is now.*

If you ever learn about this, you're going to think that I sold you out to the sus-Dariv.

She found what she was looking for—the plans and star charts and associated files for Theledau's system of hidden bases on the far side of the interstellar gap—and started copying them onto data-wafers that she stashed one by one in her inside jacket pocket.

It's true, little Zeri is going to need a place to go hide for a while where the sus-Peledaen can't find her. But I'm not doing this for Zeri sus-Dariv.

I'm doing it for the sake of the great working, and there's no way you're ever going to understand that.

Once the shuttle was safely on course for its rendezvous, Arekhon left Karil Estisk at the controls and joined the rest of his Circle—less than a full-strength Mage-Circle, it was true, but more of Demaizen in one place than he'd known in years. With the added strength of the Void-walker Mara-ganha, they might even be able to finish the working.

Narin and Ty had unstrapped themselves from their safety webbing by the time he reached the passenger compartment. Ty sat cross-legged on the foot of his couch, with his new long staff in the Adepts' style lying on the cushions beside him and his eyes gazing into the middle distance. Narin stood a few feet away, staff in hand, looking tense—he remembered that she had never cared for takeoffs and landings during her time aboard the sus-Peledaen exploratory ship *Rain-on-Dark-Water*.

"Ships go on the ocean," she'd said to him once. "Not in vacuum. I don't trust it."

The only one who seemed truly at home in space was Maraganha. The shuttle's light gravity—only a few steps above nonexistent, and likely to vanish in an instant if Karil decided to take nonessentials off-line—didn't appear to bother her; she moved in it easily as she made a slow circuit of the compartment. Arekhon wondered what other ships she was comparing the shuttle with in her mind, and whether the vessels of that future day made this one look clunky and primitive by comparison.

But that was pointless speculation, and not likely to provide useful answers. "Let's get the suits warmed up and fitted," he said. "We may need them for the transfer to the *Daughter*."

Ty turned his head enough to look at him curiously. "*Night's-Beautiful-Daughter?* After all these years?"

"It's one of House Rosselin's assets," Arekhon said. "It's been tended."

"Has it indeed?" said Maraganha. "I'm looking forward to seeing this."

The pressure-suits were supposed to be in the shuttle's main cargo hold. Arekhon went to the after end of the compartment and opened the door to the cargo bay. The inside of the bay was pitch-dark; Arekhon found the switch for the worklights on the bulkhead outside the door, and flipped it on.

The bright lights revealed a compartment empty except for the baled cubes that held the suits. Arekhon reached for the nearest bale and unslipped it from its cords. In the lower gravity it lifted easily from the deck. It was clumsily shaped and its mass made it awkward to maneuver, but he had no trouble hauling it forward into the passenger compartment.

Maraganha said, "You're the man with the local knowledge. Care to educate us on the finer points of Entiboran pressure-suits?"

"They're simple enough," he said. He pulled the zip cord on the side of the package. "And these aren't the high-end specialty stuff anyway. I got the lifeboat models. Easy to put on and pretty close to foolproof."

"I've known some pretty major fools," Maraganha said.

Arekhon looked at her.

"No one's ever called you one of them, though," she said, and grinned. "All right, here we go. Pull one out and show us the drill."

The last time that young lady ran out on a meeting, the whole building blew up not long afterward.

Vai's words remained vivid in Len's mind as he ran down the apartment-house stairs. Mages could see the luck; everyone knew that. Other people, sometimes Mages and sometimes not, *had* luck, and it came to them in different shapes and forms. Maybe Zeri sus-Dariv sus-Peledaen had luck of the conveniently-be-elsewhere variety—one of Len's old shipmates had been like that.

Without a Mage's ability to see the *eiran,* though, he couldn't tell. He could only hurry to catch up with Zeri on the sidewalk outside the apartment building, and say, "Where do you think you're going?"

"Some place that isn't Eraasi," she said, still walking away rapidly. "Wasn't that the idea to start with?"

He stayed with her, easily matching her shorter stride. The street was dark, with a lamppost at each end but nothing in the middle to break the gloom. The apartment buildings along this row weren't the kind to put up lanterns beside the front door, either. That and the lack of traffic along the one-way street made it a good site for a confidential agent's backup safe house.

"Vai and your cousin were planning to—"

"I don't care what they were planning," she said. "I don't know Syr Vai from the Mayor of Amisket—I've never even *been* to Amisket—and so far I haven't seen anything of Herin. For all I know, you and Vai were using his name to make me come along."

"What do you want, then? You can't go back to Lord Natelth."

"I want—" She stopped.

He stopped, too, catching at her sleeve as he did so to pull her a little farther into the shadows. Midnight blue made a good color for fading into the dark; he wondered if Iulan Vai had picked out Zeri's new clothing with that in mind. "What?"

"Listen."

He listened, and heard nothing except for the low rumble of a nearby engine. "It's a public road," he said. "Someone's driving this way, that's all."

"They're driving this way the wrong way on a one-way street," she said. "And they're in a hurry."

He listened again. She was right. "I think it's time to stay in the shadows and not move for a few minutes."

They stood close together as a low black groundcar sped past and pulled up to the curb outside the apartment building they'd left only a short while before. Another groundcar pulled up from the opposite direction, and both vehicles began disgorging dark-clad men.

"It's a raid, all right," Len said. "They're hunting for us now."

"What about Syr Vai? Will she—"

"She's a professional," Len said, with more optimism than he actually felt. "And she's had that house for a long time. Vai can take care of herself."

Karil Estisk found herself grateful when Arekhon headed aft to instruct his fellow-Mages in the proper way to put on and wear an emergency pressure-suit. She didn't outright dislike him—he was kind and pleasant-mannered and not at all hard on the eyes—and she trusted him as much as she was ever going to trust anybody who came from across the interstellar gap and called himself a Mage, but that didn't necessarily mean she liked him a great deal, or that she trusted him any farther than she could throw him in low gravity.

He was part of Garrod syn-Aigal's great working, and the great working had torn up Karil's life once before. Her first reaction on seeing Arekhon sus-Khalgath standing outside her apartment door a few weeks ago had been a sudden absolute certainty—*he's going to do it again*—followed by an equally absolute certainty that all her careful career-rebuilding of the last decade was going to go for nothing. She'd thrown in with his plans out of desperation, a feeling that it was better to jump wide-eyed into the maelstrom than to be thrown in all willy-nilly.

Which makes you as crazy as the rest of them, she told herself.

She reached out with one hand and dialed up the magnification and the heat-anomaly sensor on the forward screen, then sat back to wait. The speed of progress was slight, considering, at least compared with a jump run. The black band in the middle of the VU meter grew narrower and narrower as the signal strength went up.

Karil thought about what might be waiting for her back on Entibor—if, indeed, she was fortunate enough to make it home from across the galaxy a second time. 'Rekhe might be sneaky and underhanded, not to mention obsessed with Garrod syn-Aigal's working, but he wasn't stingy. He'd made arrangements to keep her pay from InterWorlds Shipping coming into her bank account for as long as his open-ended contract for her services remained in force. She might well come home from this journey a wealthy woman; on the other hand, if her last sojourn among 'Rekhe's people was any indication, she might not ever come home at all.

"What kind of pilot takes on a job like that?" she asked herself aloud, and tweaked the course a bit to keep the signal in the center of the disk of her HF/DF. "I do. If I'm crazy."

That got her to laughing a little. All she had to do was travel to the far side of the interstellar gap—to a place where everything was strange, where no one spoke her language, where no one knew the simplest things about hardware or mechanics, but where men could walk through walls and read minds—and then come back alive.

"That settles it. I *am* crazy."

Karil tweaked their course again. Up ahead, the stars were filtered from the viewscreen. They would be too bright, with the low-light turned up the way it was. But a patch of the image was a different shade of black on black. She touched up the contrast and fed in some color to saturate the field.

She sent out an active ping, and adjusted course and speed

a bit in response. Then she keyed the internal announcement system.

"We're coming into visual range of the *Daughter*. If there's anything you want aboard this vessel, bring it down to the lock. If you have suits, put them on, but don't start using air tanks yet."

Then she unsnapped herself and removed her own suit from the slide-locker behind the piloting position. She slid it on and fastened the slides along arms and legs, then pulled on the boots and gloves, clamping down the ring seals.

The dark shape on the monitor had grown in the time she'd not been looking, taking on a flattened disk shape with swooping wings outspread to either side. Even though she'd seen it before, the ship still looked horridly alien to her: its aesthetics wrong; its dimensions wrong; the very assumptions behind its making all wrong. It floated motionless in the vacuum of space, a radio-emitting buoy tethered to it.

"The hatch on the ventral surface is the one you're looking for," Arekhon said. He had returned to the bridge so quietly that Karil hadn't heard him.

"Thanks," she said. "Which side is ventral?"

"That one," Arekhon said, tapping the screen in front of her with a fingernail. "Get us close enough to float across, with this vessel's hatch oriented toward the *Daughter*'s, and be ready to come along."

"Half an hour from the time I leave the control room to the time the automatic homer takes this craft back to Eraasi?"

"Half a day would be better," Arekhon said. "I don't want to be rushed for time. Set it for standard orbit GG-12."

"Right," Karil said. "Now, if you don't mind, I have some maneuvering to do."

By the time she'd gotten the shuttle into position, Arekhon and the others were all properly suited up. Karil came down the ladder from the control bridge to join them, closing the hatch behind her and dogging it shut. She carried her helmet loose in her hand.

"All right," she said. "Time to go."

She led the way back through the cargo spaces to the airlock, and walked into it. This was the cargo lock, and large enough to hold a dozen skipsleds' worth of cargo all by itself.

"Come on in," she said, after checking the exterior controls on their panel. "Everyone who isn't standing on this side of that line when I turn this switch is going back to Entibor."

Narin went first among the Mages, then Ty and Maraganha, then Arekhon last of all. He took one last look into the ship as he left its main compartment, and Karil thought she saw his lips move, as if he were saying somebody's name. Then he too stepped across the threshold and into the lock.

"Right," Karil said. She held down the safety catch with one hand while she turned the switch with the other. The inner door swung closed.

"Now we put on our helmets, switch to internal air, and hope there aren't any leaks," Karil said, and pulled on her own helmet. She twisted the valve by her right thigh, and heard the hiss of air coming in. The fog on her faceplate cleared.

"Okay, everyone good?" This time her voice came across the radio link. "Last chance for anyone to get cold feet."

"We're all doing fine," Arekhon said.

She waited a minute longer, but nobody spoke up to contradict him. Karil turned the switch for the outer door of the lock—the door was as wide as the entire chamber—and watched as it slid up. She stepped out, and attached a lightline to the ringbolt beside the door, then switched off the magnetic pads in her boots and pushed away, floating across to where *Night's-Beautiful-Daughter*—huge compared with the craft they were in, tiny compared with a real deep-space merchant—swam above them.

Her boots clicked against the far hull, and she walked—*click*-step, *click*-step—to the airlock there. She tied off the line to a section of raised hull plate, and said, "Okay, 'Rekhe, you know this ship and how to open the door. Come on over."

———————◆———————

Evening drew on, dimming the sky outside the sus-Peledaen town house. Natelth sat alone in his study, waiting for word. He would have paced the floor, except that he had schooled himself decades ago not to do such things. Out beyond the bay window of the study, the lights of the city shone like distant stars.

No reports so far, no sightings. If one of the liveried guards hadn't thought to check all the trash bins within a half-mile radius, the searchers wouldn't even have had the dress and the bridal crown. And nobody had touched those, so far as could be determined, except for Zeri sus-Dariv herself. Somewhere between the empty withdrawing-room and that muddy alley, Natelth's missing bride had apparently changed clothes, wiped her face clean of cosmetics, and vanished.

She could have been under duress. It was possible—the sus-Peledaen had enemies, a bountiful supply of them, men and women and whole worlds who would like nothing better than to deprive Natelth sus-Khalgath of something that was his.

Or she could have gone willingly.

Could she? Natelth wondered. *Would she?*

He realized that he didn't know. He knew that Zeri sus-Dariv had blue eyes and yellow curls because he'd seen her twice—once at the formal marriage negotiations and once this morning at the wedding. He knew that she played at drama and the theatre because his intelligence operatives had included that information in the portfolio they drew up for him. He knew that she was coolheaded enough to understand that bringing what remained of the sus-Dariv into the sus-Peledaen was the best way to help them survive, and he knew that she'd been clever enough to see it on her own and send Fas Treosi to make the approach.

Did that mean she was clever enough to understand other things as well?

He knew one other thing—she was lucky. Lucky enough to escape the Court of Two Colors, when there should have been nobody in her position left alive. Clever and lucky—but if she was part of the plot, why was there blood on the carpet?

The chime of his voice comm halted the restless circling of his thoughts. He pressed the speaker button. "Yes?"

"Na'e, this is Isa. I have something for you."

He felt a surge of relief. Isayana, at least, he knew. "What is it?"

"A face and a body. Suitable for identification."

"How did—?"

"Blood can tell you all sorts of things, if you take the time to ask it politely."

He thought she sounded amused, though he couldn't imagine why. Isa's sense of humor had always been a little strange, just as Arekhon's had been. No, not quite like Arekhon's—with 'Rekhe, part of the joke would have been knowing that his older brother was missing some of it.

That didn't matter, though. Not anymore.

"Send me everything you've got, Isa. As soon as possible, if not sooner."

"You've already got it—ask the house-mind."

He was querying the main node as she spoke, bringing up a nonverbal display, a three-dimensional image of a man, hovering in the empty space above the desk: Antipodean; somewhere in the indefinite span between youngish and middle-aged; thin face; long bony blade of a nose; yellow-brown eyes. A table of data floated in the air next to the image: probable height, probable weight, numbers and yet more numbers to describe and identify a single living man.

"I knew I could count on you," he said. He closed down the display and set to work with the files, getting them moving to the right places, to people who could put names to faces, put out the word, find out who had dared—"Tell the staff that under the circumstances, we'll be staying here in Hanilat for some time to come."

"I'll make sure they know. And Na'e—don't worry if I'm not back home right away. I have some cleanup to take care of first."

Natelth keyed off the voice comm and went on to summon his chief of security—a man currently not so secure in his position as he had been this morning. Inside a few minutes, Grif Egelt was standing before Natelth's desk, looking as if he would prefer to be in any other place in Hanilat.

"My lord?" Egelt said.

"Why haven't I received a report yet?" Natelth demanded.

"An investigation like this moves slowly during the first few hours, my lord. The kidnappers have all the advantages. One interesting development—"

"Yes?" Natelth said. He crossed over to the copper *uffa* pot on the side table and poured himself a cup of the sharp, red liquid. He didn't offer one to Egelt.

"We got word through informants of a woman who could be Lady Zeri going into an apartment building in the northern suburbs of Hanilat. The house was raided."

"And? Why wasn't I informed of this beforehand?"

"The information could have turned out to be a false lead—we've seen hundreds of those so far already, and I expect we'll be seeing more of them. In any case, the house was raided, and while the woman was not found, we have reason to believe that she was there. And that she was there with at least two other individuals."

"Did one of those individuals look like this?" Natelth snapped a switch on his desk, so that the image that Isayana had sent to the house-mind appeared full-sized and floating in the air above them, rotating slowly—*like a hanged man,* Natelth thought.

"I don't know, my lord," Egelt said.

"Then find out," Natelth said. "And find out who this man is, in any case. I need him. I want him. I shall have him. Is this as clear as I can make it?"

"Yes, my lord."

And bowing, the security chief departed.

12:

Night's-Beautiful-Daughter was built of good steel and stout aluminum. Llannat Hyfid—*Maraganha,* she reminded herself yet again; *I have to be Maraganha*—was the first of Arekhon's Mages to abandon her pressure-suit, as soon as the airlock had cycled and the ship was safe. Her sturdy leather boots rang on the metal deckplates as she left the entrance bay for the narrow, curving passageway beyond. For these first few minutes, she didn't want the members of Arekhon's Circle to see her face.

I never thought I'd board this ship again. And I certainly never thought that I'd find her waiting for me at the other end of time.

She knew the layout of the *Daughter* by memory; she could have followed the ship's corridors all the way from the cockpit in one direction to the engine room in the other. She thought for a while of going to the cockpit, where a much-younger Llannat Hyfid had found—would someday find—two long-dead crew members strapped into their seats, with their throats slit and a message written on the forward viewscreen in their blood: "Adept from the forest world:

Take this message to the Domina. Tell her what you have seen."

But they wouldn't be there now. In this time, *Night's-Beautiful-Daughter* was still a living ship, and whatever had happened to set her adrift on her course through the interstellar gap was yet to come.

Llannat returned to the entrance bay instead. The two Mages already waiting in there—intense young Ty, who carried an Adept's staff in spite of his Circle training; and Narin, whom they had pulled by main strength out of salt water and the Void—gave her odd looks when she entered the compartment.

Llannat shook her head ruefully. They all thought of her as something not quite human, even 'Rekhe, who certainly ought to know better; a wonderworker, perhaps, or their own private oracle. She wished that they would stop. Not a sensible wish, since she was in this position of her own will, but good sense never stopped anyone from wishing yet.

The airlock cycled one last time, and Karil and Arekhon came aboard through the sliding doors. The starpilot turned to Arekhon and said, "Where to next, Captain?"

"Eraasi," he said. "Ty, find us food supplies if you can. The ship should be fully stocked, but if it isn't we'll have to stop somewhere before the interstellar gap to replenish our larder."

"We have to be on our way before any of the in-system ships get antsy and fire on us, or we may be permanently delayed," Karil said. "I'm going to move off a ways before I calculate the run we need."

"All we need," said Arekhon, "is to find the other side of the Gap."

"Easier said than done, maybe," the pilot said. "But we won't know until we give it a try."

"Let's go, then," he said. "Maraganha *etaze*—if you would like to come along as well?"

Llannat gave in to the inevitable. "I'd be honored," she said.

When they reached the cockpit, Arekhon took his place in the right-hand seat and gave a deep sigh. "At least I can see out. A proper spaceship."

Karil shook her head. "Eyes won't replace electronics. There's so much more I can do with viewscreens."

"If you say so," Arekhon said. "Meanwhile, let's see if we can still move. I don't trust vessels that have been sitting unused for this long."

"I don't either," Llannat said. At least neither Arekhon nor Karil Estisk were the crew members whose blood had stained—would someday stain—the floor and seats and console, and provide the ink for somebody's cryptic message. Neither of them fit the pattern of the *eiran* as she would see it on that future day when the civilized galaxy stood on the edge of war and at the end of the great working. She looked at the thick armored glass of the cockpit windows and thought about the nature of time and memory before adding, "During the transit to Eraasi, we'll need to put together a good do-it-yourself hardcopy manual on starting from a cold ship."

"I like that idea," Karil said. "In fact, I like it a lot. Given all the fancy stuff 'Rekhe's people added to a perfectly good design, the whole thing's likely to explode if you don't do everything right."

"My people didn't build the *Daughter*," protested Arekhon. "It was the sus-Radal. And what do we want a hardcopy manual for? Do you have any idea how bulky—"

"As a matter of fact, I do," Llannat told him. "And eventually somebody is going to need it. Besides—it's always good to have a hobby to keep you busy on a long transit."

"Tell me something," Zeri said to Len. "If you weren't playing bodyguard to a runaway bride, what would you be doing right now?"

The two of them were sitting together at a dim corner table in an eating establishment a few blocks outside the Hanilat starport—close enough in to attract a rougher crowd than the downtown places. In their current state, rougher was good; even if they were recognized, the clientele at Red's Fishhouse wasn't the sort to report anybody to the city watch. Len had a platter of sliced bread and meat, and Zeri was working her way through a large serving of the local deep-fried seafood—she'd always loved it, and it wasn't the sort of thing that she could cook for herself in a city apartment.

"I'd be down at the port," Len said. "Sweating the next cargo, getting the fuel and stores, worrying about port fees and about whether I counted as a sus-Dariv contract holder if most of the sus-Dariv were gone."

She dipped another strip of fried silverling into the pot of spicy green sauce that had accompanied the meal. "And if the port were closed?"

"Well, then I'd be at close-operations, raising murder about it, pointing at the clock on the wall, and shouting that time is money."

"Then maybe we should be doing something like that ourselves," she said. "Since we don't know if Syr Vai is helping us or not."

"Maybe," he said. He put together another bread-and-meat sandwich, and bit into it. A moment's chewing and swallowing, and he went on, "First you tell me something."

"Tell you what?"

"Why are you going along with this crazy plan your cousin and Syr Vai dragged me into? Lord Natelth may be a murdering bastard—ask anybody who was on Ildaon when it got space-bombed by the sus-Peledaen fleet—but I haven't heard anybody say that he treats his lovers badly. And talk like that always gets around."

They'd ordered a pitcher of summer-ale for sharing between them, because the night was warm. Zeri took the time to refill both her mug and his before she answered.

"I made the marriage-deal with Natelth because it was the only way I could think of to take care of the sus-Dariv. But I don't think Herin would have offered me a chance to get out of the bargain if he didn't have another idea in mind. I want to find out what it is."

"A little while ago you were almost accusing me and Syr Vai of doing away with Cousin Herin," Len pointed out.

"For all I knew, you could have stolen his ideas—whatever they were—and then killed him. I want to find out where he is and what he was thinking of." She ate another strip of fish and green sauce, then licked her fingers clean.

"So. If you had a female companion, who would she be, and what would she be doing?"

"Supercargo, most likely," Len said. "And since you don't have a couple of free years to learn it in, I doubt that I could teach you the job."

"Then I'll just have to pretend," she said. "If you're coming with me, let's go."

Outside on the street again, they caught the public-transit bus that made a circuit of the portside streets. The darklit back of the public accommodation gave them more time to speak.

"Am I overdressed for the port?" she asked.

"You'll do," Len said, "and so will I. The folks know me there, and they'll know that anyone who's with me is supposed to be with me."

"So I shouldn't worry."

"Not about the clothes," he said. "But with your accent, nobody's going to take you for anything less than a fleet-apprentice out on a spree."

"Then I'll need to become a fleet-apprentice," she said. "At least for the purposes of conversation."

A bit after that, in the line of bars that surrounded portside, Len and Zeri stood on the sidewalk. The humming of the glowlights punctuated the night. The air was thick and close, and Zeri smelled rotting things on the air. Streetwashers ran every day in some parts of Hanilat, but this part wasn't one of them.

"Are you sure this is a good idea?" she asked.

"If you're going to play at being a fleet-apprentice in front of the port officials, you're going to need the livery. And that's not something you can buy at a costume shop."

"I suppose not," she said. "Let me get this bit straight. We're going to wander from one drinking establishment to the next, and I'm going to go inside each establishment and look around for somebody my size in apprentice livery. When I find one, I'll persuade that person to accompany me outside, where you will relieve them of their finery. Right?"

"That's pretty much it."

"I thought so." She looked at the bright lights in the windows of the drinking places along the portside strip. "Tell me again why you can't be the one doing this part."

"Because nobody impressionable is going to follow me," Len said reasonably. "So if you want that livery—"

"I want it. Don't go away."

She left him and walked into the bar. The lights were red inside, and the burly individual by the door—*the bouncer?* she wondered—asked her for five *ahlei* to be allowed farther in.

"You freelance?" he asked.

It took her a couple of seconds to work out what he was asking. She thought for a couple of seconds longer, and said, "Yes."

"Ten percent to Syr Risa, and don't forget," the bouncer said, his bald head gleaming with sweat or oil in the flashing lights from inside.

"I won't," she said. And then she was in, and the lights were flashing around a long stage, a runway behind the bar, where a young lady dressed mostly in long hair was doing amazingly athletic things, while the bartenders in front scurried about with glasses in their hands.

She stood for a while with her back to the rear wall, waiting for her eyes to adjust to the low light level, before looking around for a suit of fleet-apprentice livery. None presented itself immediately to view. The bar formed the opening of a horseshoe shape extending from the back wall. She walked to the far end, waited, then circled the room, keeping her eyes open for an apprentice.

She didn't find one. Near the end of her transit an older fellow, white hairs showing amid the dark of his close-cropped beard, grasped her by the arm and said, "I'm looking for a good time."

"How wonderful for you," Zeri said before she remembered herself and said, "I'm hired already."

"No need to be snarky about it," the man said, but he let her go.

Then she was all the way around, and wondering if she should move on to the next place already. The music here was very loud, and everyone present was elaborately trying not to see the other people around them.

"This is impossible," she said to herself, and went out past the sweating man by the door, into what was suddenly a cool evening. She didn't see Len anywhere, but she supposed he was somewhere out of sight, lurking. She hoped he was lurking, anyway. Things might get—difficult—if he wasn't.

To her right, one door closer to the port, was another establishment similar to the one she'd left. She entered through the heavy outer door, then passed through an inner door of hanging beads, and found another man at a high table, looking down at her. A sign beside him said, FIVE *AHLEI* COVER CHARGE, LADIES FREE.

"Hello," he said, as she tried to push through his turnstile. "You freelance?"

"I'm a lady," she said. "Your sign says 'Free.' "

"That's with an escort, love," the gent said. He was perfumed, and wore a very nice waistcoat. "You freelance?"

Again she flipped a mental coin. "No."

"Who you working for?"

"Syr Risa," she said.

"You're a bit out of your range," he said, "But that's all right. Five *ahlei,* and it's in you go. I hope Syr Risa remembers, if he ever needs a favor."

"Or if you do," Zeri said, and pushed across her five *ahlei.*

Isayana's summons came sooner than Kief expected, and he was glad that he'd had the foresight to put both his prime Circle and the Hanilat Institute Circle into a state of readiness the day before. A quick head count when he reached her laboratory building showed him all of his own Mages waiting in the upstairs hall except one, and she arrived flushed and breathless a few minutes later—"I had to hand over all my case files to my backup, just in case, and there's a new rule in the office that every single one of them has to be signed for in triplicate. . . ." Giesye was a good Second, strong and reliable in the Circle, but there was no denying the fact that outside the silence of a working she babbled like water running over stones.

"It's all right," Kief said. "Let's go downstairs."

He led the way down to the lower reaches of the building, and the chambers where Natelth's sister did her work. One of Isayana's many custom-tooled *aiketen* met them at the foot of the stairs.

"If I may escort you to the robing-room?" it asked.

"Please do," he said. The sus-Peledaen *aiketen* came closer to true sapience than most of their kind, and he was willing to give them the benefit of courtesy on that account. If a device of Isayana's manufacturing should choose to hold a grudge on account of bad treatment—which was something Kief did not consider wholly impossible—he had no intention of being the object of its ill will.

Once in the robing-room, he put on his working garments as rapidly as possible, then said to the others, "I'm going to talk with our patron. Join me when you're ready; the *aiketh* will show you the way."

The setup in the main workroom had changed since his last visit, at least partly in accordance with his specifications. Nothing remained of the laboratory tables, or the specialized equipment, or the shelves laden with supplies. Only the gel-vat with the finished replicant body—*not faceless,* Kief thought, *not any longer*—waited in the center of a large circle chalked on the floor. All the overhead worklights were turned off except for the one directly above the vat.

Isayana sus-Khalgath was waiting for him next to the gel-vat, along with a thin, nervous-looking man whom Kief didn't recognize. She introduced the man as the specialist physician who had been working with her on the replication process.

"If all goes well, syn-Velgeth will be assisting us with the final stages of the vivification."

Kief nodded to the man politely, then glanced into the gel-vat at the body lying there: Lean and muscular, with a pronounced Antipodean cast to the facial features, it resembled nobody Kief knew.

"Do you have a name for him yet?" he asked.

"No. But Natelth's people are working on it."

"You gave them the image?"

She nodded. "It isn't a perfect match, of course. The process gives us an ideal body, and life . . . life isn't ideal. Scars, starvation, self-indulgence, they could all have left marks on him that we don't know about."

"A positive ID from the image and the genetic data should supply your brother with that information," Kief said. He regarded the body thoughtfully. "If you had all the necessary information in advance, how close a match could you get with this process?"

"Theoretically?" said Isayana. "An exact one. Though the process at that level would be as much art as science."

"Do you plan to tell your brother about the possibility of getting a true double?"

"No. Natelth doesn't know about the replication process; he thinks all that I derived from the blood was an image."

"I see."

He wondered who she would tell, if not the sus-Peledaen. Not another of the star-lords, surely; she was angry at her brother, not the whole family. But there was definitely somebody out there who distrusted Lord Natelth enough to back his sister in research as potentially world-changing as his own efforts with the Circles.

He already knew that—if it worked—she wasn't going to tell Natelth about filling the replicant, either.

The second bar that Zeri entered was as dim and noisy as the first, and the air was thick with smoke and sweat and the pheromones of lust. She looked around for fleet-livery, and thought for a second that she was in luck when she spotted sus-Oadlan buff and scarlet at the far end of the crowded bar. Then she got a better glimpse of the wearer—broad-shouldered, male, and taller than herself by more than a head—and her hopes faded. She scanned the room a second time, with no better result, and resigned herself to trying yet another establishment.

She was fading back through the crush toward the doorway when a recently familiar voice at her elbow said, "You're either a great deal bolder than I took you for, or a great deal stupider. Possibly both. And the mutual friend who's waiting for us outside listens to you a great deal more than he ought to, regardless."

Zeri turned, and saw a woman in a tight black bodysuit, a faux-fashionable half-mask, and a great deal of blue glitter, especially in her hair. "It occurs to me," Zeri said, "that this isn't a good place for me to call you by name."

"You're right; it isn't," said Iulan Vai.

"I have to admit that I like the outfit. But aren't you missing an accessory?" Zeri had always been under the impression that a Mage's staff never got very far from the hand of the Mage who owned it—if a staff was in fact owned, in the normal sense, which was something she'd never been clear on.

"No," Vai said. "I'm not. Now let's get you out of here before somebody on your bridegroom's payroll spots your face and makes a comm call."

"Do you really think anyone here—"

"I think at least three people here, and I've recognized one of them already. We need to continue this conversation out on the street." Vai grasped Zeri's elbow and urged her toward the front entrance. "At the moment, we're doing this the easy way. But things are moving fast, and the hard way might turn up real soon now."

Zeri and Vai made it through the crowd and out into the neon and incandescent night, where a hawker with a tray of pamphlets and text wafers was calling, "One hundred best pickup lines! Only one *ahle!* Get 'em here!"

"Now," said Zeri. "What did you do with Len?"

"He's lurking in the alley, holding my work clothes and my jacket and waiting for us to show up."

Zeri didn't think she liked Vai's faint undertone of amusement. "Show up and do what?"

"Go to his ship," Vai said. "Then leave the planet."

"The port's closed. Len said that closing it would be the first thing Lord Natelth did, and he was right."

"Nevertheless," said Vai. "We're going to his ship." They'd reached the mouth of the alley; she raised her voice slightly and said, "Len, come out and come on. The two of you have wasted quite enough time. We're off."

"Off for where?" Len said, pushing himself from the wall where he'd been leaning.

"To the sus-Dariv yards, and hope that the resources there are stretched thin."

"And will they be?" he asked.

"Walk slowly," Vai advised him. "We have every right to be here and we're about our lawful business. As for your question—nothing is ever certain, but we should have luck tonight."

She lifted her right hand slightly, and Zeri wasn't surprised to see that it held a Mage's staff. Zeri was somewhat more surprised to see that the staff was glowing a faint but vivid green—a phenomenon she had heard of, but had never expected to encounter.

Several minutes more of deliberately casual strolling took them from the entertainment strip to the starport proper, a complex of large buildings with high glass windows set about with the seals of all the fleet-families of Eraasi. They walked through the main archway, past the desk where the toteboard read CANCELED beside every lift, past the lounge where the duty-status pilots waited, out through the inner fence, and onto the field itself.

Once clear of the fence they picked up a slidewalk toward the sus-Dariv docks. Harsh yellow security lights reflected off the high clouds overhead, making the stars fade and go pale. Nobody had stopped them so far, and Zeri was actually starting to relax a little when Vai spoke up again.

"One thing that's going for us," the Mage said, "is that as far as most people are concerned, sus-Dariv is already sus-Peledaen. So we can honestly say that we've come here to check some family assets. And then we're going suborbital to another yard for repairs. We can demonstrate that we don't have the fuel on board to get to orbit. That's in the logs and it's been checked and confirmed."

"What's going to show in the logs is that I fueled up as soon as I came in," Len said. "I always do, just in case."

"A wise precaution," said Vai. "But this once, I'm afraid, you're in error. The records will show that this morning you sold what you bought."

When they reached the sus-Dariv gate, Len pushed his ID

card into the slot. "With two," he said to the *aiketh* on watch, and the *aiketh* responded, "Lenyat Irao, sus-Dariv by current contract, with two."

Len's ship, when they reached it, turned out to be somewhat larger than Zeri had expected—the three of them had to take a hydraulic lift up to the main external hatch. She felt exposed and vulnerable during the ride up, suspended on a platform between earth and air with no place to go; but nobody on the field below came running to stop them. She was grateful when the lift stopped and Len entered the combination on the keypad to open the ship. The hatch groaned open, and they stepped through.

"Welcome to *Fire-on-the-Hilltops*," Len said. "She may not be pretty, but she gets the job done."

"Where's Herin?" Zeri said.

"In the Antipodes," said Vai. "Doing business for me there." The Mage turned to Len. "Can you get local clearance to do a surface-to-surface hop?"

"If they don't give permission," Zeri said, "take it anyway. I want to find my cousin."

Kief waited while Isayana and her *aiketen* and the attending physician made final preparations. The members of Kief's Circle came in, masked and robed now, and stood together at one side of the workroom making preparations of their own—some stretching, moving in patterned exercises or in slow dancelike staff routines; others turned inward, already partway into trance. Kief had told them what would be needed, and they knew that ultimately one of them would fill the replicant. The working would show which one of them was best suited for the purpose.

He could see from their manner and movement that all of them were willing, and even eager. This was a new thing they were doing, and theirs was not a common fleet-Circle. The purpose of this Circle was to do extraordinary things.

A readout on the side of the gel-vat gave him the time. It was almost the hour; across town, the Institute Circle would already have begun their working. The lesser Circle's aim was to summon up power, to bind the cords of it together into a strong cable, and feed that cable into the pattern of the greater Circle's working.

Kief turned to the physician. "Is the body ready? Physically."

syn-Velgeth said, "Yes. It breathes; the heart beats."

"How long do we have?"

"Five hours, maybe six. If your people can't animate—"

"Fill."

"—can't fill it by then, we'll have to flush the bath with acid and let the gel revert."

"Five hours should be enough," Kief told him. To Isayana, he said, "We're ready. You've done your part; the rest is up to the Circle."

"What should we do?" she asked.

"Keep out of the way—and don't interfere, no matter what you see happening. Even if this turns out to need a great working."

He could tell from her expression that the idea of not doing anything wasn't pleasing to her, but she and the physician moved to the side without argument, standing together in obscurity outside the bright illumination thrown by the single worklight. Kief gestured to his Mages, and they came forward to kneel around the perimeter of the chalked circle with the gel-vat in its center. He waited until all the others were settled, then took the First's position, knelt, and slipped on his hardmask.

The *eiran* were everywhere.

He saw the pattern of Garrod's working, as he always saw it wherever he went and whatever he did. And another pattern, overlying it, incomplete . . . the threads that would make up this working, Kief's own working. Its lines and tracings glowed silver in the shadowed corners of the room, paler but still visible toward the center. Behind and outside the patterns lay the sturdy glowing cable of the Institute Circle's combined will, a bright loop waiting to be grasped.

Kief sank deeper into meditation, into the inner world of metaphor and imagery that shaped and directed a Mage's will. In that place, he stood on barren ground, under a hot sun in a hazy-pale sky. All around him were tangled thornbushes. He stood on a path overgrown with them, and there was something up ahead that he couldn't see, in the midst of the thorns. He was pushing his way through, pushing; the thorns caught at his flesh and tore it until it bled.

Where were his robes, his mask? Here in his inner world, he didn't have them, only the light summer clothing he used to wear as a student in Hanilat. His staff . . . he still had his staff. He was still a Mage.

A Mage, and he had to reach the thing he knew was somewhere ahead of him. It was waiting for him, it needed to be found, but the thorns were keeping him away.

Then the inner landscape changed, and he saw the world through a double vision: He was in the wilderness of thorns, and at the same time he was in the workroom under the glaring white of the overhead light. He saw himself rising to his feet, and heard his voice saying, "The working needs power; who will match me?"

Across the Circle, he saw his Second rise, and Giesye answered, "I will."

The gel-vat in the center of the chalked circle impeded them for a few moments, but not for long; Giesye held her place, and Kief came around to meet her on the far side. They had scarcely come into fighting distance when he struck the first blow, coming in hard to his Second's leg—a blow meant to bruise and weaken, to leave the other limping for the rest of the fight, while the energy of their opposition built and built.

Giesye was fast, though, as fast in movement as in speech; she caught the blow on her staff and turned it aside. Kief's hand and arm vibrated with the impact as wood struck wood. Another heartbeat, and the Second was striking another blow. Kief's head would have been in its way, but he slipped aside and felt the rush of air against his cheek as the staff whistled past.

In among the thorns, he pushed onward. The bushes grew thicker there, and the ground was rising. The *eiran* twined in and out among the thorny branches, hanging over the bushes like tattered lace. He could see patterns in the lace, old patterns discarded and new ones half-complete. One of them had the brightness of the Institute's working threaded through it. Cords from that pattern led him deeper into the heart of the thorns.

He was bleeding now where the branches parted and swung back against him, or caught at him and tried to pull him down. A pain in his side . . . Giesye had gotten past his guard, a strong blow, ribs broken or worse. Power flowed out into the working, bright silver in all the patterns. His staff smashed against the Second's right arm, breaking bone—the arm hung limp. Giesye switched the staff to her left hand, trailing sparks of silver with the movement, and struck out at him again.

Kief fought his way through the overgrown thornbushes, holding on to the strong cable of the Institute's working, letting it support him as he pushed farther inward. A last ripping and tearing of the flesh, and he was there, looking down at what lay in the heart of the thorns.

Himself. Pale and unbreathing and empty.

Giesye's blows were near to driving him down. How long had they been fighting? Minutes? Hours? He couldn't tell. He opened himself up to the power in the *eiran* and let it fill him, then let the power out again in a last desperate strike against his partner and opponent.

As the universe wills.

He looked down at his own body, lying on bare rock amid the thorns, and saw moving across it the wheeling shadows of carrion birds circling overhead. If he lay there much longer, the scavengers would take him.

As the universe wills.

He did the necessary thing. This was dream and vision, and it was easy once he made the decision—slipping out of himself standing over himself, and seeing himself fade away into the patterns before the power of the *eiran* flowed into him and he stood up and walked away.

And rose from the gel-vat in the workroom, naked and cold in the sterile air. Two bodies lay on the floor, and red blood smeared the tiles beneath them. People came forward with sponges, with towels, with thick robes, washing and drying and warming him, as though his presence were something remarkable.

He stepped over to look down at the two lying on the

floor. When he spoke, his voice sounded unfamiliar to his ears. "Are they dead?"

"No." The physician? Yes. Him. "The medical *aiketen* can deal with all of their injuries. The problem is that until they wake, we don't know which one of them—well, which one of them is *you*."

He knelt. This body differed slightly in its proportions from the one he was used to. Reaching out to the nearer of the two lying on the floor, he turned the unconscious body over and took off its plastic hardmask. Curly hair; streaks of premature grey; earring.

"This one."

13:

ERAASI: HANILAT
ENTIBOR: AN-JEMAYNE
NIGHT'S-BEAUTIFUL-DAUGHTER: THE VOID

Grif Egelt was still fuming when he returned to his office at sus-Peledaen Hanilat headquarters. The fact that Natelth sus-Khalgath couldn't be bothered to work in the same building as everybody else in the fleet-family—which meant that Egelt had to travel halfway across the city and back again every time the head man wanted a personal report—only served to increase his dissatisfaction with the way the meeting had gone.

"What a right bastard!" Egelt snarled as soon as the doorway to the outer office closed behind him. "If I didn't . . ."

"Yeah, you'd quit," said his second-in-command. Hussav lacked Egelt's aspirations toward outer-family status—as an out-islander, and one from common working stock at that, he knew that his chances were limited enough to be in effect nonexistent—and Lord Natelth's moods and caprices bore less heavily on him as a result. "Other than explaining to you that he has a really big prick, what tidbits of information did our honored employer have for us?"

"He's got a picture of the kidnapper," Egelt said. He pulled the slide on the house-mind player, and brought up the image. Only quarter-size this time—Egelt didn't feel the need to impress anyone, unlike some people he could name. "So, what do you think?"

Hussav walked slowly around the hovering image, looking at it from all angles before answering. "With that face, he's not Hanilat-Eraasian, that's for sure."

"Not by blood, anyhow. Where he lives is another question."

"Too true. We wouldn't happen to know where the image came from, would we?"

Egelt shook his head. "Lady Isayana took some of the blood, but what she did with it after that . . . let's say that I don't want to know. That woman frightens me."

"You knew going in that talking to inner family was part of the job," said Hussav without sympathy. "And better you than me."

"You warm my heart, Jyriom." Egelt tapped the player, and brought up the associated data files that had accompanied the image. "What's important right now is the information our employer has so kindly provided."

"There's certainly a lot of it," Hussav said after a moment. "We can start doing match and switch with the public databases, but that'll take a long time."

"Look for connections," Egelt said. "Start with family members—the closer in, the better. Lady Isayana, for starters."

"Because she spooks you?"

"Because she stands to lose the most if His Anxiety takes a wife," Egelt said. "Check out everybody: inner-family, outer-family, allied families, in that order." He paused to draw himself a cup of yellow *uffa* from the office pot. The sharp, spicy smell rose up to tickle his nostrils. "And the same for all the girl's families as well."

"That'll go a lot quicker," said Hussav. "Most of them are dead."

"So what are you waiting for? We aren't getting paid by the hour here." Egelt pushed a button on his desk and spoke to the outer office. "I need a secure line to Public Order and I need everything from that raid in North Hanilat, and I need them both right now."

He drank some of the *uffa*. It was too hot and burned his

lips and tongue. The pain would give him something to think about while he waited for results to come back.

"Well, I'll be a greased rocklizard," Hussav said, not too much later. "Chief, have you ever thought of taking up with the Circles?"

"I prefer my head clear and my bones unbroken, thank you. What is it?"

"A hit," Hussav said. "Look. This guy here—sus-Dariv outer-family by current contract. Merchant-captain."

Egelt walked over to look at Hussav's results. "I don't suppose you know where he is right now, do you?"

"Grounded here in Hanilat not long ago. Apparently hung around doing typical pilot-things afterward—looking for a cargo, mostly. Right now . . . I'm working on it . . . right now he's at the port."

"Get him. Get him in here, as soon as . . . no, I'll go my-self. Don't let him—"

"Too late," Hussav said. "He's moving. His ship is head-ing for—hang on; let me figure it—heading for what looks like one of the smaller fields out in sus-Dariv territory. At least that's where he said he was going."

"Get people on him," Egelt said at once. "And let the orbital station know. Do not harm him, do not slow him, do not let him know that we're watching, but I want to know where he's going before he does, and I want to arrive there first, too."

"I can get you to the Antipodes and—Serpent Station, that's where he's going. By private flyer."

"Right, get me moving. And keep a link open to me, best speed. I'll need forces when I get there."

"In sus-Dariv territory? Good luck."

"Yeah, get the fleet-Circle on it, too. I'm so gone that 'gone' is still here in comparison."

And with that, Egelt left the office, headed for the family's field behind the Hanilat complex.

The workroom smelled of sweat, and the chemicals in the gel-vat, and blood. Environmental controls labored noisily to bring the air back down to a proper laboratory coolness and sterility, but so far they'd had little success. Kief's Mages still maintained their positions around the perimeter of the white circle, but the working no longer held them in its grip. They were bone-tired and fearful, and needed only the word of dismissal to send them home.

Two black-clad bodies lay, scarcely breathing, in the center of the circle next to the gel-vat. Kief stood over them, wrapped in the absorbent robe that Isayana and her tame physician had given to his replicant body when he first stepped naked from the vat. He bent down—still learning the reactions and dimensions of this new form—and picked up the Mage-staff from what had been his own hand only a few minutes ago.

His new hand found the smooth black wood unfamiliar to the touch, but his mind recognized the sensation of grasping it, and of moving it through the basic positions. The hands of this new body were narrower than the ones before, and not so heavy-boned in the wrists and knuckles, but they were strong and sinewy, with a good grip to them. The body itself felt tough and well coordinated; it didn't yet have the long-trained skills and reflexes of his old one, but—given time and work—it could learn.

He looked at his Circle-Mages. They'd seen him pick up his staff; they'd heard him name his old body as the one emptied out to fill Isayana's replicant. Now to see if they would acknowledge his authority in this form as well.

"You've done good work tonight," he said to them. "Go home now and rest."

The senior Mage under Giesye—perhaps he should be named Third, Kief thought, if the Circle was going to do more workings of this magnitude—stood up, a little unsteady on his feet. "Will you be well, *etaze?*"

"I will be well, Chei." Kief allowed himself to smile. The expression felt different on his new face. "Both of me, and Giesye as well. Be proud, all of you—our Circle has done a new thing tonight, and done it splendidly."

One by one, the Mages stood up and left the circle, moving stiffly and wearily after the long time spent kneeling. When they were gone, Kief went back to where Isayana and her physician stood. They also looked tired and worn, as if they had kept a long vigil, but with a profound satisfaction underlying their fatigue.

He caught Isayana's eye with some difficulty—he didn't think she quite thought of this new form as human yet—and gestured toward the two bodies lying at his feet. "Do you have a place here to care for them?"

"Yes," said Isayana. "I made certain to put in a full setup when I began this project. But—both of them? You aren't going to go back in?"

"I couldn't go back now even if I wanted to," he told her. "The working is over."

The physician was frowning at him. "Making the transfer nearly killed you and the other Mage—"

"Giesye. My Second."

"—and you're saying it's going to take the same thing to put you back?"

"Not the same thing." Kief shook his head, impatient at the other man's lack of basic understanding. For the first time in years, the movement didn't bring with it a touch of metal against his neck and jaw; his new body didn't have an earring to swing and tickle against his skin. "Every working is different."

"If you say so." The physician was frowning like a man who's discovered an ugly worm coiled up inside a favored fruit. "I don't think we have an efficient process here."

Isayana said, "Efficiency isn't the point. I'm not planning on mass production."

"I don't think I want to hear any more about that," the physician said hastily. "We're getting into the realm of things that aren't healthy for bystanders to know."

"You should have thought of that when you first got into this," Kief said. "The point is, I honestly don't know how long it will take before the Circles are ready for another working. This is research, remember—we don't know the answers when we start out."

Isayana clapped her hands once, bringing the *aiketen* forward out of the shadows in the corners of the room. She indicated the unconscious bodies of Kief and his Second. "Take those to the specialized care units. The female should recover within a day; the male will probably require long-term life support. See to it."

Kief found it an odd sensation to watch his former body being carried away from him by the *aiketen*. His hardmask lay on the floor where he had removed it from the body a few minutes earlier. On impulse, he picked it up and put it on. Once again, the workroom was overlaid with the dazzling patterns of the *eiran,* and tonight they were bright and new. Garrod's working hadn't vanished—he wasn't free of it yet—but his own workings were stronger now, and maybe, just maybe, he was beginning to see a way out of the tangle that Demaizen had caught him in all those years ago.

"I'll need a Mage's robes," he said. Saying so, he noticed for the first time that his feet were bare, and that the floor was cold. "Also some proper street clothing."

"It can be arranged," Isayana said. "I will instruct the *aiketen.*"

She went off to talk to one of the quasi-organic servitors, leaving Kief and the physician standing alone together next to the empty gel-vat.

"What are you going to do while you wait for the Circles to regain their strength?" the physician asked after a few moments of awkward silence.

"Watch the patterns in the universe," Kief said. As he spoke, he thought, unaccountably, of Arekhon sus-Khalgath . . . *there's another one who's caught in the web of the* eiran *like a spider's dinner. The same web, the same working— and 'Rekhe's trying to make it stronger while I'm trying to cut myself free. That's a pattern right there, and one I don't think I like.* "See what needs to be done. And do it."

When Elaeli returned to her town house in An-Jemayne, she found a note from Arekhon waiting for her there. He hadn't left one at the summer cottage. He'd risen from her bed in the pearl-grey light of early dawn and dressed without speaking, while she lay watching him from beneath half-closed lids. She was unwilling to say anything, for fear the sound would put to flight her memories of the hours that had gone before; and 'Rekhe's face was sad. When he was done putting on his clothes, he came back to the bedside, bent down, and kissed her once on her bare shoulder where the sheet fell down and exposed her skin. Then he turned and went away, and the bedroom door swung shut behind him.

She didn't hear from him again after that—it was like him, she reflected, to make a clean break regardless of his own feelings on the matter—and the letter on her desk came as a surprise. He'd written it by hand on the stiff off-white stationery he'd used for the past ten years as her chief of domestic security. The address on the envelope was in Entiboran lettering, but the sheet of paper inside was covered with the flowing loops and whorls of Eraasian script. She had to concentrate to read it; the written language she had learned as a child was less familiar to her now than the writing of this alien world.

Elaeli [he wrote]:

This may be the last letter I'll ever write to you. I *will* come back to you if I can, you have my word— but the pull of Garrod's working is very strong, and I can't see where it will take me before the end.

One or two practical matters: I'm leaving you without a head of domestic security, and you'll need to find somebody fairly soon. You can, of course, pick anyone you like; but you could do far worse than to promote your current acting head. I've left Venner full instructions, and if he can't handle the work then I haven't taught him properly.

As Arek Peldan, I still have some money left in my local accounts. I'd be grateful if you could exert your influence to see that those funds remain available—if not in perpetuity, then for as far into the future as possible. If the working somehow allows me to return, at least that way I won't be penniless when I arrive.

I owe you apologies, too many of them. I can't say that I'm sorry for loving you, but I *am* sorry that I was too selfish to let go of you once I went to Demaizen. You deserved—you have always deserved—far better of the universe than a lover whose loyalty could never be undivided; and if I had done then what was right,

Garrod would not have been able to make you into a tool for the great working.

And I'm sorry I left you without saying good-bye. I wanted too much to say all the things that I knew I shouldn't—that I wouldn't go, that I would always come back, that the sundered galaxy could stay in two halves forever, so long as the two of us were on the same side of it—and out of fear I chose to say nothing at all. By the time you read this, however, I'll be safely beyond temptation. I love you—have loved you—will love you, and the length and breadth and height of the galaxy make no difference to it.

Live in happiness, beloved, and be well.
Arekhon Khreseio sus-Khalgath sus-Peledaen.

Galley storage aboard *Night's-Beautiful-Daughter* was a cramped, closetlike space full of boxes and canisters strapped into place with cargo webbing. Ty and Narin had a list of the supplies taken on board for the *Daughter*'s previous journey across the interstellar gap—a thick bundle of printouts, all annotated in 'Rekhe's careful handwriting—and the two Mages were trying to match up all the remaining items with entries on the list.

"Freeze-dried *neiath* fruit, fifty-seven sealed foil packets," Narin said.

Ty consulted the printout. "There should be a hundred and twenty-three of them."

"Not in this compartment. And I don't think we're going to find them tucked under 'Rekhe's mattress along with his collection of filthy pictures, either."

"No," said Ty. "They just aren't here. And neither is anything else—at least not as much of it as we're going to need. I don't think anybody bothered to restock the galley after we crossed the gap the last time."

" 'Rekhe never planned on going back," Narin said. "My guess is, he only kept the ship because in his heart he's still sus-Peledaen, and those people never let ships go if they can help it."

"Maybe 'Rekhe thinks he's still sus-Peledaen, but I don't

believe anyone back on Eraasi does—not after his brother sent armed men out to kill him. Most people probably think that he's dead."

"You know that's not going to make a difference as far as 'Rekhe's concerned." Narin checked the label on the next box. "Powdered eggs. Twenty-five . . . fifty . . . a hundred and fifty-two single-serving pouches."

"Out of the hundred and sixty that we had to start with. We didn't like the eggs very much." Ty made a note on the printout. "What do you think is going to happen when we get to Eraasi?"

"I don't know. Something to do with the working—it has to be that, if it's pulling 'Rekhe back like this, and us with him."

"And Maraganha," said Ty. "It brought her, too." He set the printout aside, and lowered his voice even though he and Narin were alone. "What do you make of that one . . . is she what Arekhon claims she is?"

"You can read the *eiran* as well as I can," Narin said sharply. "She's a Void-walker and a great Magelord—and she was strong enough to find me in the Void and pull me out again, without even a proper Circle behind her. As to where she comes from, maybe Arekhon knows."

"If he does know," Ty pointed out, "he isn't telling."

"'Rekhe's always been closemouthed. Nothing new there."

"I'm not sure I like the way she looks at us sometimes," Ty said. "At me and you, that is. Like she's wondering if she already knows us from somewhere."

Narin shrugged. "She's a Void-walker. Maybe she does."

"You don't sound very worried about it."

"There's no point in worrying," Narin said. "It's all part of the working—that much we can both see—and when it's time for us to know the answer, we will. Meanwhile—"

"Yes?"

"Meanwhile, we need to find 'Rekhe and let him know we'll have to make a port call somewhere and take on supplies if he plans on making it back across the Gap."

◆

Iulan Vai had sent Herin down to Serpent Station ahead of her.

"I can manage things in Hanilat alone," she'd told him. "But the job down below doesn't need a highly trained Mage; it needs a family member, and you're the one we've got."

Getting to Serpent was easy, in spite of the fact that Herin didn't speak or read the Antipodean language. The signs along the route from the jumpshuttle port to the sus-Dariv base were clearly marked in Hanilat-Eraasian for the benefit of travelers from the main continent. It wasn't surprising, Herin decided, that Lenyat Irao had gone first to the sus-Dariv when he was looking for contracts. The family might not have mixed with the locals through intermarriage or adoption, but they'd put enough money into the subcontinent's economy over the years to count as some sort of connection.

Herin wondered now if that connection would be enough. They should have started bringing people like Len into the outer family years ago—with a firm Antipodean power base, Zeri wouldn't have needed to go begging to the sus-Peledaen when the world fell apart. Now it lacked only the wedding night, and the sus-Peledaen would own everything.

Don't let him find you, Zeri. Trust us. We have another plan.

We hope we have another plan.

Getting inside the station perimeter had been easy; Serpent wasn't a high-security base. Once past the gate, Herin looked about him with a Mage's eyes, remembering Vai teaching him, giving him quick instructions in a bare apartment back in Hanilat: *Look for the patterns in the* eiran. *They won't lie to you, even if everything else is a fake and a setup and a trap.*

Keeping her admonition in mind, he catalogued the ships on the field. Two partial hulks, being disassembled for scrap and parts—no help there, with the *eiran* fading into transparency around them. A courier, grounded. A couple of planet-to-orbit shuttles, likewise. Base insignia on one, but ship's insignia on the other: *Garden-of-Fair-Blossoms*. And the *eiran* covered the *Garden*'s shuttle like silver curtains of knotwork and lace.

Yes.

Herin had not forgotten Lenyat Irao's story. He would investigate the shuttle, he thought, before speaking to anyone at Serpent Station. What he did after that might well depend on what he found inside.

He moved quietly across the hard-baked earth of the landing field. He already knew the physical tricks of not being seen; now he used the *eiran* as well, threading his way among the cords in such fashion as to make an observer—if there was one—look at every place and every thing except him. When he reached the shuttle, he saw that its outer hatch stood open. Still hidden and obscured, he drifted inside.

The shuttle was, on first glance, empty—nothing in the cockpit, nothing in the passenger compartment. He ventured onward, into the cargo bay. There he found a large oblong container, waist-high, its heavy lid gaping open on massive hinges. He recognized the object as a stasis box, a new development for transporting high-value perishable cargo, still in the testing phase aboard selected sus-Dariv vessels. All the versions he'd ever heard or read about were energy-hungry to an extreme degree; the question in the family's collective mind had been whether any cargoes existed that were simultaneously small enough, short-lived enough, and wanted enough to be worth the expense of running the box.

Garden-of-Fair-Blossoms, it appeared, had found something after all. The ship-mind had apparently directed the vessel's *aiketen* to put the lone survivor of the sus-Peledaen attack into the stasis box and had brought her home.

Herin felt a certain amount of guilty relief at the thought. If the *Garden*'s survivor had passed through, or remained at, Serpent Station, his present task would be a great deal easier.

He left the shuttle and followed the brightest strand of the *eiran* across the field to a low, stucco-covered building with blocky environmental control units on top of its flat roof. The thick glass door had a keycard lock. Herin pulled a card out of the inner pocket of his lightweight jacket—even that much extra clothing had him sweltering in the baking heat of Serpent Station, but he preferred looking like an out-of-

place main-continent tourist to forgoing the storage and concealment opportunities the jacket offered him.

The card was a general-purpose family keycard, but one
with levels of access that would have surprised a number of
people, had they happened to still be alive. With luck—and
he'd been making an effort, these past few weeks, to tend to
his luck and treat it properly—Serpent Station had been dragging its collective feet about changing over to the sus-
Peledaen codes.

*They don't technically have to do it until the wedding's
finished. Here's hoping they're holding out until the last possible minute.*

He slid the keycard into the lock.

The door opened; he retrieved his keycard and stepped
inside. The room was dark and shadowy after the glare of
the outside, and full of cool—no, cold—air. The personnel
at Serpent Station had apparently taken to heart the notorious
Antipodean belief that environmental controls weren't doing
their job properly unless you could shiver in midsummer and
sweat in the winter. As Herin's eyes adjusted to the lower
light, he began making out objects in the dimness: cabinets,
chairs, a desk, a nameplate.

AELBEN WINCEYT SYN-DARIV. PORT-CAPTAIN, SERPENT
STATION.

Outer-family, Herin thought. *But not senior enough to rate
an invitation to the annual meeting, or he wouldn't still be
here.*

Well, he's senior now.

The door to a back room opened, and an officer emerged—
probably the Port-Captain, from the piping on his livery. Before the door swung closed again, Herin caught a glimpse of
more fleet-livery and heard muffled voices in what sounded
like tense argument, and for an instant there was a bright
unexpected flare of silver around the edges of everything.
Ride the luck, he thought, and took a wild guess.

"Plotting mutiny, Port-Captain?"

He heard the outer door opening again behind him, and
knew without turning that there was somebody at his back
with a weapon.

He didn't bother to look around. The person he needed to

talk to was standing in front of him: a sandy-haired man i
youngish middle age, with worried lines on his face. Heri
wondered what twist of fate had given Aelben Wincey
outer-family status and then relegated him to an isolate
ground command. Was he a failure left here to rot, or wa
he an up-and-comer stashed in an undemanding billet whil
greater things were being prepared for him? A great dea
might depend on the answer in the next few hours.

"I think you'd better explain what exactly you mean b
that," the Port-Captain said. "Quickly. Your name?"

"Herin Arayet sus-Dariv. You can take a fingerprint an
blood and match me against the family database if you like
Of course," he added, "it'll probably say that I'm dead, bu
you can see how that might be convenient under the circum
stances."

"Yerris!" the Port-Captain called out. "Fetch the ID kit!
He turned back to Herin. "I'm inclined to believe you, but–
under the circumstances, as you say—it's probably best t
be sure."

"I quite understand."

The door to the back room opened again, and a youn
man in fleet-livery—presumably Yerris—brought forwar
the ID kit and linked it to the Port-Captain's desk. Heri
waited out the process in silence—the thumb-pad, the pin
prick, the flashing telltales as the kit and the databases syn
chronized—the *eiran* in this place were bright and steady
and he was fairly certain this meant he was doing the righ
thing.

*I suppose I'll get used to making decisions this way even
tually.*

Winceyt smiled. "Syr Arayet. Allow me to congratulat
you on not being dead, in spite of what the ID kit wants u
to believe." The Port-Captain nodded toward the unseen per
son with a weapon standing at Herin's back, and the sensa
tion of being in the line of fire faded away. "I don't suppos
I need to bother updating the database with a correction."

"No. The longer I'm officially a casualty of the Court o
Two Colors disaster, the better for everybody concerned."

"You're still working in the family's interest, then."

"I do the best I can. And you—I believe I asked you a question a few minutes ago. About mutiny."

"Talk," said Winceyt. "Lots of talk, especially since the *Garden* showed up with nothing but the ship-mind in charge. We sent up a shuttle, and found the *Garden*'s own boat already loaded and waiting for us with that damned stasis box aboard."

"Survivors?" Herin knew the answer, but he asked anyway—they wouldn't expect him to know, and besides, they might have information he didn't.

"Just the one, and she's still rocky." The Port-Captain's expression changed to one of frustrated anger. "But when she named the sus-Peledaen as killers outright, we knew we couldn't give them our ships, no matter what kind of marriage-bargain Lady Zeri's made for us."

"Have you got anything planned yet?"

Winceyt shrugged. "There aren't all that many options, unfortunately. We've been arguing ourselves into torching the groundside structures, then putting everything into orbit that will lift and setting the self-destruct charges."

"What if I told you there was a better way out of this than a display of wedding fireworks?"

"What do you mean?"

"I mean that Lord Natelth doesn't get your base or your ships until after his wedding night, and he hasn't had a wedding night yet because he seems to have lost track of his bride."

Amazing, Herin thought, *how sudden hope can smooth out the lines on a man's face.*

"Where is she?" Winceyt demanded.

"Lady Zeri will be arriving here very shortly—followed not long after, unless we are very fortunate, by sus-Peledaen ground security. If I were you, Port-Captain, I'd start working on some new plans right now."

14:

Winter wasn't the best time of the year at Arvedan
House. All the fields were grey and stubbled, and the trees
were bare. The sky this morning was even greyer than the
fields, and full of a harsh, gusty wind that drove before it
rain turning to spitting snow. The drops plittered and hissed
against the windows of the study where Inadal syn-Arvedan
had taken refuge from the day outside.

In spite of the foul weather, he was glad to be back in his
home district, away from the intrigues and dangers of Hanilat. He had chosen to spend the day restoring his tranquility
of mind by going through his cache of unread scientific
farming journals and planning ahead for the spring. Trade
and starships might be all they thought of in Hanilat, but
without the food grown in places like Arvedan, even the
great fleet-families would perish.

Even the sus-Peledaen, he thought, *and Isayana is right
that her brother is a fool for not seeing it.*

Nevertheless, the food had to be grown, sus-Peledaen or
no sus-Peledaen, and if Eraasi was heading into another period of unrest like the troubles of a decade ago, some of the
farming districts would fall short of their usual production

He wondered if it would be a good idea to add some more planting and harvest *aiketen* to the ones already at work on the family's various estates, in case Arvedan needed to help make up the shortfall.

Del would have had an opinion, he thought, and wondered if giving Del more of a say in the management of the family lands would have kept him from going off to the Mages and finding his death at Demaizen Old Hall. The twinge of guilt was an old one by now; he felt relief when his line of thought was interrupted by the buzzing of the voice comm on his desk.

He laid aside the journal and crossed the room to pick up the handset. "syn-Arvedan. Hello."

"This is Isayana."

She had never used the voice comm before in communicating with him, only written notes. He'd gotten the impression she didn't trust anything else. That was wrong, apparently. Maybe she was merely . . . eccentric. That was it. Eccentric.

"What—" he began, then started over. "Has something gone wrong?"

"No," she said, and he realized that the unfamiliar note in her voice was not fear or worry, or even madness, but satisfaction. "Nothing's wrong. I thought you might like to hear that we've succeeded."

We've succeeded.

Inadal thought back to the basement workroom, and the sheets of plans and drawings. Something had come of them after all. Something that moved and walked and thought like a human being. *Exactly* like. He wasn't sure that he was as happy as he should be about this.

We've succeeded.

"Do you need me in Hanilat?" he asked.

"No. Everything went well."

"How did you . . . ah . . . animate the replicant?"

"I didn't; I had a Mage-Circle do the work. One of them is currently filling the replicant."

Filling the replicant. Inadal thought about the ways something like that might have been done. Things Del had said, on rare occasions, about the body and the self and the Void.

Inadal had never understood them, really; now he wished that he had tried harder at the time.

He seized on the first detail that came to mind and asked, "You aren't planning to *keep* him that way, are you?"

He thought he heard a faint hint of laughter at his anxiety when Isayana replied, "No. His proper body is being well cared for against his return. But this was a difficult working—not a great working; nobody died; just hard—and the Circles aren't going to be up to another effort like that for a month or so at least."

"And what happened to the . . ." He paused, searching for the right word. ". . . the original? The person you replicated?"

"Nothing." Isayana's answer this time was quick and terse. "So far as we know, he's fine."

Something isn't being talked about here, Inadal thought. "What do you mean, 'so far as you know'? Aren't you going to keep an eye on him?"

"It isn't necessary. The process doesn't involve the original at all, once the necessary sample material is obtained."

And where did you get the sample material, Lady Isayana? The wind outside the manor house pushed hard against the windows, rattling the panes in their wooden frames. Long streaks of rain ran down the outside of the glass like cold fingers. The study should have been warm, not frozen like the landscape outside, but the winter chill kept getting in anyway.

I should have kept Del here, Inadal thought, *and never pushed him off to join the Mages. Del wouldn't have thought what I'm thinking now.*

"I see," he said finally. "Are you planning to tell your brother about your success?"

"Of course not. You and I still have our agreement."

He pushed again. "Does word of this go to any of the other fleet-families?"

"No."

"Then—if we plan on keeping the secret and using it later—is it wise to allow the original and the replicant free movement while they both exist?"

There was a thoughtful silence on the other end of the comm line. Finally, Isayana said: "No. If anybody happens to see the original and the replicant close together—or if they're seen at the same time by different people in different places—we lose the advantage of being the only ones who know that such a thing can be done."

Fire-on-the-Hilltops set down on the burnt earth of Serpent Station field in a roar of maneuvering jets. As soon as the ground had cooled, the *Fire*'s main hatch opened to disgorge the captain and the passengers.

Zeri had never traveled to the Antipodes before, though she knew the family had bases there, and her first impression of Serpent Station was of scattered ships and buildings dotted across a vast stretch of empty land—hot, dry, and rocky. By contrast, the main station building turned out to be dim and cold, and full of sus-Dariv fleet personnel apparently bent on suicide.

"You were going to do *what* if I hadn't turned up?"

She was angry. She hadn't expected to be, but she was— angry enough that she had made a deliberate effort to keep her voice from scaling upward with sudden outrage. A small sane corner of her mind reflected that all the hours she'd spent working on amateur and sometimes professional theatrics hadn't been wasted after all; she could keep the pitch down and make herself heard in the back row and the top of the gallery.

At close range, apparently, the effect was scathing. The Port-Captain flinched. "Set the self-destruct charges. The ones that—"

"—that give a ship honorable farewell. I know what they are."

In her peripheral vision, Zeri could see Cousin Herin looking worried, and Iulan Vai—still in her snug black bodysuit, but minus the mask and glitter—looking more amused than anything else. Lenyat Irao stood several paces away, with his arms folded; this was a family quarrel, his expression said clearly, and he wasn't family.

She drew a deep breath. "I made a bargain with the sus-Peledaen in order to preserve what was left of our ships and our family, not to see them blasted into wreckage. You would have made that bargain into *nothing*."

Port-Captain Winceyt looked chastened. "I am sorry, my lady. But suspicion is one thing, and knowledge is another. Once we heard the truth from a witness, it wasn't possible for us to contemplate becoming syn-Peledaen."

Her surge of anger was already starting to ebb, leaving only weariness and resignation behind.

"As it happens," she said, "I feel the same way. But if my cousin and Syr Vai between them hadn't come up with a better idea, I would have married Lord Natelth all the same. It wasn't a good plan, but it was the only plan anybody had."

Len Irao spoke up for the first time since they'd entered the building. "I don't think Lord Natelth would have been very happy on the morning after, once he found out that all his new-wedded ships had blown themselves to pieces instead of changing their colors from green-and-yellow to blue-and-crimson."

"Fortunately," Iulan Vai pointed out, "Syr Arayet arrived in time to keep our friends from unnecessary self-immolation. Tell them about the new plan, Herin."

Herin stepped forward and looked around at all of them with an attention-gathering glance—very much like a teacher, Zeri thought—and said, "It's this way. If we decide that there isn't going to be a finished wedding—"

"I decided *that* when I went out the window with Lenyat, back in Hanilat," Zeri said. She liked her cousin, and she was glad that he had escaped the disaster at the Court of Two Colors, but that was no reason to let his newfound Magery go to his head. "And it's not as if I can turn back now. Go on."

"If there's no finished wedding," Herin said, "and no formal union of the fleets, then something has to be done about the ships and crews. Otherwise, the sus-Peledaen will simply take them and not bother holding to the agreement made in your marriage contract. The self-destruct charges were one way to handle it, but we have a plan that we hope is somewhat better. To start with—*Fire-on-the-Hilltops* leaves Serpent Station sometime in the next hour, and we don't tell you where we're going. That way, when the sus-Peledaen security forces show up and start asking you pointed questions about our destination, you can honestly tell them that you don't know."

Port-Captain Winceyt looked unimpressed. "We could have thought of that much all by ourselves. What makes this plan special?"

"Because," said Herin, "as soon as the sus-Peledaen strongarms go away again, you take everything from Serpent Station that can lift, head for high orbit, and go from there into the Void."

Winceyt shook his head. "I won't lie to you, Syr Arayet—between a blind transit and the self-destruct charges, I know which one I'd pick for a clean ending."

"You won't be making the transit blind, any more than the *Fire* will be," Herin told him. "We'll pass you all the necessary star-chart data—and when Syr Vai is done with you, you won't remember that the data exist until after the sus-Peledaen have taken their bullyboys and gone home."

Zeri looked curiously at Iulan Vai. "You can do that?"

"At least three different ways," Vai assured her, "and two of them don't need a Mage's hand in them at all."

"One last thing," Herin said. "Nobody lifts from Eraasi who isn't willing. Because none of the sus-Dariv who leave are coming back."

Llannat Hyfid wasn't surprised, once the *Daughter* entered the Void, when Narin Iyal sought her out in the privacy of the meditation chamber. She'd locked the door earlier, but the Eraasian Mage was no more to be kept out by physical barriers than Llannat herself was. Opening a locked door was discourteous, but Narin had not struck Llannat as a person who committed discourtesies without good reason. Presumably, thought Llannat, she had a good reason now.

Llannat knelt in the white circle on the floor of the chamber, her staff lying in front of her on the painted deck. Narin came into the circle and knelt opposite her. Narin's staff was black bound with silver, in a style not dissimilar to Llannat's own.

"This isn't the time for a working," Llannat said. She

didn't think the Eraasian Mage had come for that purpose, but it never hurt to be sure.

"I'm not interested in your workings, *etaze*," Narin said. "But we need to talk."

"Yes," said Llannat. "We do—but please, call me by my name. Too much deference makes me wake up in the mornings wondering who I really am."

Narin's mouth quirked slightly in what might have been a smile. "I've been in that position myself. I didn't like it much."

"How did you handle it?"

"I quit the job and left."

"Unfortunately," said Llannat, "I can't do that. So I hope you can convince yourself to humor me instead."

Again the half-smile. "I'll try."

"Good enough. Now—you said we had to talk?"

"Yes." Narin stretched out a hand to indicate Llannat's staff without touching it. "This one and 'Rekhe's—"

"—are alike? I know."

Narin shook her head. "They're more than alike. They're the same."

"You've noticed that, have you?"

"I'm surprised that 'Rekhe hasn't," Narin said.

"He can't afford to notice it. So he doesn't."

"I see," said Narin. "Tell me one more thing: Do you mean Arekhon sus-Khalgath any harm?"

"Believe me," Llannat told her, "I wouldn't have traveled across time and the Void for the sake of something as essentially petty as all that. Which means you can stop thinking about the knife in your boot and enjoy the trip."

Egelt headed south in the private sus-Peledaen flyer that his rank as chief of security allowed him to requisition. Along the way he radioed back to the sus-Peledaen ground office and spoke with Hussav. "I'm en route to Serpent Station— I'm going to see if I can persuade them to tell me what's going on down there. If we can manage this without getting rough, in the long run everyone will be happier."

"Right," said Hussav. "Want me to start checking that picture against anything?"

"We'll know when I get there. Put a team together to escort our missing friends back home, but do it quietly. We don't need the boss to get any maybe-mistaken ideas about how close we are."

"No disappointment for the boss. Check."

Egelt broke the transmission, and settled back in his seat. Off to his left, the sky was going grey. He'd had a long night after a long day, and if he called ahead he'd alarm a number of people whose loyalties, in all likelihood, remained uncertain. No sense in telling them how close pursuit was—assuming that it was close. But if the mysterious kidnapper had fled to Serpent Station, there was always a chance that he'd needed the extra time on the ground to pick up fuel and supplies outside the Hanilat surveillance net, and hadn't yet left Eraasi.

Egelt called Hussav again. "Do we have any guardships orbiting over or close to Serpent?" He'd long ago committed to memory those portions of the family's defense and security structure that fell into his formal area of responsibility—but he hadn't needed to know about the family's space defenses until now. He felt his ignorance keenly, and promised himself that he would take steps to rectify it as soon as the current problem had resolved itself one way or the other.

"You want me to call up the Fleet-Captain?" Hussav asked. "Do you know what time it is?"

"I'm painfully aware of what time it is. Consider that closing the ports may not be one hundred percent effective, and that we're dealing with people who may not ask permission to leave."

"I'll see what I can do. What message do you want me to pass along?"

"Tell Fleet-Captain sus-Mevyan I consider flight from the southern zone to be a possibility, and that she should be prepared to block, board, and capture anyone who makes the attempt."

"Right."

Egelt sat back again, and tried to close his eyes. There was nothing else to do right now, so he might as well sleep. The red plush of the seat was inviting, even if the hum and whistle of the atmospheric passage wasn't especially conducive to sleep or anything else. Just the same, no sooner had he stretched his back and composed his mind than the flyer's pilot came on over the intercom.

"We're on approach to sus-Dariv control. They're asking us what we want."

"Tell them we want to land and inspect their field," Egelt said. "Since the marriage we have the right to do so, and I'm exercising that right."

"I'll relay," the pilot said. A moment later he was back. "The sus-Dariv want to know if you know what time it is."

"Doesn't anyone on this planet own a pocket watch?" Egelt demanded "Tell them yes, I know what time it is, that this is a matter of some urgency, and that I want someone with decision-making power awake and ready to talk with me on my arrival."

"They won't like that."

"Our likes and theirs aren't of much concern to the ones who cut our paychecks," Egelt said. "How long until we land?"

"Couple of minutes. Strap in if you aren't already."

"No rest, and no help for it. I'm wrapped and strapped."

The landing was no more bumpy than usual, and the air when the door was opened no more breathable than he expected. It was hot and bone-dry, like stepping face-first into a brick oven, and it smelled of smoke and burnt clay. A young man in sus-Dariv colors with his tunic misbuttoned stood outside the safety perimeter.

"I'm here because a ship arrived here from Hanilat a few hours ago," Egelt began before he was fully down the ramp. "I want to visit that ship, if I may."

"This is most irregular," the young man said. "From Hanilat, you say?"

"Yes. Did a ship arrive?"

"Perhaps before I came on duty? Come with me to Control," the young man said. His nametag read YERRIS, and he'd pinned it on upside down. "We can look at the logs and see where it is, if there is one."

Control was a one-story building at the edge of the field

with no windows on the field side, and it was locked. Yerris opened it with a keycard. The lights came on as they entered.

"Isn't there anyone on duty in here?" Egelt asked. "Who did my pilot talk to on approach?"

"Oh, that's the surface side," Yerris said. "This is ships' operations. You asked about a ship?"

"Yes, I did. But the one I'm looking for would have come point-to-point surface. Maybe we should ask at surface control."

"Of course, sir, you're quite right. Let me call them." Yerris left the room, and the door swung shut behind him.

Egelt waited. A few seconds later, the air around him and the floor beneath him rumbled and vibrated, and the windows on the side of the building away from the port lit up with the glaring orange of reflected light. Someone out there was lifting ship—Egelt turned, and pushed on the door. Locked.

A few minutes later, the door opened, and Yerris stood there, still looking frowsty and misbuttoned and shaking his head. "I'm sorry, sir; no ship arrived from Hanilat last night."

"You know that we'll be able to track the arrivals and departures," Egelt said. "What was that launch just now?"

Yerris blinked. "Launch, sir? An engine test over in the yards."

"Really?" Egelt had decided when he saw the orange flare of liftoff that Yerris couldn't possibly be as stupid as he was acting, not and remain in a fleet-family's employ. "If what you've said isn't true, things will go hard with you people now that you're sus-Peledaen."

"We aren't sus-Peledaen until after the wedding night," Yerris said. "That hasn't happened yet, has it? We'd have had word."

Definitely not as stupid as he's acting, Egelt thought. *And he knows entirely too much.*

But all he said was "Thank you for your time. I suppose it wouldn't be helpful for me to show you some pictures and ask if you'd seen certain people?"

"My time is yours. I'd be happy to look at the pictures."

"At some future point," Egelt said, feeling certain that if Yerris was that willing to look at his pictures, the pictures weren't likely to do any good. "Right now it's time for me to leave."

"You won't be staying for breakfast? Port-Captain Winceyt will be disappointed. We so seldom get visitors from Hanilat."

"My compliments to the captain," Egelt said. "And please inform him that he'll certainly be my guest in Hanilat, soon."

Yerris gave no sign of noticing the veiled threat. "Of course, sir. Will there be anything else?"

"Nothing, for now," Egelt said. "I'll find my own way back to my flyer."

As soon as he was in the air, he contacted Hussav again at the Hanilat office. "Anything happen while I was out of range?"

"I got in contact with the fleet. No guardships in place around the south. But listen to this: I've gotten a report from the orbiters that there was a launch from down there, a few minutes ago."

"I know. I saw it. Has he headed for a jump point?"

"I don't know."

"Find out. Get the fleet to board him if they can. And while you're doing that, get a guardship assigned to us, and get us an unlimited letter of credit, and pack a bag. We're going traveling."

"Traveling?"

"When Lord Natelth finds out that we've let his bride slip off to space, I want to be a long way away and already on the job of tracking her down. Pack a bag for me, too, and be at the spaceport when I get there."

Egelt settled back into his seat again, while the sky to his right went pink, then bright and blue. Try as he might, he still couldn't get to sleep.

Kief attracted little notice as he made his way home from Isayana's workplace. Mages were no oddity in Hanilat, even Mages robed for a working, and masks were all the fashion these days. His own building always had Mages coming and going at odd hours, since his Circle did most of its ordinary workings there; the neighbors were used to it, and one more Mage, as they might see it, wouldn't matter.

His new body, now that he had dressed it properly in street clothes, robes, and a hardmask, felt much less alien. The world still looked odd; this body was slightly taller than the old one, and the angles on things were different. Sounds were different also, sharper and more distinct, and he realized that this body had better hearing as well.

The door to his apartment had a cipher lock. He laughed under his breath as he entered the keycode. It was a good thing he hadn't wasted money on one of the new blood-and-thumbprint high-security models. He could force one of those, if he had to, but he preferred not to do it for his own apartment. If he did, he'd probably break the lock anyway.

Inside the apartment, everything was bare and dusty as always. He'd never been a man to care about personal possessions, not since the Old Hall burned, and having none to speak of gave him less to worry about.

He hung up his robe and hardmask on their customary peg, and went into the kitchen. He knew that he should be hungry after such a working, but he wasn't, and a sudden flash of insight told him why: His new body had been nourished until scarcely two hours ago in Isayana's gel-vat, needing nothing.

The image and the realization together sickened him. He gripped the edge of the counter, knuckles white—*breathe in; breathe out*—willing down the unexpected nausea. After what felt like a long time, the ringing in his ears subsided and the dots that swirled in his field of vision like angry insects faded and went away.

With the waning of the sickness, however, came knowledge: If he didn't eat something right now, and force himself to become accustomed to taking ordinary nourishment, he would keep on avoiding the very thought of it. And this body—*his* body—would waste and die.

Lady Isayana needs to know that there is a chance of this, he thought; *that it must be guarded against.*

The preserving-cupboard in the kitchen held bread and sliced meat. He took out a quarter-portion of each, and forced himself to eat them slowly. He found no pleasure in the meal; eating it was like chewing and swallowing pulped paper. At least he was able to finish the bread and meat without his body turning against him, and the next time would be easier.

With the unwanted food lying heavy in his stomach, he went to bed. He stretched out fully clothed on top of the covers and lay staring up at the ceiling. Mind and spirit were both exhausted, but his body refused to take the offered rest. Too tired to meditate, too spent to put his intention behind anything at all, he drifted.

The silver cords of the *eiran* shifted and changed against the shadows above him, and he made no effort to touch them. He only watched. He saw his own working, and Garrod's working, and all the myriad lesser workings of a galaxy filled with Circles. They shifted and spun and connected and parted again, and he felt himself being pulled inexorably from his place of rest into the dance of the patterns.

Somebody's out there, he thought. Somebody was working the luck, and something about the working had called to him, had drawn him out of even this strange exhausted stupor. He could almost believe that the Mage was someone from the old days at Demaizen—no other Circle had ever held him as strongly, for good or ill, not even his own—except that all of Demaizen's Mages were dead or exiled. He would have to investigate—so strong a tie was dangerous—but not now, he was too tired—and the voice comm was shrilling on the bedstand by his ear.

Coming fully back to consciousness was like surfacing from deep water. He fumbled for the handset. "Diasul."

"Kiefen *etaze.*" It was Isayana's voice. "I'm sorry to disturb you at this late hour—"

Late? he thought groggily, and looked over at the windows. It was dark outside; he must have slept after all. "It's all right."

"That's good. I need you to come back here for a little while, *etaze,* to make a proper report on the filling process while it's fresh in your mind. I should have thought of it earlier and asked you to stay—but frankly, I was so head-in-the-clouds over the fact that everything had actually worked that I simply forgot."

"I understand." Though he didn't, not really. Isayana had struck him at their first meeting as the kind of person who never forgot anything. Of course, he'd never before seen her on a day when she had accomplished something new in the universe. "I'll come."

"There's no need to trouble yourself with riding the public transport at this hour," Isayana said. "Wait where you are, and I'll send one of the family's groundcars over with a driver."

He closed the connection and sat on the edge of the bed, deep in thought. He remembered that he didn't know Isayana, not well—but one of the things he *did* remember about her was that she was capable of working against someone who had every natural reason to expect her loyalty.

Also, she was Arekhon's sister—*and face it,* Kief said to himself, *'Rekhe could talk rocks and stones into behaving unwisely if it suited his purpose.*

Thoughts of betrayal made him remember another day, long ago now, when armored vehicles came growling up the road to Demaizen Old Hall, and armed men poured out of them to kill Garrod and Del and Serazao. Only luck had saved him then, and he suspected—he believed—that it was time for him to make his own luck now.

He rose from the bed, put back on his robes and mask, and slipped out into the dark.

15:

The sus-Peledaen courier ship *Last-Day-of-Summer* hung in high orbit over Eraasi, awaiting the signal to depart. The *Summerday* was a small runner, set for light and fast cargoes, designed to travel without a large fleet escort. It was cramped, at least compared to the large merches, but comfortable enough.

Under normal circumstances—which these were not—the *Summerday* would be used for security and for message carrying, not for passenger transport. The pilot had been articulate on the subject, to say the least, and more than a little disgruntled when the pair of high-level operatives from family security answered his complaints with an equally high-level authorization chit.

Egelt and Hussav didn't care about the pilot's opinion one way or the other. They had problems of their own, and they had to come up with solutions for them soon. They stood on the *Summerday*'s cramped bridge and spoke to each other in a tense undertone.

"Well," Hussav said, "our boy definitely made his Void-translation and took the lady with him. So what are we going to do now?"

"What we've been doing. Follow him."

"The boss won't be happy—finding out that he can say 'Shut the spaceports!' all he likes, but not everybody is going to listen."

Egelt grimaced. "That's one reason I like the idea of being under way."

"What if he recalls you, wants you to give your report?"

"I'll tell him that I don't want to lose the momentum of the case, and that he should hang tight."

"*That'll* go over well."

"I've always wanted to be a beachcomber anyway," Egelt said. He took a step forward to look out of the forward bridge window, even though the pilothouse was so small that it hardly rated the title of "bridge." There wasn't anything outside the window but black space and stars—Eraasi wasn't visible from this angle. The view helped Egelt to think clearly, though, and to make plans that weren't shadowed by worry about the whims and the temper of Lord Natelth sus-Khalgath sus-Peledaen.

"Give me a minute," he said, looking out at the distant stars. "Let's see. Our boy's probably going to Aulwikh. Main port is Firreka. Nice place, big enough to get lost in, no sus-Dariv interests to draw our attention. It's on his arc. So we'll go to Aulwikh. But in case he's pulling a fast one, I'm going to get some help. Messenger drone to every system, house cipher, with pictures of the malefactor—the one Lady Isa generated, and the matching images our people pulled out of port security—a description of his ship, a description of the happy bride, and a request to send replies to me at Firreka on Aulwikh."

"The boss won't like having his shame discussed on all of the settled planets, not to mention most of the unsettled ones."

"The idea you're groping for is 'apoplexy,'" Egelt said. "As in, if he drops dead of one, his sister will succeed, and she's reasonable. But if Lord Natelth truly wants his new-wed lady back—well, when we show up in his office with her, he'll be so grateful that he'll kiss us, and never mind the methods we used to do it."

"You hope."

"I hope. So, anyway, let me get busy. I want the messages away before we jump, and I want to jump for Aulwikh soon. The longer we delay, the colder the trail will get."

It was still night outside when Kief left the apartment. He kept to the shadows—his working robes were dark, and should suffice to keep him obscured from watching eyes. He didn't want to expend energy on hiding himself from view if he didn't have to, not when he remained exhausted in mind and spirit from the rigors of the working.

He supposed it was possible that Isayana had been telling him the truth—that Arekhon's sister had only wanted to get his report on the filling process, and not to capture and detain him indefinitely. But Kief was neither optimistic nor trusting, and hadn't been for years. As far as he was concerned, his best course of action was to make certain he was elsewhere when the sus-Peledaen groundcar arrived.

But which elsewhere? He couldn't run to his own Mages for help. Kief was the First of their Circle; it was his responsibility to take care of the unranked Mages, not the other way around. And the sus-Peledaen enforcers would be certain to check the Circles before they looked anywhere else. Nevertheless, he had to find a place, somewhere he could go to ground for a few hours until he either figured out a long-term plan of escape or decided that Isayana sus-Khalgath wasn't a threat.

His legs hurt; this new body wasn't yet accustomed to traveling long distances on foot. He glanced around, and saw that he'd walked all the way from his apartment to the grounds of the Hanilat Institute while he was lost in thought.

Kief had been a Mage too long to ignore the obvious. There was at least one place on the Institute's campus that would welcome him. He'd been there—had it been only a day ago now? It seemed much longer. Shaking off the urge to ponder the relationship between time and experience, he headed for the Institute Towers, and within minutes was tapping the code for Ayil syn-Arvedan's apartment into the front-door pad.

After a short wait, he heard a sleepy but familiar voice come over the annunciator. "Who's there?"

"Ayil? It's me. Kief."

"Again? I thought you'd gone back to wherever it is you're living these days."

"Things—happened. Can you put me up for the night?"

"Of course." She sounded puzzled but agreeable. "Come on up."

The front door opened, and shut again behind him. He took the elevator up to Ayil's apartment, and pressed the entry-button. The apartment door opened and showed him Ayil standing there in a night-robe, yawning and hair all awry.

"Come in; come in," she said. He entered, and she closed the door again behind him, saying as she did so, "You could have stayed here overnight in the first place, you know. I'd have lent you a key."

"I'd have asked, believe me, if I'd expected to need it. There was a working, and—" he shrugged "—like I said, things happened."

He knew that the next part couldn't be put off any longer; she was already regarding his masked face with a puzzled expression. The Institute apartments, as he recollected from his student days, were reasonably soundproof. He took off his hardmask and threw back the hood of his robe.

She didn't scream, only caught her breath quickly and followed up that slight gasp with a long, long stare, looking him up and down. He should have expected that; but it was always easy to forget that under Ayil's mild and innocuous surface lay a first-class mind.

"Kiefen Diasul," she said finally.

"Yes. Despite appearances."

"If it's really you—tell me what was I thinking about working on before I decided that studying interstellar gas clouds would actually result in more useful data and less unproductive theory?"

"The sundering of the galaxy," he said. "Root and proximate causes."

It was a good question. Ayil had played with the topic over a period of about six months, but she'd never taken it past the talking-in-the-office stage—too much mysticism and not enough fact, she'd said at the time.

He smiled in spite of himself. "You told me that the Teleological and Cosmological Studies Departments had their hooks in the topic and weren't going to let it go."

"It *is* you, then." Her eyes weren't sleepy any longer; instead, they were suddenly bright with curiosity. "Come, sit down—I'll make us a pot of *uffa*. And we can talk."

Arekhon had always known that there were more habitable—and inhabited—planets on this side of the Gap Between than there were among the homeworlds, but he'd never seen any of them except for Entibor. Making a new life for himself on Elaeli's world had been hard enough work without making the task more complex with visits to other, and equally alien, places. Now, with *Night's-Beautiful-Daughter* grounded on Ophel for the first time and probably the last, he found himself wishing that once or twice he'd taken the chance. At least a few of those other worlds might have been as restful and pleasant to the eye as this one.

He sat in a wicker chair on the terrace of a seaside hotel in the city of Sombrelír, sharing a late luncheon with the other members of the *Daughter*'s crew. Other tables, some occupied and some not, dotted the black-and-white tessellated pavement. On the far side of the bay a fishing boat set out to sea, down the crystal-sparkling channel. The sky overhead was an even blue without a trace of cloud, but the air was only pleasantly warm.

The local inhabitants had seemed unsurprised when a spacecraft as clearly alien as *Night's-Beautiful-Daughter* landed at the Sombrelír spaceport. The port, such as it was, lay on the high ground outside the city, an hour's ride away by wheeled jitney and even longer by draftbeast-carriage. Already during their stay here, Arekhon had noted that hovercars, so common on Entibor, were rare items on Ophel—the few that he'd seen were import items, and certainly not cheap enough to be used for public transit.

The *Daughter* was docked at the port, topping off her fuel reserves and restocking the galley supplies. Those charges—

and the crew's room and board here at the hotel—had come close to wiping out Arekhon's money supply, but he had decided not to worry about the problem. Once the *Daughter* was resupplied, they would have enough food and fuel to get from Ophel to Eraasi and then back, if the working allowed it, to Entibor. And he still had money left on Entibor.

On the other hand, he reflected, when the *Daughter* got to Eraasi money would be the very least of his problems.

Narin, meanwhile, was watching the distant fishing boat with a combination of nostalgia and expert interest. "This is a nice place," she said eventually. "I think I could live here. Maybe when this is all over, I'll come back and give it a try."

"It's all right if you don't mind being at the tail end of nowhere." Karil Estisk, the pilot, was nibbling on a plate of crumb biscuits and sipping at a cup of wine. "There wouldn't even be a standard course between Ophel and Entibor if one of InterWorld's pilots hadn't taken a blind jump during a running pirate-fight about fifty years back."

"It's definitely the farthest-out world on this side of the Gap Between," agreed Maraganha. "Looked at another way, though, it's the closest of our worlds to Eraasi."

"I wouldn't exactly call it close," said Karil. "Everything from outside the Ophelan system is strange here, and they like it that way. Foreigners come and foreigners go—we could tell 'em we were Khesatan, or Miosan, or even Gyfferan, and there's no one in a hundred miles would know to say different. We knew the port frequencies, and I speak a bit of pilot-Galcenian, and that's good enough for the authorities. No problems."

"Unless you count getting overcharged on our temporary visa fees." Ty had made himself into the keeper of the *Daughter*'s petty cash—Arekhon, he maintained, didn't worry enough about money to be trusted keeping track of it—and he remained certain that between the currency exchange rates and the language barrier, they'd been cheated somewhere in the process of converting their bank drafts into Ophelan coin.

"It's all Entiboran money and not worth anything on the other side of the Gap," Arekhon said. "So we might as well spend it here." He turned to Maraganha. "Tell me—when the Gap goes away, will 'here' still be here?"

Maraganha shook her head. "That I can't tell you."

"Do you mean that you can't, or do you mean that you won't?"

"I mean that I don't know the answer," she said. "But if we're going to get philosophical here, then let me ask you a question: When we can freely come and go across the Gap, is there really a Gap at all?"

"I suppose not."

Karil spread her hands in a dramatic gesture. "Then, *poof!* Your working is finished already, and we can all go home. Right?"

"Wrong," said Arekhon. "We have to make certain that the fabric of Garrod's working extends to both sides of the galaxy. And so far, there's scarcely enough threads of luck and life in the Gap to make the pattern with." He gazed thoughtfully out into the middle distance. "I wonder about what might have happened, though, if Garrod's Void-walking had relied on the stargazers' disciplines a bit more, and on the *eiran* a bit less ... would he have found this world, and not Entibor?"

"Better for everyone, maybe, if he had," said Karil.

There was a moment of uncomfortable silence. Finally Maraganha said, "What's done is done. And we'll never know, so there's no point in fretting about it."

"There's one thing we can do, though," said Arekhon. "We'll need an off-world rendezvous point in case things go bad on Eraasi and we get separated on the way out. We might as well make it Sombrelír."

"You're forgetting one thing," Karil said. "We only have a canned course from the Entiboran side. And setting up a course by hand coming from the other direction isn't something most of us can do—I could, maybe, with a big enough comp system on board; and 'Rekhe, you might be able to—"

"Once, maybe. Not now."

"That leaves us with one person who can set a course by hand, and that's me. Anybody who isn't riding with me when it all falls apart is going to be flat out of luck."

Maraganha shook her head. "Don't borrow trouble, my

grandmother always said. The trick is to somehow make the planet visible to Mageworlders—that's your lot—looking around the Void for emergence points."

"Void-marks," Arekhon said. "The fleet-Circles set them, for the families' star charts. But Garrod was the Void-walker in the Demaizen Circle, not me."

"Don't worry," said Maraganha. "We'll do it together."

Kief sat on the uncomfortable plastic chair in Ayil syn-Arvedan's tiny kitchen, waiting in silence while she brewed up a pot of *uffa*. He heard the kettle singing as the water inside came to a boil, and then the kitchen filled with the sharp blossoming scent of *uffa* as she poured the water over the leaves. She steeped it meticulously by the kitchen timer, and poured it out into two cups when it was done. She kept one cup, and handed the other across the table to him.

He tasted the *uffa* cautiously. But his new body seemed to be growing reconciled to ingesting food and drink in this manner; its rebellion this time was only a fleeting uneasiness, and soon passed.

Finally Ayil spoke. "So. Kief. Am I looking at some kind of illusion here, or is what I'm seeing actually flesh-and-blood real?"

"It's real."

"I'm not even going to ask how you did it," she said. "Just—did you *mean* for this to happen?"

"It's a long story. But yes."

Her eyes widened a bit, but otherwise her expression remained calm. "That's playing the game at a higher level than I can even imagine," she said. "And I suppose now it's gotten you into some kind of trouble . . . why else would you turn up on my doorstep at this hour, wearing another man's face?"

Kief finished his *uffa* in a long gulp. The hot liquid had brought with it an unexpected rush of new energy—this body, unlike his old one, was not yet habituated to the drink's stimulant qualities.

"You're right," he said, setting down the empty cup. "The people I'm working with may possibly have decided that they'd sooner keep me locked away someplace than have me wandering around loose."

"Why?"

"I'm not certain. But I decided not to wait for them and ask."

"Good idea." Ayil stood and put the cups into the sink. "I'll go get some sheets and a pillow."

"Thanks." A thought struck him. "Do you mind if I check the news channels? There may be—there almost certainly is—stuff going on that I don't know about, and I'd like to see if it's common knowledge yet."

"Go right ahead. The display switch is on the desk."

She disappeared, presumably into the bedroom or the necessarium or wherever the sheets-and-towels closet was. Kief went into the apartment's main room, which held a couch, a guest chair, a low table—piled high with stacks of paper—and a fully equipped desk. A scholar living in the Institute Towers wouldn't have anything less than state-of-the-art.

He found the switch and flipped it on, and watched the display take form above the desktop. He kept the sound low; so far there wasn't anything that looked like it might be of interest. Weather reports, mainly . . . "mild and temperate in Hanilat, chilly in the northern and central districts." Ayil returned with her arms full of bedclothes; he heard her making up the couch behind him, thumps and rustles and the whisper of cloth on cloth.

The news channel changed over to doing sports scores, long strings of names and numbers that he wasn't interested in; he never had been interested, either, though Ty and Delath in the old days had argued the merits of city versus country teams for almost half of every year. He wished he could remember now what sport it was that they had so enjoyed.

Somewhere in the room a voice comm buzzed. Ayil reached past him and picked up the handset. Kief listened to her voice with half his concentration and tracked the changing news display with the other.

" 'Adal? . . . What are you doing, calling me this time of night? . . . I see . . . I see . . . frankly, 'Adal, I think you've gone crazy . . . no, I haven't seen him anywhere . . . I'll let

you know if he turns up, all right? . . . Now, if you don't
mind, I'm going to go back to sleep."

He heard the click of the handset settling back in its cradle,
and said, " 'Adal?"

"Inadal," she said. "My brother. You were right; they're
looking for you."

"Thanks for keeping quiet about—"

He broke off. The news channel wasn't doing weather and
sports any longer, and there were new pictures in the display:
a small blond woman; a masked woman dressed all in black
and glitter; and a man. A man with his face. With his body's
face.

". . . from security cameras at the port," the voice-over was
saying. "If you see any of these people, please notify . . ."

The image came from the port. Which meant that the man-
with-his-face had been seen leaving Hanilat, possibly leaving
Eraasi, in the company of a pretty blonde who almost had
to be the kidnapped sus-Dariv bride—though she hadn't been
looking particularly kidnapped at the time.

And then there was the third person, the woman in black.
Her face was masked, but something about the way she
moved stirred up memories at the back of his mind . . . "Ayil.
Make it go back and play that last bit again."

Ayil fiddled with the desktop controls, backtracking the
news stream to the sequence showing the man-with-Kief's-
face and his two companions. This time Kief concentrated
on the unknown woman.

He knew somebody . . . had once known somebody . . .
who moved like that, and who always wore black. But it was
hard to be sure, with the glitter in her dark hair and her facial
features hidden by the mask.

"Could you do it again, please?" Kief said. "Just the dark
woman? And larger?"

"Trying my best."

Ayil tinkered with the controls some more, blocking out
the man-with-his-face and the sus-Dariv heiress completely.
Kief watched the larger image of the dark woman alone—
she had a compact, well-collected body, and he had known
somebody once who moved with that same economical
grace. Then she turned slightly, and he saw what was in her

hand, and had been hidden all this time against the dark fabric of her garment. A Mage's staff. And recognition came.
Iulan Vai.

Arekhon and Maraganha set the Void-marks in the hotel room in Sombrelír. It wasn't the sort of place Arekhon would have picked for a working, even a small one: high ceilings, a polished wooden floor, tall window-doors opening out onto a balcony with a view of sunset and the bay. A lazy ceiling fan turned slowly overhead. The hotel provided luxury, it was true, but faded luxury—a glossy establishment nearer to the spaceport would have had environmental controls and imported entertainment gear. Arekhon liked the seaside hotel better; it reminded him of the summer cottage he was increasingly sure he would never see again.

It wasn't a proper meditation room, though. He said as much, fretfully, and Maraganha replied, "We have to do it on-planet, not on-ship."

The Void-walker, for the first time since he'd met her, was looking a bit tense herself. He found this disturbing; the more so when he remembered her claim that he himself had once been—and someday would be—her teacher.

But this, at least, she *is teaching* me. *Does this mean that the working binds time together, as well as the galaxy? And if I looked at the* eiran *properly, could I see it?*

"What about marking out the circle?" he asked her. "I don't think the management will be happy if we mess up their nice hardwood floor."

"Draw it in your mind, Arekhon *etaze.*" It wasn't quite a reprimand, he thought, but it was close. "You of all people should know that the circle is an aid to meditation, and nothing more."

The rebuke was a just one, and he bowed his head in acceptance. "You're right, *etaze.* When do we begin?"

"Whenever you want to."

"Then let it be now." He knelt on the cool, matte-polished floorboards and laid out his staff in front of him, a cubit and a half of ebony and silver wire. Handmade on Ninglin, it had been, made at the request of the First of the sus-Peledaen fleet-Circle, as the Circle's parting gift to a young Mage and fleet-apprentice who was leaving the family's service. Arek-hon had taken the staff with him to Demaizen, and in all the years since, he had never seen its like.

Until now, when Maraganha knelt opposite him and put down her staff only inches away from his—and he saw what he had been willfully not seeing, before.

Yes, he thought. *The great working does bind time as well as space, and the proof of it lies here before me.*

He shivered at the magnitude of it all. *If Garrod had known the scope of what we were undertaking, would we even have dared—?*

Such questions, he knew, could not be answered. He put speculation aside and said to Maraganha, "I'm ready."

She nodded. "Then let's begin."

Arekhon closed his eyes and tried to slip into the usual mental landscape of his workings. The attempt failed—Mar-aganha was leading them this time, and they were standing in the grey mist of the Void. He wondered if they were completely there, or if they were there in spirit only; with difficulty he resisted the temptation to drop into double-vision and see.

Maraganha pointed out into the Void with her staff. The direction seemed random; there was nothing to distinguish any quarter of the Void from another.

"We go there," she said.

The mist parted in response to a wind he couldn't feel, and he saw the façade of their seaport hotel emerge from the fog only a little distance off. The front door of the hotel stood open, and save for themselves, nobody was in sight.

They traversed an expanse of chilly fog, and entered. The hotel lobby was dim and empty. No clerks stood at the front desk behind the long wooden counter; no guests relaxed in the high-backed, deep-cushioned wicker chairs; and beyond the swagged-back window curtains he saw no view of the sunlit bay, only grey nothingness pressing against the glass.

"We set the Void-marks here?" Arekhon's voice echoed strangely in the silent room.

Maraganha shrugged. "Apparently so. I didn't go into the Void looking for a good hotel—but when I pointed toward where the marks would be, this is what we got."

"Sometimes it occurs to me that the universe has a sense of humor," Arekhon said. "But I'm not certain I understand all of its jokes."

"I'm fairly certain I don't understand any of them," Maraganha said. She went down on one knee and struck the wood of the lobby floor with her staff. "What I will, becomes so. *Here*."

A bright glowing spot sprung into being on the polished floor, sparkling like an inset gem. Maraganha stood up and looked at Arekhon expectantly. "Now you."

Copying her actions, he knelt and struck the mark. "What I will, becomes so. *Here*."

In response he saw a sudden flash of white light, as much inside him as all around him, and then he felt it—the presence of a new beacon shining out across the Void.

The satisfaction of accomplishment faded in an instant, pushed away by fear. This world was too pleasant a place to be threatened by danger from the homeworlds—dangers like the heavy-armed warships of the sus-Peledaen, the ones his brother had started building a decade or more ago.

Arekhon scrambled ungracefully to his feet. "We have to hide the marks somehow," he insisted. "Not all the charts should read them—only ours. Can it be done?"

"This is the Void," said Maraganha. "If that's what we want, then it's already done. But everything here comes with terms and conditions, and this means we'll have to take the back way home."

"The back way—I don't understand."

Maraganha pointed. "There."

He followed the gesture. And at the back of the lobby, where there should have been stairs and elevator, he saw a door—a heavy thing of rough stone, two posts and a lintel, nothing like the rest of the room at all. Except that the rest of the room was gone now, and there was only the door, opening onto black.

Arekhon looked at it. "The back way. Right."

"You've got it, *etaze*," said Maraganha, and after that there was nothing for it but to go.

They crossed the intervening stretch of mist—the door

was farther away than it looked—and stepped through.

Now there was darkness all around them, behind them as well as before, and the smell of stone. Arekhon remembered Councillor Demazze's cavernous underground base, where he had lost Elaeli for so long to the great working and to the wars on Entibor. He hadn't liked caves much since that time; in fact, he hadn't liked caves after that at all.

He kept his voice calm with an effort. "Which way do we go now?"

"Ahead."

Maraganha's staff was glowing with a bright green light; belatedly, Arekhon did the same for his own. The glow revealed that they were in a stone tunnel, its walls and overhead fairly rough, the surface underfoot smooth.

Constructed, then, thought Arekhon, *wherever we are.*

They began moving forward—or at least, moving in the direction they had been facing when the door shut behind them and the dark closed in.

"What exactly are we looking for?" he asked. This place wasn't the grey mist; he didn't think that the point-and-summon method was going to work here very well.

"Doors." Maraganha was frowning slightly, looking not so much distressed as thoughtful. "This place has a lot of them. The trouble is picking the right one."

16:

Eraasi: Hanilat
Aulwikh Orbit: *Fire-on-the-Hilltops;* Sus-
  Peledaen Guardship *Cold-Heart-of-Morning*
Ophel: Sombrelír
The Void

Ayil syn-Arvedan woke up to the vague awareness, even before rational thought returned, that something strange had happened during the night. Half-drowsing, she cast her mind back over the events of the evening before, looking for the nagging worry that had drawn her out of sleep.

I made dinner, I worked on that paper for the conference, I went to bed . . . I was asleep and the door woke me up again . . . Kief was here; he needed a place to sleep. . . .

The rest of her memories snapped into place, and she sat bolt upright in bed. Kief would still be here, sleeping on her couch, wearing somebody else's face. *That* was what she had forgotten while she slept, and then remembered.

She dressed quickly and quietly, and went out into the main room of the apartment. The morning wasn't as early as she'd thought; streaks of sunlight reached into the dimness through the slats in the window-blinds. She saw Kief kneeling on the floor, his staff lying in front of him and his eyes closed. The sheets and pillow on the couch behind him weren't even rumpled; if her sleep last night had been uneasy, Kief had clearly never slept at all.

Looking at him, she found the whole thing strange and

hard to believe. She'd found it beyond strange, last night—hearing the familiar speech patterns and the familiar accent in a voice pitched several notes deeper than Kiefen Diasul's had ever been, seeing his familiar gestures and attitudes and expressions displayed by a body nothing at all like the one she'd known.

She wondered how it had been done, and knew that she didn't dare ask. Something he'd said yesterday implied that the body was a true double, not some kind of Magework-impelled takeover. The creation of a new body implied groundbreaking accomplishment on the part of a physician or a savant or both, in addition to the help of his Circle. Ayil knew that Kief worked for the sus-Peledaen, who were dangerous to entire planets when they were crossed; but after her voice-comm talk with Inadal last night, she suspected that Kief was also working for somebody else—somebody who, if her brother was involved in it, wasn't on the sus-Peledaen side at all.

It looks like he's decided to go on the run from all of them, for reasons of his own. . . .

Mages were like that, she knew. Her brother Del had been the same way after he'd found the Demaizen Circle. He'd come home from his summer hiking trip, and he'd unpacked and cleaned himself up and taken his place at the family dinner table as if everything were normal. Then he'd told their parents to take his name off the family tablets because he was going to the Mages. The yelling and the arguments had gone on past midnight—Inadal and their father shouting, mostly, while their mother cried—but Del hadn't budged, and he'd never explained his reasons.

She didn't think Kief was going to explain much, either. He hadn't bothered to turn off the frozen image of the masked woman in black, hovering above Ayil's desktop, and she had the unnerving impression he was still looking at it, even though his eyes were closed.

She left him to his meditations, or whatever they were, and went into the kitchen nook, where she found refuge from strangeness in the mundane necessity of providing a breakfast for her unexpected guest.

Fresh uffa, she thought. *And flatbread, and a platter of baked eggs.*

She pulled out the ingredients from the pantry shelves and the preserving-cupboard, started the oven heating, and turned on the cooktop, while trying not to think about whatever Kief was doing in the other room. The flatbread came from a mix packet. She added tap water, patted out the the thin rounds, and set the first ones to toasting on a hot griddle. Maybe the smell of fresh bread would bring him back.

She didn't want to rouse him; was half-afraid to, if she was honest with herself. On the other hand, she didn't want him staying here past morning, either. If her brother took it in mind to leave Arvedan and come up to the city, he might decide to visit the sister who'd warned him once already that Kiefen Diasul was doing something strange with the Institute Circle. Kief needed to be long gone by then—she didn't know where to. But somewhere.

Finally, sounds of movement were coming from the other room. Ayil broke the eggs into the cooking platter and slid it into the oven. She closed the oven door and set the timer, then turned to see the stranger-who-was-Kief standing there in his rumpled clothes.

"Good morning," she said.

He seemed to think about it for a few seconds before replying. "Yes."

"Breakfast is almost ready."

"I see that. Thank you."

She'd forgotten—over the years since her brother's death—exactly how exasperating conversations with Mages could sometimes get, but this one was starting out even worse than usual. Making an extraordinary effort, she said brightly, "Have you decided yet what you're going to do? Next, I mean?"

"Yes," he said. When she didn't say anything this time in reply, he added, "I need a starship and a pilot."

Mages, she thought.

She put a cup of *uffa* and a plate of flatbread on the table, and gestured him into a chair. "Sit. Have food." She watched him put tangleberry butter on a piece of warm flatbread and roll it up to take a bite. Then she said, "I can see how leaving

town for a while might be a good idea—but just buying a
ticket at the station isn't going to work?"

"No. I have to go off-world. And I can't risk taking a fleet-
family courier."

"Then what else is there?"

She had to wait while he rolled up and ate another piece
of flatbread before answering her question. "A contract carrier," he said finally. "Those are fleet-family on paper only,
and they shift contracts whenever a new arrangement looks
better than the old."

The oven timer went *bing,* and Ayil took out the baked
eggs. "Only one problem with that," she said, setting the
platter down on the table. "Hiring a contract carrier is going
to cost you a lot of money. And I mean the kind of money
that fleet-families and mercantile associations have—not the
kind that people have."

Kief paused in the act of spooning himself out a serving
of eggs. "The money doesn't matter. I've been trying to get
rid of it for years."

Saying it, he smiled—Kief's smile on a stranger's face,
even more disturbing in the light of morning than it had been
the night before—and Ayil knew suddenly that she would
be relieved to have him gone.

I won't tell anybody where he went, she thought. *I owe
him that much for old times' sake. But if he comes back here
again, I'm not going to let him in.*

Fire-on-the-Hilltops had a crowded passage through the Void
to Aulwikh. The former sus-Radal courier ship had never
been intended to carry passengers on a long transit—especially not three of them, and none of them friendly enough
to share rack space.

Len settled for bedding down Zeri sus-Dariv in the pilot's
cabin, on the grounds that she had the most rank and the
least experience at sleeping in bad conditions, and telling the
Mages to make do with the acceleration couches in the passenger pod. He made his own bed for the duration in the
pilot's seat on the bridge, where the swirling grey pseudosubstance of the Void pressed against the armored glass win-

dows and the *Fire*'s ancient, cranky ship-mind clicked and whirred in the instrument consoles and the interfaces.

The journey was nevertheless strangely restful, as Void-transits so often were.

"Ships can't attack in the Void," Len explained to Lady Zeri on the first ship's-night in transit, over a dinner of spiced meat-paste and crunchy wafers. The food was basic Antipodean quick-meal fare. Zeri took to it at once, while her cousin Herin and Iulan Vai ate their dinner with varying degrees of resignation. Too bad; Len had stocked the *Fire*'s galley for his taste, not theirs. "If you can make it in, you're safe until you have to come out."

"So they can't follow us now?"

Len decided it was time to hedge a bit. Lady Zeri didn't need to know about blind transits and other risky business, not unless they had to do it.

"You can make a guess about where somebody's going to drop out," he said. "You base it on what they may have told the spaceport, and on what other planets are on the arc of their approach to the Void—but there's nothing that says a ship has to tell the truth about where they're going, or that they have to go all the way there."

Zeri licked the last of the meat-paste off her fingers. "I don't remember us telling Eraasi inspace control anything at all."

"We didn't," said Iulan Vai. "Anyone tracking us is going to have to take a look at the arc and guess."

"Do we have a plan for dealing with that?"

"What we can't hide, we disguise," Vai said. "Get new paperwork for the ship, take new names all around, and make ourselves anonymous as fast as possible. Your husband's family has more resources than we can fight directly."

"Prospective husband," Zeri said. "The contracts aren't in force until after the wedding night."

Vai snorted. "Tell *him* that."

Zeri's cousin Herin said, "He knows. If he's going to have a shred of legal right to take over the sus-Dariv resources, he has to get Zeri back. Otherwise, it's theft. Once he gets angry enough, he won't care about that any longer, but he's going to try doing things the more-or-less legal way first."

"Sounds like the farther we get from Eraasi, the better," Zeri said.

"In part," Herin said. "On the other hand, the farther we get from Eraasi, the more willing he'll be to use force."

"So." Zeri turned to Len. "You're the pilot here—when do we stop running and head for that rendezvous point Syr Vai talked about back at Serpent Station?"

"Not yet. We drop out at Aulwikh and dally there long enough to let them see us leaving on a projected course for Ildaon, then drop out again at Ninglin and wait there a few days to see if anyone's tracking us. After that, if we turn up clean, then we can see about making the rendezvous."

Egelt and Hussav stood in the pilothouse of the sus-Peledaen guardship *Cold-Heart-of-Morning,* in high orbit over Aulwikh. Patience and forethought, it appeared, were about to be rewarded.

At Egelt's urging, the pilot of the courier *Summerday* had pushed the fast-runner at max speed all the way from Hanilat. The *Fire*'s official specs made out the sus-Dariv contract-courier to be an older-generation craft bought as surplus from the sus-Radal—and therefore no match for a sus-Peledaen ship in a transit through the Void. If Zeri sus-Dariv and her renegade captain had done as Egelt predicted and headed for Aulwikh after lifting from Serpent Station, the security chief wanted to be in position and waiting for them before they arrived.

And so he had been, safely anonymous behind a misleading identifier beacon and assured of the full cooperation of Aulwikh's local defense force—as it happened, a flotilla of four guardships on semi-permanent loan from the sus-Peledaen fleet. The contract-courier had emerged from the Void a full two ship's-days later, but hadn't bothered to land. As Egelt had suspected, Aulwikh was only serving as a misleading dropout in a longer course.

A light on the *Cold-Heart*'s main console flashed. The guardship's captain plugged in the earpiece for the comm set, and listened briefly.

"Report from Aulwikh surface control," he said to Egelt.

"The *Fire*'s given notice they're leaving orbit and heading for Ildaon."

"Good, good," Egelt said. "Put the flotilla in position for a block and board. We're bigger than him, we're faster than him, and we know where he's heading. We've got him."

"Where do you want to put the *Cold-Heart?*"

"Out beyond the jump point," Egelt said. "So that when we have him, we'll be in position to board at once. I won't be happy until that sus-Dariv female is safely back in my possession."

"You and everyone else," Hussav told him. "So far she's been more trouble for her size than anybody else I've ever met."

"Three around the path to jump," the *Cold-Heart*'s captain said, ignoring the byplay. "We'll be in the point out spaceward. We have it logged in and running."

Egelt smiled. "Good job. This time, for certain."

"Careful," Hussav warned. "Don't jinx it."

"Don't we have a Circle to take care of things like that?"

"Not one of our own," the captain said. "It's part of our deal with Aulwikh. We send them our guardships to chase off pirates, and the Aulwikhi Circles handle everything to do with tending the luck."

"And whose bright idea was that?" Hussav asked. "A Circle down on the planet somewhere—and not even a sus-Peledaen Circle at that!—isn't going to give a damn about Lord Natelth's married life."

"That bright idea was probably the price of our ship-loan treaty with Aulwikh," Egelt said. "Which means that without it we'd be trying to stop the *Fire*'s entry into the Void with nothing but an unarmed fast-runner. So we make do."

Zeri and the two Mages were strapped down on the acceleration couches in the *Fire*'s passenger pod when Len's voice came crackling over the intraship speakers.

"People, we have a problem. There are guardships hanging around our jump point."

"Whose?" Zeri had to speak loudly enough for the pod's audio pickups to catch her words; she considered it an accomplishment, under the circumstance, that her voice remained steady and free of obvious panic.

"You need to ask? His."

"Somebody," said Iulan Vai thoughtfully, "has been a very clever boy. Or girl, of course, but not if I remember who's who in Lord Natelth's security service."

"Grif Egelt," said Herin. "And he's certainly no fool. If he's taking a personal interest in this project, we have our work cut out for us."

"When it's all over you can send him a card and flowers," Zeri said. To the audio pickups, she added, "How are we going to get out of this?"

"Good luck and clever maneuvering," came Len's reply. "I'll supply the maneuvering; tell your cousin and Syr Vai it's their job to handle the luck."

"They hear you," she said.

"Good," Len said. "Get ready. We're building speed for entry into the Void."

"Matching course and speed," *Cold-Heart-of-Morning*'s captain said to Egelt. "Looks like *Watch-where-the-Wind-Blows* has him."

"Maneuver to where they'll be when they come dead in space," Egelt said.

"Take me a minute to figure the course," the captain said.

"Damn!" Len's voice crackled again over the intraship speakers. "They're alongside us now."

"Shoot them!" Zeri ordered.

"With happiness, my lady, but we're unarmed. Merchant, remember?"

"Damn," said Zeri in her turn. In a quieter voice, she said, "Herin?"

For a moment there was no answer; then he answered her in a voice that sounded distracted and far away. "Yes, cousin?"

"I don't want to be captured and taken back to Lord Natelth," she said. "It would humiliate me and disgrace whatever was left of the family. Don't let it happen."

"We're working on it, Zeri."

"I wasn't thinking about that. I was thinking that you probably know how to—well, to put a quick end to someone."

"Yes. That too."

"Don't do anything stupid quite yet," Len said. Over his voice came the metallic sound, echoing through the bulkheads, of magnetic grapnels attaching to the courier ship's hull. "I'm still working on being clever."

"Be *very* clever," said Zeri. "And do it now."

"Portside forward thrusters, fire," Len said. "After starboard thrusters, fire." Abruptly *Fire-on-the-Hilltops* began to spin around the point where the magnetic grapnels had attached. "Reverse thrusters." The spin stopped, making Zeri's head slew around despite the safety webbing. "Engines, fire, full."

"Just got the word," the *Cold-Heart*'s captain said. "We've caught him. The grapnels are all in place and he's cut his main engines."

"Head toward him," Egelt ordered.

"Heading toward him, aye," the captain said. Then, in tones of incredulity, "What the fuck? The slippery bastard isn't slowing down. He's rotating."

"They can't do that!" exclaimed Hussav. He sounded as though the *Fire*'s maneuver was a personal affront.

"They're doing it," Egelt said. "For a contract-captain in an obsolete ship, our man has got a definite venturesome streak."

"He's accelerating," said the *Cold-Heart*'s captain.

"Match him," Egelt ordered. "Follow him. Get ahead of him. Hell, ram him if you have to—just don't let him get away."

"*Watch-where-the-Wind-Blows* reports that the grapnels have broken free," the *Cold-Heart*'s communications officer reported.

"He's venting atmosphere to space," the captain said. "He's torn the skin and he's holed and leaking."

"We've got him," Hussav said. "He can't go far that way."

"Make sure he goes no farther." Egelt leaned back against the *Cold-Heart*'s bulkhead and rubbed his forehead. He was beginning to get a headache. "Do not disappoint me, Captain."

"We're the only ship headed in the proper direction right now," the captain said. "It's us or no one."

"Then it's us," Egelt said.

In the *Fire*'s passenger pod, the loss-of-pressure alarms whooped.

"Don't panic," Len said over the speakers. "We're okay as long as we stay in here and the internal airtight bulkheads hold."

"What are you doing?" Zeri asked.

"Just following your instructions," he said. "One way or another, we aren't going to be taken alive. That's what you wanted, right?"

"Right," Zeri said. "Do what you have to do."

"He's approaching the necessary speed for Void-translation," the *Cold-Heart*'s captain said.

Egelt snapped, "Make sure he doesn't get in."

"I don't know—"

"I said, *make sure*."

There was a brief moment of silence, and then the *Cold-Heart*'s Pilot-Principal said to the captain, "He's in."

"What was his heading?"

"Nowhere," said the Pilot-Principal. "That wasn't a standard translation point. There's nothing out that way."

"Did you mark the position?" Egelt asked him.

"Yes."

"Then make our translation the same way, in the same place. Wherever he's gone, we're going to follow."

The *Cold-Heart*'s captain paled. "That's suicide!"

"No more than telling Lord Natelth that we've failed again," Egelt told him. "Make your translation."

"I didn't want my pension anyway," the captain said, and took the ship through.

Arekhon and Maraganha were walking through a tunnel cut in the rock, the muted green glow of their staves the only light. The tunnel was a labyrinth of forks and curves; Maraganha picked right or left each time without hesitation.

"How do you know where we're going?" Arekhon asked her, after she'd made the choice for the fifth time.

"I don't," she said. "Not in the usual sense of the word."

"In what sense of the word *do* you know it, then?"

Even in the dim light, he could see that Maraganha looked amused. "I didn't think all that deference and respect would last very long—not in a great Magelord and the First of a famous Circle. I'm looking for marks at the turnings."

"Marks. At the turnings." He looked harder, and found that he could see them after all—faint pinpricks of white light, not so much on the stone as somewhere inside it. "Like Void-marks, only quite a bit smaller?"

"Yes."

"Somebody was here before," he said, after a moment's thought. "And they left a trail for the rest of us."

"A lot of people have been through here," Maraganha told him. "Sometimes you'll find yourself following your own marks even though you haven't left them yet."

"I don't think these are mine." His own marks, he was convinced, would have a different feel to them—he remembered the blaze of white light when the Ophelan Void-mark set. "Are they yours?"

"Not mine. Maybe a friend's, though. If I'm reading them properly, they lead upward and out, not deeper in."

He hoped she was in fact reading them properly. If she was wrong, the two of them would be heading into the core of whatever this place was. He decided not to dwell on that aspect of their journey any longer; too much thought along those lines only served to make him hot and sweaty and oppressed by a conviction that the walls were closing in.

They hiked on in silence for some time, until they came to the first door. It was made of heavy wood bound with iron, like a door out of legend, and it blocked the whole passage.

"We could go back," Arekhon said. "Maybe we took a wrong turn somewhere a few junctions ago."

Maraganha shook her head. "No. The marks on it are clear."

Arekhon gave it a push. The door was hard and unyielding; he thought it might be locked in some fashion on the other side. "It's not going to budge."

"Then we go through it."

"How?"

"Very carefully," Maraganha said. "Relax, keep your eyes on the marks, and let them guide you as you slip through."

Suiting her action to her words, she stepped up to the door, then passed through it and out of sight. Arekhon was alone in the labyrinth.

"Right," he said under his breath. "Relax."

He looked for the marks, and as before he saw them inside the wood of the door—sparkling like a string of jewels, leading him through. He took a deep breath and walked forward to touch the first mark. As soon as he reached it, the second mark flared up like a nova, farther in. Then the third, then the fourth, and he was standing with Maraganha on the other side of the door.

The tunnel here looked much the same as before, only now it was illuminated by a dim, sourceless light. Maraganha had dampened the glow of her staff in response; he did the same, and was able to see how the marks continued on this side. Maraganha gestured at the marks with the tip of her staff.

"See?" she said. "I was right, by the way. They're leading up."

She moved on, and Arekhon followed her. The walls of the tunnel became smoother and smoother as they progressed, until at length the tunnel wasn't cavelike at all anymore, but even-surfaced both underfoot and overhead, in a manner reminiscent of passageways on the fleet-family vessels of his youth. But those corridors had been made of metal and glass and hard plastic, not of stone, and he found the resemblance not so much comfortable as oddly disquieting.

There were doors again, suddenly—not blocking the passage, but appearing along it to either side at irregular intervals. This time he saw no marks lighting the way.

"Now what?" he asked.

"This is your journey, Arekhon *etaze*. Choose a door."

He stood in the middle of the passageway, looking at doors stretching out ahead to the limits of his vision. Doors upon doors, and all of them the same—and at the same time, he knew that picking the right one was vital, that things bad beyond imagining lay behind all of the others. He could have chosen, but he had nothing left to guide him in the choice. The marks were gone, and looking for the *eiran* in the Void was a pointless exercise.

But the passageway wasn't the Void, or at least it wasn't the unliving no-place, no-time of grey mist without substance that he had always thought the Void to be. This place was other. He looked again, searching now for traces of the *eiran*—and he saw them, looping and coiling along the corridor walls and lacing themselves in a familiar pattern across the surface of a particular door.

"That one," he said.

He opened it with a touch—it slid open; it wasn't even locked—and stepped through before he could lose his nerve. Maraganha followed close behind him.

They were standing on an observation platform, a bare room that was mostly floor and a half-dome of ceiling, opening up above them to show clear glass and a view of the surrounding stars. Other lights were winking into being out in the darkness as he watched—they were still too distant for detail, but in his heart he knew already what they were.

Ships. Warships. Coming here.

"This is the wrong room," he said, fighting down a rising terror. "It has to be. We can't stay here any longer—they'll destroy us."

"This is the right place," said Maraganha calmly, as if life had never given her reason to fear warships coming out of the Void. "Follow the marks, and they'll take us home."

"But there aren't any more—"

He stopped. There *were* marks now, out beyond the armored glass, out in the deep of space. All he had to do was trust them—

—and step through—

—onto a balcony in Sombrelír, with the sun going down

across the bay. He looked over his shoulder and saw Mara-ganha coming out through the windowed doors of the hotel room to join him.

"It was real," he said. "It wasn't just the Void."

She smiled at him, the proud smile of a teacher to a be-loved student. "It was real. And now your own marks are there as well, in case you ever need to find your way through that place again."

17:

ERAASI: HANILAT; SERPENT STATION
SUS-DARV GUARDSHIP *GARDEN-OF-FAIR-BLOSSOMS*:
  ERAASI NEARSPACE
FIRE-ON-THE-HILLTOPS; SUS-PELEDAEN GUARDSHIP
  COLD-HEART-OF-MORNING: THE VOID

Zeri sus-Dariv felt the vibration of the *Fire*'s run for the Void subside to the quieter, more familiar sensations of normal operation, and allowed herself to start breathing normally again. Lenyat Irao—"captain," Iulan Vai called him respectfully, now that they were in space, and if Syr Vai, Iulan *etaze*, gave someone a title of respect, then custom doubtless required the head of what remained of the sus-Dariv to do likewise—*Captain* Irao had called the *Fire*'s earlier departure from Serpent Station a hurried mess when he spoke of it afterward. She wondered how he was going to describe this one.

Zeri hadn't been afraid when she heard the noise of magnetic grapnels attaching to the *Fire*'s outer hull, and felt the shock travel through the metal of the ship clear into her bones. What she knew was going to happen next and what she wanted Herin to do for her before it did were the only things she'd had room for in her mind. She'd been too cold and too clearheaded for anything like fear.

That was then. Now that the crisis was over, she knew in her heart and stomach, as well as in her head, why it was that spacers liked the Void. All she could do was lie on the acceleration couch, and look up at the lights in the overhead, and shake.

She heard the sound of the bridge door sliding open, and turned her head. Captain Irao—the name didn't work right inside her head; she'd thought of him as "Len" for too long while they were on Eraasi—came into the passenger pod. The captain looked like she felt: pale and sweaty and exhausted. Zeri wondered if he hadn't started shaking until afterward, either.

Iulan Vai was the first one to speak. "That was good ship-handling, Captain."

"Thanks." He gave her weak grin. "Tell you the truth, I'd just as soon never have to do it again."

Zeri unstrapped and sat up on the edge of the acceleration couch, the better to speak to the captain herself. "I'd just as soon you never had to again, as well. But I'm extremely grateful that you could."

"You're not the only one." Herin was also looking bad. It wasn't a kind thing that she'd asked of him, Zeri knew, but it was something better asked for from family than from a stranger like Iulan Vai. "I'm a man of boundless curiosity, Captain. Where did you learn a trick like that?"

"I didn't. I heard someone talk once about having been there to see it done."

Herin closed his eyes and looked ill. "Oh."

Zeri stood up. Her knees had stopped shaking, which surprised her somewhat. She crossed the passenger pod to look at Len directly. "In that case, Captain Irao, you have my admiration as well as my personal gratitude."

"I could hear what you said to him." Len jerked his head at Herin. "Over the audio. Made it sound like a good time to try anything that might work."

"And you were right," Iulan Vai said. "So don't lose sleep worrying about it afterward."

At the mention of sleep, Zeri had to fight against an involuntary yawn. She was more exhausted than she ever remembered being in her life, in spite of having done nothing except ride out the crisis in the passenger pod. "Is that what we do now? Sleep?"

Len nodded. "And eat, and maybe play solitaire against

the ship-mind. Work on inside repairs, if it turns out that we need any. Then sleep some more, and so on until we get to Ninglin."

"Sounds like an excellent schedule of activities," said Herin. Her cousin was looking better, Zeri reflected, now that he'd worked out what the captain's untested maneuver had saved him from having to do.

"Glad you approve of it," Len told him. "But I warn you—the ship-mind cheats."

Kief had never gone into space before, despite the fact that he'd studied the stargazers' disciplines before going to the Demaizen Circle. Nor was riding second-seat in a cargo courier his idea of the best way to start; but nothing else had advertised itself as available for hire, and he was uncomfortably aware that he lacked the expertise to seek out a better alternative.

Chartering the courier ship for an indefinite term—in theory from the sus-Radal, who held the captain's contract—would also come near to wiping out Kief's share of the Diasul fortune. The money didn't matter; he'd spoken the truth to Ayil syn-Arvedan when he'd said that he never used it anyway. He'd lived off his stipend as a sus-Peledaen Mage for the past ten years, partly from a reluctance to touch his share of the family's assets, but mostly because he'd lacked the desire for anything more.

The great working had bound and controlled him in that as in so many other things, and he had never fully comprehended the magnitude of that binding until now. Stepping away from his old body had taken him outside of the *eiran* that surrounded it, and had finally made him understand. He was no longer one of the Demaizen Mages, and it was time to do what was necessary and set himself free.

There was, he had to admit, a distinct possibility that once the job was done, he might not be a sus-Peledaen Mage any longer, either. That didn't matter any more than the money did. He was the First of his own Circle, and First above the First of the Institute Circle, and nobody in history had ever linked two Circles in that way before. Someone on Eraasi would always need the kind of luck-working that such combined power made possible, and those who needed it would always pay.

Given time, he could cut himself and his Circle-Mages free of patronage and the fleet-families altogether. They could be truly free, as only those with power could be free—but Kief's glimpse of Iulan Vai in the news-channel image, and his long meditation afterward, had brought him to a realization of what first had to be done.

He had to free himself from Garrod's working. If all his efforts so far had been worthless, it had to be because Arekhon sus-Khalgath sus-Peledaen was still alive, still the First of a remnant Demaizen, still tending and maintaining the *eiran* of the great working. Kief had thought his fellow-Mage lost forever by now, or even dead, but the working wouldn't be resisting Kief's efforts to break free if Arekhon weren't caught up in it as well. Iulan Vai had been one of the Demaizen Mages who'd gone with Arekhon when the Circle split; if she was still a Mage, she would be with 'Rekhe now.

If he wanted to find 'Rekhe, he had to follow Iulan Vai.

Kief had known better than to try explaining his decision to Ayil. She was a scholar and a stargazer; she'd never seen the silvery threads of the *eiran* and known beyond certainty that one of them gleamed brighter than all the rest. But he had that thread now, and his firm grip on it and his determination to follow where it led gave Kief his first real sense of steadiness and purpose since he'd stepped out of Isayana's gel-vat.

He forced himself out of his light meditation and back into reality, where the courier ship's pilot was waiting on launch permission from port control. Only vital traffic was lifting—the port had been full of gossip about Natelth sus-Peledaen's stolen bride, and the courier's pilot was disposed to be chatty.

"Some people say she wasn't kidnapped," the pilot said. "That she figured out what was really going on, and she ran away."

"I'm not much for following the news channels," Kief said. "If you could enlighten me . . . what *is* 'really going on,' that it should distress a young woman so to find it out?"

The pilot cast a disbelieving look in Kief's direction. "Huh. Word is, wasn't pirates that did for the sus-Dariv fleet, any more than it was an accident that blew up the Court of Two Colors—and the lady got herself proof of it from somewhere."

"You're verging on dangerous speculation, my friend. The sus-Peledaen make bad enemies."

"Did you hear me say anybody's name but the lady's?" the pilot demanded indignantly. "You did not—" An amber light began blinking on the main console. "There's the port."

He flipped the switch underneath the blinking light. "sus-Radal contract carrier *Waves-Breaking-Softly*."

"*Waves-Breaking-Softly*, you have permission to lift for orbit with one passenger."

"*Waves-Breaking-Softly*, preparing to lift. Out."

The pilot flipped switches and pressed buttons in a sequence that Kief made no pretense to himself of understanding, and the world closed down around him until there was only the roar of engines and the pressure of liftoff. This was it; he was leaving Eraasi. If he'd had the breath for it, he would have laughed. Star travel wasn't supposed to be for him; it was supposed to be for fleet-family scions like 'Rekhe had been, or for Void-walkers like Lord Garrod . . . *strange*, he thought, *what necessity compels*.

The pressure eased, replaced by a new sensation. He had no weight, and he was floating inside the constraints of the safety webbing. For an instant he teetered on the verge of nausea, but the courier's pilot flipped another switch, and the floating sensation was replaced by the return of normal gravity, or by something that mocked normal gravity well enough for all practical purposes.

The pilot gave Kief a sympathetic look. "First time up, eh?"

"Yes."

"We can rest here in orbit a bit," the pilot said kindly; "let you get used to it. I need to file a projected Void-transit with inspace control."

Kief was not so distressed by the experience of liftoff that he missed the pilot's subtle inquiry. The courier ship had been hired for lift to orbit and a Void-transit to be filed later:

a mildly shady deal, but not illegal. Anybody watching the boards at the port would see only the first destination, the lift to orbit, and not the second. The maneuver bought time, not safety; inspace control wasn't in the business of keeping anybody's secrets.

Now that the courier had made it into orbit, Kief needed more than the name of a world to give the pilot. He needed the course that would take him to Arekhon sus-Khalgath and the end of the great working. Iulan Vai, he told himself, Iulan Vai was the thread he needed to follow, wherever she was going and why. She'd been the last Mage to join the Demaizen Circle and the first Mage of Arekhon's teaching, and the combination made her life and luck into a glowing thread in the great working.

He let his mind tell over the roster of the settled planets: Eraasi, Ildaon, Rayamet, Ruisi, Ninglin, Aulwikh, Ayarat, Cracanth . . . those were the heartworlds, the worlds where Mages had found each other and spoken across the deeps of space. Then came the lesser worlds, settled from the greater ones; the bright thread that was Iulan Vai didn't touch those, but instead wove through and around them in the pattern of the great working and came to rest on—

"Ninglin."

"If they went into the Void, they'll come out of the Void," Egelt said. With *Cold-Heart-of-Morning* safely in the Void, the sus-Peledaen security operatives had time to consider exactly where they were going next. "Did the captain get a fix on their likely point of emergence?"

"After much profanity and repeated assertions that doing something crazy like this was a good way to end up inside a star someplace in the middle of nowhere—yes." Hussav laid a printout on the wardroom table. "Here's the arc."

Egelt studied the printout carefully. "So . . . Cracanth if they want to get lost in the crowd, or Ninglin if they want to go somewhere obscure. What do you think?"

"sus-Dariv has assets on Cracanth."

"Then we'll go to Ninglin," Egelt said. "Whoever's running their operation isn't stupid, or we'd have grabbed them by now. They have to know that *we* know about those assets, and after getting ambushed at Aulwikh they know that we're faster than they are in the Void. So they'll be looking for us to put on speed and catch them at Cracanth."

"You're the boss."

Egelt sighed and pinched the bridge of his nose. "No, Lord Natelth is the boss. I'm only the guy who has to obey his whims. If some girl was that dead-set against marrying me, I'd tell her to go with my blessing, and find me a different one that I dared to close my eyes around."

"You don't think she was kidnapped?" Hussav asked.

"Not really," Egelt said. "You remember questioning those guys from Serpent Station? They all seemed to think she'd gone of her own free will."

"Assuming that they weren't all fibbing, too."

"We asked them pretty persuasively."

"Not so persuasively that someone couldn't be prepared to resist," Hussav said. "I'm not a monster."

"The fangs and horns aren't real?"

"Nope. Stuck on with tape."

"And here I'd always thought—" Egelt paused as a message alarm beeped. "That's odd. The drone must have come in at Aulwikh before we jumped, and squirted off its messages at the last minute."

"If the captain's routing it down here, it's tabbed for us. What does it say?"

"Give me a moment." Egelt tapped his authorization code into the table display, then read the text as it scrolled in. "This is damned odd. You know our guy Len? He's just been spotted leaving Eraasi."

"Ignore it," Hussav advised. "Any time you start looking for someone, tips start coming in that put him all over the place. Seen simultaneously on two planets a hundred light-years apart."

"I don't know," Egelt said. "Hanilat spaceport security says that the fingerprints match."

"No kidding?"

"No. But we don't know for sure he left on that ship we've been chasing. They could have picked up a pilot at Serpent Station for all we know."

"So what do we do now?" asked Hussav.

"We follow the girl. That guy who helped her out the window—yeah, I want to talk with him. At length. In some detail. But the girl is why we're drawing our pay."

Natelth had been working at the desk in his study since early morning, and he intended to keep on working until dinner. His outward demeanor, as far as family and associates were concerned, remained as calm and deliberate as ever, but to himself he admitted the need to keep himself occupied while waiting for news of the missing Zeri sus-Dariv. Inactivity, in his experience, only made waiting more difficult; and if all the news, in the end, turned out to be bad, at least he would have the work that he had done.

Today's project was an intensive review of the sus-Dariv assets currently in the process of being transferred to sus-Peledaen family control. He was pleased to see that matters were going smoothly, despite the technical hitch of the un-completed wedding. He'd made a point of offering the hired employees and outer-family members a chance to transfer into the sus-Peledaen ahead of schedule. A good number, he saw from the rosters displayed on his desk, were taking the offer—young workers, mostly, with less time to form habits of attachment to a particular employer; as well as various outer-family members of more than ordinary ambition.

The former would do well, he reflected, so long as they were paid promptly and treated no differently than other hired crew. The latter, on the other hand, would bear close watching, in case their ambition should someday override their family loyalty a second time.

The majority of the sus-Dariv, however, appeared to be holding to the letter of the marriage contract. Until the wedding morning, they would continue to remain separate. Annoying, but not unexpected, and loyalty wasn't a bad thing. Most of them, once they'd been subsumed into sus-Peledaen, would be equally loyal to the new family. Those who weren't loyal would doubtless make the fact obvious soon enough, and could be dealt with appropriately at the time.

The few absolute holdouts, of course, would require making an example of. Natelth was worried, though not excessively, about the handful of ships remaining in the sus-Dariv fleet. Based on reports from Security Chief Egelt and from sus-Peledaen sources at Hanilat inspace control, they'd been showing signs of recalcitrance. The example, Natelth had almost decided, would come from there.

It hadn't been the ships that he'd wanted in the first place, but the family's other assets. Their policy of leasing yard space and most port facilities, instead of building their own dedicated orbital and heavy ground bases, meant that the sus-Dariv purse was, for a fleet-family in these troubled times, almost unnaturally plump. All the same, if things went on as they had been, the fleet remnant would require chastisement with a strong hand.

His thoughts were interrupted by the gong-tone of the office door. "Come in," he said—and when the door opened before he had time to properly finish the phrase, he continued, "Ah, Isa. What keeps you busy today?"

Isayana, dressed in her usual work clothes, with a smudge of ink on her forehead and a stylus thrust through her hair, wandered into the office with the distracted air of someone who has forgotten the errand she came on. Granted, Natelth thought, Isa looked that way most of the time, as though she usually had forgotten necessity in favor of an interesting technical problem or an elegant new theory.

"I've been tinkering, mostly," she said. "Tuning the house-mind. We're here so seldom, these days, that it grows forgetful."

This was a complaint he'd heard before, and he knew by now the response that was expected of him. "The new-style systems are less so. It might be time to consider purging the old one and doing a complete changeover."

"Let the orbital station have the new systems; playing with the old house-mind will give me something to amuse myself with when we visit Hanilat."

"If it pleases you, Isa, we can keep it for as long as you like." He regarded his sister fondly, while reflecting that she hadn't been well served by recent events. All the work of arranging the wedding banquet had fallen to her, and the disappearance of Lady Zeri had ruined it all. "I'm afraid you haven't had the most enjoyable of visits so far. Once the marriage has been regularized, though, things should get better."

"I hope so." Isa paced over to the bay window and back again, her hands shoved into the pockets of her working coat. She was frowning. "Na'e—what are you going to do if they can't get her back?"

This was a new worry, not one of the old ones already worn smooth by time and use. "I have every trust in Syr Egelt's capabilities," Natelth said. "He'll find her."

"Even the most capable man can sometimes run out of luck. This could be Egelt's time, and what will you do then?"

"If Lady Zeri can't be brought back," Natelth said, "then she'll have to be dead."

"But will that work?"

"There's a precedent for it," he told her; "I had the legalists make certain. 'If one party or the other should die between burning incense at the family altars and greeting guests on the wedding morning, it shall be assumed for the purpose of inheritance that the marriage was in all things made complete.'"

In the main office building at Serpent Station, all the lights were out. The only illumination came from the outside sunlight. There wasn't even the usual background flicker of displays and readouts and I'm-alives—Port-Captain Winceyt had purged the station's house-mind hours ago, as soon as he remembered what Iulan Vai had told him before she hid the memory from the sus-Peledaen. He'd copied the new star charts onto data wafers and personally hand-carried them to the ships' captains, and then had given the house-mind its last command.

"You are the house-mind of sus-Dariv's Serpent Station. Now we release you from your service and set you free. Initiate sequence. Go."

After that, there was nothing left except a large quantity of quiescent mind-gel, possibly salvageable for remaking into low-grade *aiketen* or cheap data storage, but probably not. There was certainly nothing left of the sus-Dariv in it anywhere.

With step one done already, Port-Captain Winceyt turned to Command-Tertiary Yerris and said, "Are all the charges set?"

"Everything's wired and ready, sir," Yerris replied. "Even the plonkball court."

"We definitely wouldn't want to leave that for the sus-Peledaen," Winceyt agreed. "How are the constructs coming?"

"Rigging-Chief Olyesi says they're done and ready to lift. They'll go off with a bang as soon as you give the word."

"Noise isn't important. We need them bright and flashy and eye-catching."

"She's got all that covered, Captain," Yerris said. "A bright light and a long burn. Nobody's going to miss it."

"Good. Let's go."

They left the office—Winceyt didn't bother locking the door, in spite of regulations about the proper way to leave an empty building—and crossed the field to the grounded ships, the two shuttles and the fast courier. The repairs on the courier weren't finished, but it was good enough to lift. Also waiting on the field were the huge tangled masses of metal and plastic and scavenged engines that Olyesi and her work crews had labored on without rest ever since the sus-Peledaen inquisitors had departed. Winceyt ignored the constructs for now; their time would come later, when they would lift and then self-destruct to provide cover for an escape into the Void.

Once aboard the courier, he strapped in and gave the orders that would take the small ships into orbit where the larger ones waited. There weren't that many of the large ships, either: the guardship *Garden-of-Fair-Blossoms,* that had been orbiting above Serpent since limping in under control of the ship-mind after the sus-Peledaen attack; and two space-only heavy-cargo carriers and one light lander, currently shifting their orbital positions from Hanilat to Serpent.

Iulan Vai had been worried that not every sus-Dariv ship would choose to go along with the plan. Syr Vai was a Mage-lord and a very dangerous woman, Winceyt reflected, but she wasn't part of the fleet. The word brought in by *Garden-of-Fair-Blossoms*'s lone survivor might not have made the public news channels, but it had gone through the family's surviving ships and crews like a rushing flood. And like a flood, it had washed out all desire to be sus-Peledaen. Even most of the hired crew had chosen to stay, and the ones that hadn't chosen knew only what all of Eraasi would know before tomorrow morning.

The courier ship broke free of Eraasian gravity; Winceyt felt the homeworld let them go. This was the turning point, these last minutes spent on the journey between the old life and something strange and new and only half-planned. For a while, he felt outside of time and space, existing in neither one place nor another, in a state where all things remained possible.

The loud noises and jarring sensations of the shuttle docking broke the illusion. Time was passing again, and passing quickly. Winceyt sat through the docking process with suppressed impatience, and unstrapped as soon as possible to go aboard the hastily repaired and re-crewed *Garden-of-Fair-Blossoms*. The *Garden*'s captain—two days ago, he'd had been Pilot-Principal on the grounded courier, and new in the rank at that—was waiting for him outside the lock.

"Welcome aboard, Fleet-Captain."

Winceyt struggled briefly with cognitive dissonance. The *Garden*'s captain was not the only person suddenly holding down a job far above his rank and training. But this was in sober fact all that remained of the sus-Dariv fleet, and he, Aelben Winceyt, was in command of it.

Very well, he would act the part. He and the *Garden*'s captain were already heading for the guardship's bridge—they both knew time was short. Everything was moving fast now. So little a span of time remained in which to take such an irrevocable step.

"Are *Sweetwater-Running, Blue-Hills-Distant,* and *Path-Lined-with-Flowers* in position yet?" Winceyt asked.

"They're taking station now. The *Path* says inspace control was frothy about the move from Hanilat to Serpent."

"Any movement yet from the sus-Peledaen?"

"Not so far. But Fleet-Captain sus-Mevyan is nobody's

fool. She'll be after us as soon as Lord Natelth gives the word."

"It's time to do it, then," Winceyt said. "Send a message to all ships in the fleet: Stand by to jump on my command. *Sweetwater, Distant,* and *Path* will take their course from *Garden-of-Fair-Blossoms;* they'll get their copies of the new charts once we reach the rendezvous point."

The *Garden*'s bridge, when Winceyt and the captain got there, looked disturbingly bare and thin of crew for a guardship. The customary depth and redundancy were absent; the handful of command-ranked officers at Serpent were spread out to cover all the ships that had to lift. The *Garden*'s Pilot-Principal—and only surviving original crew member—was pale and thin in her newly tailored officer's livery. She'd been a mere fleet-apprentice only days before, and was barely half-recovered from her near-death at the hands of the sus-Peledaen.

We'll have time later to even things out, Winceyt told himself. *We don't have time now.*

Outside the armored glass of the bridge windows, he saw the darkness of space and the curved bulk of Eraasi below: a view of baked red Antipodean earth, blue-green coastal ocean swirled with clouds, inland vegetation in patches of jade and emerald. Home.

"Pilot-Principal," he said.

"Yes, Fleet-Captain?"

"What's the status on the jump into the Void?"

"All ships have the course laid in and ready to execute, sir."

"Signal to all ships: Commence jump run now."

A vibration began in *Garden-of-Fair-Blossoms*'s deck-plates; her engines were putting on speed for a straight-line run into the Void. The vibration grew stronger and louder, and Eraasi began to fall away below the bridge windows, so that what had been a great curving shoulder of the world dwindled rapidly in the bridge windows to a distant parti-colored sphere.

"Communications."

"Yes, Fleet-Captain?"

"Time to give Lord Natelth his wedding present. Transmit

he first signal to receiving units at Serpent Station."

"Transmitting."

Nothing that happened next would be visible from orbit.
But Winceyt knew what would be going on down below as
he receiving units picked up the signal:

Rigging-Chief Olyesi's constructs would respond to it
irst, lifting ponderously from the baked earth in a roar of
eavy engines. As soon as the constructs had cleared the
ield, the incendiary charges on the ground would start going
off one by one, and the sheds and buildings and storage
angars of Serpent Station would be consumed in white and
ll-devouring flame.

Let the sus-Peledaen have it. We're done.

The Pilot-Principal spoke again, her voice thin but firm.
"Stand by for jump."

"Communications. Transmit the second signal."

What happened next, Winceyt in part experienced and in
part could only imagine. Rigging-Chief Olyesi's constructs,
oushing their way toward low orbit, would receive the signal
nd respond by blowing themselves up—becoming dazzling
white fire-blossoms, filling the sky over Serpent Station with
a pale and dreadful light and sending hot debris raining down
nto the coastal sea.

At the same time, the faint queasy sensation of a jump
ippled along Winceyt's nerves. Outside *Garden-of-Fair-*
Blossoms's bridge windows, the bright dot that was Eraasi
winked out, and the velvet black of space changed inside a
heartbeat to the all-enfolding greyness of the Void.

18:

The engines of Kiefen Diasul's chartered courier fell si
lent, and the spacecraft settled onto its landing legs. The pilo
waved a hand at the portion of the local landscape that wa
visible outside the bridge windows.

"Welcome to Ninglin, the back end of the heartworlds. /
wonderful place to be from."

"You sound as if you know the place," Kief said.

"Damn straight I know it. I left here as hired crew on a
sus-Radal merch as soon as my legs were long enough to
hike to the port. And this is the first time I've ever bee
back."

That explained the accent, Kief reflected. He had to admi
that the charter pilot was right. Ninglin was a long way from
Eraasi.

The planet was the most recently found of the heartworlds
the Ninglinese had barely qualified as a spacegoing peopl
when their Mages made contact with Eraasi's across th
Void. Garrod syn-Aigal had been the Void-walker who firs
touched Ninglin's soil, some years before he left the Hanila
Institute and founded Demaizen; the working had been th

last one of any major consequence done by the Institute Circle.

The last one until now, Kief reminded himself. *The Institute Circle was part of our working for Isayana; now they can call themselves true Mages again.*

Ninglin's backward status meant that the world had only one spaceport, and that one a low and muddy thing—except on the landing field, of course, where the jets of arriving and departing spacecraft had already fused the soil into a glassy hardness.

"I have business here of an unpredictable nature," Kief said to the pilot. "I may need you to stay in port for quite some time."

"It's your money." The pilot leaned back in the control chair and put his booted feet up on the console. "I'll be sacking out on board ship, but there's flophouses in town if you're tired of sleeping in back like cargo."

"Thanks," Kief said. "I think I'll see what the port has to offer."

Actually, he'd found the quiet of the empty cargo bay a good thing. He'd spent most of the Void-transit in its echoing space, part of the time occupied in meditation, and part in teaching his new body the moves and forms of combat with a Mage's staff. Intent counted for much when dealing with the *eiran,* but it was skill that gave a working its highest intensity and drew out of it the greatest power.

"You might want to take this with you, then." The pilot fished around in the storage drawer under the main console and extracted a small but menacing-looking handgun, which he held out to Kief butt-first. "Ninglin Spaceport isn't Hanilat, and if you run into trouble you can't count on Fire and Security to pull you out."

"Thank you," Kief said, although he privately considered the handgun unnecessary. Ninglin Spaceport was unlikely to harbor anything that could take out an Eraasi-trained Mage.

"Yeah, well . . . portside nightlife can get rough. If you have to come back to the ship in a hurry one night, you won't be the first person it's ever happened to."

Kief thanked the pilot again, pocketed the handgun, and headed into town. The pilot hadn't mentioned any ships from

Eraasi in port; perhaps he had beaten Vai to Ninglin in spite of her head start. That was good; it meant that he could wait and keep watch, and take her unawares.

Nobody looking at him would realize that he was a Mage. He'd taken pains not to look like one, wearing ordinary street clothes and a long loose coat that did well enough to hide the staff at his belt. It might have been wiser to forgo the staff altogether, but he found himself no more willing to leave it behind than Iulan Vai had been.

The main street outside the Ninglin landing field was wide and muddy, a grey silty mud that splashed up onto the wheels and sides of the boxy little locally made groundcars. Somewhere else on Ninglin, Kief assumed, there must be paved roads for the groundcars to run on properly—maybe there was even a pavement here, somewhere under all the mud.

A block past the port gate, his aesthetic senses reeled under the assault of a large, gaudy, internally lighted sign, so big it covered one whole wall of the building it advertised:

HANILAT LOUNGE —HOSTS AND HOSTESSES TO SERVE YOU ANYTIME —BAR AND CAFE —GAMES OF CHANCE — ROOMS BY THE HOUR, THE NIGHT, OR THE WEEK.

Kief looked at the sign in stunned appreciation and began to smile. He hadn't had much time to know Iulan Vai before the Demaizen Circle split in two and she followed Arekhon sus-Khalgath across the interstellar gap, but he remembered her peculiar sense of humor. She would find the façade of the Hanilat Lounge intensely amusing—he was certain of it.

Today, or tomorrow, or another day, that horrible sign would draw her in without any need for him to work the *eiran* at all.

Then I will ask her where to find Arekhon, and she will tell me.

By the time *Fire-on-the-Hilltops* reached Ninglin, the former sus-Dariv contract carrier had acquired a new name, a new port of origin, and a new ID transmitter. Zeri was impressed by the high level of technical knowledge her cousin Herin and Iulan Vai brought to the process of making the forgeries. She was convinced by now that Vai had been somebody's confidential operative before she became a Mage—which explained a good deal about Herin's former life as well. She'd always wondered what it was he did for the family; the dilettante act had never struck her as all that convincing.

Me, though . . . I really was a dilettante. At least I could tell when somebody else wasn't.

Making the forgeries had proved simple, compared with the job of convincing the *Fire*'s ship-mind to agree to the disguise. The ship-mind was old and cranky, and not fond of change; it required many iterations of the new data before the *Fire* would agree to answer, for public purposes, to the new name *Once-Over-Lightly*.

"If anybody digs down into the deep files, we're gone," Herin said. The *Fire*'s new paperwork had already convinced inspace control, port control, and the local customs office, as well as the desk clerk at their lodgings, but he still looked dissatisfied.

They'd locked up the ship after landing, and taken a quartet of rooms at the Far Call Guest Home, a faded but respectable rooming house at the edge of the port district. The windows in the Far Call's bedrooms were uncurtained, and the bright lights of the strip cast flashing patterns on the walls: an uncomfortable reminder that ships came and went daily even on Ninglin, and that any one of them might bring pursuit.

On the other hand, while the mattresses on the guest home's narrow beds were thin and lumpy-looking, at least the rooms had beds instead of acceleration couches. Zeri felt guilty about having been granted the relative luxury of bunking in the captain's cabin during the transit from Eraasi, and was glad the others would have a chance at some comfort.

"Don't worry about the deep files," Len advised Herin. "Anybody who gets close enough to read those will have already spotted the old serial numbers on the outer hull. And we can't fix those without spending time in a repair yard."

"You cheer me unspeakably," Herin told him.

"Stop it, both of you," said Zeri. "I want to know what we're going to do on Ninglin now that we're here. We've been running nonstop ever since I climbed out of that window in Hanilat, and I'm tired."

Iulan Vai answered her. "What we're going to do on Ninglin is lie low, get some rest, and wait for the hue and cry to die down. The last thing we need is one of Lord Natelth's operatives following us out of here to the rendezvous point."

"No," said Zeri. "We definitely don't want that."

The upcoming rendezvous was another thing that was causing her to fret, and she already knew that spending time on Ninglin in forced inactivity was going to make the fretting worse. At least as long as they were on the run, nobody had expected her to make decisions on behalf of what remained of the independent sus-Dariv.

And a pitiful lot we are, too, she thought darkly. *A handful of ships and a fine-arts dabbler who's only alive now because she couldn't be bothered to pay attention to business in the first place.*

On the other hand, while she might not have much by Eraasian standards, Ninglin was currently doing a good job of reminding her that Eraasian standards weren't the only ones around. On a world like this one, three cargo ships, two shuttles, and a fast courier would look like a star-lord's fortune. Given time, they might even be able to bring the sus-Dariv remnant back to . . . well, maybe not wealth, as they'd known it before, but something like comfortable prosperity.

The trick, of course, was going to be finding somewhere out of reach of the sus-Peledaen.

And where in the galaxy is that *going to be,* she wondered, *when we can't even trust someplace as backward as Ninglin to be safe?*

Cold-Heart-of-Morning had been in orbit over Ninglin for almost a week by the time the merchant ship *Once-Over-Lightly* landed at the port below. Egelt and Hussav were passing time at playing flipsticks in the *Cold-Heart*'s wardroom when word of the *Lightly*'s arrival came in.

"Think this one's our boy?" Hussav asked.

Egelt studied the message on the table display. "Hard to say. The configuration's pretty close, but he's got a sus-Oadlan contract ID and the ship's log says he's come straight here from Ayarat."

"Damn. I'm starting to think we outsmarted ourselves by coming here, and the pretty sus-Dariv and our mystery man are somewhere else laughing themselves silly at our expense."

"They're coming to Ninglin," Egelt said. "Care to place a bet on it?"

"We already have."

"Our jobs, yeah." Egelt frowned at the message again. "Something still doesn't look right about this guy. We'll see what our contacts have to say about him after they get done working over his ship."

"You think that's going to be worth the trouble?" Hussav was disposed to be gloomy—the last round of flipsticks had not gone well for him, and he was usually better at the game than Egelt. "Those chase-and-go-homes are some of the wonkiest pieces of technology I've seen in a long, long time. Expensive sons-of-bitches, too."

"But if they work," Egelt said, "and our guy runs again, this time we can follow him without having to make a blind jump and take a wild guess at the dropout."

All the same, he reflected, it would have made life a lot easier all around if they could have used the chase-and-go-home technology on ships leaving Eraasi—but Hanilat's port security was too tight, and its groundside crews were too honest. Ninglin, on the other hand, with its low traffic and its lax standards, was an ideal place for deploying the *Cold-Heart*'s limited store of the devices.

The door of the wardroom slid open and admitted the captain of *Cold-Heart-of-Morning,* with a message pad in his hand. The captain approached the wardroom table with a purposeful stride, causing Egelt and Hussav to look at each other with barely suppressed apprehension. Anything that had a full guardship captain doing message delivery—a job usually given to fleet-apprentices, in order to further their general ship-knowledge—could only be bad.

"Message for you, Syr Egelt." The captain of the guardship handed over the message pad to Egelt as he spoke.

The display screen on the message pad showed the Eyes Only sigil. Egelt entered his personal passcode, and the sigil dissolved and re-formed as blocks of text. The message itself wasn't the most shocking that Egelt had ever read, but it came close.

"Thank you, Captain," he said. "Have you decrypted this?"

"No, of course not."

"You will have had similar instructions?"

"I wouldn't know, Syr Egelt, not having seen that."

"Blast it, did you receive any eyes-only messages? And where did this one come from?"

"A message drone just now dropped in-system from Eraasi," the captain said. "This was part of its payload."

Egelt blanked the screen of the message pad and slipped it into his shirt pocket. "Make the *Cold-Heart* ready to leave orbit on my word. We need to shape a course back to Aul-wikh."

"Those are your orders? May I see them?"

"I'm sorry, Captain," Egelt said, making no move to retrieve the message pad. "These are eyes-only. But I will have more for you before we jump. Meanwhile, my partner and I require the services of one of your landing shuttles—we have business to transact in port before we leave."

"What's all this about?" Hussav asked as soon as the captain had left. "Why are we going back to Aulwikh?"

"We aren't," Egelt said. He pulled out the message pad, then brought up the text and extended it to Hussav for his perusal. "We've been recalled to Eraasi and our unlimited letter of credit has been canceled."

"Then what in the name of the Six Fountains do you think you're doing?"

"I'm not sure yet. But you and I are going to go down to Ninglin Spaceport and have a talk with the captain of *Once-Over-Lightly*. I have a very good idea where the blushing bride went, and I think he does, too. Now—" and here Egelt blanked the pad's screen again, and entered a string of numbers instead "—take this codefile to the ship's registrar and tell him it's the accounting data he'll need to use for paying fees and making purchases on our next jump."

"And this number really is—?"

"Accounting data," Egelt said. "For a different family ship, one that's currently outbound in the Void. No one will notice that the *Cold-Heart*'s been accessing the wrong line of credit until that other ship makes it all the way back to Eraasi."

"You're planning something, I can tell."

"Let's say I'm not quite ready to give up and head home. Even if Lord Natelth has decided to declare his lady bride dead and dispense with the morning after."

"You're crazy," Hussav said. "But what the hell, I think I'm going crazy, too." He took the pad full of numbers and departed.

Several hours later, Lenyat Irao sat at a table on the roofed-over dining porch of the Far Call Guest Home, drinking cold beer and waiting for the cook's helper to bring him the afternoon special. They didn't have *aiketen* to wait on tables on Ninglin, and the afternoon special was something whose name he couldn't even read—only the prices on the menu had an Eraasian translation—but he was looking forward to the meal. Even if the main dish turned out to be broiled tree-rats on toast points (which hadn't been all that bad, the one time he'd had them), at least it wasn't going to be ship's rations again.

Of the *Fire*'s passengers, Zeri was the only one whose exact whereabouts he currently knew. She was upstairs in her room, having expressed the intention of standing under the waterfall in the necessarium until either she felt clean again or the water ran out, whichever came first. Cousin Herin was off lurking somewhere, or at least that's what it had sounded like he'd been planning to do . . . soaking up local gossip along with, probably, a distressing amount of the local beer. And Iulan Vai had gone to try her wiles, Magish and otherwise, on the officials at the port.

The guest home had other customers, of course—it apparently catered to the more respectable end of the spaceport trade, and Len wasn't surprised to see a man dressed in business drab come up the porch steps and call out to the cook's helper for a beer. The man's Hanilat-Eraasian accent did make him somewhat uneasy, but most spaceport cities relied on some version of Eraasian for a common tongue.

All the same, Len reflected, it might be a good idea to

give up on the afternoon special and slip off the porch before the stranger noticed him.

He had, unfortunately, arrived at his conclusion too late for it to do him any good. The man in drab had gotten his beer and was heading straight for Len's table.

"You know, they don't see many travelers from the Antipodes here on Ninglin," the stranger said. He took a chair on Len's left without waiting to be invited. "And people tend to remember it when they do. If I asked if you knew an Antipodean ship captain named Lenyat Irao, what would you say?"

"I might say that I've never heard of him," Len said. *If this is a sus-Peledaen agent,* he thought, *why is he bothering to talk to me when Zeri is alone upstairs for the grabbing?* "On the other hand, I might ask why you want to know."

" 'Why do you want to know?' is definitely the wiser option," said the man in drab. "Because it turns out that Captain Irao has made some very powerful enemies."

"He was afraid something like that might happen," Len said. "You wouldn't happen to know anything more specific about those powerful enemies, would you?"

"I know that Lord Natelth sus-Khalgath wants Lenyat Irao dead, and that he sent a couple of top sus-Peledaen operatives all the way from Eraasi to make sure."

"That's old news," Len said. He took a pull of his beer. "Captain Irao would tell you he's been dodging sus-Peledaen operatives ever since leaving Hanilat."

The man in drab gave him a tight smile. "In that case, the captain might be interested to know that Lord Natelth has called back his operatives and cut off their credit."

"That's a star-lord for you," Len said. "No patience, and no gratitude, either. If I were one of those operatives, I'd be worrying right now about whether I'd have a job when I got home."

"The operatives have been worried about that for some time," said the man in drab. "And they've concluded that they don't want to operate on Lord Natelth's behalf any longer."

"Risky," Len said. "Natelth sounds like the kind of guy

who thinks a bullet in the back of the head makes good severance pay."

"That possibility has also crossed their minds," the man said. "That's why they're going to tell Captain Irao they want to jump ship and join his team, so they can help him make a clean getaway."

"All that helpfulness might be a ruse," Len said. "They could be trying to get him to tell them where he's got the girl stashed—everyone knows about the girl, too—and it could be that he's already made a clean getaway and doesn't need any help."

"It could be," agreed the man in drab. He picked up the beer with his right hand, sipped, then put it down using his left hand.

Across the street, Jyriom Hussav was watching. *That's the signal*, he thought, and headed over to join Grif Egelt and Captain Irao.

Iulan Vai regarded the main street of Ninglin Spaceport with the jaundiced eye of someone who has just spent several hours on a profitless errand. The hike from the Far Call Guest Home out to the landing field and back had left her boots splotched with slippery grey mud, and likewise her clothing below the knee. The muddiness irritated her. Unrelieved black could be unobtrusive or intimidating, depending upon necessity and her mood; all-black with pale grey mud stains, on the other hand . . . maybe the guest home had a laundry.

Her visit with the Ninglinese port officials hadn't yielded much by way of useful information. The disguised *Fire-on-the-Hilltops* excepted, Ninglin Spaceport had only one Eraasian ship on the field, a contract carrier nominally working for the sus-Radal. Without more data, there was no way to tell whether or not the ship represented a threat. It could well be legit; the sus-Radal fleet-family had maintained regular trade ties with Ninglin ever since the planet's reunion with the heartworlds.

If we're still here when they lift, she thought, *then we're probably safe. At the very worst, they'll have come here looking for us and gone home empty.*

The port officials had been a great deal more closemouthed than she'd liked, and she'd been afraid to try outright bribery. She didn't have an infinite amount of ready cash, for one thing; more to the point, a bribe in the amount necessary to break down a port official's reticence would draw unwanted attention.

Just the same . . . they were hiding something. She remembered the sus-Peledaen guardship that had been waiting in ambush for *Fire-on-the-Hilltops* over Aulwikh. Somebody on board that ship knew how to think more than one move ahead, and a guardship was faster in the Void than an obsolete sus-Radal-built cargo hauler.

If I had a guardship, and Natelth sus-Khalgath's money to spend and Natelth sus-Khalgath's authority to back me up, where would I be right now?

Lurking in orbit, that's where I'd be. Maybe using something straightforwardly sneaky, like a false ID. Or maybe something complicated and flashy, because I'm sus-Peledaen and that means I can.

Cloaking, say. The technology had been in development among the fleet-families for over a decade; the lamented *Night's-Beautiful-Daughter,* now long gone across the Gap, had been outfitted with one of the sus-Radal prototypes. The device at that stage had been small-scope, cranky, and only good in short bursts, but Vai was not so foolish as to think that the sus-Peledaen hadn't built themselves a better one by now . . . and being sus-Peledaen, they'd have built it big enough and powerful enough to hide a guardship the whole time a little vessel like the *Fire* was inside sensor range.

There was no way to prove any of that, of course, but Vai was morally certain it was true. The certainty, however, didn't change her projected course of action for the *Fire* and its ragtag crew: Become one with the local ground, and don't move until the big predators go somewhere else.

The wall-high sign of the Hanilat Lounge flashed and dazzled its way into view on the corner ahead, and Vai's mouth quirked into a smile in spite of her bad mood. She hadn't seen a place that unashamedly tacky and whorish since the days when she worked full-time for Theledau sus-Radal.

Even better, the Hanilat Lounge looked like the sort of all-day, all-night dive that would attract a ship's crew on liberty. People in there might be more willing to talk than the port officials had been, or at least cheaper to bribe; she could find out if anybody else had been poking around asking questions, and whether or not there had been any sus-Peledaen crews coming into town on liberty.

As soon as she entered the lounge, she was hit by a combined blast of bad music and bad air. Environmental control was apparently not a well-developed local technology, and the lounge atmosphere was a mixed funk of old cooking oil, unwashed bodies, stale beer, and sex. Vai made her way inside, blinking in the sudden dimness, and found the bar.

Eventually the bartender noticed her presence. "What're you having?"

"Beer."

"Tap?"

She shook her head. "Bottle."

The barkeep slid a bottle of something local across the bar, along with a glass. She ignored the glass in favor of drinking straight from the bottle—even in the low light the bottle looked cleaner—and put down a couple of Eraasian banknotes on the bar next to the empty glass.

The formalities having been observed, she commented, "Business looks a bit slow."

"Bad season for it."

"Nobody in town?"

"Couple of small ships, not big party types from the looks of them." The bartender eyed her up and down, in a way that made it clear he'd noticed and catalogued her off-planet clothes and her Eraasian speech. "You'd know about that."

Vai shrugged. "Some people are stingy. Working for them's a pain, but you take what you can get, sometimes." She glanced around the barroom. "I take it the rest of these guys are local?"

"Short-hoppers, mostly," said the bartender. "In from the lunar mines and the asteroids."

"Down at the port, they said there was a sus-Peledaen guardship up in orbit somewhere, come all the way from Eraasi. You'd think those guys at least would be ready to have fun and spend some money."

"If they're up there, they sure haven't come in here."

His replies earlier had been evasive, but this one, Vai thought, held a note of genuine grievance. *Conclusion—there is a guardship in orbit, and the whole port knows it.*

She finished her beer, added another couple of Eraasian banknotes to the stack on the bar—"for your time"—and turned to go.

And there was Len. She'd thought he was staying back at the guest home, sticking close to Zeri sus-Dariv . . . it looked like there might be a bit of something developing there, and maybe that wasn't a bad thing. Under normal circumstances, high inner-family was a long way above an Antipodean contract-captain; circumstances for the sus-Dariv weren't normal anymore, though, and they might not ever be normal again.

Zeri sus-Dariv or not, she thought, *it looks like a spacer's a spacer when it comes to the joys of a portside strip.*

"I see you decided to check out the local action after all," she said to the contract-captain.

"Yes," he said. "I've been here awhile, watching people come and go. Then I saw you."

He sounded a bit off, and she wondered how many drinks he'd had while he was people-watching. Maybe he'd cherished thoughts of making a night of it—he looked like he'd broken out his port-liberty clothes for the occasion, Hanilat-tailored shirt and trousers and a good loose coat.

Vai wished she had a coat like that herself; then she wouldn't have all the extra work and headaches of making sure that nobody noticed her Mage-staff who wasn't supposed to. Literal headaches, sometimes. The necessary constant subliminal awareness of the *eiran* caused a disquieting flicker at the edges of her vision—

Damn.

The man in the loose coat wasn't Len. And he *was* a Mage.

If the sus-Peledaen have gotten to the Circles on Ninglin already, we're dead.

She met his eyes—yellowish-hazel eyes, like Len's, but the expression in them now was not one of Len's at all—and said, "I'd be glad to try the will of the universe with you, my friend, but not in here. Shall we walk outside?"

"Yes. There's an alley not far off. We can make our working there."

They walked together out of the Hanilat Lounge. Vai tried to calm her mind as best she could—it was not going to be good if she went into this affair cursing at the inconvenience of it all. On the other hand, if she could prevail in this back-alley working and shake the Ninglin Circles loose of the sus-Peledaen, then the others, Herin and Zeri and Len, the real Len, would be safe.

The alley proved to be as muddy and unappealing as every place else she'd been on Ninglin. But empty, which was good—not that anybody was likely to disturb a pair of Mages busy at a working.

"Do you want to draw the circle, or shall I?" she asked politely.

The Mage-not-Len, in his turn, was equally polite. "Neither one of us, I'm afraid."

He took his hand from his coat pocket, and he had a weapon in it. Vai had time for one last, disgusted thought—*Magecraft is ruining me for fighting dirty; I should have seen this coming*—and then he shot her.

19:

Hussav mounted the steps to the dining porch of the Far
Call Guest House and pulled a chair up to the table. He was
careful not to sit too close to Captain Irao—this wasn't the
time to screw things up by appearing to make threats. So far,
though, things appeared relatively unscrewed. Irao was still
listening, at least, and looked more cautious than anything
else.

"It's like this," Hussav said. "When we left Eraasi, Lord
Natelth was red-hot to get his bride back and have himself
a proper wedding morning, and we could have asked for the
codes for his private bank account and the services of half
the fleet if we'd wanted, so long as we found the lady and
brought her home."

"I noticed that, back at Aulwikh," Captain Irao said. "Four
guardships chasing an obsolete cargo hauler. Very sus-
Peledaen."

"That was some good piloting, though," said Egelt. "We
were impressed. Not enough to stop us putting on speed and
beating you to Ninglin . . . but still, we were impressed. And
pleased with ourselves, when it looked like we'd finally
nabbed you."

Hussav picked up the tale again. "So you can probably imagine our state of mind when we received that message from our honored employer. Cut off, called back . . . never mind picking up you or the girl, just quit spending his money and get ourselves home."

Captain Irao didn't look particularly sympathetic. "I don't know about your state of mind, but I'm relieved."

"What *we* think," said Egelt, "is that Lord Natelth has decided it's a lot simpler to finish the wedding by declaring his lady-bride tragically deceased."

Hussav nodded. "No more expense of chasing her, no need to bother with a wedding night, and no need to worry about keeping her around the house afterward. All the advantages of marrying the head of the sus-Dariv, and none of the trouble. There's only one problem, and guess what it is? A pair of security operatives who happen to know that Zeri sus-Dariv isn't really dead."

"The more we thought about it, the less we liked the look of our long-term prospects," Egelt said. "And our choices for a sudden change of career are somewhat limited. Given the choice of becoming spaceport bums on Ninglin—"

"—with a chance of working our way up to barroom bouncers or small-time thugs inside a couple of years—"

"—or throwing our lot in with you people and whatever you've got cooked up with the rump end of the sus-Dariv, it appears that the better choice is you."

"Don't let it go to your head, though," added Hussav. "For a while there, 'spaceport bums' looked like it was going to be the big winner."

"I'm rolling on the floor laughing," Irao said. "But your story does sound plausible. You told it to me—are you willing to tell it to a Mage?"

"I'll tell it to anyone," Egelt said.

"Then we'll wait here for a little while," Captain Irao told him. "If Lady Zeri sees you here, she won't come down. But her cousin Herin is going to be back any minute now, and he's the Mage I'm thinking about. If you're lying, he'll boil your brains until they run out of your ears. But if he says you're telling the truth, then unless Lady Zeri says otherwise, you're in. Fair enough?"

"Sounds reasonable to me," Egelt said, and picked up his beer. He drained it in one long swallow.

When Vai came back to full consciousness, she was in a large, echoing space. Overhead worklights set in metal brackets shone down at her and made her turn her head away. She knew that she ought to be able to recognize where she was, or at least put a general name to it, but the pain in her arm was making it hard for her to think straight.

The Mage-not-Len had shot her, that much she was clear on; shot her in the upper part of her left arm. From the way it hurt, the bullet must have struck bone. She had vague memories of the Mage-not-Len manhandling her—half-dragging, half-walking—back out to the landing field and up the ramp of a grounded courier ship. Somewhere between the alley and the top of the ramp a voice had said, "She's a friend. I was supposed to meet her here—you were right; we ran into trouble," and not long afterward she passed out completely.

Somebody had bandaged and splinted her arm while she was out. Peculiar, she thought, to shoot her in one moment, and then to take care of her in another. No, not peculiar. Crazy.

It took her a moment more to figure out the rest of her situation. She'd been bedded down in emergency passenger berthing: absorbent foam pads and lots of heavy-duty safety webbing, made fast to recessed attachment points in the hold's deckplates, a standard setup for converting cargo space into something safe for liftoff. It was also damned good for holding someone prisoner if you didn't have a brig.

Given time, she thought she could probably get free, even hurting and with one arm splinted and useless. Emergency berthing wasn't a specialized prisoner-holding setup, and Vai was a pro.

At least I used to be a pro. Getting captured like this— they ought to make me turn in my license.

But one thing she wasn't going to have enough of, it seemed, was time. A brain-wiping roar filled her ears, the deckplates underneath her started vibrating with the rattle of a thousand jackhammers, and the pressure of liftoff came down on her and pressed her flat like a giant's heavy, smothering hand. Then the pain in her arm expanded to fill the whole universe, and she passed out for a second time.

When she came to, things weren't any better. She was still webbed down in the cargo hold. This time the Mage-not-Len was in there with her, holding his staff loosely in one hand, squatting on his heels a bit more than arm's length away, and watching her out of those yellow-hazel eyes.

"You've got it wrong." Her voice came out in a dry croak.

The Mage-not-Len blinked. "What?"

"You've got it all wrong. This is the part where you're supposed to loom over me and make threats."

He shook his head. "I don't want to threaten you, Vai."

Wait a minute. He knew her name. She hadn't used it once on Ninglin that she could remember, not even in the privacy of the guest home.

"Who the hell *are* you?" she demanded.

His expression was one of sheer bewilderment, and he shook his head in apparent frustration. "Don't you remember—no. You wouldn't know me, not anymore."

Now she was starting to get really frightened. It was a disturbing experience to watch someone with Lenyat Irao's face but another man's expressions, way of moving, turn of phrase . . . "Did you kill Len before you took his body?"

"Kill?" For a brief instant his expression changed from bewilderment to distraction. Then he said, "No. The sus-Peledaen want him for questioning, I think, but they haven't found him yet. Is his name Len?"

Damned amateur, she thought. Her head ached. It would almost be better if she were being interrogated by professionals, complete with drugs and intimidation and calculated doses of pain. At least then she'd know what was going on. This—this was only making her tired and confused, and she hurt all over, not just in her injured arm.

She closed her eyes against the glare of the overhead lights—and so that she wouldn't have to look at the Mage-not-Len's face.

"Why don't you go ahead and tell me what you want,"

she said, "so we can move on to the part where I don't give it to you?"

"It's . . . complicated," he said.

"Well, don't expect any sympathy from me on that account." Her arm was throbbing; she could feel the low vibration of the courier vessel's engines all the way up and down the broken bone. She wished she could pass out again and end all of this, but her body remained stubbornly conscious. "I'll settle for the grossly oversimplified version if you've got one."

He laughed. Not a cardboard villain's gloating laughter, or the easy contempt of a torturer with the upper hand, but a laugh of genuine amusement colored with overtones of friendship and regret. And with her eyes closed—without the distraction of seeing Len and not-Len at the same time in the same body—she knew him.

"Kief?" Her eyes snapped open again—and now that she knew the truth, she could see that the other Mage's nervous, awkward posture was all Kiefen Diasul. "What in the name of the twice-damned, bleeding, sundered galaxy do you think you're *doing?*"

"I'm sorry," he said. "But I need you to tell me how to find Arekhon."

" 'Rekhe? He's gone for good, Kief. We both know that."

He gave an angry shake of his head. "No. If 'Rekhe were dead, I'd be free of the great working. But I'm stuck in it, like a bird in a net, and it won't let me go."

Oh, Kief, she thought sadly. *Aren't we all?* "Finding 'Rekhe won't change that."

"Yes, it will. I'm strong now, Vai; if I can find 'Rekhe the two of us can break the working together."

"He wouldn't help you," she said. "The great working meant everything to him—he was as tied into it as you are. The only difference was, he didn't mind."

"Then when I find him, we'll have to try the will of the universe and see which one of us prevails."

She looked away, back up at the worklights overhead. "What makes you think I could show you how to find 'Rekhe, even if I wanted to?"

"You're running from Eraasi, and you're a Mage. Arekhon

is the First of the only Circle you have left—where else would you go?"

"You're crazy, Kief, do you know that? Stark, staring, raving mad."

"Maybe. I don't want to hurt you, Vai; I don't bear ill will toward anybody who was at Demaizen." He reached out and struck her injured arm lightly with the tip of his staff. "But I *will* hurt you if I have to."

The pain was nauseating; she had to struggle not to vomit. As soon as she could control her voice again, she gasped, "All right. All right." *Amateur. He's an amateur, and he doesn't know that you are—that you used to be—a pro. He's not going to have any high expectations about how long you're going to hold out before you cave.* "If you're so dead set on getting to 'Rekhe that you have to beat me up to do it, then I won't try to stop you."

She could hear his sigh of relief. "Just tell me where I need to go."

"My jacket—you took it off me when you splinted my arm. Or somebody did."

"Yes."

"Look in the inside sealed pocket and you'll find a data-card. It's a star chart, and it'll work with any standard interface. You'll know the rendezvous when you see it—it's a flashing purple marker out beyond the Edge, and there aren't any others like it on the chart."

"Thank you." He stood up and started to move away. "I'm sorry I have to leave you like this while we make the transit, but I can't have you giving my pilot wrong ideas before we even get there. I can bring you some medicine for the pain, though; the ship's kit has some of that."

"No," she said. "I don't want to risk choking on my own vomit while I'm unconscious."

"Suit yourself."

And he went away, leaving her alone with the throbbing in her arm and the blood-loss-induced fuzziness in her head.

Those ships from Serpent Station had better be on their way to the rendezvous by now. Otherwise, she was going to end up stranded on the sus-Radal asteroid base with a mad-man.

Len waited with the two former—or nearly former—sus-Peledaen security operatives for some time. He was afraid at first that they'd get impatient and go away, but they didn't; they sat there drinking beer in silence.

The cook's helper brought Len's afternoon special out of the kitchen while they were waiting. It wasn't grilled tree-rat after all, but some kind of stew, heavy on the vegetables and smelling almost spicy enough for his Antipodean taste. The aroma made his mouth water, but he didn't feel comfortable about eating a full meal while the two operatives had nothing in front of them except a couple of beers.

"Should I order you—" He made a vague gesture at the afternoon special.

"No thanks," said the first operative, and the second one shook his head. Len went back to not eating.

The food on his plate had cooled completely by the time Vai's cousin Herin appeared. He was coming down the street at a fast walking pace—almost a run for Herin; he normally ambled—and Len knew at once that something had gone awry.

Herin reached the bottom of the porch steps and saw the two security men, and his face went dead pale.

Looks like he recognizes one of them, Len thought. *Maybe both of them.*

Herin came up the steps without breaking stride. "Egelt," he said curtly to the first man. Then he gave a stiff nod to the other. "Hussav."

"Relax," Len said. "They're here to talk friendly."

"We can sort that out later." Herin sat down where he could watch both men. His expression didn't change. "Right now we have another problem."

"What is it?"

"Gossip from the port—I went out looking for some."

"I remember," Len said.

"Well, the last place I stopped, I found it. Nice and fresh. Somebody shot Iulan *etaze* in the alley back of the Hanilat Lounge, then dragged her off to the landing field."

" 'Somebody'?" The question came from the man Herin

had named Egelt. "You mean you didn't try to get anything better than that?"

Herin gave the man what clearly would have been a scornful look if he hadn't been so distressed. "Of course I tried. The witnesses said the shooter was an off-worlder with yellow eyes."

Everybody looked at Len, who shrugged helplessly. "I've got an alibi." He gestured at the plate of food and the bottle of beer on the table in front of him. "Ask the cook's helper if you don't believe me."

"We believe you," said the man called Hussav. "But that does explain how we could get a message saying an individual matching your description had been spotted leaving Eraasi, right after we'd gotten through having our tails twisted by you at Aulwikh."

"You wouldn't happen to have a twin somewhere, would you?" Egelt asked.

"I don't even look that much like my own cousins, Syr Egelt," Len said impatiently. "And my mother would have told me if I had a twin."

"Peace, peace—it's always best to eliminate the improbabilities as soon as possible." Egelt turned to Herin. "Did your sources at the port say anything else?"

"That a ship lifted what would have been a few minutes later."

"Which ship?" asked Len. If the *Fire* were stolen . . .

"A chartered contract-courier in from Eraasi," Herin said. "It had been waiting on the landing field for almost a week, local, and it left without filing a destination."

"That's not good," Len said.

Egelt shrugged. "Pay a contract-captain enough, and he'll forget to file and pay the fine later."

Len stiffened. "I have *never*—"

"Len." It was Zeri's voice, from the shadows inside the guest-home door. She came out onto the dining porch looking proud and imperious— by now Len knew her well enough to tell that she was scared to death. "He didn't mean to give you insult."

Len swallowed a cutting remark about the general trustworthiness of spies. "I'm sure he didn't. How long have you been listening, my lady?"

"The whole time." She gave him a faint smile. "I heard you say that I wouldn't be coming down if I saw these men here . . . so I stayed inside out of sight. Herin—"

"Yes, cousin?"

"I'm sorry that your friend is in trouble. But you have to tell us—is there any more news from the port that we need to know?"

That's a good guess, Len thought. Herin was nodding, his face still pale.

"Yes. The sus-Peledaen guardship—"

"*What* sus-Peledaen guardship?" demanded Zeri. "Nobody mentioned one of those when we landed."

"That'll be the ship these two came in on," Len said, indicating Egelt and Hussav. "And probably the same one we got away from over by Aulwikh."

"I'm sure of it." Herin wasn't looking any better. "The port said it pulled out of high orbit as soon as the contract-courier lifted, and followed the courier's projected arc of transit into the Void."

"Damn," said Egelt. "I hate smart ship captains."

Hussav gave a gloomy nod. "I don't think he believed that fake accounting data."

"On the good side, now we know he doesn't decrypt private messages. He thinks that the chase is still on."

Zeri glared at the two operatives. "Would you *mind*—"

"Right," said Egelt. "Sorry. What happened was that the courier dropped off a chase-and-go-home when it entered the Void."

" 'Chase-and-go-home'?" Len asked.

Egelt nodded. "New tech—military stuff. A message drone that can latch on to a ship-mind and pull stuff out of it. We couldn't get away with using them on Eraasi—but as soon as we'd beaten you to Ninglin, we handed over a whole cargo container of them to some cooperative port workers, and they've slapped a chaser on to the hull of every ship that's come in since."

"You put one of those things onto *Fire-on-the-Hilltops?* Onto *my* ship?"

"Well . . . yes," said Hussav. He looked a bit embarrassed. "But we were going to tell you about it, once we'd officially switched sides."

"Anyway," said Egelt, "it's the one on the courier that's the problem now. It would have given the guardship captain an exact course to follow—"

"No blind jumps," Hussav contributed.

"—including the projected dropout point. So unless the courier's pilot changes plans in mid-transit, the guardship is on him start to finish."

"And Iulan *etaze* falls out of the hands of someone who shot and kidnapped her," said Herin, "and into the hands of the sus-Peledaen."

Zeri's cousin looked shaken, and pale around the mouth. *He's taking it hard,* Len thought. Then he remembered that Vai and Herin were Mages together, and not just fellow-operatives in the shadowy world of fleet-family security, which meant there were bonds at work that he didn't even pretend to understand.

"This is not acceptable." Herin was talking again. "We have to do something."

"We can't." Zeri had gone all straight-backed and firm-voiced, like she'd been at Serpent Station, and Lenyat Irao realized that he was hearing the head of the sus-Dariv declaring someone to be a casualty of war. "We don't know who has Iulan *etaze,* or where she's gone, and we don't have the means of finding out the answer. But we do have a rendezvous to make, and a plan to carry through—and she was the one who set them both up for us. We go on."

Vai lay on the pads in the hold of Kiefen Diasul's ship, in pain and drifting.

It occurred to her that she had absolutely no idea how long the transit to the sus-Radal asteroid base was going to take. She knew that the base was supposed to be on the far side of the Gap somewhere, and she recalled that the first transit of the Gap had taken months to complete.

But that was a first transit, when they had nothing to guide them but Garrod's Void-mark. 'Rekhe knew ships, and he'd explained to her once about how initial transits always took so much longer.

She missed Arekhon. Ten years since she'd last seen him, and she'd been firm with herself about not thinking of him except as the Mage who'd brought her into the Demaizen Circle and changed her life. Friend and teacher. Respect and admiration. That was it. Nothing more.

Only now it wasn't working. She couldn't move, and she was hurting, and Kiefen Diasul had gone insane. She'd been afraid for years that she'd be the one who would lose it—a Mage without a Circle was by definition half-mad—but the universe had a sick sense of humor and in the end she wasn't the one who had snapped.

Kief's made up his mind to look for you, 'Rekhe. And when he doesn't find you at the asteroid base, he isn't going to stop. He'll keep right on going, unless somebody kills him.

And nobody *would* kill him—not even the sus-Dariv, when they showed up at the rendezvous point and she didn't—because when he wasn't talking about finding Arekhon sus-Khalgath and tearing apart the great working, he looked and sounded sane. Sort of sane, anyhow. More or less sane. Sane enough to convince the sus-Dariv, which was the only thing that would count.

So he'd get away, probably. And—because he *was* a Mage, after all—he'd keep on working the luck to get closer and closer to Arekhon. Until eventually, someday, it worked.

Somebody would have to warn 'Rekhe. And tied down and hurting as she was, there remained only one way to do it. Vai closed her eyes against the bright lights overhead, relaxed as much as she could under the pain and the safety webbing, and let herself fall into the meditative trance.

. . . she was alone somewhere, standing in an empty wilderness—not the stony place of the great working to repair the galaxy, but a high rolling landscape like the Wide Hills District back on Eraasi. It wasn't Eraasi, though, not even in dream. The ground cover underfoot was the wrong shade of green, and the sky overhead was the wrong shade of blue, and the trees that grew here and there in the folds of the hills were the wrong kind of trees.

She wondered if this was Arekhon's new world. Or was

this only the way that she, who never saw it, had created it in her mind? It didn't matter, really—it was enough that it existed to show her where Arekhon was, and to help bring her to him.

It was a cold place, this landscape of her mind; she was glad that she'd had the forethought to bring her jacket along with her when she started walking. But where should she go?

Vai remembered the Wildlife Protection League's safety pamphlets on how to stay alive in the woods: going downhill was almost always a good move when you were lost. Downhill would put you on the way to finding things like water, and roads, and people. She headed downhill.

She walked for a long time, and still didn't see anybody. She didn't see any sight or sound of wildlife, either, which would have made her uneasy if she hadn't known that none of this was real. It was a long hike down to the low ground— she felt like she'd been walking all afternoon, although she didn't get hungry and she didn't feel the sun getting warm on the back of her neck.

After a while she came to a grove of the not-quite-right trees, with a jumbled pile of boulders in the middle of the grove. The pile had been there for quite a while, from the look of things; grass grew on top of it, and more grass was growing out of the cracks in between the boulders.

Something about the place made the small hairs along her arms and the back of her neck stand up and vibrate. She circled the pile of boulders. She wasn't surprised, not really, to find an opening on the other side, with two standing stones topped crosswise by a third to make a door.

I love it when my mind sends me invitations I can't turn down.

She went in. Her nostrils were full of the smells of damp loam and cold air. The ground underfoot sloped steeply downhill; soon the light from the mound entrance faded, and she was in the dark.

Vai thought about calling light to her staff, but rejected the idea as too pretentious. She'd done it once to impress Herin, back in the basement of Demaizen Old Hall, but there was nobody to impress in this tunnel but her. She carried a perfectly good mini-light in the vest pocket of her jacket, and it would do the job.

The incandescent beam lit her way farther downward. The tunnel was a single path, with no turnings—she supposed that her mind was telling her that the journey was urgent, and that she couldn't afford any distractions from her goal—and it coiled and spiraled ever inward and became narrower as it went.

Tighter and tighter it grew, and the ceiling grew lower. She could stretch out her hands to either side and touch the dirt walls, reach up and touch the weight of the earth over her head.

She went on. The tunnel kept on getting narrower. She didn't even have to lift her arms to touch the sides; all she needed to do was flex her wrists, and her fingernails scraped against the dirt. She had to bow her head to keep from grinding the earth into her scalp.

Then the light in her hand went out.

She stood there, wrapped up in absolute, utter darkness, and felt its pressure so intensely that she couldn't breathe. Then the paralysis lifted. She drew a loud, shuddering gasp—the air in here smelled ghastly, like something dead for so long it had gone past rotting—and took a step to turn and back away.

Only she couldn't. The tunnel had narrowed behind her as well as before, and she was trapped in the dark.

She forced herself to breathe deeply. *Calm. Never mind what the air smells like, take a good breath. Remember, you asked to be here. You won't have left yourself without a way out.*

No. Understanding came; this was something new she was teaching herself, under the pressure of her need. *Not out. Through.* She stepped forward, and the dirt walls fell away from her and the light came on.

She was in a corridor, a familiar unmystical passageway built out of steel and glass and plastic and paint, and she knew at last where she was. Over a decade had gone by since she'd last stood on the deckplates of *Night's-Beautiful-Daughter,* but she hadn't forgotten. She felt a brief surge of triumph—*'Rekhe is here; I've done it!*—and reminded her-

self that she hadn't yet done it all. She had to find Arekhon
and give him her warning.

She needed to look for him in crew berthing on the
Daughter. She hadn't had a chance to see much of the ship
before Arekhon took *Night's-Beautiful-Daughter* away
across the Gap and the rest of Demaizen went with him, but
she remembered how to find crew berthing from where she
stood.

The cabin locks were nothing to her; this was her meditation, after all, and she knew all the codes. The first door
that she tried showed her Narin Iyal asleep in her bunk, and
the second cabin belonged to Ty. Watching Ty sleep sad-
dened her a little: He'd barely been out of boyhood when
she first met him, and not much older than that when she
saw him last, and now he was a man nearing middle age,
with tired lines on his face that not even sleep could erase.

She was prepared, then, when she came to Arekhon. The
shock wasn't as great—he'd been older than Ty before, and
had already grown into the face he would wear for most of
the middle part of his life—but she felt a pang nevertheless,
seeing how threads of silver had stippled his thick black hair,
like the threads of the *eiran* against the dark. Maybe that was
why so many Mages went grey early, to remind them of what
they worked with, and how much it sometimes cost.

Stop it, she thought. *That's done and gone. Do what you
came here to do, and then go.*

20:

NIGHT'S-BEAUTIFUL-DAUGHTER: SOMBRELÍR
SUS-RADAL ASTEROID BASE
SUS-OORADAL GUARDSHIP *EASTWARD-TO-
DAWNING;* SUS-DARIV GUARDSHIP *GARDEN-OF-
FAIR-BLOSSOMS*: SUS-RADAL ASTEROID BASE
NEARSPACE

Vai reached out and touched Arekhon on the shoulder.
" 'Rekhe! 'Rekhe, wake up!"

Arekhon gave a full-body shudder, said, "What!," and sat
up on the bunk with the crumpled bedsheet falling down
below his waist. It was an excellent view; Vai wished she
had the time to admire it properly, even if it was only a
construct in her mind.

" 'Rekhe," she said. "It's me. Iulan Vai."

He was still half-asleep. He smiled, the smile that in the
old days could convince anyone to do anything—make a
lover out of a stranger or a Circle-Mage out of a sus-Radal
spy—and said, "I haven't forgotten. You talk to me in
dreams, Iule, and tell me I need to come home."

"Not this time, 'Rekhe. This time it's different. Kief's
gone mad, and you have to stay away."

"Mad? How?" His expression grew sharper; he was all the
way awake in an instant. "Something is wrong, Vai—I can
see that you're hurt."

She looked at herself. Arekhon spoke the truth. The self-
image she'd worn while walking through the hill country was
gone. The jacket she wore now had its left sleeve empty, and

her arm was in a sling. Bloodstains covered her sleeve and the front of her shirt.

"Damn it, 'Rekhe—you always were too good at seeing things for what they really are."

"Did Kief do that?" Arekhon demanded. "If he did, you're right—he's mad."

Just for a moment, she let herself rest in the caring and the concern. There was nobody left on Eraasi to care for her like that anymore; now she was the one who was taking care of things. She wasn't even part of Demaizen anymore, not really—if there *was* a Circle, it was only her and Herin, and she was the First of it.

She gave a deep sigh. "Yeah. It was Kief. He thinks that if he can find you, you'll help him break Garrod's working . . . or fight with him for it, and he'll break the working if he wins."

"I see. Where is he now?"

"No!" she said. " 'Rekhe, you can't fight with him. He's crazy—he doesn't even have his own body anymore; he's gotten hold of somebody else's somehow—and by the time he finds you he might not even give you the *chance* to fight."

"Then I need to find him now," said Arekhon, "before it gets worse."

Anger rushed through her, hot and sudden. "I came all this way to warn you—to tell you to stay away from Kiefen Diasul no matter what—and now you tell me you're going to *find* him? I'd forgotten what an ungrateful bastard you can be sometimes."

He hung his head, and the long dark hair fell across his bare shoulders to hide his face. "I know. But I can't let Kief destroy the great working—if he keeps on like this, he'll pull it apart whether he fights me or not. Tell me how to find him, Iule. Please."

She felt it now, as she realized he must feel it all the time—the inexorable weight of the working, pressing in.

"All right."

Vai reached with her good hand into the inner pocket of her jacket, and took out the star chart she'd kept there ever since leaving Hanilat. She put it on the pillow next to where his head had lain.

"This will take you where you want to go."

"Thank you."

He lifted his head, and looked again at her face. In another heartbeat, she thought, he would reach out a hand and touch her.

But there was no time for it; there was never any time. The world of her meditation was coming apart around her, and she was falling, falling, down and through and backward into the glaring bright emptiness of the cargo bay.

Bertan Hafdorwen syn-Radal, captain of the sus-Radal guardship *Eastward-to-the-Dawning*, was sleeping in his bunk when the *Dawning*'s Command-Ancillary sounded the message call. Hafdorwen pushed the Answering light on the bulkhead next to his pillow and listened.

"We have contact from the listening posts in the BK-two area," the Command-Ancillary reported. "Someone's come out of the Void."

"Someone? Who? A man or a ship?"

"Ships, sir. The listening posts went dark after one challenge, per doctrine. We have three contacts, at least. No reply on the family channel."

"I'll be right up," Hafdorwen said. He was already sitting up and pulling on his trousers, and had the lights up to half-intensity to enable him to find his way.

Command of *Eastward-to-Dawning* was a prestigious position, and meant that the fleet-family had trust in him. Bertan Hafdorwen knew that he was one of perhaps half a dozen people in the entire galaxy who possessed the secret charts needed to reach the refuel and repair station Theledau sus-Radal was building, here on the other side of the interstellar gap. Hafdorwen suspected that there were other stations—he would certainly build more than one of them, if *he* were Theledau sus-Radal—but he had no way of knowing for certain, nor any need to know. He didn't think about it often in any case; that sort of decision was fleet-family policy far above his present level.

But duty at the station was a long journey out of the way, and aside from the return trips to Eraasi to replace the crews and pick up supplies, it was dead boring. Ship's-day in and ship's-day out, the little line of fabrication drones picked at the substance of the smaller asteroids nearby, and refined them into building materials. Then they transported the materials to the larger asteroid that was being converted into a base.

The routine had gone on for months so far—months that were rapidly turning into years. Only Captain Hafdorwen saw the charts, or knew where the ship was jumping to; the crews were never told, and since one piece of space looked much like another, they had no way of finding out for certain where they were located.

But now, apparently, someone had found them. Someone who wasn't responding on the family frequencies.

Hafdorwen arrived on the *Dawning*'s bridge, and looked at the stack of intercept reports.

"Everyone dark?" he asked the Command-Ancillary.

"We broadcast once, narrow and compressed. The drones have shut off. The base is silent. So yes, we're dark. Our friends—" and here the Command-Ancillary tapped her fingernail against the intercept on the top sheet "—know that at least one listening post exists, because they would have heard the challenge, and they know that at least one ship exists, because they would have heard our broadcast."

"And from that they'll logic out that there are more ships," Hafdorwen said. "Because we wouldn't be talking to ourselves, eh?"

The captain strode over to the bank of bridge windows and looked out. The brilliant, unblinking stars were as they'd always been: no sign of intruders, not that he'd have been able to see them in any case. The unimaginable distances of space would have swallowed them whole.

"Whoever it is," the Command-Ancillary said, "they know that we're here. Otherwise a fleet would hardly pick here to drop out of the Void. So we have to assume that they know everything, including the location of the base."

"They must be unsure of themselves at best," Hafdorwen said. "For all they know, there's another layer of secrets, and a whole fleet waiting to gobble them up."

"So," the Command-Ancillary said. "What are we going to do?"

"Prepare for battle, of course," Hafdorwen answered. "That's why the family put us out here."

In the spaceport at Sombrelír, Karil Estisk sat in the pilot's chair on the bridge of *Night's-Beautiful-Daughter*. Outside the *Daughter*'s bridge windows, the sky was turning rosy-grey with the coming dawn.

Everybody else on board was still asleep; they'd boarded the starship last night for a morning departure. The *Daughter* was fueled up, resupplied, and ready for Karil to take her back across the interstellar gap, to the home of Arekhon sus-Khalgath's murderous relatives and entire fleets of space pirates. All for the sake of a working Karil had never seen and didn't especially believe in.

That settles it. I am *crazy.*

The door behind her slid open with a click and a sigh, and footsteps sounded on the deckplates. She turned around in the pilot's chair and saw Arekhon.

The Eraasian looked like he'd experienced a severe shock. His pupils were so dilated that his grey eyes appeared almost black, and there was feverish red color along his normally pale cheekbones. He was carrying something in his hand—she couldn't tell what.

" 'Rekhe," she said. "What's up?"

"Do you have the course for our Void-transit?"

"Worked out and laid in," she said. It wasn't like Arekhon to be so abrupt; something was definitely wrong. "Just like you asked for."

"Scrub it." He held out the thing he was carrying. "Use this instead."

Karil looked at it, and saw a stiff flat piece of card plastic with no distinguishing marks. Light danced off it, quick flashes of brightness there and gone again, and she realized that Arekhon's hand was shaking.

She took the card. "I've never seen one of these before. Use it how?"

"It's a star chart. An Eraasian star chart." He was fretting now, gazing wildly about the bridge—he had to be looking for something, only she didn't know what. "There must be a reader on board that will interface with the *Daughter*'s systems; they would have intended her to use the family charts . . . aha!"

He'd found a shallow sliding drawer under the edge of the main console. Karil had seen it before, but she'd never understood what it was for—the *Daughter* was full of inexplicable things, and she'd forgotten that one almost as soon as she'd first noticed it. Arekhon placed the flat piece of plastic into the drawer and slid it closed.

"There." His voice held a note of satisfaction, and some—though not all—of his visible tension went away.

An image was forming over the main console. It was flat, like a rumpled grey carpet, full of folds and ridges and valleys. Colored lights shone here and there on the carpet: a big bunch all on one side, and a white one standing alone a long way off. And also a long way off from the main group, a single light colored a deep, pulsing violet.

A few seconds later, a new light—bright golden this time—winked into existence and joined the others on the grey carpet.

"What is that?" Karil demanded.

"The new light—the gold one—that's Ophel. The chart picked it up from the *Daughter* now that we've set a Voidmark here."

"That's what you and Maraganha were doing the other night?" she asked. "Setting Void-marks?"

"Yes," he said. "The white Void-mark, that's Entibor— Lord Garrod set it, at the start of the great working." He pointed to the cluster of lights. "And those are the homeworlds. Eraasi, there, and Ninglin and Cracanth and all the others."

"Uh-huh. And what's that purple one, over here on the same side as us?"

"That's the place we have to go."

Karil stared at him. "What?"

"You need to scrub the old course," he told her, "and set up a new one for that mark."

" 'Rekhe, I can't even *read* this chart of yours, let alone interface it with the navicomps!"

"I'll help you. My fleet-family days were a long time ago, but 'Prentice-Master syn-Lanear wouldn't have turned me loose if I couldn't set up a straightforward course from a standard chart."

"I am never going to understand you people." She looked at him with concern. "Listen to me, Arekhon. Last night you were bound and determined to head home to Eraasi, the same as you've been ever since you showed up on my doorstep and talked me into making this trip. Then this morning you come bounding onto my bridge with a star chart you've apparently pulled out of your left ear, and you point at a blob of purple light and tell me that we have to go there instead. Before we do anything, I think you need to tell me what's going on."

Arekhon sat—no, collapsed—in the copilot's chair. "Iulan Vai—remember her?—"

Karil nodded slowly. "Dark hair, wore black a lot. One of your people, not the, whatever you call it, the family."

" 'Fleet-family.' Yes. That's Vai. She stayed behind on Eraasi. And she brought the chart to me last night."

"If anybody else in the galaxy said that to me, 'Rekhe, I wouldn't believe them." She looked again at the star chart, and the glowing white light that was Entibor. "But I've seen what you can do."

"You'll set the course, then?"

"Maybe," she said. "You've told me how; now I'm waiting for you to tell me why."

He sighed. "Kiefen Diasul. You don't know him—he was the Mage I fought with at Demaizen Old Hall, before the *Daughter* came and took us away. He's looking for me, Vai says—he wants to end the great working, and he needs me either to help him end it or to be dead so I can't stop him."

"And let me guess. Instead of heading in the other direction as far and as fast as you could, you talked Iulan Vai into giving you a map to Kief's location with 'X marks the spot' written on it in big red—excuse me, big purple—letters."

He looked away; but not before she saw the color rise in his cheeks. "Something like that."

"I still think you're crazy. But I'll set the course."

The tension went out of him like a taut string being loosened at the peg. "Thank you. Because it's not just the working. Vai didn't say so, but I think Kief has her with him. And she's been hurt."

For Iulan Vai, the transit to the sus-Radal asteroid base passed in a long, confusing blur. After her walk through the landscape of her mind in search of Arekhon, she lay strapped down and feverish in the ship's cargo hold, with no clear awareness of the passage of time, or even of whether she was sleeping or awake.

When her head finally cleared, she was still in the cargo hold, but she was no longer strapped down. There were clean sheets on the emergency cushion, and—except for her matted and unwashed hair—she herself was also clean. She was naked under the sheet that covered her, but her clothes lay clean and folded in a neat pile on the deckplates by her head.

Somebody, then, had taken care of her. She didn't remember who—Kief, most likely, or the unknown person whom Kief had addressed when he first brought her aboard. That would have been the pilot, Vai decided. Kief was a scholar, and his family were merchants; he didn't know how to handle a starship.

Her staff lay atop the folded clothes, and a ship's-first-aid-kit standard sling lay underneath the staff. Vai dressed herself slowly and carefully. She was still weak, and her splinted arm hurt whenever she touched it or moved it wrong. The sling helped, once she got it into place. The shirt wasn't hers—the old one would have been a total loss anyway—but a cheap man-tailored one from a chain of clothing stores in Hanilat. The left sleeve had been thoughtfully slit down one seam to allow for the bulky splint on that arm.

There weren't any shoes; she had to stand barefoot on the cold deckplates. She clipped the staff to her belt—it had to have been Kief who provided the clothes; leaving the staff was definitely the act of a fellow-Mage—and finished by running the fingers of her good hand through her tangled hair.

I wish I had a hairbrush, or even a comb. My head itches.

She heard the door of the cargo hold opening, and turned toward the sound. As she'd anticipated, it was Kief. He was wearing the loose coat again, and she knew that he was carrying his little handgun in the right-hand pocket.

"Do you have spy cameras in here," she asked him, "or is this just an example of good timing?"

"It's timing," Kief said. "But I don't know if it's mine or yours."

"What do you mean?"

There was a look in his yellow-hazel eyes that she didn't quite understand. "According to the chart you gave me, we've reached our destination."

"And?" she said.

This is the part where he shoots me dead out of spite. I knew it might happen, but it was going to be worth it, to keep him away from 'Rekhe . . . then I had to go and bungle even that.

"We're at an asteroid, or something that looks like one." Surprisingly, Kief looked intrigued, not angry. *He was a stargazer,* she thought, *before he came to the Circles. He knows what's natural and what isn't.* "And there appear to be quite a lot of ships in the nearspace vicinity."

Vai felt a rush of dizzying relief, so strong that she had to struggle to conceal it. At least one thing had finally worked out right—the sus-Dariv were here as scheduled. She tried to appear curious but not too happy. "Whose?"

"Fleet-families, the pilot says. sus-Radal, and some that he doesn't know." Kief gave her a sharp look. "Are you sure Arekhon is here?"

She let out a deep sigh. "He isn't yet. But he will be. I gave him the same chart that I gave you."

Aboard *Garden-of-Fair-Blossoms,* the senior surviving guardship of the sus-Dariv fleet, emergence from the Void came calmly, at least on the surface.

"Passive sensors show fast task element is on time, on

station," the *Garden*'s captain said to Fleet-Captain Aelben Winceyt. "We all made it."

"Good job," Winceyt said. The words came out muffled; he had his face buried in the lightshield around the sensor readout, the better to see any low-level traces. He straightened up and added, "I want this approach to be as fast and quiet as I can make it."

A light on the starboard readout flashed yellow, and the *Garden*'s Pilot-Principal said, "Fleet-Captain—someone's transmitting."

"One of ours?"

"No." The Pilot-Principal remained a bit thinner and paler than she ought to be, but overall the time spent on the Void-transit had done her good. She didn't look on the verge of collapsing any longer, and her voice was steady.

"I suppose it's inevitable," Winceyt said. "If we've come out where we're supposed to be, then there are bound to be people out here. Do you have a position on the transmitter?"

"No, sir," she said. "It went up and down too fast. We have it to about a hundred-eighty half-sphere."

"Do you have any ID on it?"

She shook her head. "It's in a code that we don't recognize."

"Get traces on all the background, with permanent recordings."

"Sir." The Pilot-Principal turned to the duty logmaster—one of Serpent Station's handful of fleet-apprentices, who in happier times would have been barely senior enough to carry messages and tend the wardroom *uffa* pot—and the two of them started on the record, in constant hard and soft readout.

The other members of the bridge team, meanwhile, stood and waited. "Well," said Command-Tertiary Yerris eventually, "we don't have charts from out here, but this is certainly an interesting—"

The yellow light came on again, and the *Garden*'s communications officer interrupted Yerris, saying, "Second transmission. Attenuated. Short. I expect that it's a guardship giving orders to a fleet."

"Background is dropping," said the *Garden*'s captain, who had replaced Winceyt at the low-light hood.

"Very well," Winceyt said. "Find the things that vanished when the orders went out. Find their records. Backtrack them, then project their courses outward. That should give us the location of their base."

"Or not," the *Garden*'s captain said.

"Or not," agreed Winceyt. "They know we're here. So— message to the two outlying couriers. Get me lines of bearing on that last transmission. With those, and our line of bearing, get me a fix on the transmitter. That'll be the flagship. That's where we want to be."

"But whose flagship is it?" said the *Garden*'s captain. "That's the question."

"I wish that Syr Vai were here," Yerris said. "She claimed that she'd cover us."

"Well, she's not here, Command-Tertiary," Winceyt replied shortly, "and she didn't tell me what she intended to do after we got here. So for now we walk wary, try not to look vulnerable, and remember our pride."

"And remember that someone in this bright galaxy sold us out and tried to kill everyone in the fleet," the Pilot-Principal added. "The people who did that are still out there somewhere. And *we're* still sus-Dariv—we don't take charity from anyone."

"Meanwhile," said Winceyt, "send a narrow beam to the location of that last signal. Tell them who we are, and say that we want a palaver."

"What code?" asked the communications officer.

"None. We don't have any friends out here."

By the time Kiefen Diasul's hired ship landed in the docking bay of the asteroid base, Vai was riding in the copilot's seat, with Kief standing close behind her. The seating arrangement was an uneasy one, made even more so by her awareness that she had a madman with a handgun at her back. She knew that Kief bore her no malice—not that he truly bore anyone malice, not even Arekhon—but she also knew that he was, in his own polite and reasonable way, completely insane.

Her first sight of the sus-Radal base, however, was almost overwhelming enough to take her mind off her problems altogether. She was impressed at how close it had already come to matching the rendered image she'd seen in Thel's office. Parts of it were still being built: during the approach she saw a number of hard-vacuum *aiketen* moving about, at work transforming the base's outer surface into something like natural rock. The docking bay itself was huge, as if someone had taken the entire Ninglin Spaceport landing field and shoved it into an enormous vaulted cave.

"They hailed us on sus-Radal frequencies," the pilot said as the ship settled onto its landing legs. "Well, I'm sus-Radal by current contract, and I've got those. So I answered up and asked for permission to land or dock or whatever the local custom might be, and they gave me a beacon to home on. Slick as you like."

The pilot was talking mostly to Vai; he'd plainly realized by now that she knew more about starships and piloting than his employer did. Vai wondered if he'd also realized by now that his employer was crazy.

If he doesn't know, she thought, *there's no point in scaring him to death by telling him.*

"I'm sorry that I can't tell you exactly how long we'll be here," Kief said to the pilot. "I'm expecting someone, and I can't leave until my business with him is finished."

"Fine with me," said the pilot. "There's something strange going on outside—a bunch of ships jumping and signaling like crazy in a couple of different codes—and I'd just as soon stay in here out of the way until they get themselves sorted out."

Damn it, thought Vai. *It's a battle.*

For the first time, she felt true anger at Kief. She should have been out where she could talk to the sus-Radal before all this started, not locked up in a cargo hold; she'd been counting on using her family connections one last time to get safe harbor for the sus-Dariv ships. She felt anger at herself as well: The plans and files she'd taken from Thel's office along with the secret chart had only mentioned crew transports going back and forth, not armed guardships, and she had believed them.

You believed them because Thel never mentioned guardships when he told you about his secret base, she said to herself. *And Thel never used to leave out things like that when he told you about his plans.*

Kief's voice brought her back from her interior recriminations. "We'll wait for Arekhon down on the floor of the docking bay," he said. "It should be an excellent place for a working."

"It could be days and days before 'Rekhe shows up," she protested.

"I don't think so. The threads of the working are too tight for him to be that far away." Kief turned to leave the courier's bridge, then stopped and looked back at Vai. "Come on. If we have a few hours of free time, we can use them to find this place's infirmary. A proper set of medical *aiketen* can take better care of your arm than I was able to with a handbook and a kit-in-a-box."

"We have a message coming in," *Eastward-to-Dawning*'s Command-Ancillary said to Captain Hafdorwen.

"What code?"

"None."

"It could be from anyone, then," Hafdorwen said. "What does it say?"

"Sir," said the Command-Ancillary, looking startled. "They identify themselves as sus-Dariv."

"Why not invite the sus-Peledaen to the party, too?" the captain demanded rhetorically. "It looks like Lord Natelth's using what's left of his new wife's people in order to take down our family as well."

"I don't know," the Command-Ancillary said dubiously. "They're not requesting anything other than that we identify ourselves."

The captain shook his head. "They want to see how much we have out here, and they want to take or destroy the station."

"For what purpose?"

"For all intents and purposes, they're sus-Peledaen. This station is an asset, and they want either to take it or to deprive the fleet-family of its use."

"Damn," said the Command-Ancillary. "They sure picked

the right time for an attack, if that's the case. The station's too close to completion for us to abandon it and start over on a new one, but not close enough to defend itself or go into complete camouflage mode."

"Passive shows minimum five ships," the *Dawning*'s Pilot-Principal said. "Three of them talking among themselves, unknown code."

"They're getting a fix on us," Hafdorwen said. "Rig two transmitters on different frequencies. We're going to play some games."

"The intruders have turned," reported the Pilot-Principal. "Their new axis of advance is toward our current location."

"Let's draw them off from the station," said the captain.

The Command-Ancillary looked shocked. "And leave the station unguarded?"

"You have a better idea?" Hafdorwen asked. "We can't fight five ships. We'd be hard-pressed to fight two. No, listen—what I want to do is transmit a message to myself, drop into the Void and back out again, make a reply to myself, do another in-and-out of the Void, and then send a message again. Jump back and forth, sending a message on a different frequency each time, so it'll look like two ships transmitting."

"That'll be tough, Captain."

"Do it," Hafdorwen ordered. "The family expects more of us than merely making the attempt."

21:

SUS-RADAL ASTEROID BASE
SUS-DARIV GUARDSHIP *GARDEN-OF-FAIR-BLOSSOMS*;
SUS-RADAL GUARDSHIP *EASTWARD-TO-DAWNING*;
SUS-PELEDAEN GUARDSHIP *COLD-HEART-OF-
MORNING; NIGHT'S-BEAUTIFUL-DAUGHTER*: SUS-
RADAL ASTEROID BASE NEARSPACE

"The whole board's lighting up," Command-Tertiary Yerris said to Fleet-Captain Winceyt, aboard *Garden-of-Fair-Blossoms*. "Lots of communications coming in. We can't break them."

"Then get me lines of position on them," Winceyt said. "And everyone look sharp. One way or the other, before we sleep again this will all be over."

"We have a ripple," Yerris said. "Dropout. More ships coming in."

"They're getting reinforcements," Winceyt said. "Where?"

"By a cluster of large asteroids, Sector Three Green."

"We're working on that problem," said the *Garden*'s Pilot-Principal. Her eyes were hot and eager—she at least, Winceyt reflected, had a good reason for hoping to find someone to fight. "Using the stored data—if we assume anything that vanished after the second squawk was a ship—we have a number of tracks, converging over there. Confirm Sector Three Green."

"Put a beacon in that direction," Winceyt ordered. "Mark it. Now tell me more about those people who are out there doing the transmitting."

"Working . . . working . . . got them!" exclaimed the Pilot-Principal. "Their locations are jinking all over the place. I can't make a course or speed on either one, but we have a bunch of signals from locations TA-38 and RN-22."

"I want everything you can pull out of those numbers," Winceyt said. "And while you're working on that, I want to see where everyone was heading. The ones who went dark. Signal to *Sweetwater-Running*, *Blue-Hills-Distant*, and *Path-Lined-with-Flowers*. Guide on me. Now turn toward, as soon as you have a position plotted."

Aboard *Night's-Beautiful-Daughter*, Arekhon and Karil Estisk had stood watch-and-watch for the duration of the transit to the Void-mark on Iulan Vai's chart. Arekhon had remained firm in his conviction that the *Daughter* needed to reach that position with all possible speed, and Karil gave up arguing with him on the first day. Now Arekhon sat sipping at yet another cup of *uffa*—at least the *Daughter*'s original sus-Radal owners hadn't stinted on that vital part of the ship's stores, for all that it had gotten stale. He was leaning back in the *Daughter*'s copilot's seat, with Karil in the pilot's seat next to him.

"I don't know how you can drink that stuff," she said, with a nod toward the cup in his hand. "If we ever get trade going across the interstellar gap and your people start importing proper cha'a, the *uffa* growers of Eraasi will all be going on the dole."

"I grew up with it," Arekhon said. "I still remember my first cup. Did I ever tell you about it?"

"I don't think so."

"I was twelve, and there was some kind of get-together going on in the lower reaches of the house. It was late at night, but I wasn't sleepy. Na'e was head of the family already by then—our parents had died a long time before—and he and Isa were down there with the rest of them. So I got dressed, and walked down."

He paused briefly as Karil touched a dial, making sure of the reading, and then continued when she glanced his way again.

"I went down to the forecourt, all candlelit, with quiet groups of adults standing about, and a low murmur of conversation going on. Walked right in, and stood against a wall. I knew I didn't belong there; I knew someone would notice and send me off to bed. And I'd be so embarrassed. Publicly humiliated. And my hands were so empty. An *aiketh* was passing by, with a tray of *uffa* cups, each with a warmer. I reached out, and picked one up. If I had a cup of *uffa* in my hand, I belonged, right? Well, there it was, and it was warm in my hand. So to make it look like I belonged, like I was as sophisticated as the rest, I raised the cup to my lips and I took a drink."

"How did you like it?" Karil asked.

"Thought I was going to die," Arekhon said. "It was awful. Sour and scalding and nasty-tasting all at once. But if I sputtered, if I spit it out, if I vomited, everyone would have looked at me, right? But I was all grown up; I belonged there. I took another drink. And another. Until the glass was empty. I set it on a tray beside the door as I left. And that was the first time I drank *uffa*."

"And the second?"

"Nothing as dramatic. I was a fleet-apprentice by then, and I needed to stay awake."

"Ah." Karil smiled. "We're coming close to drop-time. Want to warn the rest?"

"I suppose I should." Arekhon switched on the amplified circuit to the rest of the ship. "We'll be dropping out to realspace in a few minutes," he said. "Stand by the engines. Depending on how well Vai's chart has guided us in, we should be at a sus-Radal base."

"There," Karil said, not looking at Arekhon, her concentration on the V-meter in front of her. She twisted the silver knob below it until the two glowing green sides of the V just met, but did not overlap. Then she pressed the Lock button. She closed her eyes and rolled her shoulders to release the tension. Then she opened her eyes again and glanced out of the pilothouse window to her right. The grey mist swirled past.

"After dropout?" Arekhon tried to make the question sound casual, but his own tension came through in it despite his effort. He forced himself to relax and lean back in the copilot's chair.

Karil moved three sliders to the right-hand end of their tracks. "This ship has the beacons set to identify us to the sus-Radal."

As always, when she spoke in the language of the homeworlds, her speech was strongly accented. Arekhon would not have recognized the family-name if the context had not helped him, even though she was fluent enough to make herself understood on Eraasi if she needed to.

How does my Entiboran sound to her? he wondered. He thought of the accent that Maraganha wore on her words—more of a harsh growl, not the elongated vowels Karil's An-Jemaynan dialect added to Hanilat-Eraasian. It struck him that he'd never heard the Void-walker speak in her native tongue. The thought of speech brought another thought to mind.

"If someone comes up on comms," Arekhon said, "let me answer them. Going by the charts, we're going to be dropping out a long way from anywhere."

"Well then." Karil was looking at the dropout timer. It faded from violet to yellow. "Here we go." She pulled back on the transit lever until it clicked into its safety slot.

The shift from Void-transit to normal space was as disconcerting as ever; Arekhon shuddered, and the light of the stars blazed up outside of the cockpit windows. Karil looked into the position-plotting scope. She paused, then adjusted the scope's brightness and focus, as if not believing what was displayed. "This may be a long way from anywhere, but there's a goodly number of sus-Radal ships here just the same. One big one radiating, and they're . . . my goodness. Jumping."

"Who else is out here?"

"Can't say . . . want me to broadcast an Any Ship message?"

"No. Stay quiet; stay dark. See if you can find that base. Are the charts good here?"

"Oh, the charts show the same position as realspace," Karil said. "This wasn't that far a jump."

"Then get us to the base. I don't want to get in the way

of whatever's going on. And I *do* want to find Kiefen Diasul before he tears apart the working."

"Well . . . the base should be over in that . . . looks like that large asteroid is probably it. Recognition beacon?"

"Yes."

Karil reached to the overhead control panels, and turned a rotary switch. It made a clicking sound.

"Response . . . and wait a minute." The emission-warning light was glowing, and an alert tone was coming from the bulkhead speaker. "Someone out there is using fire control."

"Get to the base," Arekhon repeated. "Are they searching for us?"

"No, that evaluates as a side lobe."

"Switch on cloaking, then, and move us in."

"That cloaking thing you guys have isn't a hundred percent," Karil warned him. "I'd call it thirty-five, tops, on a good day. More of a hardware enthusiast's fantasy than anything workable."

"Use it anyway," Arekhon said. "If going in cloaked manages to make us thirty-five percent less obvious, I'm all for it. If there are weapons around, that is."

"If there are weapons around?" Karil laughed. "To judge by the detection board there's nothing but." She ran a finger down the line of switches marked Cloak. "You got it."

"Now, how about getting me a list of everyone out here, and positions, and all that."

"Do I look like a fully manned bridge crew?" Karil swung her chair around until she faced Arekhon. She gestured with her hand to take in the whole of the pilothouse. "Does this look like a cruiser?"

"I have utmost faith in you."

Karil sighed and turned back to the control console. "I expect double pay for this," she muttered, and started scribbling notes on a scratchpad.

Arekhon noticed that he'd never turned off the intraship amplified circuit. He spoke to the audio pickup. "Maraganha, could you come up here? I need your talents."

He sat back. His *uffa* mug was empty. Well, he could get more later. Right now he needed to get to a place where he was safe, and where the crew was safe, then see if he could link back up with Iulan Vai. She'd have a handle on what was happening. She always did.

"Somebody out there is shooting," Karil said, looking up from the plotting scope. "It isn't just ranging and marking anymore. And . . . yep, it looks like someone took a hit. Your friend Vai dropped us into a hot war zone."

"Damn," Arekhon said. "I thought I wasn't going to make a habit of that."

"Yeah," Karil said. "Well, as long as it doesn't spread to the galaxy in general, I'm happy. I left all my stuff back on Entibor."

Arekhon sighed. The threads of the great working stretched out across the starfield before him, and all of them were dipped in blood. From the moment when Garrod had walked through the Void to Entibor, and all of the Demaizen Circle had joined to pull him back, the great working had claimed them all, and taken their lives to give itself strength.

"The universe will come together," he said. As he spoke he was uncomfortably aware that he wasn't telling all of the truth.

This is where I earn my outer-family adoption, Hafdorwen thought. Command of *Eastward-to-Dawning* and the right to call himself Hafdorwen syn-Radal were a great honor and a doorway to future advancement, but they came with a price attached and now it was time to pay up.

Hafdorwen looked at the color bar on the main display console. It showed more ships coming in, the knot in space-time that indicated a dropout from the Void. This one had arrived near the under-construction base.

"How many do they have now?" he asked.

"Minimum five," his Command-Ancillary replied. "Maximum—who knows who hasn't dropped out yet, or who's dropped out and isn't talking?"

"Let's see if we can make it minimum four," Hafdorwen said to the Command-Ancillary. "Transmit multiple frequencies, in the clear, asking them to state their name and business."

"Is that wise?" she asked. "We already know why they're here."

"The request will come from a chase-and-go-home," Hafdorwen said. "Launch one with the message, then do a quick in-and-out Void-transit to put us astern of them. Put me in their shadow zone, so I can see how they respond to the challenge."

"Preparing chaser, aye," said the Command-Ancillary. "Captain, you're made of stone."

"There were only four real sons-of-bitches in the universe," Hafdorwen said. "Now two of them are dead, and I'm looking for the other one. I want three things to happen all at once. I want the chase-and-go-home's message to arrive at their location, and set it to reencipher and retransmit, in case they have directional on it. I want us to drop out behind them at that same moment, while they're distracted. And I want a firing solution on one of their vessels."

"Aim for engines?" That was the *Dawning*'s Weapons-Principal, who'd been listening to the conversation between Hafdorwen and the Command-Ancillary with considerable interest.

"Negat," Hafdorwen said. "I want a destruct solution. People who've been destroyed can't shoot back. The opposition can afford to lose half of their ships better than we can afford to lose just us. And oh, yes," he added, to the *Dawning*'s communications officer this time. "Prepare a message drone. Send our log back to Eraasi, so that Theledau sus-Radal will know where to start looking for us if we don't come home."

Night's-Beautiful-Daughter made her careful approach to the asteroid, to a seemingly innocent shadow that held an opening. A light force field shimmered across the cave mouth, set to allow large, slow-moving things like spaceships to enter and depart while retaining small, fast-moving things like air molecules. The scoutcraft traversed what at first looked like a cave of natural stone that opened out at last into a docking bay. Then she made a slow descent to the metal deckplates of the asteroid base and eased down onto her landing legs.

"Wait here," said Arekhon to Karil. "What has to be done

here is a thing for the Circles, and you'll be safer staying out of it."

"And what do I do if you don't come back?"

"Like we discussed on Ophel," he said. "Make certain the survivors get back to Sombrelír."

"Take care of the survivors. Right. That's all I'm good for? Have you ever wondered why I agreed to come along with you this time?" Her voice was quiet, as if she wasn't sure she wanted him to hear. She looked away from him, out at the docking bay. In a louder tone she said, "In case I don't get another chance to say it: I wish I'd never had to meet you, but since I did . . . good luck, 'Rekhe."

"Thank you." He left the *Daughter*'s cockpit and made his way to the main exit hatch, where Ty and Narin and Maraganha were waiting.

They were a ragtag excuse for a Circle, he thought—no robes, just the ordinary clothes they'd worn about their daily work. Even Maraganha the Void-walker looked less like a great Magelord than she did like a small-town schoolteacher from some country district on Eraasi or Entibor. And yet— in their hands lay the future and the continuation of the great working.

"Let's go," he said to them. "Kiefen Diasul is waiting for us. It's time to finish what we began."

Together, they left the ship, walking down the ramp between the landing legs. Outside, the docking bay was cold and empty of life: its echoing walls spread wide, its top lost in shadows far above. Aside from the *Daughter,* the only things living or nonliving visible in the huge expanse were a number of construction *aiketen* in various stages of repair, and a grounded fast courier displaying sus-Radal temporary colors. Deep within the bay's recesses, a cascade of welder's sparks sluiced down, bouncing yellow-hot on the deck before they faded to black grit. The stars burned outside of the force field that blocked up the entrance, as hard and far away as the welder's sparks were close and soft.

Arekhon stood shivering, looking out at the stars. In his right hand, his silver-bound staff hung loosely. A hammer, or perhaps it was a hatch, clanged behind him. Beneath his feet the station quivered with the distant thrum of machinery.

Later, perhaps, it would be filled and braced, and the vibration would be damped. He feared the coming war: the loss, the betrayal that it would entail, the thousands and hundreds of thousands who would give their lives, unwilling, for the great working.

Truly, the threads I hold are dipped tonight in blood.

The air ducts sighed above him in the dark. A worklight glowed. A shape stepped between him and the stars. A man. Kief. And Iulan Vai beside him, with her left arm as he had seen it aboard *Night's-Beautiful-Daughter,* broken and bound up in a sling.

"Iule," he said, using the form of affection despite himself, even though he knew she preferred to brush such terms aside. But it wasn't every day that old friends and former lovers came together from opposite sides of the interstellar gap, especially with the fate of the universe at stake. "Are you well?"

"I'm well. Or repairable, at any rate."

"Good."

He turned to Kief. Vai had spoken truly, he saw—Kiefen Diasul had stolen another's body, and if it hadn't been for the unmistakable way in which the *eiran* of the great working twisted and warped in the air around him, Arekhon would never have recognized the man who had been his fellow-Mage in Garrod's Circle for so many years.

"Iulan *etaze* tells me you want to try the will of the universe," Arekhon said, "for the maintenance or the destruction of the great working."

"Yes," Kief said. "We're bound into it, you and I, and neither one of us will ever be free of it while the other one lives."

"Is that so bad, Kief? To draw the galaxy back together?"

Kief laughed bitterly. "It's killing me, 'Rekhe; I'm not alive but it won't let me die. There isn't a working I turn my hand to that isn't warped by what Garrod tried to do, and failed. It has to stop."

"Garrod began something that was too big for one person to finish," Arekhon said. "The rest of us have to see that it goes on. If you want to fight me for it . . . all that remains of Demaizen is here. Let's form the circle and begin."

Kief looked from Arekhon to the others, one by one, ending at Maraganha. "First tell me who this is that's come with you. She was never a part of Demaizen."

The Void-walker chuckled, a surprisingly warm sound in the cold of the docking bay. "Oh, but I am. The very last of Demaizen, as it happens, with more right to be here than you'll ever know."

Kief frowned at Maraganha a little longer, then seemed to cast the thought of her aside as inconsequential. "Very well," he said to Arekhon. "Let it begin now."

Kief raised his staff into guard—a swift move, then into attack—while Arekhon's staff was still at his side. Arekhon threw himself backward, out of the way of the blow, fell, rolled to his feet, and raised his staff to guard.

Kief was nowhere in sight. *Where—?*

The question was answered when the tip of Kief's staff came whirling out of the dark to strike him a glancing blow above the eyebrow, enough to open a gash and flash a bright light behind his eyes, not enough to stun or slow him. He turned to face his attacker.

"Isn't it customary to say 'As the universe wills'?" Arekhon asked, spinning again on the balls of his feet. He could feel blood trickling down the side of his face.

"No," Kief said. "Not as the universe wills. As I will. As you will. As Garrod willed. The universe has nothing to do with it." He lashed out again, a combination to head and flank that made Arekhon block and fall back, all thoughts of a counterattack driven from his head by the fury of the assault.

Kief surged in, catching Arekhon's staff between their bodies, one arm behind Arekhon's back, the protruding tip of his staff stabbing down and in as he drove his fist again and again onto Arekhon's left clavicle, trying to break it, to sever the subclavian artery with fragments of bone, to destroy with pain and without hope of succor.

Arekhon pushed against him, but Kief had a younger and stronger body now, slab-sided with hard muscle. Arekhon could not raise his knee to kick. His left arm had lost feeling after the first blow; his right was trapped.

He smashed forward with his head into the other man's

face, then went limp and dropped as Kief gasped in pain and surprise. A moment later and Kief fell, his legs scissored from beneath him by Arekhon, lying on the deckplates. Then Arekhon smashed downward with his elbow into Kief's solar plexus, making him gasp and fold at the center, shoulders and heels coming off of the deck.

The two rolled apart, then came to their feet facing each other, almost at the same time.

"You won't say it, so I will," Arekhon gasped. His staff began to take on a scarlet color, pale at first, then burning brighter. "As the universe wills."

Kief's breath was also coming hard and fast. "No. I'll see this damned working of yours stopped, 'Rekhe, if it takes me half a thousand years to do it."

"Half a thousand years is a long time to wait," Arekhon said.

"Twice a thousand years wouldn't be too long."

"What we have is now," Arekhon said. He turned his strong side toward Kief, at the guard, not yet ready to attack. His shoulder ached. Perhaps the bone was cracked. "We should make the best of it."

"True. Guard yourself."

Kief advanced, his staff glowing reddish-orange. Arekhon stood his ground, his weight equal on his feet. As the other man came into range, Arekhon stepped forward, lowering his staff and stabbing the end forward toward his opponent's chest.

Kief shifted his own staff to push the lunge aside, and slid his staff down Arekhon's in an attempt to smash fingers, while spinning to take advantage of his opponent's momentum. He found himself opposing only air, as Arekhon landed a stinging blow across his lower back.

A flurry of blows followed, faster and faster, none of them touching flesh, as the two fighters grew cautious. To Arekhon it seemed as if a woman stood far off in the shadows, watching. Vai or Maraganha, perhaps, though he didn't dare turn enough of his attention from the struggle to make sure. The end of the world was upon him, and the memory of Elaeli filled him with longing, like the long-drawn-out autumn sunsets of home.

He knew then that he would never return to Eraasi—but the reality of the wood seeking to crush his bones for the will of the universe and the restoration of the galaxy was too much for him, and he staggered, and in that moment, he thrust, and felt his staff go deep into soft and yielding flesh.

"Hold!" Kief gasped, and raised his hand to call a halt.

"For you or the universe?"

Arekhon too was in need of breath. His lungs hurt as he sucked in the cold air of the docking bay. He saw the *eiran* around him, tangled, in the deep of the wild worlds beyond the interstellar gap, where no one could find safety or salvation. Beyond the force field that crossed the docking bay's entrance the endless stars burned like ice.

"You gave me quarter?" Kief asked quietly, and for an instant it was as if they were still young men at Demaizen Old Hall, fellow-Mages in Lord Garrod's Circle and full of an eagerness to do great things in the world.

"Surprised? You shouldn't be. You spend all your strength and passion fighting without meaning. Don't fool yourself."

Kief shook his head. "You're the one who was always good at seducing other people with your words, and dragging them into all kinds of foolishness. But not any longer. Ready?"

"Ready."

Kief raised his staff and sketched a salute. Arekhon returned it, and they fell to the combat again. Flames crackled around them, the blazing light of air thick-charged with energy as two great Magelords strove to make manifest the power inherent in the universe. Arekhon felt himself entering the place where he could see and pull on the *eiran* and bring them into line, securing the pattern of the great working for all the time to come.

Almost, almost, he could touch them—but before he could reach out across the gap he felt the strength of Kief's resolve settling like a loop of fire around his chest, drawing him back into the world before he could touch the one cord that he needed above all others to pull.

—————◆—————

Interesting, thought Fleet-Captain Winceyt. The unknown contacts ahead of *Garden-of-Fair-Blossoms,* the recent emergences, headed out along a vector that would take them to where the unknowns, the ones that had gone cold, would also have been heading. Aloud, he said, "Something over there."

Then, "Mark, on the scan," said the Pilot-Principal. "We have a signal. From the near target. Signal. We have a second signal, from . . . it correlates with one of the asteroids, sir."

It's some kind of secret base, Winceyt realized. *Iulan Vai must have been intending to get here ahead of us and arrange for safe harbor.*

Well, that *plan took a blind jump into the Void a long time ago. We'll have to do the best we can with the situation we've got.*

"Interrogation and answer," he said to the Pilot-Principal. "Did you record?"

The *Garden*'s communications officer answered, "Recorded."

"Keep it handy," Winceyt said. He stood in the command position, on the raised walk by the big armored glass windows, and looked out over the *Garden*'s bridge crew. "People, I intend to fight this ship as I see fit. But if anyone has any thoughts or suggestions, I'd like to hear them now."

Before anyone could answer, the communications officer said, "Signal coming in, in the clear."

"On audio," Winceyt said.

The *Garden*'s bridge speakers came on with a pop and a crackle. ". . . unknown vessels. You are in sus-Radal space. You are required to stop. Identify yourselves."

"Where's that coming from?" Winceyt demanded. "Does it correlate with anyone we've identified already?"

Command-Tertiary Yerris said, "Negative."

"We will not stop," Winceyt said. "Make course for that asteroid. Something's over there, and my guess is that it's important to the sus-Radal. That family's one of a kind with the sus-Peledaen, these days—building stations and warships instead of sticking with honest trade."

"Are we going to reply to the signal?" Yerris asked him.

"Give them a minute," Winceyt said. "Better to let them

wonder if we're friend or foe, than to answer and remove all doubt."

"Captain, look at this," the Pilot-Principal said. She pointed to a graph on the display console, two lines overlaid, one in red, one in light brown. "Those two who were talking to each other before. The signals were on different frequencies, and they came from different positions, but look at this. There's a beat frequency in both of them that looks a lot like they're using identical antennae, with an identical power source. See, here?" She poked a finger at a jagged set of lines near the right side of the display. "I'd be willing to bet my pay against yours, sir, that these two signals came from the same physical pieces of metal."

"They were on entirely different bearings," Winceyt said.

"Yes, sir, but look at this." She laid in two more graphs. "These are Dopplers on the carrier frequencies. Both of those ships were engaged in one-hundred-eighty-degree turns at near-jump speeds. Not just once, but every time they were talking."

"Two ships?"

"One, sir. Talking to itself. I'm sure of it."

"That means—"

An alarm started wheeping before Winceyt could finish. "Sir!" Command-Tertiary Yerris exclaimed at the same time. "Someone's lighting us up with fire control!"

The sus-Peledaen guardship *Cold-Heart-of-Morning* stood by to drop out of the Void. The *Cold-Heart*'s captain paced the bridge. If the chase-and-go-home had done its job, this was where that fleeing courier ship had been heading, and this was where Zeri sus-Dariv was going to be.

Egelt and Hussav, damn their eyes, had tried to put him off the trail and keep the honor of bringing home Lord Natelth's missing lady all to themselves. *Forged accounting data, indeed. Do they think I was born yesterday?* But now he was here, and the two civilian operatives were cooling their heels back in muddy, exciting Ninglin Spaceport.

"On three," said the *Cold-Heart*'s Pilot-Principal. "Two, one, mark. Drop out."

"What do you have?" the captain asked the Command-Tertiary once the blackness of deep space had replaced the swirling grey pseudosubstance of the Void in the *Cold-Heart*'s bridge windows.

"Asteroid field," the Command-Tertiary replied. "And I'm seeing power sources in use. Five, no, six ships."

The *Cold-Heart*'s captain felt a pang of apprehension, and suppressed it. "Emissions?"

"Picking something up. Clear transmission, identifying the transmitting station as . . . sus-Dariv, sir!"

Damn. Egelt and Hussav are turncoats, and we've been had.

"That's the mutineers from Serpent Station, damn and blast them," the captain said. "Let them know that we're here and that we mean business. Range them with fire control. Communications, give me all-frequencies. Max gain. Family cipher, the share-with-the-sus-Dariv version."

"You have it, sir."

The *Cold-Heart*'s captain keyed on the ship-to-ship audio. "Unknown sus-Dariv craft. This is sus-Peledaen guardship *Cold-Heart-of-Morning*. You are under our command and control. Stop your engines; switch on your locator beacons. Send us your crew lists. Prepare to be boarded."

22:

SUS-RADAL ASTEROID BASE
SUS-DARIV GUARDSHIP *GARDEN-OF-FAIR-BLOSSOMS*;
SUS-RADAL GUARDSHIP *EASTWARD-TO-DAWNING*;
SUS-PELEDAEN GUARDSHIP *COLD-HEART-OF-
MORNING*; *FIRE-ON-THE-HILLTOPS*: SUS-RADAL
ASTEROID BASE NEARSPACE *NIGHT'S-BEAUTIFUL-
DAUGHTER*: ERAASIAN FARSPACE

Vai knelt on the deckplates of the docking bay with the other members of Arekhon's Circle—Narin and Ty, and the stranger who had named herself the very last of Demaizen. The cold air of the bay made her injured arm ache bitterly, distracting her from proper meditation; she thought with longing of the infirmary back at the Old Hall, and its first-class medical *aiketen*. The sus-Radal base didn't have anything nearly as good, only a basic care setup and a stasis box for transporting home anything worse. The ships would have better gear than the station did.

Of course, the people who usually work here spend most of their time trying not *to get hurt . . . in the Circle, it's different.*

Then the universe flared up in silver light all around her as she saw Arekhon go down under Kief's last crushing blow, and she knew why the meditation had not claimed her as it should.

I'm not part of Demaizen anymore. The insight came down on her with an impact as profound as the strike that had driven 'Rekhe onto the deckplates. *I am the one who watches, and who keeps safe what is needed for the finish of the working.*

A few feet away, the woman who had come with 'Rekhe in *Night's-Beautiful-Daughter* rose from her kneeling position and stepped forward.

"Kiefen Diasul," she said, lifting her staff in salute. "I am the last of Demaizen and the First of all the Mage-Circles, and I challenge you for the great working. Let it be done as the universe wills."

To Vai's amazement, Kief's battered and bloodstreaked features lit up in a smile of pure delight. "So in one thing, at least, my workings *do* prevail!" he said—and then staff met staff in a blow and counter that echoed off the walls of the bay.

Vai didn't have time to watch them any longer. Arekhon was lying motionless a few feet away from where they fought, and the *eiran* around him twisted and flickered with a fitful, diminishing light. She got to her feet, her balance awkward with one arm useless, and went over to kneel beside him.

" 'Rekhe," she said. Then, louder, " 'Rekhe!"

He opened his eyes—barely opened them; his face was swollen from the blows it had taken—and said, coughing, "What? Vai—"

"Get up," she said, under the noise of the fighting nearby. She struggled to work her good shoulder under Arekhon's arm on what looked like his less-injured side. "I'm going to try and move you out of here. Help me as much as you can—"

"I don't know if I—I'm hurt, Vai."

"You're damned near *dead!*" she snapped, and had to shake her head to dash away the tears that threatened to fill her eyes and destroy her vision. "But there's an infirmary here, and if we can get you in there, you'll be all right."

"Kief—"

"Your friend is with him. Your fight is over."

"It's not," he insisted. "It's just beginning. I should be dead. I should give my power to the working."

"Be quiet," she said. "Save your strength. The universe

will need it later." And as she spoke, she knew that she spoke true.

He *was* quiet, which was worse, as she dragged his increasingly limp and unprotesting body across what felt like an infinity of docking bay. She looked back once, and wished she hadn't—the blood trail stretched out behind them in one long, red streak.

Inside the infirmary, all the lights were dim. She ignored the medical *aiketh* that had done the patch-and-go on her arm—it had done better for her than a kit-in-a-box, as Kief had promised her it would, but it wasn't anywhere near equal to mending the damage Kief had done to Arekhon. The base's stasis box, an ugly thing that looked like nothing so much as a locker for frozen meat, occupied one whole corner of the room, powered down into resting mode, its lights and telltales dim. That would be her only hope, if she could force it open and put Arekhon inside. Then she could load the box onto a ship and get it under way for Eraasi, making sure that the line current didn't bobble the whole time.

Working the clamps and opening the lid one-handed seemed to take forever, and heaving Arekhon up from the deck and manhandling him over the side of the box took even longer, but at last she was done.

"There," she said. The controls on this box were automatic—stasis would kick in as soon as she clamped the lid back down and would stay in effect until the medical *aiketen* in Hanilat unclamped it again. "You're safe now."

Eastward-to-Dawning's communications officer looked up from the console and said, "The new contact is transmitting in one of the sus-Peledaen ciphers, Captain."

"Didn't I say that we should have invited them?" Hafdorwen said to nobody in particular. "I knew it. Put a spread of missiles out; that'll get them thinking. Then let's start fighting this thing."

"We're being targeted," said his Command-Ancillary.

"Launch decoys, and give me some speed," Hafdorwen said. "At least let them know they've been in a fight. And put a flock of antiradiation missiles back down the beam at whoever's illuminating us."

"One thing in our favor," said the Command-Ancillary, as acceleration pushed them all toward the rear bulkhead, forcing the bridge crew to grab the handholds on their seats. "Everything we see out here is a target. Those guys have a different problem. They have to keep from shooting their friends."

"I'd trade problems with them in a heartbeat," Hafdorwen said. "Get me into fifty percent hit range on somebody. Anybody. Now."

"Yes sir."

Out in the asteroid base's docking bay, Llannat Hyfid circled Kiefen Diasul, her staff blazing green in her hand. Narin and Ty knelt to either side, backs against the outboard bulkheads, marking the entire bay as a circle, the ground upon which they did their work.

Arekhon says this man has stolen another's body, Llannat thought. *But I know the truth. He is a replicant—perhaps the first of them all.*

That was bad and good at the same time. Kief was strong and fast, and the new body he wore was unmarked by the accumulated subtle damage of living—on the other hand, it didn't yet have the reflexes of staff combat built into its neural pathways through years of painful practice. She could make herself open, and let her body think for her. He would have to make a conscious decision for everything he did. She threw a series of rapid blows at him, not attempting to hurt him as much as to tire him, to keep him from thinking of anything more than his own defense.

"I *will* break the great working," he said. "Even if the last of Demaizen has come from the other end of time to keep it whole."

"I'll follow you to the other end of time if I have to," she said.

"Not if I end it here."

Kief launched into his own series of blows, attempting to use the power of his wrists and shoulders to overmaster Llannat's defenses, forcing her back, smashing through. She slipped and turned his blows, but with each one she gave up ground, a pace at a time, backing toward the archway where the force field kept in the air. One cracking, stinging blow sent pins into the palm of her hand, and she gasped and leapt backward.

"You've seen the interstellar gap. What could be more broken than that?" she asked, regaining her breath and slashing under Kief's guard to crease his abdomen, nearly losing her weapon as it caught in the fabric of his shirt. She took a step back, away from the deep recesses of the station, closer to the force field and the stars. "Why keep apart what needs to be drawn together?"

"Knots and threads and cords and ties," Kief snarled. He slashed down with his staff against her exposed forearm, at the same time taking her wrist in his free hand, grasping cruelly, fingers digging into her flesh. He pushed her and she staggered back a step, farther still from where Narin and Ty knelt, closer to the bay's opening. "They're all snares to catch and bind us, to keep us prisoner and force us into the working. I want none of it."

"And the galaxy bleeds for centuries because one man stood aside and said, 'This is no work of mine.' " They were almost at the force field now. Llannat twisted her wrist outward, breaking Kief's grip, at the same time laying her staff into the crook of his elbow, where it caught like a toggle— and let herself fall backward.

Her booted foot caught him in the abdomen as she lifted him up and over and threw him, flailing, into and through the force field at the mouth of the docking bay. Designed to let through spacecraft and other things larger and slower than molecules of air, the force field let him pass. He fell out and away, continuing his arc, freed now from the station's artificial gravity. His staff clattered to the deck.

"May the Void take your refusal, and all of your workings with it," Llannat said at last. She lay on the deck, panting, and did not stir.

------◈------

"The sus-Dariv always were a sneaky bunch," the *Cold-Heart*'s captain said. "Who'd have thought they were tight enough with the sus-Radal to use their base for a fallback position? We should have suspected."

"We're being targeted," said the *Cold-Heart*'s Pilot-Principal. "Someone's got fire control on us."

"Launch decoys, and gang all the controls to my panel," the captain said. "Put some antiradiation missiles back down the beam at whoever's illuminating us. Centerline pod. At least let them know they've been in a fight."

"One thing in our favor," the *Cold-Heart*'s Command-Ancillary said. "Everybody we see is a target. The sus-Dariv have to keep from shooting each other."

"I'd trade problems with them," the captain said. "Because let's be honest, they've got some powerful incentives to miss each other and hit us—most of a fleet and half a family's worth of incentives. Do you think they'll care that we were on pirate-chasing duty over by Aulwikh while their fleet was getting destroyed?"

"Say what?"

"Word is, Fleet-Captain sus-Mevyan was wiping out all of their friends and drinking buddies."

"How do you know?" asked the Command-Ancillary.

"If you haven't heard, then you weren't listening in the right places. sus-Mevyan was off on some secret mission at the exact same time as the sus-Dariv had their problems, and in the same sector. When she came back, she wouldn't talk. I know her, and that isn't like her. I can add two and two as well as the next man, and so can the sus-Dariv. There are no secrets."

"If that's what was done, it was badly done," the Command-Ancillary said. "People can't go breaking custom like that."

"We not only could; we did," said the captain. "No one asked me up front. But it's our problem now. sus-Dariv'll fry us the second they get the chance. Engines, stand by. And get a report drone ready to launch."

———◆———

Zeri sus-Dariv was sitting in the second seat on *Fire-on-the-Hilltops* when Lenyat Irao dropped his ship out of the Void. "I know I don't know anything about starships," she'd said earlier, when Len looked dubious. "But neither does anybody else on board now, except for you. And I *am* the head of the sus-Dariv."

That had been several minutes ago. Now Len said, "Stand by for Void-emergence," and she felt the ripple of internal disquiet that had accompanied all of their dropouts so far. The swirling iridescent grey pseudosubstance of the Void fell away from the bridge windows, and she saw the stars.

"Now I know why you like this job," she said, after her breath returned.

"Nothing like it," Len agreed. "The first time I ever saw it, I said to myself I was damned if I was ever going to look for dirtside work again. And so I—wait a minute."

Zeri didn't like the sudden change in his voice. "What's wrong?"

"Too many ships out there," he said, "and the ship-mind is reporting signals in at least three different ciphers. sus-Dariv and sus-Radal—"

"Syr Vai said that the rendezvous was technically in sus-Radal territory," Zeri said. "I don't think she expected to find a ship here, though."

"Well, for once Iulan *etaze* guessed wrong," Len said. "The ship-mind says that we're looking at sus-Radal's *Eastward-to-Dawning*. A guardship, damn all the luck. And the other cipher—"

"Yes? Don't just sit there, Captain Irao—*tell* me!"

"The other cipher is sus-Peledaen. It's the *Cold-Heart*." Len said something in his native Antipodean language that Zeri didn't understand, and added in Hanilat-Eraasian, "Another luck-rotted guardship. Just what we needed."

"At least Cousin Herin will be happy," she said, after a moment. "If the *Cold-Heart* is here, then—if you believe Syrs Egelt and Hussav and their chase-and-go-homes—so is Iulan Vai."

Len was busy donning headphones, and turning his attention to the *Fire's* high-frequency direction finder. "In the meantime, all we can do is stay well out of the way of things and listen."

He pulled back to bare minimum on the control yoke, sending retro blasts forward to bring them to a near halt in space, cutting power and gravity to minimal levels as well. Zeri felt herself begin to float a bit against her safety web every time she moved.

"Now, let's see how things sort out. As soon as things have calmed down, if our friends are on top, we'll tell them we're here. If they aren't . . . well, we'll find somewhere else to be. Do you think I'd look good with a mustache and an eye patch?"

Zeri looked at Len critically. "Neither one would do you a bit of good. I like you fine the way you are."

"Ah, the sweet promise of youth. But changing our names and habits might not be a bad idea regardless, as long as I can still go into space."

"Not . . . wait a minute," Zeri said. "What's this light?" She pointed to a flashing telltale on the console beside her.

"Damnation. Something's shifted back aft. Started drifting when I shut down to minimal. That's a motion detector. I'll go secure whatever it is, okay? You keep watch up here. Anything happens," he pointed to a silver knob, "call me on the intraship comm. Flip that to turn it on, it'll sound back aft. Just talk normally. Okay?" He was already unlacing his safety webbing.

"Okay."

"Don't touch anything else," Len said, and headed aft, dogging down the airtight door behind him.

Kief twisted through the vacuum outside the force field. Nothing to hold, nothing to touch, his eyes stabbed agony into his brain as if they were pierced with white-hot knives—he clamped them shut. His lungs . . . he twisted the corner and dropped, panting and gasping, into the Void. Lost, without a Circle behind him, with nothing to show the way. He could die here, he knew, but perhaps not as soon as he would have with his blood boiling out of his lungs in hard interstellar vacuum.

The grey mist that marked the Void surrounded him, the silence eerily total. He saw nothing in any direction. But then, ahead, a shape moved. A black thing disturbed the chilling mist like a rock disturbing the surface of the sea. It approached. A ship, a spaceship, moving in its Void-transit. In the way the nature of the Void demanded, the vessel seemed to be heading straight for him, at a sedate walking pace. Kief sprinted toward it, the battering he'd sustained in his fight with Arekhon and Maraganha making his legs, arms, and ribs ache, even as the Void sucked the warmth from his bones.

He grasped the leading edge of an atmospheric-control surface on the spacecraft and pulled himself up onto it, pressed against the cold, real-feeling metal, with hands that had begun to lose their strength. Crawling, he made his way to the main body of the craft and closed his eyes. He pressed flat against it and twisted. He was through, falling to the deck, and breathing in the warm, humid air of the ship.

Wherever this ship was going, he would go. It would be a world. He lived.

Abruptly, an alarm sounded. Then he felt the sensation of disquiet that marked a Void-transition. The engines sounded different now, through the deckplates. A dropout, so soon? Kief wondered where they were.

He lay motionless, delighting in having air and warmth. Then the sound of the engines changed again, dying to nothing. He felt himself growing lighter, until the slightest motion was enough to push him from the deck. Gravity had been shut off.

Kief pushed back with his elbows and floated to a standing position, grabbing a handhold to brace himself. A locker was fastened on the forward bulkhead. Kief opened it. It held ship's coveralls, with patches for *Fire-on-the-Hilltops. Luck*, Kief thought, *has not deserted me*. He pulled the coverall over his torn and sweat-stained clothing, fastening it up the front. He didn't have a staff—for the first time in years—and that was upsetting. But no matter. There had to be something on board that could be fashioned into a makeshift. He started to move forward, pulling himself from handhold to handhold.

Time to find the crew and introduce himself. He felt lucky. Lord Natelth would reward him well for returning his escaped bride.

Len moved aft. The motion had been in number-one cargo hold, and he didn't recall any cargo being in there. Maybe the sensor was wrong. Sometimes—more often than he liked to think—the sensors were wrong, and a realspace translation was often the thing to knock them off.

But here . . . the dogs on the hatch to number one were moving, apparently by themselves. Something was trying to get out. He stood, holding an overhead ring, amazed. The door swung open, and someone emerged. He saw a man dressed, as he was, in a ship's coverall. The man had a trickle of blood at each nostril, but his face was oddly familiar. Len wondered where he'd seen the man before. He was about Len's own height and build.

"Who are you?" Len asked. "How did you get on my ship?"

"Lenyat Irao," the stranger said.

"You know me?"

"No, that's my name, and I have your body," the man said, and launched himself forward, striking Len and bearing him up against the far bulkhead, all elbows and knees and grasping hands.

Zeri sat back in her chair, looking out the windows. Nothing appeared out there but the stars. They were in unfamiliar patterns, but that didn't surprise her. She was a long way from home. Len said they were on the other side of the great Gap.

A voice came up on the amplified outside circuit, from *Eastward-to-Dawning,* broadcasting in the clear, calling, "Any sus-Dariv."

"I am sus-Dariv," Zeri said aloud. "I am *the* sus-Dariv."

But she didn't key the external microphone. Instead, she twisted the internal communications switch. Before she could speak, though, she heard the internal pickups.

"Who are you?" Len was asking.

A stowaway? she thought. How long had the intruder been on board?

Then she heard a voice that sounded a great deal like Len's answer, "Lenyat Irao."

Zeri unbuckled her safety webbing. She was certain that if she were more familiar with the ship she'd be able to do something clever, like dialing the gravity in that one compartment up to about three times normal, then going back to sort out what was going on among the people lying flat on the deck unable to move. She could mend her ignorance in the future, she decided. For now, voices had given way to the sound of what could only be a fistfight.

Whatever else Zeri could do, she knew theatre.

"Time for me to make a dramatic entrance," she said, and headed aft.

Len struck back, but the stranger with his face had apparently been trained as a hand-to-hand fighter. The two men fought, battered, and screamed, twisting in midair, each movement sending them to one side or another of the compartment rebounding with bruising force from the hard surfaces.

Abruptly, the echoing roar of a slug-gun sounded, and Len was deafened. The man he was grappling jerked and went limp.

Zeri was standing braced in the doorway, the weapon held in two hands before her.

"What?" Len asked.

"A girl has to protect herself these days," Zeri said. "Herin picked it up for me on Ninglin. You just can't be too careful."

"But . . ." Len said. "How did you know which one of us to shoot?"

"I'd know you anywhere," Zeri said, and kissed him.

On board *Eastward-to-Dawning*, Captain Hafdorwen said to his Command-Ancillary, "Now that's something you don't see every day, even in space."

"What is it?"

"That sus-Peledaen guardship who just showed up is shooting at his friends."

"I don't know how friendly they think they are, sir," the Command-Ancillary said. "The sus-Dariv are shooting back."

"Take the sus-Peledaen guardship under fire," Hafdorwen said. "And make a signal to the sus-Dariv. Offer them temporary alliance with sus-Radal."

"What?" demanded the Command-Ancillary. "You want to make alliance with mutineers?"

"Better with mutineers than with the sus-Peledaen. I've heard some rumors about what really happened to the sus-Dariv fleet."

"I'll be damned, sir," Command-Tertiary Yerris said to Fleet-Captain Winceyt. "The sus-Radal guardship is shooting at *Cold-Heart-of-Morning*."

"I didn't think Lord Theledau's people would trust the sus-Peledaen for long," Winceyt replied. "Weapons-Principal, take the *Cold-Heart* under fire as well."

"Sir!" said *Garden-of-Fair-Blossoms*'s communications officer. "Message coming in—the sus-Radal guardship *Eastward-to-Dawning* offers temporary alliance."

The *Garden*'s Pilot-Principal looked up from the sensor display. Her expression was one of fierce delight. "Fleet-Captain, the sus-Peledaen just took a hit!"

"Whose?" Winceyt asked.

"sus-Radal."

"Tell the *Dawning* that *Garden-of-Fair-Blossoms* accepts the offer. Weapons-Principal, keep the *Cold-Heart* under fire."

In a hidden room in Hanilat on Eraasi, the empty shell of Kiefen Diasul stirred and his eyes opened. His wandering self, bound to his body by a silver cord none but he could have seen, had finally returned. This body was weak, damaged by its prolonged emptiness. He raised his hand and pushed himself upright, pulling free from the tubes and lines that had fed his shell.

Staggering—both from the weakness of this long-unused flesh and from the fight that his mind had sustained—he stood and pulled on a robe, and made it to the doorway one halting step at a time. He leaned there against the doorjamb for a minute, his breathing ragged and heavy, then stumbled on.

"Isayana," he said to the first *aiketh* that he encountered. "I need Isayana, now."

And so she found him that morning when she entered the laboratory. "Diasul," she said, in shock, and he raised an emaciated hand to touch her face, flesh against flesh.

In that same moment his mind flowed into hers, and she knew his memories as though they were her own, childhood and the love of learning and the fellowship of the Circles—and one memory more strong and bitter to her than all the others, of the night among the ruins of Demaizen Old Hall, when he had betrayed 'Rekhe his Circle-mate into the hands of gunmen at the behest of Natelth sus-Khalgath sus-Peledaen.

Isa was helpless then; Kief's will overrode her own. She was aware that he was seeing through her eyes, and that the words that she spoke, for all that the voice was hers, were his words.

Her body bore Kief's mind within it as she left her laboratory and returned to the sus-Peledaen town house, where her brother Na'e was finishing his breakfast and going over the morning messages from the orbital station.

"Isa," he said, surprised. "I thought that you were gone."

Isayana didn't answer, except to pick up a silver jelly-knife from the breakfast table and drive it through his right eye into his brain. Then, speaking aloud, she said to the part of her mind that was Kiefen Diasul and not Isayana sus-Khalgath, "I will make a new body for you to fill, a fresh replicant seeded from the wreck of your corpse, so that our work may continue."

Kief's mind fled back then, to his own body, leaving Isayana alone. "I see now," she said, "that it's one thing to suspect the truth, and something else to know it."

Then she summoned the household *aiketen* and told them, "Lord Natelth has met with an accident; see to it that his body is dealt with according to the customs of our family."

23:

"You're safe now."

The lid of the stasis box closed over Arekhon, and he struggled vainly against panic for a drawn-out, excruciating moment—he had to get out, he had to push open the box, but his body didn't have any strength left in it and he hurt too much even to move—before a grey lassitude swept over him and he was . . .

Nowhere at all.

I am. Here. I am here. I am here I am here I am here.

Grey mist around him. Cold.

A place, then. This place.

The Void.

This was the Void, and someone, once, had shown him the way to go through it.

Look for the marks, and go through.

Movement now, ahead of him in the mist. Movement and light. He stood and walked forward—this was the Void, where what he willed became what was real, and if he willed himself into health and wholeness then it would be so—and found the first Void-mark, and stepped through.

The mist vanished. Arekhon stood on the observation deck

of the asteroid base, looking out at the stars as he had when he and Maraganha set the Void-marks on Ophel. The starfield beyond the half-dome of armored glass was alight with flashes of energy and sudden bursts of colored light.

"It's beautiful," said a voice at his elbow. He turned, and saw Ty standing there beside him, looking up at the stars with the light of the *eiran* silvering his face.

"Yes," Arekhon said. Part of him would always be sus-Peledaen, and the sus-Peledaen were star-lords above all; the glory outside the observation deck was part of his inheritance. "So beautiful it hurts to leave."

"People will die out there," said another voice. "People have died." Narin Iyal stood at his other side, and her face was full of an old sorrow. "They'll die out there, and their ships will be their graves, because there's nobody left to bring them home."

"Their lives go into the working," Arekhon said. "Someone will bring them home."

"Not if it fails for lack of tending," Narin said. "And who can tend a working over half a thousand years?"

The question struck him like a knife into the heart. "I would," he said, "if there were any way that a living man could do such a thing."

"Do you give us your word?" Ty asked. "Your life to the working, from now until the galaxy is mended?"

"My life to the working," he said. "I swear it."

Narin smiled then, and her square plain face was beautiful in the starlight. "Then our lives will go with you and keep you through all the years of the working, until the end of it brings us home. We will keep the working, with our lives, while you are gone."

He embraced her, and Ty embraced him, and they stood for a long while in companionship under the roof of stars. At last Narin said, "You have to go now, and see to the working. Live in honor, 'Rekhe, and be well. I must rejoin my Circle." 'Rekhe noticed then that when she talked her mouth did not move.

A trickle of dried blood ran down Ty's chest. "I have my family altars to attend, with at least one memorial tablet," he said.

Once again, the Void-marks shone brightly in the starfield beyond the glass. Arekhon withdrew reluctantly from the closeness of his friends, and stepped through.

Aboard *Fire-on-the-Hilltops,* Lenyat Irao tore the headset from his ears. "Ow, dammit! That hurt!"

"What?" Zeri asked.

"Major noise." He looked at the high-frequency direction-finding sensor, and touched the maneuvering jets to swing the *Fire*'s nose around, so that the cockpit windows pointed to one side. The needle on the sensor swung to centerline.

Zeri pointed at the needle. "And that—?"

"Energy burst. And that means . . ."

Outside the *Fire*'s bridge windows, a pinprick of light appeared, blue at the center, then white, then large, larger, then fading back through red to darkness.

". . . someone isn't coming home," Len finished.

"What—who—was on that bearing?" Zeri asked.

Len checked back through the ship-mind's sensor readouts. "sus-Peledaen guardship *Cold-Heart-of-Morning,*" he said finally. "No going home for anyone now."

"I promised Arekhon that I would see the survivors back to safety on Ophel." Karilen Estisk's voice was courteous, but her expression was immovably stubborn. "And what I promised him, that I will do."

The sus-Radal asteroid base was an artificial construct. It had conference rooms, engineering spaces where power and life support were maintained, machine shops, and berthing compartments, as well as the infirmary. It was still unstocked and unmanned, nor were most services on-line, but what they had was good enough—in the aftermath of the space battle, a conference turned out to be sorely needed, and one of the upper rooms, adjacent to the observation deck, was finished and furnished.

Representatives from the sus-Radal and sus-Dariv fleet elements, as well as the remnants of the Demaizen Circle and the leader of the sus-Radal construction team, had all gath-

ered there for discussion and negotiations. An *aiketh* supplied
uffa from the general mess, in cups with sus-Radal house
crests. Len sat beside Zeri, his hand resting over hers on top
of the table, between the sus-Radal and sus-Dariv sides, opposite Ty and Narin. Herin leaned against the wall, behind
the remnants of the Demaizen Circle, and Maraganha stood
beside him.

Iulan Vai still sat on the sus-Radal side of the table, though
from the way Captain Hafdorwen regarded her, Vai didn't
think she would be enjoying that honor for long after she
returned to Hanilat. Stealing family charts and handing them
over to the sus-Dariv was not something that Hafdorwen—
nor, she suspected, Theledau himself—would take lightly.

It doesn't matter, Vai thought. *I'm not planning to wait
around for fleet-family justice anyhow. As soon as I hand
over 'Rekhe's stasis box to a really good medical center,
Zeri's cousin Herin and I are going to be long gone—to our
own Circle and our own workings, somewhere a long way
away from the great Magelords in the big city.*

At the moment, however, that resolve still left Vai with
the problem of *Night's-Beautiful-Daughter.* The black wing-
shaped craft had been given to her by Theledau, and no one
here, she resolved, had the authority to take it away from
her. She needed the craft for the purpose of taking 'Rekhe
home, and now she said as much.

"He may be sus-Peledaen," she said, "but he's also Demaizen, and he's never played anyone false."

"He's Natelth sus-Peledaen's own brother," Winceyt said.
"And that family is no friend to anybody here. There isn't a
person in this room who hasn't lost family, friends, or livelihood to them."

"I'm as much sus-Dariv as you are," Herin reminded him.
"I've lost as much to the sus-Peledaen as anyone who wears
the fleet-livery. But this man himself has done us no wrong.
From what I've heard, he left his family altars years ago."

"Taking him to Eraasi, any one of us, would expose us to
more danger," Len said. "Why there? Aren't there a hundred
other worlds where he could be healed?"

"My understanding is that there were promises given,"

Herin said. "And isn't it true, Syr Vai, that you yourself have urgent business there?"

"I do," she said.

"Family business?" Fleet-Captain Hafdorwen asked. He was the spokesman for the sus-Radal, and had been watching Vai narrowly since the conference began.

"Yes."

Fleet-Captain Hafdorwen sat back, and sipped his *uffa*. "That this base's existence is compromised is due to you. I say that taking the lot of you back to Eraasi is the proper thing to do, all right—aboard my ship, to be turned directly over to house security."

"No, let her go," Herin said. "She's a Mage, like Arekhon sus-Peledaen, and they do their own work—so why not give the whole ship to the Mages? Who would risk their luck to do anything else?"

"That's not your decision to make," said the sus-Radal construction boss. "It's a family ship, and I say we should put our own crew on it and take it back to the family."

"Captain Estisk, syr." Zeri sus-Dariv was far more polite than Vai had thought of being. *Of course,* Vai added to herself, *she's still fresh and well groomed by comparison with some of us in here—I look like I've been mud-wrestling with a mortgaunt.* "Can you answer a question for me?"

"Perhaps," Karil said. "Or not—I have no answers for some things."

"Did you promise Lord Arekhon that you would take the *Daughter* back, and call her by name in the promise?"

"I told you. I promised to take care of the survivors."

"Not people by name? Just 'survivors'?"

A reluctant half-growl. "No names."

"Then, if you're willing, you can keep your promise by sharing your Ophelan charts and Void-marks with us. We're all that's left of the unbroken sus-Dariv, and we need a place where we can settle and carry out business, away from the grip of the sus-Peledaen."

"Arekhon would approve," Maraganha added in her low-pitched, lightly accented voice. "Having the sus-Dariv on this side of the interstellar gap is one more thing to further the great working."

"Always the working," said Karil. "I am sick to death and beyond of this working. It sucks the life out of everyone who touches it." She sighed. "Very well—I will guide the sus-Dariv to Ophel. And you can bring who you like with you, your ships and your people, even those two that sit to one side and say nothing."

"Syr Egelt and Syr Hussav," Zeri said. "They were in sus-Peledaen employ, but that's no shame—they did their work honestly, and left it when the sus-Peledaen stopped working honestly with them."

"I will return to Eraasi," Herin said. "Iulan *etaze* is returning, and I'm a Mage in her Circle now."

"That's done, then," said Vai. "If Captain Hafdorwen will provide a pilot for the *Daughter* for courtesy's sake—and because I'm only qualified to handle a ship's controls in normal space—then I think we part ways here, sus-Dariv and sus-Radal, for Ophel and Eraasi."

"The pilot will be mine," Hafdorwen said. "And that makes the ship mine, and so honor is satisfied. Lord Arekhon will heal in the house of sus-Radal, and afterward Theledau sus-Radal himself can judge what should be done with him."

The sus-Dariv fleet was gone in the morning, with Karil Estisk acting as Pilot-Principal for them all. Vai watched their departure from the asteroid base's control room. Then came time to load the stasis box into *Night's-Beautiful-Daughter* as she sat in the landing bay. But when the construction workers arrived in the infirmary with a portable generator at the ready to maintain stasis until the box was hooked to ship's power, they found the lid open and the box empty.

"Didn't anyone bother to stand watch?" Vai asked.

"Apparently not," Narin said. She was stoic as always. "The best of plans can fail when the *eiran* pull them strongly enough awry, and the *eiran* pull strongly on 'Rehke."

"He's gone to Ophel with Karil, most likely," Ty said. "Then back to Entibor. His lover is still there, and if he told her that he would come back, he would do a great deal to keep his promise."

Narin turned, and walked back to *Night's-Beautiful-*

Daughter without a word. Vai followed a moment later.

Night's-Beautiful-Daughter departed later that same day, but without a stasis box on board. Captain Hafdorwen had indeed supplied a pilot, and the transit, while long, was unremarkable.

Once across the interstellar gap, Vai, Herin, and Hafdorwen's pilot took the *Daughter*'s own shuttle to *Eastward-to-Dawning,* as she orbited Eraasi near the sus-Radal shipyards.

"I have to settle accounts with Thel somehow if I'm going to live on Eraasi and make myself a new Circle," Vai said to Maraganha before departing. "He's going to have to build another asteroid base now that the old one is compromised, and that's all my fault. On the other hand, Natelth sus-Peledaen and his most powerful Magelord are both dead, and the sus-Dariv are going to need a homeworlds trading partner once they've set up shop on Ophel, so with any luck he'll think that the family's gained more than it's lost from what I've done."

"You're a Magelord yourself," Maraganha said. "You'll have the luck."

Vai hoped that Maraganha was right. Thel had wasted no time in asking for his accounting, as it turned out; representatives of sus-Radal groundside security were waiting for Vai aboard *Eastward-to-Dawning,* with instructions to convey her directly to the planet's surface and thence to an interview with Theledau himself.

Herin's presence disturbed the security operatives at first—Vai suspected that Thel's instructions had not mentioned what they should do with him. She identified him, firmly, as a Mage of her Circle, and was pleased to see that the *eiran* responded to her intent, lulling her escorts and allowing Herin to remain with her during the journey by shuttle from the *Dawning* to Hanilat Starport, and by groundcar from the Starport to sus-Radal headquarters.

Theledau sus-Radal was waiting for her in his office. Outside the windows, the glass-walled towers of central Hanilat dazzled in the midafternoon sun. Thel sat behind the broad desk from which she had stolen the charts for the hidden base and watched her enter, accompanied by Herin sus-Dariv and the team of security escorts. She couldn't read his expression.

"Syr Vai," he said.

"Theledau."

He looked at Herin, standing silent beside her, and at the security detail. "Go." Vai heard the office door open behind her, and then close after the security operatives had left. Thel looked at Herin again. "You too, Syr Arayet."

Herin glanced over at Vai, a question on his face. "Iulan *etaze?*"

"No." She turned back to Thel. "Herin is my Second. He stays."

Thel said nothing for a few seconds. When he did speak, he sounded more sad than angry. "It's like that now, is it?"

"I'm afraid so."

He sighed and shook his head. "I should never have sent you off to spy on Lord Garrod's Circle . . . it ended up costing me a starship, an observation post, and the best Agent-Principal our family ever had. I suppose you're the First of Demaizen now?"

"Demaizen is broken. This is a new Circle."

"I see." He paused again, and she wondered briefly if he was about to offer her his condolences—or worse, his congratulations. It came as almost a relief when he said only, "You can't make your Circle in Hanilat, Iule. Not here, and not in any other place where the sus-Radal have a presence. After what you did, there's no place for you with us anymore."

In spite of herself, she smiled a little. "You're saying that if I'd ever made it onto the family tablets, you'd be taking me off of them now?"

"Just so." His answering smile was even briefer than hers, but it was genuine.

"Fair enough," she said. She would go back north, she decided, into the wilderness where neither fleet-families nor land-families had any real authority, and put together the rest of her Circle there. With Herin for a Second, she could gather enough Mages to pass along what she'd learned—from Garrod, from Arekhon, from Narin and Ty and Delath and Serazao, and yes, even from Kiefen Diasul—and make certain that there was always at least one Circle on Eraasi that wasn't bound to fleet or land or mercantile wealth. "Give me a few minutes' head start before you turn loose the hunters—I think I've served you well enough over the years to ask for that—and you'll never so much as hear word of me again."

"Take as long as you need, within reason. But go."

"Thanks," she said. "And Thel, one more thing—"

He regarded her warily. "Yes?"

"I gave Lenyat Irao and Zeri sus-Dariv my private cipher. Take a good look at any messages that show up in it . . . if half of what I heard about where they're going is true, a trade connection with those two will be worth more in the long run than a dozen observation posts."

After the shuttle had left, Llannat Hyfid went to seek out Ty and Narin. Vai had not argued when the three of them remained behind on *Night's-Beautiful-Daughter*, and Llannat suspected that in her heart the other woman was relieved not to have to explain their presence to Theledau sus-Radal. The three Mages sat at the table in the *Daughter*'s galley, drinking *uffa* more for sociability and to pass the time than because any of them needed the stimulant or was in the mood to relish the taste.

"So," Ty said eventually. "Do we wait around for whatever friendly persuasion the sus-Radal have in store?"

"No," Llannat said. The question didn't surprise her, and from Narin's expression, she wasn't surprised, either. The three of them had no place on Eraasi; Iulan Vai had known it when she left them behind on the *Daughter*. And Vai had never mentioned returning the *Daughter* to Theledau sus-Radal. "I can fly this ship—Arekhon knew how to fly it, and where the *Daughter* is concerned, I know what Arekhon knows—and our place is on the other side of the interstellar gap."

"If we're going to do that, we're going to have to do it soon," Ty said. "I expect that someone on-planet is going to remember us any minute now, and we won't like the plans they've made for us."

"My crew is over there, on the other side of the gap," Narin said. "I've been away too long. I have my own place, and this is not it."

"And I have no place," Ty said. "So it doesn't matter if I go."

"Then let's do it," Llannat said.

She went to the *Daughter*'s pilothouse, and strapped herself in. "Narin, you take copilot."

"Got it." The other Mage sat in the left-hand seat, but did not turn on the exterior comm rig. They stood against the door behind them.

"Like a thief in the night," Llannat said.

"Well, in the *Night,* anyway," Ty observed. "And we're certainly stealing her."

"I have the jump point for Entibor," Llannat said. "It's one of the courses Arekhon and Karil set into the board. We can do it if we don't care how long we spend in the transit."

"Do we have enough fuel?" Ty asked. "Remember, we had to top off on Ophel before."

"It doesn't matter," Llannat said quietly. "Shifting out of orbit in three, two, one, now!"

She fired the main engines to take them away from planetary orbit surface and the sus-Radal shipyard. They ran fast, neither listening to external comms, nor caring. The jump point came; the stars blazed and died, and were replaced by grey blankness outside the pilothouse.

"Now, lunch," Narin said. "Ty, do you want the first watch or shall I take it?"

"Mine," Ty said.

"I'll be in the meditation chamber," said Llannat. She unstrapped and headed aft, leaving Ty to take the seat that she had abandoned.

Llannat knelt for a long time in the center of the meditation chamber's white tiled circle. She waited, feeling the ship pulse around her, feeling the waves of the years about her, like black tapestries brushing her face as she walked through the dark.

She was watching the *eiran*. They surged around her,

forming patterns, slipping away, never knitting into a pleasing form.

How long, she thought, *how long? The cords stretch out from one side of the universe to the other, lost to sight with distance, but which to pull?*

Then the darkness was split, and the cords became clear, and she knew that it was time.

Llannat rose to her feet, her knees creaking. *I'm getting old,* she thought. *And I've been kneeling here too long.* She left the meditation chamber and walked forward, back up to the *Daughter*'s cockpit.

As she had known that she would, she found Ty and Narin waiting for her there, looking out through the cockpit windows at the swirling, iridescent greyness beyond. The vision of the *eiran* was lost to her here, for the *eiran* did not enter the Void.

"Drop out," she said. "Drop out now."

"Etaze?" Ty said. "We're nowhere near—"

But Narin reached forward and pulled back on the control lever, and the stars appeared before them in all their glory. Llannat could see the *eiran* where they should be and where they would be, when the pattern of the great working was at last complete—but only, only if she grasped the silver cords with greater power than was in her. Power that required lives.

"We know," Narin said, before she could open her mouth to speak. "We've already pledged ourselves to Arekhon, and to the continuation of the great working. Do what you must."

Ty nodded. "As the universe wills."

Narin pulled out the knife that she'd worn in her boot top since the days when she was the First of a Circle from a fisherman's town. She offered it to Llannat.

"This will be a little different," she said. "Not the usual working. My Circle is calling to me. I've been away too long."

"Not the usual working at all," Llannat agreed.

"Shall we get started, then?" Ty asked. "Our wills oppose. And when the power is greatest, *etaze* . . . then you can strike."

"Yes," Llannat said. "For the sake of the working," and the other two echoed, "For the sake of the working."

Ty turned toward Narin and shut his eyes. A glow sprang up around him, as did a matching glow in the air around Narin—so dim that it would be unseen in the light of a natural sun, but visible here in the dim pilothouse of a starship gliding through a starless lane.

The glow grew brighter around them. The tendons stood out in Ty's neck. Narin's breath grew ragged. The light grew stronger around them both, streaming away from their fingertips, outlining their bodies in coronae. The two light-circles touched. The boundary between them flared, and the flare spread outward.

The light was growing stronger, magenta shot through with green. Now it was overpowerering the illumination in the pilothouse—it was as bright as day, as bright as noon, as bright as the heart of a sun.

"For the working!" Llannat cried out. "As the universe wills!"

She shaded her eyes with one hand, and flicked out her wrist, knife gleaming, and slashed Narin's throat, so that the blood spurted over her hand. She struck again, and this time Ty's throat was under the knife. She felt their power rush into her as the blood poured forth.

The power they had called up was too much for her to hold—it was more than one person should ever have to hold—and she pushed it as hard as she could into the working, and into the *eiran* where they made the pattern of the working all around her, and on through the *eiran* into the universe again. Then she grasped the threads of the *eiran* where they stretched out into the interstellar gap from either side, and pulled and twisted them together, so that a cord was formed from one side of space all the way across to the other.

But something was still lacking—the pattern was not yet fixed. It wouldn't be fixed until she came aboard *Night's-Beautiful-Daughter* for the first time, and began to understand what she would have to do. She had to leave the message that would bring her to this place.

She reached into her memory, and summoned up the words. Then she dipped her finger in the flowing blood—Ty's, it was—and wrote a letter to herself on the cockpit window, in the formal second-person familiar that she had learned from speaking in this time and place with Arekhon sus-Khalgath sus-Peledaen: "Maraganha *etaze:* bring this message to she-who-leads. Tell her what thou didst learn."

She wrote in the script of Eraasi, for it was fitting that the great working end so, and that Ty have a proper memorial tablet even in a starpilot's grave.

"Narin, my friend, your Circle waits," she whispered, and kissed Narin's forehead. Then she bowed her own head, and walked back to the galley, closing the bridge door behind her.

In the galley she opened a bottle of wine, and splashed a bit on the deck, so that Narin and Ty's ghosts could find their ways home. Then she took the manual, the one she had helped to write during the passage to Ophel and across the Gap, and followed it step by step in an orderly shutdown.

Most of the ship's atmosphere she gathered into the holding tanks, ready against future need. She switched off life support, gravity, the power generation, the engines. At last she put on one of the EVA suits, the last one remaining, opened the inner airlock, and wedged it.

The ship was nearly airless itself by then. She hand-cranked the outer airlock door open, and the wind of the last ghosts of air barely disturbed her. She wedged the outer door. Then she launched herself out into the darkness between the stars. As she did so she twisted, turning the corner into the Void, and began the long walk homeward to her proper time and place.

Epilogue

OPHEL: SOMBRELÍR

Arekhon Khreseio sus-Khalgath sus-Peledaen, Magelord and Void-walker, stepped out through the last of the Void-marks on his long journey from the asteroid base, and found himself standing on a black-and-white tiled terrace on a summer's evening in Sombrelír. The street below the terrace bustled with activity—hovercars and jitneys and draftbeast-carts, laden with passengers and piled high with merchandise—and the fiery dart of a lifting starship rose skyward against the blue-purple dusk beyond.

He turned to look at the building behind him, curious to see if it too had changed. It had been a hotel once, not long ago as his mind remembered it, a pleasant place with a certain faded grandeur. Now a different building stood there, solid and foursquare and weathered by the passage of many years, with a metal plaque set into the masonry next to its heavy bronze doors:

> DARIV-IRAO MERCANTILE AND TRANSPORT
> PRIDE—PROSPERITY—PROFIT
> OPHEL—NINGLIN—ENTIBOR

It was a good thing to know, Arekhon reflected, that not everybody bound by Demaizen into the great working had served it with pain and blood—that some had served it by loving and doing well. He would call on the Dariv-Irao in the morning, and make arrangements through them, if he could, for a journey back to Entibor.

Arekhon had always prided himself on his service, and he had a promise to keep to Elaeli.